Elisabeth's writing career began when she finished third in Harlequin's *So You Think You Can Write* contest in 2013 and she hasn't looked back. She teaches primary school but would rather write full-time because, unlike her five-year-olds, her characters generally do what she tells them. She spends most of her spare time reading and is a pro at cooking one-handed while holding a book.

She lives in Cheshire because the car broke down there in 1999 and she never left.

elisabethhobbes.co.uk

 twitter.com/ElisabethHobbes
facebook.com/ElisabethHobbes
instagram.com/elisabethhobbes

THE SECRET AGENT

ELISABETH HOBBES

One More Chapter
a division of HarperCollins*Publishers* Ltd
1 London Bridge Street
London SE1 9GF
www.harpercollins.co.uk

HarperCollins*Publishers*
1st Floor, Watermarque Building, Ringsend Road
Dublin 4, Ireland

This paperback edition 2021
1

First published in Great Britain in ebook format
by HarperCollins*Publishers* 2020

A catalogue record of this book is available from the British Library

ISBN: 978-0-00-840013-2

Printed and bound in Great Britain by
CPI Group (UK) Ltd, Croydon CR0 4YY

For J, A1 & A2 for putting up with my 'writer's head' at much closer quarters than usual during Lockdown and for riding the elephant with me in Nantes.

Chapter One

An Unknown Location

1944

'My name is Sylvie Duchene, and I am a dancer.'

'Liar.'

The voice cut through Sylvie's protestations with the violence of a whip.

'Tell me the truth! Tell me your mission!'

Sylvie licked her dry lips and swallowed before answering, hoping the small delay would give her time to keep her voice even.

'I've already told you this' – she craned her head in the direction she believed the voice was coming from – 'I am Sylvie Duchene.'

She heard footsteps and sensed the man come closer. When he spoke, his mouth was close to her ear. The sensation of his breath on her neck made her hair stand on end and her skin crawl.

'You are a liar,' he said, his voice lower and harsher. 'We've been watching you for weeks. You are working with the Allied forces. You are a member of the Resistance. Admit the truth.'

A hand slammed onto the table Sylvie was seated at. She jumped in alarm, but her hands were securely cuffed behind her and the chair was pushed close, giving her little room to move.

'Admit it. We know who recruited you.'

Another thump on the table. From the change in tone, it sounded like a fist now rather than an open-palmed slap. Sylvie wondered how soon it would be before the next thing to be on the receiving end of that hand would be Sylvie herself. She'd already been slapped harshly when she had fought against the two soldiers who had dragged her from her bed. They'd cuffed her and put a heavy cloth bag put over her head then carried her kicking and screaming from the building. She had been thrown into the back of a car and driven for what felt like miles to wherever she had been brought, dragged into a cell and commanded to stand under blindingly fierce lighting while she was bellowed at repeatedly. After an hour or more, her legs threatened to give way. When she had been taken from that cell and shoved roughly onto the wooden chair, it had almost come as a relief.

'What you say is not true,' she said as firmly as she could manage.

Silence.

Sylvie tensed, holding her breath.

The next voice to speak was new. Also male, but higher than the first and with a much more pronounced German accent to his French. Sylvie imagined him to be younger than his colleague.

'Your whole network has been captured. Even now your associates are admitting the truth under interrogation. Tell the truth and your life might be spared.'

'There is no network,' Sylvie insisted. 'I don't know what you're talking about, I'm just a dancer.'

'You are a liar and a whore, *fräulein*. Your circuit was betrayed. Perhaps you were the one responsible?'

The second voice was quieter now, but more menacing for it. Sylvie almost denied she would ever do such a thing, but caught herself. Protesting she was not a traitor would be tantamount to admitting there was someone to betray. Another chill raced up her back. That had been too close, but she was becoming too disoriented to think straight. She shivered, partially from fear but also because wherever she had been taken was close to freezing, and she was still dressed in her nightgown.

She flattened her bare foot against the floorboard, grounding herself with the sensation of the wood knots against her toes. She had been dragged from her bed without any idea of what time it was, but her sleep had felt so unusually deep, she wondered if she had been drugged.

She tried to remember everything her training had covered about arrest and interrogation.

Admit nothing. Deny all knowledge.

'Tell us what you know of *Icarus*,' the first voice commanded.

'Is that a nightclub?' Sylvie asked. 'Not one I've ever danced at.'

Her reward for the deliberately insolent answer was a ringing slap across her cheek and she gasped with shock and pain. Despite her determination not to show emotion before her interrogators, she felt tears swimming in her eyes. She was grateful they were quickly soaked up by the blindfold she wore before they could make their way down her cheeks.

'*Icarus* is a network of British agents working with the French Resistance. Your cell is part of that network. Tell me the names of your contacts. Who is the courier? Who operates the wireless? Which *résistants* are you working with?'

'I'm telling you everything I can,' Sylvie said, her voice trembling. She doubted that slight tremor would be enough to soften her captors' hearts, but she would try anything.

'I am just a dancer. I grew up in Rennes in Brittany. I don't know of any *Icarus*. I don't know any Resistance cells.'

The cover story was easy to remember. It was her own life or that which it should have been had her mother not died when Sylvie was thirteen.

'We checked your past. There is a gap in your whereabouts from the age of thirteen. Where did you go?'

'I was living in a convent,' Sylvie said.

'Why?' the second voice asked. 'A cheap little slut like you hardly seems the type to consider a life under the veil.'

This was where Sylvie's cover story and the truth parted

company, but the memorised and rehearsed lies slipped off her tongue with ease.

'I became pregnant,' she said, hanging her head to demonstrate shame. 'My mother sent me to the convent so I did not disgrace her, and our neighbours would not find out. I had the baby, but my mother refused to take me back, so I had nowhere else to go. Then I moved from place to place, trying to find work. It is not my fault the records were destroyed in the bombing.'

She gave a small groan, an idea coming to her.

'I may be with child again now. Please don't hurt me. Please don't hurt my child.'

If her hands were free, she would have cradled them over her belly for emphasis. The cuffs ground into her wrists whenever she tried adjusting the position of her arms. She began to sob loudly in great, dry heaves. She conjured everything from her past that had ever caused her sadness; the death of her mother, the real reason for her absence from French records, her disastrous love affairs. She forced tears to her eyes, this time hoping they would fall down her cheeks below the blindfold, where they might be seen as evidence she was telling the truth. Finally, she let her outburst subside to the occasional sniffle. The men had been silent while she sobbed, but without her sight, she could not guess what affect her performance was having on them.

'You think you are pregnant but you are unmarried.' The voice sneered. She hadn't helped herself with that story, only lowered their opinion of her. 'You are a fond of men, are you, *fräulein*?'

A hand fell heavily on her knee, fingers pointing towards her inner thigh. Sylvie bit back a cry of revulsion as the warmth of the man's hand spread through the thin cotton nightdress.

'Would you like to get to know me? I wonder what I could make you tell me if I was inside you.'

Sylvie bit the inside of her lip and remained still. Don't let them think rape was the key to loosening her tongue. For the first time, her fear was replaced with contempt; men were men, and they would try to use sex as a weapon. The hand moved beneath the hem onto the flesh of her thigh, squeezing lightly, then abruptly lifted.

There was silence again, then the second voice spoke.

'Do you smoke, *fräulein*?'

Sylvie licked her lips, relieved that they had decided, for the moment at least, that an assault was not the best course of action.

'Occasionally,' she admitted. 'There's nothing wrong with that.'

'So you smoke and you fuck. No doubt you drink too?'

Sylvie nodded, wishing she had a large tumbler of whisky to hand. There was the scrape of a match and then the smell of tobacco. One of the men – she couldn't tell which – took an audible drag and blew smoke in her face. The smell was sickening, and she retched. Then she felt a bright spot of heat grow close to her cheek, dancing over her skin. Panic flared brighter than the tip of the cigarette and coursed through her veins.

'How much do you think it would hurt if I ground this

into your eye? Unless you tell me what we need to know, that's what I will do.'

Sylvie pulled her head as far back as she could, straining against the back of the chair.

'Where is *Icarus*? This is your final chance before I pass you to the Abwehr so they can loosen your tongue. They will not be as tolerant as we have been.'

Sylvie grew cold. The rumoured methods of interrogation used by the German military intelligence service would be the real test of how strong she was. Through the panic and coldness, the stiff joints and pain, she marshalled one piece of advice her instructors had told her during training.

Think of your family and loved ones. Keep their faces in mind. They are the ones you are protecting throughout your interrogation.

As hard as she tried, Sylvie couldn't bring anyone to mind. Who mattered enough to her, and who did she matter to? The recruits had been warned that they should try to hold out for twenty-four hours to give other members of the cell time to close down operations and escape. Radio equipment could be hidden. Other lives could be saved. Men and women could continue to sabotage and disrupt and strive towards freeing France.

France. The word was a beacon. Her beloved country no longer ground beneath jackbooted heels. That was what she had joined the Special Operations Executive for. She lifted her head and sat as straight as she could. In the steadiest voice she could muster, she spoke.

'I have nothing to tell you. My name is Sylvie Duchene and I'm a dancer.'

The heat from the cigarette danced closer and then without warning it vanished. The hand went to her face again, causing her to recoil, but instead of pain, the blindfold was lifted. A light shone so brightly that Sylvie had to screw her eyes shut again, and when she opened them she was looking into daylight.

'Thank you, Miss Crichton.'

The voice spoke in English, and the Scottish accent was instantly recognisable. Sylvie looked into the corner of the room where it had come from and gave a small gasp of surprise. Donald Ashton, one of the SOE trainers in interrogation techniques, had been the older voice that had been questioning her.

'I expect you would like some cocoa,' Ashton said, stepping forwards. Sylvie nodded and promptly burst into tears. The other man, dressed in an SS uniform, produced a key and unlocked Sylvie's handcuffs.

'Well done, Miss Crichton,' he said warmly as he helped her to stand up. 'I'm so sorry for your treatment.'

He was nobody Sylvie recognised, but he had spoken in German to Ashton and had interrogated Sylvie in fluent French. Sylvie wondered if he was either of those nationalities or British. As he helped her from her chair, he placed a hand in the small of her back but removed it immediately as she tensed. Had he been the one who had grasped her knee and slid his hand far too close to her crotch? She wondered if he had enjoyed that part of the play acting. She tried not to think about it as she put her hand on the crook of his elbow. Her legs shook and needed the support or else she might faint, and she was determined that would not happen in front of the men she had held out against for so long.

Ten minutes later, Sylvie was sitting in a comfortable armchair in front of the fireplace in a small sitting room. She had discovered her own dressing gown and slippers waiting for her. On the card table beside her was a mug of watery cocoa, two slices of toast with a generous scraping of butter, and a very small dish of plum and carrot jam. A wireless played quietly in the background. It was so English that Sylvie could scarcely believe this was the true reality and the horrific interrogation room had been the pretence.

'How are you feeling now, Miss Crichton?' asked the middle-aged man sitting opposite her in the second armchair. He spoke in French flawlessly, despite Sylvie knowing for certain that he was English through and through, with a line of ancestors stretching back to the seventeenth century.

He didn't wait for her to answer, but filled in her response himself.

'You'll be disoriented, I expect. Weary. Sore and possibly a little bruised.'

Anthony Carmichael often did this, Sylvie had noticed; supplying the answer he wanted to hear in clipped, telegram-like sentences, and assuming it was the right one. It would take a strong person to contradict him. In this case, there was no need because he summed up Sylvie's emotional and physical state perfectly.

Sylvie nodded. She put her hand to her left cheek where she had been slapped. 'I'm tired,' she admitted. She took another piece of toast and ate it enthusiastically. 'It felt so real,' she explained between mouthfuls. She shivered and pulled the red-and-green tartan rug a little higher over her knees. Carmichael helped himself to a piece of toast. And the last of the jam, Sylvie noted indignantly.

'It's supposed to feel real. Before you commit to working for SOE, we need to know how you will bear up. More crucially, you need to know what you might face. We obviously stop short of inflicting real or significant lasting pain. If you are captured by the SS or Gestapo, they will not be as considerate. They will use whatever methods necessary to wring the information from you.' Carmichael sat back and looked at Sylvie with a grave expression on his face.

'It's not only your life that will be at stake if you are sent to France, Miss Crichton. Any weakness could put in jeopardy the lives of your fellow agents. Allies in the French Resistance. British airmen and soldiers. Can you handle that responsibility?'

Sylvie reached for her cocoa and drank half the mug while she digested Carmichael's words. How much more would it have taken before she broke and admitted to anything the interrogators had wanted to hear? *Icarus* was a fiction: one of the invented networks that SOE used to train the potential field agents who would be sent out to work in genuine networks all over France. The next network she might be asked to betray would be real.

'Good. Don't answer yet,' Carmichael said. 'Additionally, you are under orders not to breathe a word of what has occurred this morning to anyone.'

The other potential agents would be faced with the same assessment and would have to believe, as Sylvie had, that their ordeal was real. In all probability, some of the women had done so already and were under the same restriction. If a woman couldn't keep secrets, she would be utterly useless as an agent. Sylvie wondered how the women she had grown closest to would bear up to the ordeal. She wondered how she had done herself.

'Of course I won't tell anyone,' she answered.

Carmichael nodded approvingly. 'I'll debrief with Mr Ashton and we'll speak to you again. Go to bed. You're off duty until three this afternoon.'

'To bed?' Sylvie wrinkled her brow and glanced around, not sure whether she was expected to curl up in the armchair.

Carmichael gave Sylvie one of his rare smiles. 'Your room is in the north wing, I believe.'

Sylvie looked around the room once more, this time with curiosity. Carmichael pulled back the thick velvet curtains and Sylvie looked out onto the familiar front lawn with the ornamental fountain and low box hedges. Despite her aching body and extreme weariness, she laughed. She hadn't even left the stately home that had been taken over by SOE for training. Her bedroom was almost directly overhead, two floors up. She drained the last of the cocoa and stood. Her legs felt more solid now. As she made her way to the door, Carmichael called after her.

'There is one delicate matter of your interrogation I would like to clear up before we proceed any further, Miss Crichton. You were in a relationship before you joined us. Is there any likelihood you are really pregnant?'

Sylvie gave him a brittle smile. The term *relationship* lent far too much dignity to the pitiful affair she had walked away from. Nevertheless, it was a fair question. Some of the other recruits she was training with had left husbands and children to do their part in the war effort. That was acceptable, but no department would knowingly send an expectant mother into occupied lands. Enough time had elapsed since she had left Dennis's bed for the final time for her to be completely sure.

'None whatsoever.'

She left without waiting for an acknowledgement and made her way to her room. The corridors were empty, which she was glad of. Everyone else would be engaged in training of one sort or another somewhere in the grounds or house. She didn't have any urge to discuss what she had gone through, but wasn't sure she would be able to hide that something had happened.

Her room had been left in a state of disarray when she had been taken. The bedclothes had been trailed across the rug as they'd tangled between her feet. She dimly remembered grasping for a vase containing dog daisies and trying to dash it across one of her attacker's heads. Water had gone everywhere. Now everything was as neat as it always was, and her bed had been made.

Sylvie slumped onto the bed and stared at the ceiling. She had done well, surely? She had not given in, even when threatened with violation or burning. She wrinkled her nose, knowing it would be a long time before she was able to smell a cigarette without imagining singed flesh. Wearing the nightgown that carried the lingering smell of the interrogation room any longer was unbearable. She stripped it off and threw it into the corner of the room, resolving to buy pyjamas to wear from now on, and clambered into bed naked. The mattress was lumpy and had seen better days, but Sylvie was asleep within minutes of pulling the covers over her head.

Chapter Two

Two weeks after her fake interrogation, Sylvie sat in the SOE's flat in Baker Street to finally learn where she was to be sent. She had been interviewed in this same room when she first applied to join SOE, back before she had really understood what it entailed.

No one had given her a grade for her performance in the interrogation room, but she got the impression that she had done well. Not all the women had proven to be as resilient to the threat of torture and had surrendered information. Those who had not succeeded had been taken from the training house without a chance to say farewell. Sylvie had no idea where they were now.

Two people sat on the opposite side of the desk to Sylvie. Vera Atkins, who was the personal assistant of Major Maurice Buckmaster, the head of SOE's French operation, and Major Swift, better known to Sylvie as Uncle Max.

'Why do you want to go to France, Sylvia?' Uncle Max asked.

'Sylvie,' Sylvie corrected automatically.

Her father had insisted on changing her name to the more English-sounding Sylvia when he had brought her from France to England as a child. She still bristled on hearing it. Maybe more so now she was being asked to justify why she wanted to serve in France.

'Why do you want to go to France, *Sylvie*?' Uncle Max asked.

He looked over the top of his spectacles. His hooded eyes and beaked nose made Sylvie feel like a mouse being scrutinised by a hawk. She held his gaze. If she couldn't even hold her nerve when speaking to the man she had known for almost a decade, she wouldn't do very well under interrogation.

Sylvie smoothed the khaki serge skirt of her FANY uniform. Recruitment into the First Aid Nursing Yeomanry corps was the starting point for all female candidates for SOE. She had answered all these questions when she applied, but now she was reaching the end of her training and her superiors were sizing her up for a role. She could work as a wireless operator, in encryption, drive cars, work as a personal assistant. All important roles, but all behind the lines. Even now she might be deemed inadequate and shunted into a desk role, receiving 'skeds' – the scheduled messages from agents abroad – or translating codes to be sent back.

'France is my home and I have not been there for her.'

'England is your home too, Miss Crichton,' Miss Atkins said. 'There are many roles in which you could serve France and Britain without leaving these shores and putting yourself in danger.'

Sylvie drummed her fingers on the arm of the chair. The surname was a minor irritation, but here it was again. This was a new line of questioning, however.

'Perhaps it would be more accurate to say that I have never felt like England is my home.'

Uncle Max raised his eyebrows. He was not a real uncle, but he had served with Sylvie's father in the trenches during the Great War. He might even have been nursed by Sylvie's mother in the Normandy field hospital where Angelique Duchene and Arthur Crichton had met. Before the war Uncle Max had visited the house in Scarborough frequently, and once Sylvie was deemed old enough (and English enough) to join the adults, they lunched together. Uncle Max had always been kind to her, and she had a sense that she was being ungracious.

'Not everyone made me feel like a stranger,' she admitted, giving him a gentle smile to show she counted him in that number. Uncle Max acknowledged the compliment with a silent nod of the head.

'I heard General De Gaulle speak on the radio in June 1940. He called on all French citizens to contact him and fight to free our country. I didn't answer that call. I thought I had no skills. Now I know I do,' Sylvie said.

'If you had believed your skills were useful, would you have responded?' Miss Atkins asked.

'I…' She straightened her posture. 'Honestly, I'm not sure. I was younger. I was studying. I'm wasted in England when I speak French fluently and could be of use in France.'

'No other reason?' Uncle Max asked.

Running away from a failed relationship. Not wanting to live with a stepmother. Not very admirable reasons.

'What would you answer if I asked *you* why you wanted to defend your homeland?' she asked Uncle Max. 'I detest what has happened to my country. I was born there. I wish I had never been forced to leave. Now my father is dead, there is nothing to keep me in England. If I can do anything in the slightest to hasten Hitler's overthrow, I will not hesitate.'

The corner of Uncle Max's eye twitched. Sylvie suspected he would rather be in France than stuck behind a desk, training agents to send to places he could not go himself. Sylvie stopped and brushed her hair back from her forehead. The outburst was out of character. She had worked so hard for years to conceal the emotions that her father had termed 'un-English', that to have them burst through was unsettling.

The two interviewers exchanged a glance.

'You were right,' Uncle Max murmured to Miss Atkins.

Sylvie bristled. Here she was, sat in the room alongside them, being referred to as if she was absent.

'Please,' she said, 'tell me what exactly Miss Atkins was right about and I will confirm it myself.'

'I told Major Swift that you notice people,' Miss Atkins said. 'You size them up.'

Her voice was low and soothing. Even though Sylvie knew on an intellectual level that she was being placated, the tone was motherly enough that it tugged a little at her heart. She thought she had got over the longing for a mother and the long-buried yearning to be nurtured and comforted took her by surprise.

'I may as well observe,' she said, shrugging in an offhand manner to disguise the unwanted emotions. 'I've been excluded enough times, and it gives me something to do to pass the time.'

Miss Atkins scribbled something on the pad in front of her. 'The role we have in mind for you would require a particular set of skills and attributes, Miss Crichton. One that you might be alone in possessing. You began training as a dancer before your father brought you to England, is that correct?'

Sylvie permitted herself a smile. She'd travelled with her mother, Angelique, from birth, and had begun her stage career aged thirteen when puberty had hit with a hard fist and reshaped her body so dramatically that she could easily pass for seventeen. Her developed figure and precocious manner had been a source of concern for Sylvie's father and his English wife when they brought Sylvie to live with them after Angelique's passing.

'I didn't exactly train,' she admitted. 'Not with a teacher, but I was dancing from almost as early as I could walk. I danced in the chorus of the show with my mother before her death. It was all I wanted to do. Father let me take ballet lessons when I came to England. What do you have in mind for me?' she asked. 'I hardly imagine you are planning to install me in the Paris Opera House, are you?'

'I'm afraid our reach does not extend that far,' Uncle Max said.

He chuckled in what seemed to Sylvie to be a rather

patronising manner. She tried not to bristle openly, knowing that Uncle Max would have a great degree of influence over when, where, and if at all she was used as an agent.

'I'd be happy to demonstrate my credentials. Would you like me to audition for you?'

She sat back and waited for Uncle Max to elaborate.

'We won't ask you to demonstrate your proficiency on the stage – we've already observed the way you move. The question is whether you think it would be possible for you to take instruction from a choreographer in French?'

Sylvie permitted herself to laugh out loud at this.

'Uncle Max,' she said. 'Any ballerina in England is able to take direction in French. From *pliés* to *jetés*, the language of dance is in French.'

'In that case, I see no issue with assigning you on that basis,' Max said. 'There is a nightclub in a particular city – never mind the name at this point. You will find out if it becomes necessary for you to learn it. This club has lost a number of dancers and our network operator in the city has told us they are currently looking for a young woman who is capable of performing. The proprietor is a loyal supporter of our campaigns. If you were to work there, it would raise no questions.'

'A club,' Sylvie remarked. Not a theatre or ballet troupe. Her mind filled with music and she could almost feel the heat of spotlights, smell the cigarette smoke and liquor on the clientele's breath. A dozen different perfumes mingling together. Sultry female voices crooning songs of love and deceit in her ears. *Dieu*, how she missed it. How she missed her mother and the smell of powder and paints. The longing and homesickness were almost physical in their intensity.

'Are you all right, Miss Crichton? I think we lost you for a moment,' Miss Atkins asked.

Sylvie shook herself out of the reverie and smiled widely at them both.

'I'll do it. I want to go home. See France again, even if it will be the last time. No one knows what the outcome of the war will be. Whatever is necessary, there is no one better positioned than me.'

'Whatever is necessary,' Max mused. He exchanged a glance with Miss Atkins. 'Whatever it takes might be another matter completely.'

***

Somewhere over France

The interrogation and interview played themselves over and over like a Pathé showreel in Sylvie's head. It served as a useful distraction against the upcoming events of the next quarter of an hour.

What was about to happen was landing in occupied France on a (hopefully – unless they were shot down) unwatched field, to be met (hopefully – unless they had been discovered and arrested) by agents working for the local network who would assist Sylvie in beginning her onward journey to Nantes and the *Librarian* network Sylvie would become a part of. So many uncertainties.

The message had been sent out over the BBC radio

broadcast earlier that day: *'An umbrella and a parasol are for sale in Rue Candide.'* The code that one male and one female agent were to be arriving inland near Bordeaux. Being referred to as a parasol made Sylvie want to giggle, the image was so absurd. The man who sat alongside Sylvie didn't look much like an umbrella for that matter.

It was a balmy evening, and the moon was full as the Lockheed Hudson flew across the Bay of Biscay, though a bank of low clouds gathering ahead threatened to make landing tricky. The drops were always made on the nights of a full moon to enable pilots to fly low without lights. Shadows illuminating the faces of passengers and crew made for an unsettling experience.

'At least the cover will help mask us from German searchlights,' the pilot reassured Sylvie and her travelling companion. 'I've made this drop twice now, and aside from a couple of tricky streams running across the fields, it makes for a perfect landing strip.'

'At least we're not jumping.' The man beside Sylvie gave her a patronising smile. 'Wouldn't want to be ruffling your hair now, would you?'

Sylvie rolled her eyes. 'At least that is a problem I have to consider,' she replied sweetly and a little unfairly. The agent was reasonably young – no more than thirty – but had a very receding hairline. His cheeks reddened and his fingers twitched as if he was about to check his thinning locks were still there. Sylvie hid a smile.

'Why aren't we jumping?' Sylvie asked the navigator. 'I was told that was the original plan.'

'We need to make a collection,' he replied. He jerked his

thumb at a consignment of wooden crates held in place with a cargo net. 'Saves having to send those down on 'chutes as well.'

Sylvie nodded. She had hated parachute training, which had taken place at an airbase outside Manchester, and was relieved that she was unlikely to risk twisting an ankle or worse. Her mission would be over before it started if she was unable to dance.

'The coast is coming up now,' the pilot said.

Sylvie peered through the window, cupping her hands around her eyes to try to get a better look at the long, straight coastline with the unending dunes. Of course, there was barely anything visible. The plane had taken a circular route, arriving from an unconventional direction, to avoid the German gun turrets that defended the coast against Allied attacks.

Home. Sylvie swallowed down the emotions that filled her belly.

The pilot banked the plane sharply.

'Are you all ready?' he asked. 'I need you off as soon as we land and reload. A reception committee should be waiting for you. No red carpets or china tea, I'm afraid.'

The man grunted and Sylvie laughed dutifully.

'We want to be gone within ten minutes. We have to unload and collect a return passenger.'

'Who is it?' Sylvie asked.

'We don't get told details. We just arrive, drop and pick up,' the engineer said. 'Waste of a good plane, if you ask me.'

The pilot nodded in agreement. 'This girl has better things to do with her time.'

Sylvie detected a note of hostility. She'd been warned about that. The use of planes had been restricted since the RAF protested that landing in France was putting their men at risk and a waste of fighting machines.

'We'll be quick,' Sylvie said.

'Quicker than you can get your knickers up and down,' the balding man joked.

Sylvie eyed him coldly. 'Which is still not as quick as you could do the deed.'

She smiled to imply it was meant to be a joke, causing the pilot to snigger. The bald man began to fuss with his shoe. Sylvie sat back, wondering if she had been foolish to rise to his jibes. She had no idea where he would be going once they landed, and as far as she knew, they may have to work together.

The plane was met almost as soon as the wheels down. The seemingly empty field came alive as shadows rose out of the surrounding forest. Three separate groups of men appeared. They were obviously well practised. The first began unloading the crates from the plane. The second group ushered Sylvie and her companion away quickly through the damp undergrowth and into the safety of tree cover. She had a brief moment to look behind and spot the third group helping a limping figure onto the steps of the plane.

Sylvie had been briefed on what would happen next, but it still happened in a rush, her head whirling. She and the other agent were hurried through the forest on foot. It was hard to move quickly through the tangle of roots and bushes that clutched at them while holding their bags. Before long, Sylvie was hot and breathless. From the direction they had left, the distant sound of gunfire punctured the night. Sylvie's instinct was to freeze and huddle down in the undergrowth, but one of her guides urged her on.

'Not our affair. Keep going.'

When they eventually reached a rutted track they were ushered onto a flatbed truck and nestled among various pieces of what Sylvie thought might be farm machinery. By the time the German sirens were screaming through the night, a tarpaulin had been placed over the top and they were making a jolting journey from the landing site into occupied France.

Chapter Three

Rural France

After, perhaps, half an hour, the truck jerked to a stop, and the tarpaulin was removed. Sylvie and her companion were ushered into a farmhouse and taken through the kitchen, straight into an upstairs bedroom. The room smelt of cigarettes and sweat. The scent was markedly different to English tobacco, the pungent, thick aroma reminding Sylvie of her childhood.

They were motioned up a wooden ladder into a cramped attic, where two agents were waiting for them. A man in his late thirties and a woman who was closer to fifty in Sylvie's estimation.

'Welcome to France,' said the man in French. 'I am Hugo. This is Marianne.'

Not their real names, or even the ones that would appear on their identification papers. These would be field names designed to protect them when they were carrying out missions that involved meeting other people. Sylvie's was Monique. It was confusing but gave her confidence knowing how much care was taken to protect the agents and résistants from accidental discovery or intentional betrayal. Hugo spoke with a slight inflection to his vowels; Sylvie marked him down as not being a native speaker. A genuine French accent was one of the advantages she had over British agents who might be fluent but who had not grown up speaking French as a first language.

'You'll spend the night here and leave at first light,' Hugo continued. 'Marianne has instructions for each of you. Memorise them. It would be safer if you do not share the contents with each other. You know the names of your final destination and contacts, of course.'

'We do.' Sylvie nodded. *Librarian*'s chief went by the name Marcel. She would finish in Nantes but knew nothing beyond beginning the next morning with a walk across the countryside to the nearest small village. At each stage, she would give the same greeting to the courier and introduce herself by the name of Monique. The courier would take her onwards.

'We will bring you food,' Marianne said as she handed over two envelopes. She really was French. There was something in more than her accent that distinguished her, and Sylvie felt a momentary twinge of anxiety that she had been in England too long and would not pass as a native of her own country. She studied Marianne with interest, taking note of her hairstyle and planning to fix hers into similar chestnut waves before she had to appear in public.

The farmer's wife brought a tray of bread and cheese and, even more welcome, a jug of weak cider. Sylvie and the other man devoured the food while Marianne filled four earthenware cups that she passed around.

'To your success and safety,' Hugo said. They all raised their cups and toasted each other.

'You should get some sleep now. You leave before dawn,' Hugo said.

Marianne took Sylvie's hand. 'Monique, I thought you would prefer to sleep with the farmer's children.'

Sylvie nodded. She shook hands with her fellow traveller. 'Good luck.'

'And the same to you, *mademoiselle*.'

She followed Marianne down the ladder and into a small bedroom. A mattress had been laid between two cots that each bulged with a small body. The largest bundle made a snuffling sound and shifted as the child roused and settled almost instantaneously. A scratched leather suitcase, patched up with parcel tape, stood at the end of the bed. It contained Sylvie's new clothes and her identity papers. Sylvie had acquired a very good suitcase recently, but she had to leave it safely stored in London because it had the name of the English company engraved on the lock plate, so would immediately reveal her as a foreigner. She put her snakeskin leather bag beside it. That was French and had been a gift from her father and her stepmother, Maud, on Sylvie's twenty-first birthday. It was the most fashionable thing she owned and also the most useful, being large enough to carry a great deal more than the type of dainty little clutch bag that had been in fashion before the war.

'There's a biscuit tin in the bottom of the case wrapped in your slip,' Marianne whispered. 'When you get to Angoulême, tell the *charcutier* to give it to Jean-Pierre. He'll know who you mean.'

Sylvie nodded. Marianne leaned forward and kissed her cheek, then hurried away. Sylvie settled down on the mattress, not bothering to undress. None of it felt real. She wondered what was in the biscuit tin, then decided she would rather not know. Better to be able to deny knowledge if she was caught and questioned.

If she was caught...

She shivered and pulled the crocheted blanket over her head. That didn't bear thinking about. She reached for the gold cross on the chain around her neck and felt reassured. She did not put her faith in the God whose symbol she wore, but rather in the ruby-coloured paste gem in the centre. Concealed within was a small pea-sized ampoule filled with cyanide. If she was arrested by the Gestapo, it would most likely mean her death one way or another, but poison would ensure a quicker end. As she closed her eyes, she fervently hoped it would not come to that.

Looking back, Sylvie would remember the early-morning hike across the fields to the village as a time of serenity and peace before the consequences of war in France sunk in. The sun quickly burned away the dawn mist, and the air smelt of wheat and wildflowers. Aside from one alarming encounter with a bad-tempered nanny goat, Sylvie reached the village without incident. The goat had been standing on her rear legs, chewing at the low-hanging leaves of a tree, and had taken exception at having her breakfast interrupted by a walker. She let out a bleat that would have rivalled an air-raid siren and lunged towards Sylvie, teeth bared. Sylvie scurried past before the sound drew every German patrol from miles around, clutching her bag and suitcase high, thinking she'd happily face the Gestapo a dozen times than that mad-eyed creature!

She walked into the village and encountered the first evidence that she was in a country under occupation. The village, like so many in France, was centred around a small square with a small-windowed church and a town hall. The church doors were closed and instead of a Tricolore, a swastika hung in front of the *mairie*. Sylvie stared at the flag. It was the first time she had seen one in the flesh, and the red, black and white seemed disturbingly normal in the sunshine. A handful of old women were milling around the square, waiting to buy bread. They looked Sylvie up and down with suspicion, and she shivered. She had no idea how great the German presence was in this prefecture, or what the attitude to the occupiers might be. These women could go to the grave denying having seen a stranger or could rush straight to inform the authorities.

She hurried on to the address she had been given and took possession of a bicycle that had seen better days. She began her long and arduous bicycle ride to Angoulême, glad to leave the silent village behind, but full of foreboding at what she might yet encounter.

Things were even more shocking there. The next town

had been devastated by Allied bombing a fortnight before, and streets of houses had been reduced to rubble. Small children of both sexes climbed through window frames devoid of glass, throwing fragments of brick at each other while adults wearily passed by. She edged her way through the streets, taking in the pock-marked walls where bullets had lodged or chipped away the stone.

She stared in dismal resignation at the swastika flags hanging proudly outside the town hall. Pedestrians walked purposefully, avoiding eye contact. Though hair of all shades passed by, every face was a hue of white. No one Jewish. No one black or olive-skinned. This was not the France she had longed to return to, where the theatre had buzzed with people of all colours and nationalities. Not the country she had missed with such heartfelt misery from across the English Channel for almost a decade.

She took a deep breath, remembering the way she had argued her case with Uncle Max and Miss Atkins to be sent to France, and counted to ten as she let it out slowly. These sights made her all the more determined to succeed in her mission.

The charcutier who introduced himself as Claude explained the safe house where Sylvie spent the night had narrowly escaped being destroyed. He took the biscuit tin without question and poured Sylvie a small cup of something fiery. They toasted their mutual good luck before he showed Sylvie to a small guest room.

'Unless you'd rather share with me?' he asked hopefully.

He wasn't bad-looking, and the promise of sex on her

terms with absolutely no repercussions was almost tempting, however, Sylvie declined with a smile.

'Bad timing, I'm afraid,' she lied, patting her lower belly.

Claude left her to sleep, seemingly bearing no grudge at his rejection.

From Angoulême the next morning, a softly spoken elderly man who introduced himself as Papi drove her all the way to the outskirts of Cholet in a Peugeot baker's van. Sylvie sat beside him and learned of his youngest daughter who had died in an airstrike on Paris and his wife who had died in the bombing of the city two weeks previously. He brushed off condolences but gripped Sylvie's hand tightly.

'I am too old to fight, so I play my part how I can,' he said. 'I will take you to my daughter. She will look after you.'

He delivered Sylvie to a café in a small square. The sign pronounced the café was closed. Papi knocked and when the door opened a crack, he was greeted by a grey-haired, handsome woman who pulled Sylvie and Papi inside and was introduced as Eloise. They had no sooner sat down at the table when a young man banged on the window. He gave a signal that meant nothing to Sylvie, but Eloise and Papi sprang into action.

'You have to hide! Quick!' Eloise dragged the table out of the way, kicked the rug free and pulled open a trapdoor. 'Down there.'

Sylvie had been trained to obey orders. Without question, she lowered herself into the hole. Papi passed her luggage down.

'Stay silent.'

The space was not big enough to stand up in. Sylvie crouched in blackness, clutching her knees, and listened to the sounds from above. There was a dull flopping sound, then the dragging of wood as Papi and Eloise returned the furniture to its rightful place, then creaking as they sat down.

Sylvie waited, hoping desperately her mission was not at an end before she had even reached her destination. Sylvie had never suffered from claustrophobia, but the air was too hot and thick to breathe comfortably. She tried not to think of coffins. Of her father last August, lying in his. Of her mother, eleven years previously, so delicate against the cushions. Dying in France and being buried on the same soil as Angelique would be some comfort, but not much.

The sound was muffled by the rug and thick floorboards, but when the soldiers came, the noise reached Sylvie's ears. Hammering on a door. Male voices followed by female pleading. Different male voices, then weeping, begging. More shouting and then the piercing sound of glass breaking. She huddled into a smaller ball, clutching the cross with her suicide pill and waiting for the burst of light and discovery.

But discovery never came. After what felt like hours, she heard the sound of the table being moved overhead and the trapdoor opening. Sylvie clambered out of the hole and together, not speaking, she and Papi covered the trapdoor again. It was only when they were seated at the table dipping stale brioche into bowls of coffee that Sylvie began to tremble. 'I thought they were here for me,' she said.

Papi sighed. 'So did I.'

'It appears my neighbour's son has been making his opinions about the Führer known rather loudly in places he should not have been. He had Jewish friends who disappeared in the night and he doesn't know where they went.' Eloise closed her eyes. 'The Germans who took him were in uniform, not men in black coats with black cars, so maybe he will escape with a flogging or short imprisonment.'

Sylvie said nothing. There was nothing to say. The boy may come back, or he may not. His friends could have been among the lucky ones who escaped, but most probably not. Eloise gathered the empty coffee bowls.

'You can sleep on the top floor in my room. The bus to Nantes leaves at eight. Make sure you are on it, and God protect you in your fight.'

The next morning, Sylvie finished her journey to a village on the outskirts of Nantes on a local bus, sitting beside a garrulous woman who spent the entire journey telling Sylvie about her ailments. Whether or not the woman was part of the Resistance network or not, Sylvie never found out, but it meant that when she left the bus, the pair of Germans patrolling saw two women, who had obviously known each other for years, saying goodbye.

Sylvie completed the final part of her journey alone with a sense of awe. She had been smoothly passed from person to person. So many lives were being risked for her sake and that of France. Now she was here, she now had a much fuller appreciation of the network that stretched across France. A network she was now a part of. She might be tired and travel-stained, but her sense of determination was redoubled. SOE and the Resistance had to succeed. She must not appear nervous or suspicious or she would get no further than the first control point. She hoisted her bag and suitcase – lighter now she had passed on whatever the mysterious contents of the biscuit tin had been – and continued on her way.

She followed her nose as she walked the two miles into the *centre-ville* then sat on the edge of a fountain in the square. Nantes was a city Sylvie was unfamiliar with, which meant that she was unlikely to be recognised and exposed. It also meant, however, that when she sat on a wall outside the Nantes-Orléans railway station at the appointed time and Marcel did not arrive to meet her, she had no one to turn to for help. At first she was not worried. She waited for a quarter of an hour, keeping her eyes peeled for a blond man with a red band in his hat to approach and give her the first part of the code exchange. She left at twelve fifteen precisely, having been told to wait no more than fifteen minutes. She was supposed to return at two o'clock and then again at four and six and every even numbered hour until Marcel appeared. When eight o'clock came and went that evening, Sylvie began to grow more concerned. She wondered if she or the final contact had made an error and the meeting should have been at the Paris-État station where freight was brought into the city. If that were the case, the meeting would have to wait until the following morning. The Paris-État station was now entirely for the use of the German army, and anyone French who frequented the area was unlikely to be an upstanding member of society. To go there on her own in such a place at ten at night would attract unwanted – and probably unpleasant – attention. At every stage of the journey she'd seen women loitering on the streets, offering themselves with resignation or desperation to passers-by. To Sylvie's mind, the curiosity of German authorities was barely worse than the interest of French men looking for a good time with a prostitute.

She found a bistro and ordered some food. While she ate the bowl of thin onion soup, she ran through the implications. They were stark. Something had prevented Marcel from making the rendezvous. Did it mean the entire unit had been discovered? And if so, had Marcel managed to hold out for the expected twenty-four hours needed to abandon the safe houses and cover all traces of other members? She might have come to a town deserted by the network. If that were true, it had happened in the past three days because otherwise her mission would have been pulled before she left England.

The sky was completely dark when Sylvie left the bistro, wincing inwardly at the cost of her meal. Inflation had hit France hard, and it seemed people had become resigned to paying more to receive less. Nevertheless, her brief rest had fortified her spirits, and now she had a plan. There was no way for Sylvie to contact anyone in England. She was in limbo, waiting, but at least she knew where she could begin her search for someone in the network who might help her.

She had a cover story and an identity. A job was waiting for her in the city.

Swinging her suitcase and trying to keep her spirits high, Sylvie wove her way through the narrow streets of the old town in search of the nightclub named Mirabelle.

Chapter Four

From the outside, Club Mirabelle looked run down. It stood halfway up a narrow road on a hill leading away from the river. Perhaps before the destruction wrought on Nantes by the war and subsequent occupation, this would have been a high-end establishment, but now it showed evidence of neglect.

The club was double-fronted in one of the three-storey buildings that lined the street. A plain black door was set between wide windows that at some point had been boarded up with black-painted wooden planks. It could have been due to the war and the need to block out any escaping light, but Sylvie suspected the alterations had been done prior to that in order to create an atmosphere. The sign outside looked strikingly old-fashioned. A laughing woman held out the flounces and ruffles of her skirts to display one leg raised in a high kick. In her right hand, she held a flute of champagne that appeared to defy the laws of physics given the tilt of the glass. The club's name curled in cursive script from leg to arm. Perhaps this was Mirabelle herself.

If she had been in England, Sylvie would have turned her nose up at any suggestion she spent an evening there. Still, she reasoned, disreputable might mean it was less likely to be frequented by Germans and she would stand less chance of being discovered for who she was.

Sylvie pushed the door ajar ever so slightly and was greeted by the sound of laughter and piano music. Seedy and down at heel it might be, but Mirabelle was busy tonight. She hesitated, wondering if the middle of a busy evening was the best time to try to make contact with someone, or whether she should return tomorrow when there would be fewer witnesses to the conversation she needed to have.

She was still wavering indecisively when voices speaking German made her start. A quartet of soldiers in uniform were making their way down the empty street towards the door. Sylvie tensed, recalling the brutal arrest of the boy in Cholet, but they were strolling, not goose-stepping. They were off duty, not a patrol out to round up suspects for interrogation.

They walked two abreast, and one in the first pair nudged his young companion and gestured towards Sylvie. The two walking behind spoke in German to each other, laughing. It was obvious to Sylvie that the young man was being teased and that she was the subject.

'Are you going inside, *fräulein*?' asked the man who had begun the joke, switching to halting French.

'She is waiting for you, Valter,' said the oldest and, from

the insignia on his uniform, the most senior officer of the group.

The young soldier looked visibly relieved that the attention had moved on from him and stepped aside to let his superior – presumably, 'Valter' – pass him and kept his eyes firmly ahead as if he was standing to attention on the parade ground. Sylvie suspected nothing short of a direct order from the Führer himself could have induced him to meet Sylvie's eye.

'Maybe she is waiting for all of us,' Valter replied.

Sylvie's scalp prickled. She could probably fend off one man, but not four. She hid her revulsion and gave him a smile, hoping it was just bravado. He straightened up and looked pleased with himself. Men were men, it appeared, whatever nationality they were.

Without replying, she opened the door fully and stepped inside.

Mirabelle had seen better days inside as well as out. The room went on further back than Sylvie had expected from the outside. Small circular tables were set for couples or groups in front of both sides of the door and throughout the room. Most were occupied. A raised stage area ran along the left side of the room. The bar covered the back-right-side wall. Between them was an arch covered with a pair of burgundy velvet curtains.

Besides the stage was a piano where a dark-haired man in a black dinner jacket sat with his back to the door. He was currently playing something almost like jazz, with a languid rhythm that made Sylvie's fingers begin to drum against the side of her leg. His lean frame moved sinuously from side to side as his fingers worked along the keyboard. As Sylvie watched, he reached up and caught the lit cigarette that was tucked behind one ear, took a quick drag and put it back without losing his rhythm. Though he was only half facing the audience, Sylvie was sure he must be aware that all eyes were on him.

The club was dimly lit and the air was hazy with smoke. The intense odour of French cigarettes made Sylvie blink. Colognes and perfumes added another layer, and beneath that were the smells of warm bodies and alcohol.

It was sleazy and exciting.

The Germans had followed Sylvie inside and stood in the doorway, letting the cool air in. One of them clapped his hands and whistled loudly, a piercing sound that cut through the buzz of conversations harshly. The pianist stopped playing and glanced over his shoulder. He caught Sylvie's eye, and she smiled instinctively. He remained stone-faced, shrugged and resumed playing, clearly dismissing her. Conversations resumed and the patrons went back to flirting or listening to the music.

From between the curtains, a middle-aged man appeared, wearing shirtsleeves and a waistcoat. He walked across the floor with a smile.

'Good evening, gentlemen, mademoiselle. Is it a table for five?'

'Well, *fräulein*,' asked Valter, raising his eyebrows towards Sylvie. 'Is it our night of fortune?'

'Not tonight, gentlemen.' Sylvie smiled with an air of regret she did not really feel and turned back to the waiter. 'I am here to speak to the proprietor, on business.'

'Business?' The waiter narrowed his eyes. 'What do you want?'

Sylvie was aware of the four Germans behind her who were undoubtedly listening to the conversation. She was making a complete mess of things. Any second now she expected to feel hands on her arms, dragging her away on suspicion of being a spy.

'I am a dancer. I wanted to ask him if he needs any girls to work here,' she said. 'I'm trying all the clubs in Nantes. If you don't, do you know anywhere that might have an opening?'

Behind her, the Germans made enthusiastic noises of encouragement. The waiter pursed his lips. Sylvie was dimly aware that the pianist had finished the song and had begun another, languid and quiet. Everyone in the club would be listening in to the conversation.

'I am Monsieur Julien,' the man said eventually. 'I own this club. It is me you need to speak to.'

Sylvie blushed. She had been convinced from his attire that he was staff, not management. 'I'm sorry, I didn't realise.'

Monsieur Julien scrutinised her and seemed to come to a decision.

'Let me attend my customers, then we can talk. Adele, see to these gentlemen, please.' He snapped his fingers and a young, very pale blonde woman dressed in green silk came from behind the curtain. Adele paused to look Sylvie up and down then led the party of Germans away to an empty table, leaving Sylvie alone with Monsieur Julien.

'Well, mademoiselle,' he said. 'You have made quite an entrance. Do you have a name?'

'Sylvie Duchene.' It felt good to be reverting to her old name.

He sucked his teeth. 'I do need another dancer. My best girl got herself in the family way and left. But why should I employ you without credentials? Where have you been dancing?'

Sylvie hesitated before answering, gathering her thoughts. 'In Angoulême. The theatre was hit in the bombing raid two weeks ago. Fortunately, no one was performing at the time, but the troupe was disbanded as there was nowhere for us to perform.'

'Let her dance, Herr Julien!'

They both turned to the voice that had hollered from the back of the room. The Germans who had followed Sylvie inside were seated at a table now with a bottle of wine. They raised their glasses and cheered. Monsieur Julien crossed his arms and looked at Sylvie, assessing her. She wasn't sure if the intervention had done her any favours, or quite the opposite.

'I am quite particular in who I employ. You might not have all the skills I require.'

He was right to be wary. Sylvie knew he was sympathetic to the Resistance, but she should have been introduced by Marcel, not appear alone. He was risking a lot by allowing a SOE agent to come within his walls, and Sylvie could not openly admit to the existence of the organisation. Not when surrounded by Germans.

'Please,' she begged, feeling desperation well inside her. 'This wasn't how I planned to ask.'

She looked into Monsieur Julien's eyes and was met with scrutiny in return. They looked like they belonged in an older face, dark and sharp. He glanced down at the suitcase at Sylvie's feet then looked her up and down, taking in the sensible lace-up shoes and woollen skirt beneath her bottle-green coat.

'Do you have clothes you can wear to dance?' he asked after what felt like forever.

'Most of my costumes were destroyed, but I have one good dress and my shoes,' Sylvie answered. She had no idea what it must have taken to obtain them, but in the suitcase Marianne had given her there was a dress that would be perfect stage outfit along with a second dress, a skirt and two blouses for day to day wear. SOE prepared their agents well.

'Good.' Monsieur Julien drew Sylvie towards the back of the room, slipping his arm into hers, and leaned close. 'You have a trial for one week. If anyone else arrives who I think is better, you will have to leave. Is that understood?'

'Thank you.' Sylvie let out a breath of relief.

'Céline,' Monsieur Julien called out sharply. A few moments later another pretty blonde woman stuck her head out from between the curtains. 'We might have found a new dancer.'

The woman raised an eyebrow in Sylvie's direction.

'You can put your things behind the curtain for now,' Monsieur Julien said. 'Watch tonight. Speak to the girls when they're not onstage and see if you can learn some steps. Tomorrow afternoon, come here. You can perform with them, and I'll decide then if you are suitable.'

Sylvie held out her hand. 'Thank you, monsieur, you won't regret this.'

He gave her another level stare. 'Make sure I don't or, I can tell you, Mademoiselle Duchene, I won't be the only one who does.'

Tossing that veiled threat over his shoulder, he walked back behind the curtain, leaving Sylvie standing alone. She put her suitcase behind the velvet drapes and then sat on one of the stools beside the bar. She ordered a small glass of the cheapest wine and sipped it slowly as she watched Adele and two other women performing and tried to learn some of the routines. After the dancers left the stage to enthusiastic applause, the blonde woman Monsieur Julien had called Céline sashayed onto the stage.

Dressed in a silk floor-length gown with a beaded fur draped around her neck, she would have been striking in any case, but above her elegant costume she was stunningly beautiful with blonde curls and wide eyes. She sang in a sultry, throaty voice that left Sylvie reeling with envy. Dancing was one thing, but she had never been able to sing. Céline held the room as she performed, coming into the light or receding into the darkness; Sylvie knew without looking that every pair of eyes in the room were on Céline. She finished the performance leaning against the piano and looking into the eyes of the pianist with seductive intensity. He held her gaze, rising to his feet as he played. The effect was electric. Sylvie wondered if they might be sleeping together.

After the three songs had finished, Céline joined Sylvie at the bar. Sylvia congratulated her, which Céline accepted with a gracious shrug of the shoulders that suggested she was well used to such compliments and knew her talent. Now there was no one performing, and the bar was buzzing with conversation and gramophone music. Two wide-rimmed glasses appeared in front of the women. Sylvie looked at the bartender in surprise.

'I didn't order these.' She glanced at Céline who had already picked up her crystal glass and was sipping the cocktail.

'It was the officers at the table in the corner,' the bartender answered.

Sylvie swivelled on her stool and looked across to the four Germans she had come in with. Seeing her looking, they raised their own glasses.

'I can't accept this.' Sylvie pushed the glass away from her, shaking her head towards the men. They looked disappointed.

'Don't be foolish,' Céline said. 'It's only a drink, and a free one at that.'

'But what is the real price?' Sylvie asked.

Céline dimpled and smiled. She lifted her glass towards the Germans, then took another sip. 'Probably none. But ask yourself, what would be the cost of refusing it? You're new in town, aren't you? Don't make enemies on your first evening.'

'They are the enemy,' Sylvie pointed out.

Céline drummed her long fingernails on the top of the bar. 'Of course they are, but these particular men have done nothing to you, so why antagonise them? We all have to accept what has happened and do our best to make the best of it.'

Sylvie considered the singer's words. France was full of collaborators who had, if not welcomed the occupation, done little to oppose it to it. She wondered if Céline was one of them. Or perhaps she spoke sense, and it would be foolish to cause a scene and bring attention to herself. She picked up the glass and raised it to her lips, smiling at the Germans over the rim. This was met with their approval. They shouted a loud toast in German and went back to talking among themselves.

'Where are you staying?' Céline asked.

'Nowhere yet,' Sylvie replied. 'I hoped an old friend of my mother's might put me up for a night or two, but when I went to her address, the whole street was rubble. I suppose I'll try to find a hotel.'

She glanced at the stage, wondering if she might resort to sleeping on the bare wood wrapped in her overcoat. The pianist was in the process of arranging sheets of music and caught her eye. He gave her a measured look that made the roots of Sylvie's hair stand up on end.

He was very handsome, with intense blue eyes and dark hair parted to the left. It was grown long to flip over his forehead and almost cover his right eye. Sylvie's cheeks began to grow warm at being subjected to such open appraisal. He took the cigarette from behind his ear and put it to his lips, taking a long drag before stubbing it out on the ashtray balanced on top of the piano. He never took his eyes from Sylvie. When Sylvie kept her face perfectly immobile, he curled his lips slightly and carried on rearranging the pages as if she was beneath his notice.

'There is a room in my building,' Céline said. 'It's quite a walk from here, but it's away from most of the places the army are quartered and probably not near enough to anything worthwhile that the Allies might try to bomb. Come home with me tonight, and I'll speak to Madame Giraud and see what she says. The previous girl left a few weeks ago and it has been sitting empty.' She tipped back her glass and smiled at Sylvie. 'I have to go sing again. Stay here, and if any more drinks come that you don't want save them for me.'

She glided across the floor, hips moving in a sultry fashion as if inviting the whistles and cheers that inevitably followed. She paused and spoke to the pianist, placing both hands on the top of the piano and leaning over. He scowled and muttered something, which caused her to laugh. She seemed unperturbed and, in fact, playfully swatted him across his arm with the fringe on her stole. From the body language, Sylvie was even more convinced that they were lovers or had been in the past.

Chapter Five

Céline's apartment was above an *épicerie* in the middle of a row of tall houses. While Céline discussed whether Sylvie could have the room with her landlady, Madam Giraud, Sylvie looked around. This had probably been a thriving and well-to-do neighbourhood once, but now the shopfronts told the story of a city under the yoke of occupation. The *charcuterie* next door barely contained enough meat to fill one, let alone two, of the double-fronted windows, and Giraud et fils fruit-and-vegetable shop itself looked sorely empty. The hat shop, with gilt Art Deco lettering advertising its wares, on the other side was boarded up. The words *Juden hier* and a six-pointed star painted across the door and windows was a sickening explanation of why the business was no longer open. Sylvie had seen the same words and symbol repeatedly since she had arrived in France, and it chilled her to the bone to think of the owners being rounded up and taken to work camps simply on the basis of their faith.

'I don't know. Can I trust her?' Madame Giraud eyed Sylvie coldly.

The woman was bound to be worried. Who would want to risk letting a stranger into her house? Sylvie could be an informer. But it seemed Madame Giraud's concerns were more financial rather than for her safety because she added, 'The last one ran off without paying what she owed.'

'I can pay now,' Sylvie said. 'I can give you a month's rent in advance.'

Madam Giraud's eyes lit, and Sylvie was warmly ushered up to a small room on the third floor. Apparently, any reservations Madame Giraud might have had about inviting a stranger into her home were quashed by the prospect of regular and available rent money.

Like many buildings of its type, the ground floor was given over to the *épicerie* and storerooms. The first-floor was occupied by Madame Giraud, though there was no evidence of the son whose name was painted above the door. Céline, who turned out to be a great niece of Madame Giraud, occupied the large room on the top floor, leaving Sylvie a tiny room in the attic. At one end, it held a cast-iron bedframe and mattress, and a dressing table, closed off by a threadbare curtain. The other end of the room contained a table and a wooden chair. A single ringed oil stove was just big enough to heat a pan of water or milk.

It was a far cry from the bedroom at Sylvie's father's house and reminded her unpleasantly of the years she had spent at boarding school, sharing a dormitory with nine other girls. Nevertheless, it would certainly suffice until she managed to make contact with someone from the network.

The room contained no windows but had a skylight set at an angle in the roof. She opened it as wide as she could, then went to the tiny bathroom opposite Céline's room. She could hear her new friend humming one of the songs she had sung.

All things considered, Sylvie decided, as she climbed into the narrow bed that night, it could be a lot worse.

She slept deeply and longer than she could remember. Her travels from the landing site to Nantes had taken their toll, and the first night in a bed in a room to herself lulled Sylvie into a state of relaxation. The safe houses had been welcoming but had not felt particularly safe – the irony not escaping her – being temporary and shared. Other bodies had occupied the mattresses hidden in corners and attics. The mornings had started early, with Sylvie ushered furtively out and on her way. This room felt safer than all of them. A home, rather than a house. 'A room of one's own', as Virginia Woolf had written; words that had struck Sylvie with such poignancy as she had moved into her father's house, and then into the boarding house at the school he had rapidly sent her off to.

Even as she was returning to consciousness, stretching out in the shaft of sunlight that slipped through the open skylight, she was making plans to stay.

Later, when she broached the subject with her new landlady, Madame Giraud readily agreed to Sylvie staying indefinitely and at a price that was not too eye-wateringly extortionate. She softened the blow by promising to throw in breakfast each morning and handed Sylvie a bread roll.

'I know what you girls are like,' she said agreeably. 'Céline is always out all night and coming in at odd hours, then sleeping late.'

Sylvie chewed the small roll and sipped a cup of bitter coffee. It was not much of a bargain but would at least save her having to hunt for food herself. Madam Giraud's clock struck nine. Sylvie looked at it in surprise. She really had slept in much longer than she had expected. She would have to hurry if she hoped to make it across town for her first attempt at the rendezvous point at ten.

As she was returning to her room, Céline's door opened a crack and the singer peeked out. Céline looked very tired but smiled. 'What are you doing up so early?' she asked.

'I planned to take a walk into town and look around,' Sylvie answered. 'I didn't have much time to see it yesterday.'

She felt a quick burst of anxiety in case Céline offered to accompany her, but Céline yawned and stretched. She was wearing a red nightgown made from some silky fabric that clung to her, highlighting the few curves of her slender frame to great effect. Nightgowns like the one Céline wore were made for wearing with lovers, not for sleeping alone, and Sylvie wondered who the fortunate man was who got to see it. Since the day of her mock interrogation, Sylvie had not been able to rid herself of the memory of the interrogator's fingers creeping up her bare thigh beneath her nightgown. Now she always wore pyjamas to sleep in and had no worries that a lover would ever see them.

'What time will Mirabelle open? I need to go learn the dances,' Sylvie asked.

Céline wrinkled her brow as if this question was unfamiliar. 'I never arrive before six, but Antoine – Monsieur Julien – lives on the third floor, and I dare say he would let you in earlier. Are you really going to walk around all day?'

'I don't know,' Sylvie said. 'I'll see how the fancy takes me.'

Céline yawned again and stretched her arms above her head. 'Take care,' she said. 'The city has been peaceful for a while, but there are checkpoints everywhere. Mostly the soldiers are well mannered, especially if you smile nicely. They don't often check bags if you are coming from the market, which is very useful, but then again you are a new face, so they might be interested in you.'

Sylvie thanked Céline for the advice, noting it for the future. Nantes would undoubtedly have a thriving black market, but she did not intend to get caught up in that if she could help it. It was useful to know that searches were not common because if she ever managed to contact a network, one of the duties she would be expected to carry out would be to take messages and equipment from place to place.

She wondered if her new friend knew anything about the black market. Céline was well dressed and did not look as if she was lacking in food. She had already shown that she had few qualms when it came to accepting drinks from the occupying forces, so perhaps she was equally lax about trading with black marketeers. Sylvie gave herself a mental shake. What rights did she have to speculate or to criticise

Céline? In Britain, the black marketeers were generally despised as opportunists, profiting from the needs of a population beset by rationing. Perhaps things were different in France, and they were fighting against the occupation in their own way by providing morale as well as extra food and clothing.

Sylvie walked through the streets back towards the station and arrived a few minutes before ten. During daytime, the street was more alive. Shop doors were open, old men chatted on street corners and in cafés and housewives went about their daily business, carrying baskets and bags. If it had not been for the presence of German soldiers dressed in uniforms, the scene would have been as familiar to Sylvie as any day from her childhood. Few people seemed alarmed or cowed by the patrols, but Sylvie's shoulders and jaw tensed whenever she passed them. She forced herself to try to relax, knowing that nothing would draw attention to her more than appearing to have something to hide.

As she had done the previous day, she sat on a wooden bench and waited in the hope that a blond man might approach her and offer the first part of the exchange they should make. No one appeared at ten, nor again at twelve.

Between times, she spent the time walking and trying to orientate herself with the streets of Nantes. But now she was more conscious of returning and sitting alone, drawing attention to herself. She had been a stranger the previous day, but since then a handful of people now knew her face from Club Mirabelle and she did not want to risk being seen. Céline had already found it odd that she intended to spend the day out. She found a *boulangerie* and handed over one of her precious stamps in exchange for another bread roll and a sliver of cake. A wafer-thin slice of ham from the *charcuterie* completed her lunch. She tried not to feel guilty about where the stamps would have come from. The Resistance carried out raids on the town halls to obtain extra so that agents could eat, and she couldn't shake the feeling that someone else was being deprived for her benefit.

By half past four, Sylvie was so disheartened that she gave up and made her way to Club Mirabelle. The front door was locked, and no one answered her knock. When Sylvie pressed her eye against a small knothole in the board covering one of the windows, she could see no lights inside.

She walked past the club to the alley beside it and looked down there in case there was a side door. As with most of the buildings in the street, the club was in a three-storey building, and on the alley side had small windows set one above the other going up each floor. There was a door, but there was no handle on the outside and piles of rubbish and rags littered the uneven cobbles around it, suggesting it was rarely used. Something small scurried over and away, and Sylvie decided she did not wish to investigate too closely. If she listened hard, she could hear the sound of an accordion playing a melancholy tune coming from inside, though it could be a gramophone recording and she was not even sure it was coming from that building.

She went back to the front and walked along the street to the end where the road split into two. There were narrow alleys at regular intervals of five or six houses. It was a warm afternoon and windows were open. An intoxicating mixture of food smells made Sylvie's mouth water. Salty, savoury cheeses that she could picture oozing across the plate and stews of rabbit in cider.

With the rationing that had been imposed in Britain, she was used to eating small repetitive meals and had grown to live with the constant sensation that her stomach was emptier than it should be, but these scents reminded her of her childhood and made the hunger rawer and more urgent. The portions would be small, but she longed to taste them again. She decided that the following morning, she would shop properly. In the meantime, she took a table in the bistro at the foot of the hill and ate her way through a plate of greasy rillettes and hard bread until she spotted Céline walking up the hill.

She wiped her lips, paid and called after Céline. Together, they walked into the club. Already the other dancers were there. Three women, all of roughly similar height to Sylvie but with figures ranging from delicately slender to voluptuously curvy. Clearly, Monsieur Julien had chosen them to appeal to as wide an audience as possible. Sylvie estimated her own figure would place her between the narrow-waisted, high-breasted blonde she had seen the previous night and the curvaceous brunette. The pianist was already sitting on his stool. He was not wearing his dinner jacket but a pair of black trousers with braces and a loose cream-coloured shirt with no collar. His dark hair had not been slicked back and had a slight wave to it.

'Well then, mademoiselle, are you here to show us what

you can do?' Monsieur Julien said. 'Do you think you can remember anything you saw last night?'

'I'll try,' Sylvie replied.

Monsieur Julien settled back into his chair. 'Watch once more, then see if you can join in.'

He nodded at the pianist, who started to play. Sylvie recognised the introduction to one of the dances from the previous night. Sylvie stood at the edge of the stage and watched the three women work through the steps. She tried to discreetly mimic them without actually moving. A twist of the foot here, legs kicked to hip height, a toss of the head and flick of the wrist, and so on. The routine was not complicated by the standards of the ones Sylvie's mother had performed and taught her as a child, nor did they require the technical expertise of her ballet lessons. Her physical memory for dance had always been strong, so when Monsieur Julien clapped his hands and asked everyone to stop, Sylvie felt confident that she would be able to remember them.

'Your turn, mademoiselle.'

The three dancers moved to one side of the stage where they assumed various states of interest. The pianist began to play again. Knowing that all eyes were on her, Sylvie began to dance.

Chapter Six

London, England

Two weeks previously, 1944

Whatever is necessary.

Sylvie considered Uncle Max's cryptic words over and over after her interview. She had been trained in various skills since being recruited: she could use explosives to destroy infrastructure and buildings; she was able to memorise complicated messages to pass on; and she knew how to carry weapons and equipment hidden about her person and belongings without detection. She had proven that she could hold her nerve under interrogation. She knew how to kill in a number of ways. Was that what Uncle Max had doubts about? If it came to it, did Sylvie believe she would have the strength necessary to end lives?

In the service of her country, she believed so. The

following day she made her way back to the Baker Street house where SOE was based. She sat in the strangest waiting room she had ever been in: a bathroom tiled entirely in black, until she was summoned into Uncle Max's office.

'Tell me what you meant yesterday,' she said to Uncle Max.

Uncle Max paused and glanced at Miss Atkins, who had again joined him. Sylvie noted the exchange of looks and swore to herself that whatever they asked of her, she would agree to. And, moreover, be capable of.

Uncle Max spoke first. 'You will act as a courier, scouting out sites for drops and liaising with safe houses and the local Resistance. You will be asked to transport equipment and take part in sabotage missions. In short, all the duties that we have been training you for over the past months.'

'I accept that,' Sylvie said. She was relived she would not be asked to be a wireless operator. Whenever they practised receiving or sending scheduled messages, Sylvie's skeds were some of the least accurate in the group.

'What else do you require me to do?'

Miss Atkins took up the tale. 'The cover story that we hope you will accept might bring some other possibilities that we have not trained you for, Miss Crichton. You will be working in a nightclub in occupied France. The Germans are treating the country as their own and for many of them life is comfortable as they oppress the population.'

Sylvie nodded slowly. She wondered if the inkling that was growing in the back of her mind was the right one.

Uncle Max spoke. 'The officers take full advantage of the

nightlife that is available, both legitimate and otherwise. It is highly likely that you will encounter men who are responsible for making decisions that directly influence if not control German strategy as a whole, certainly the day-to-day management of the occupied area.'

Uncle Max stopped speaking and looked at Sylvie over the top of his fingertips. This was a test, she realised; one to see how acute her understanding was.

'If I understand you,' Sylvie said, 'you are suggesting that I listen and pass on anything I hear. Am I correct?'

'To a certain degree,' Max acknowledged. 'Although, do not expect that you will hear tittle tattle as you dance. I imagine our opponents are as disciplined in avoiding loose talk as the Allies are – I must credit them with that at least.'

Miss Atkins shuffled her chair forward a little. 'What we are suggesting is that certain tongues may become slightly looser in the company of a charming companion. In certain circumstances, of course.'

'Pillow talk,' Sylvie supplied. A creeping sense of revulsion began in her lower belly and spread up through her stomach until she tasted acid at the back of her throat. They might as well have suggested sending her to work in a brothel. 'You want me to seduce German officers and learn their secrets while I fuck them?'

Uncle Max and Miss Atkins exchanged another glance at Sylvie's crudity. She noticed with abstracted amusement that Uncle Max appeared more shocked than Miss Atkins.

'I would not perhaps put it so bluntly,' Uncle Max said.

Sylvie leaned forward, mirroring his gesture by linking her own fingers on the table top.

'You might not, but I would. How far would you expect me to go in the name of learning secrets?'

'No more than you would be comfortable with,' Miss Atkins assured her, smiling.

Sylvie's cheeks began to burn. She hoped it wasn't too visible. Of course they would know every detail of her life, including the reason she had left her job as secretary in the firm of solicitors where she had been working since completing her degree. Miss Atkins clearly thought Sylvie would be comfortable with a great deal.

'Your life will be dangerous enough as it is,' Uncle Max broke in. 'We would not wish you to compromise yourself.'

'Can you give me time to think about it?' Sylvie asked.

'Of course. This decision is not one that we would expect you to make lightly. Everyone would have to be completely satisfied before we proceed.'

Something in Uncle Max's tone sent Sylvie's nerves jangling.

'You have reservations about my capabilities?' she asked, raising her brows.

'Not about your abilities in the field,' Miss Atkins assured her.

She looked at both of them. 'Do you believe I am not capable of that part of the mission? Do you think I'm too shy and don't have the guts to seduce men?'

Miss Atkins smirked. 'Hardly. If anything, our reservation is that your shell is so hard and your manner so cold that no one would be fooled into thinking you cared for them.' She sat back and folded her arms, keeping her eyes level on Sylvie. 'I dare you to contradict me,' her expression appeared to say.

'Perhaps I am,' Sylvie said. 'But that doesn't mean I can't pretend to be otherwise. We are talking seduction, not devotion – I don't imagine the German officers will be sighing over a *Hausfrau* and looking for someone to stroke their head as much as a pair of knickers they can climb inside.'

'Sylvie, you are very hard for someone so young,' Uncle Max said. 'It always made your father sad to see.'

'It is partly my father's behaviour that made me so cynical.' Sylvie leaned forward. 'Uncle Max, you have read my file. You knew me as a child. You know everything about me, including why I am happy to assure you I have no intention of becoming besotted with any man. I don't truly believe I am capable of falling in love again.' She straightened the cuffs of her sleeves and raised her chin. 'If you choose me, you can be guaranteed that I won't have my own head turned by a handsome young example of Aryan perfection. If you don't trust me, pick someone else and use me however you see fit. If you have another dancer, of course.'

Uncle Max and Miss Atkins looked at each other and nodded.

'That is the answer we hoped for,' Uncle Max said. 'The role is yours. I have word sent to the *Librarian* network to expect you in the next fortnight.'

———

Nantes, France

1944

As the music wound itself about her, Sylvie felt completely at ease for the first time in longer than she could remember. This was what she was good at. She felt more alive dancing than doing anything else and finished the routine with barely a single error.

It came as a great disappointment to her then, when Monsieur Julien shrugged his shoulders and gave a half-hearted nod.

'Yes, you can dance,' he said. 'Technically, you're good and you learned the routine quickly. But my patrons need to be entertained, and to be entertained they need to be attracted to my girls. You dance like you don't mean it. Like you are a machine. Can you make yourself into a seductress, Mademoiselle Duchene?'

Sylvie could feel a blush rising between her breasts and spreading over her throat. Monsieur Julien's words uncomfortably reminded her of the doubts Uncle Max had expressed at her ability to appeal to men. Cold, and now lacking in sex appeal. Mechanical. It was a bitter indictment, and one she found hard to swallow.

'Play something slow, and I'll see if I can do better.' Sudden inspiration struck her and she turned to the pianist. 'I heard someone playing the accordion earlier. Was it you?'

The pianist's eyes flickered with suspicion. 'Were you here earlier?'

'I knocked, but no one answered,' Sylvie said. 'I wasn't sure if the music came from here. Was it you?'

He didn't look any less suspicious, but he nodded. 'My instrument is in the room upstairs. Wait one minute.'

He disappeared between the curtains backstage and returned a few minutes later with the accordion. It looked old and well loved, with dull patches where the varnish had been rubbed off by repeated touching. He moved his piano stool to the edge of the stage, sat and played an experimental trill, squeezing the bellows while his fingers ran up and down the keys. He paused and looked at Sylvie, tilting his head and giving her a questioning look. There was an air of challenge about him.

Sylvie knelt and removed her shoes. Her fingers shook as she undid the buckles, and she wondered if she was about to embarrass herself further. If they wanted sultry, she would give them sultry. She walked to the centre of the stage. The other dancers had joined Monsieur Julien at the table. Céline sat at the bar, a glass of wine in her hand. They were all watching her closely, so she was not sure why the pianist's attitude bothered her so much. Perhaps it was only that it had been a long time since a good-looking man had appraised her in any form.

'What is your name?' she asked him.

'Felix.' He sounded a little surprised at being asked.

'If you want passion, I can show you that,' she told Monsieur Julien. 'Can you play anything from ballet, Felix?'

'That is not really my area,' he answered. 'But if you want slow, I can give you slow.'

Felix held Sylvie's gaze as he replied, and the expression

in his eyes made her shiver. The challenge was still there, and she did not know why he seemed so determined to unnerve her. Once more, he began to play, drawing long notes from the instrument in a rhythm that seemed closest to a waltz. Sylvie began to dance again, throwing in some of the steps from the dance she had performed before but interspersing them with ballet steps. Arms extended gracefully and body held erect, she bent and extended, using the whole stage. She was Odette, dying of grief. Giselle protecting Albrecht.

Remembering how Céline had sung to Felix the night before, Sylvie worked her way over to the stool he was sitting on and danced for him alone. She bent towards him, then as he leaned forward she drew back. As she moved closer once again, Felix sped up a little. He changed the rhythm from a loping waltz into something that seemed more like a Charleston. The song was one Sylvie recognised. She changed her posture. Now she was a chorus girl like her mother had been, feet twisting and kicking, arms held rigid by her side. She tossed her head and winked at Felix, flashing him a wide smile, then pouting provocatively. He didn't return the smile. In fact, his expression looked more belligerent, though his pupils had widened and his thick black lashes flashed. He dipped his head slightly but kept his eyes on Sylvie. His fingers began to race faster, and now his lips curled into a determined smile, as if daring Sylvie to keep up with him. She rose to the challenge and began to add in a series of pirouettes and *jetés*. She improvised rapidly, becoming breathless and was relieved when, after a minute or so, Felix slowed and changed the rhythm again.

Though she was intent on the dancing, the moment he played the long, drawn out notes in a minor key, Sylvie was thrown back across the years to her teens. Traditional music. The sort that made you want to bob and kick, sway from side to side. Intoxicating and exotically foreign.

A name sprang to Sylvie's lips, but she managed not to release it aloud. Jakov. A young Jew who had performed songs from his native Russia on the fiddle in one of the theatres Sylvie's mother had performed at. The first man who Sylvie had ever persuaded to kiss her. She hadn't minded about his faith, but Angelique had later informed Sylvie that Jakov was a homosexual, crushing Sylvie's first infatuation. Still, the kiss had lit a fire in Sylvie's breasts and loins, and she did not regret it.

What has happened to Jakov? Doomed on two accounts by Hitler's new regime. Was he in a work camp somewhere, or had he been lucky enough to escape from France at the first sign of invasion? The joy flooded out of Sylvie, and she stopped abruptly, letting her hands hang limply by her side. Felix carried on playing for a few seconds longer until he realised Sylvie was not about to continue dancing.

His eyes flashed to hers. He wrinkled his brow in what might have been concern. Sylvie gave him a curt nod, one performer to another, not caring what he thought.

'Have you seen enough?' She addressed the question to Monsieur Julien, putting her hands on her hips with one foot slightly out as if posing for a photograph. 'Do you think I will pass as a performer?'

Monsieur Julien blinked and ran a finger under his collar. Sylvie hid her triumphant smile. Oh yes, she had definitely done enough to prove that she could be seductive when she wanted to be.

'You can stay,' he said. His expression darkened, and he pointed his finger at her, jabbing it to emphasise his words. 'But I'll have none of that sort of dancing or accompaniment, do you understand? My establishment will not be tainted by any association or suggestion of partiality to Jewish culture. You dance what the customers want, and Felix, you play the songs they like'

'I understand,' Sylvie replied. 'I'm sorry.'

Felix had stood and was strapping his accordion closed once again, pulling the leather straps tight around it. He had his back to Monsieur Julien.

'Felix? Tell me that won't happen again. You're lucky Mademoiselle Duchene had the sense to stop dancing. If anyone outside heard that!' He broke off and threw out his arms wide in exasperation.

'Understood. Of course,' Felix said, his voice dead. He picked up the accordion in his arms, as if it was a beloved child, and disappeared behind the curtain without making eye contact with anyone. Sylvie watched him go. Monsieur Julien followed him through the curtain.

Felix's manner and words continued to trouble her as she sat on the edge of the stage and put her shoes back on. He had sounded angry at the very public reprimand. She didn't doubt that being told she had shown more sense than he had would not endear her to him. As much as she disliked it, Monsieur Julien had talked sense. To be Jewish was dangerous and to even show an interest in anything Jewish was risky. She glanced again to the curtain. Had

Felix accidentally revealed something about himself he had not intended to, or had he been trying to trick Sylvie into revealing something about herself? She wasn't sure, but she had a sense now that there was more to the musician than she had suspected.

Chapter Seven

SEO Basic Training, Scottish Highlands

1943

'You will be working undercover. New names. New histories. Do you understand what that truly means?'

Sylvie nodded, seeing that the other women seated in the room were doing likewise. There were a few murmurs. Sergeant Kintour waited for them to die down and for silence to settle over the room once more. His piercing blue eyes ranged over the women, and Sylvie felt like a schoolgirl again. She had to resist the urge to pull her skirt down to cover her knees. The lectures were an essential part of training. The syllabus had been devised to prepare recruits as fully as possible for their work which, until they arrived at what were termed 'finishing schools', they had not been completely aware of.

'The work you carry out will be dangerous at times. Most of the time. But it will also be lonely, and that is something which is harder to anticipate or deal with. You will not be able to share your true identity with anyone, and that can leave you feeling isolated. Even the other members of your networks will not know your true names or past. You will be a part of the jigsaw, but you will not even know who the other pieces are. It is possible you could be sharing a dinner table with another member of SOE from a different unit and you will never know. The woman sitting beside you on the bus could be carrying transistor radio crystals in her bag from a safe house to a wireless operator. The man pushing the barrow of vegetables to market might have fuses and explosives hidden beneath them that he plans to detonate on the railway lines that night.'

She caught the eye of Lucy, a dark-haired woman in her early thirties, who sat to her left. They grinned at each other. It was a comical image to imagine a barrow full of carrots and bombs, but there was nothing funny about it in reality.

'Lucy. Sylvia. Are you listening?'

'Yes, sorry, sir,' Lucy answered rapidly.

Sylvie winced. Sergeant Kintour had switched from French to English, and Lucy had been so quick to assure him she was paying attention that she had answered in English. Sergeant Kintour said nothing. He didn't have to. Lucy covered her face with her hands, turning scarlet with shame. A slip like that overseas would mean detection and capture.

'Betrayal could come from anywhere,' Sergeant Kintour snapped. 'Deliberate or accidental. The less you all know about other missions being carried out, the less you will be able to reveal and the fewer associates you will incriminate.'

He lowered his voice and walked around the room, his stick tapping softly on the stone floor.

'If you are captured, lives will be in your hands and you might never know whose. Similarly, your life will be in the hands of unknown others.'

All eyes were on him.

'Wouldn't it be safer to have as little contact as possible with anyone?' asked Lucy.

Sergeant Kintour shook his head. 'No, for two reasons. First, it would raise more suspicion to ignore your colleagues. Not to say hello to the old woman in the queue at the bakery, to shy away from any social or public event. You must go about your daily lives with the confidence that comes from knowing you have nothing to hide and every right to be where you are.' He permitted himself another smile. 'Even though that will be far from the truth.'

'And the second reason?' Sylvie asked.

'Because people need company, and it is not normal to be without it. I spoke of loneliness. You cannot become hermits. For your own sanity, you will need to reach out to other people and live in whichever society you are placed in. Learn your new identities until you are perfect. The more you become that person, the more confidence you will have.'

Sylvie sat back in her chair, thinking of the evenings she had spent sitting alone, turning down offers from workmates in case Dennis might pay her an unexpected visit. Before that, all the days at school where she moved among the other girls silently and with aloofness that they returned. She had always declared she was happy to be solitary, but perhaps she was wrong.

For the rest of the afternoon, they practised their cover stories until they were word-perfect. They took turns to try to catch each other out. Lucy, visibly shaken by her blunder at speaking in English, slipped up again when asked by another trainee if her shoes had come from Harrods and proudly said they had.

That evening, Sylvie sat with Lucy by the small fire in the drawing room as they drank weak tea. Lucy's thirty years were showing on her face, and she looked anxious.

'I don't know if I can do this.' Her mouth trembled and she seemed to be fighting back tears. 'I'm making too many mistakes.'

'Of course you can,' Sylvie reassured her. 'You're the best wireless operator of all of us. My messages have twice the number of mistakes that yours do. And don't forget, you were the only one of us who could hit the head target from fifty feet away.'

'But none of that will be any use if I blunder on my first day in France. What if I'm not strong enough to hold up? I thought it would be easy to pass as French, but it's been so long since I lived there.' Lucy sat back and teased at a thread on her skirt. 'I have to do this. I *have* to. For Claude's memory.'

Sylvie poured out more tea. Lucy's husband had been a minor French aristocrat, but when the situation on the continent became unsettled and the threat of war loomed closer, he had sent Lucy back to live in England. He had been killed in the first year of the war. If Lucy thought that being out of France for five years would make it challenging, what did that mean for Sylvie's longer absence?

'How easy do you think it will really be to begin as a new person?' Lucy asked.

'Easier than you think,' Sylvie replied. She shifted her legs beneath her and settled to face Lucy on the overstuffed sofa. 'When my father brought me to live in England, I was too French for the school I went to – I had to learn to act more English.' She squeezed Lucy's hand and gave a merry laugh she didn't quite feel. 'If I can pretend to like hockey and swimming in cold pools, then you can pass for a native French woman.'

'Thank you,' Lucy said, squeezing Sylvie's hand in return. 'Sergeant Kintour is right. It does no good to hide away and not talk.'

Nantes, France

1944

'I thought Antoine would fall of his chair when you started doing those jumps,' Céline exclaimed, rushing over to the stage as soon as Monsieur Julien left. 'You must come and sit with us for a drink.'

Be sociable. Sylvie reminded herself of Sergeant Kintour's words. Don't reject the opportunities to talk with people. Sylvie stepped off the stage and looked around the club at the remaining people who had been her first audience. Three dancers, Céline and the barkeeper.

The training officer's other warning jumped into her mind. The problem with working undercover was that Sylvie had no idea who else was working undercover. As such, she did not dare to say anything that might reveal her true purpose or identity.

She knew from what Uncle Max had told her in England that Monsieur Julien was a supporter of the work SOE were doing and the Resistance, otherwise he would not have agreed to her joining his staff, but she had no idea what else he might know. She had no way of guessing whether any of the others were sympathisers, members of the Resistance, other agents, collaborators or spies for the Gestapo.

This was the prime reason for the secrecy, of course, but she reflected it would have been helpful to be able to ask out right who she could contact.

She slipped onto a chair at the table and smiled around at the new faces.

'You were superb. Wasn't she, girls?' Céline said. She sounded enthusiastic, but her smile ended before it reached her eyes. She was not completely happy. Was it because of how Sylvie had danced directly for Felix? The flirting had been harmless, but if Céline had a claim on him, she might be possessive.

Céline introduced the dancers: Adele, who Sylvie remembered had taken the party of Germans away the previous evening, Emily and Estelle. Two blondes and one brunette. Sylvie decided her own chestnut-brown hair would balance the act out well.

'Is that how you dance in Angoulême?' asked Adele. 'Was it in a nightclub or a circus?'

'Don't be rude,' said Emily, the brunette, nudging Adele in the arm.

Adele got up and walked away, scraping her chair on the floor. 'It's your turn to cook tonight, Céline,' she tossed over her shoulder. 'Hurry up, I'm hungry.'

'We all eat together,' Céline explained. 'It's never much, but Antoine's brother is a butcher and gives us the bones and scraps he has left over. Antoine likes to call it his "family dinner".'

Antoine. Sylvie hid her amusement at the way Céline tossed about Monsieur Julien's first name. Clearly the privilege was something that mattered to her.

'Of course, none of us are his family,' Emily explained. 'Though he'd happily marry any of us.'

'Marry! I don't think so.' The voluptuous woman with honey blonde hair, who Céline had introduced as Estelle, laughed. 'Watch where you let him put his hands when you're in the dressing room. Who do you think got Marie-Elaine in the family way?'

'That's not true,' Céline said. 'At least it's only half possible. She'd been walking out with a *Stabsgefreiter*. She must have done something in return for the chocolate he kept saving for her.'

Everyone laughed – Sylvie included, though she didn't know the woman. Her mouth watered a little. If she was going to have to seduce a German officer, then one who worked as a corporal wouldn't be a bad choice in times of rationing and food shortages.

'Well, if Marie-Elaine is planning to have a German baby, she had better not come begging to me for help minding it,' Estelle said primly. 'No self-respecting French woman would lower herself to do such a thing.'

'You were happy enough to share the chocolate!' Céline snapped. She and Estelle began to argue; listening to them, Sylvie realised that there was more to this than she was seeing. Remembering Céline's willingness to accept drinks from strangers, she wondered if Céline's reputation was as marred as the absent Marie-Elaine's.

'Anyhow, no one has seen Marie-Elaine for weeks,' Emily said to Sylvie. 'I do hope she's safe wherever she is.'

'Don't you know where she is?' Sylvie asked. 'Wasn't she your friend?'

Emily squeezed her hands together. She wore expensive-looking rings, Sylvie noticed.

'Not really anyone's friend. She kept to herself.'

'From the women at least,' Estelle threw in. 'She liked the men. She didn't come into work one afternoon, and after that no one saw her.'

Céline shrugged. 'She told me she was going back to her family who would look after her when the baby came.'

Sylvie hoped the girl was all right and had, indeed, simply gone home. People disappeared. They were taken and never seen again. Marie-Elaine's family might think she was in Nantes while the dancers assumed she was with them. She could be somewhere else entirely.

'I need to pay a visit to the ladies' room. Where do I go?'

she whispered to Emily, who was watching the back and forth between Estelle and Céline with interest.

'Through the curtain and under the stairs,' Emily replied, not taking her eyes off the other women.

Sylvie found the toilet; a cramped cupboard beneath the stairs where she had to step over a mop and bucket and duck her head to stand in front of the sink. After relieving herself, she didn't go straight out to the club again. She had seen the backstage area briefly when she had dropped her suitcase there and wanted to explore further. There were two rooms. A quick look in the one to the right confirmed it as the girls' dressing room, which looked onto the alley that Sylvie had walked down. The other must have been Monsieur Julien's office, as Sylvie could hear him whistling through the half-closed door.

A hand landed heavily on her shoulder and she jumped in alarm, giving a small squeak.

'What are you looking for?'

It was Felix. Sylvie had not heard him come downstairs. He was dressed in a black overcoat with a grey fedora pushed back on his head. He folded his arms and studied her, his eyes narrowing in suspicion.

'I was just wondering where I would get changed later,' Sylvie said.

Felix cocked his head in the direction of the first room. 'In there. No one goes into Monsieur Julien's office unless asked.'

'Thank you.' Sylvie smiled, but something about him was forbidding. 'I'm sure it won't take me long to find my way around.'

Felix leaned back against the wall of the narrow passage. His right leg was pushed out so his knee was out at an angle and blocking Sylvie's way. Sylvie wrinkled her brow in confusion. He seemed disinclined to talk, but did not look as if he was planning to go anywhere. Perhaps he still suspected her of snooping.

'You played very well,' she said. 'It was hard to keep up.'

'I was interested to see how much endurance you had,' Felix said. He pursed his lips. 'What made you stop in the end?'

Sylvie shrugged. She had no intention of sharing her personal memories of Jakov or explaining the reason. 'I thought Monsieur Julien had seen enough to decide.'

She leaned her back against the wall opposite and extended her legs a little into the passageway, crossing her ankles. She was careful not to touch his legs, but there wasn't much distance between them. She folded her arms and stared him out.

'It was an interesting choice of tune, your final one. What made you pick it?' she probed.

The musician's lips curled into a sardonic smile. He reached into the pocket of his trousers and pulled out a packet of cigarettes. Instead of lighting it, he held it between the finger and thumb of his left hand and pointed it at Sylvie.

'Are you hoping to lead me into an incriminating admission? Subversive talk or behaviour? Are you a German spy? Will I soon find myself installed in a cell for questioning?'

Sylvie's mouth fell open. Did he really suspect her of spying for the Abwehr? He saw her astonishment and laughed.

'I'm teasing you, mademoiselle.'

Sylvie didn't laugh and he grew serious again.

'You can play whatever you want. I'm not in the business of informing anyone of anything,' Sylvie sneered. She tried not to blush, conscious that was a lie. She lifted her chin and looked him straight in the eye. 'And when it comes to endurance, I have more than you would expect.'

Felix's eyes widened, and he grinned wolfishly. 'Do you now? Maybe I will look forward to finding out how true that is, mademoiselle.'

Sylvie bit back the retort that sprang to her lips. She knew damn well he was not talking about dancing any longer. She glanced at his hands, now twisting the cigarette between long, elegant fingers. Musicians' hands. An image filled her mind of them deftly teasing at her underwear, and a flicker of eagerness made her belly tighten.

'I don't know what you mean,' she said haughtily. She pushed herself from the wall and stalked past him. Her thigh brushed against his out-stuck knee, conjuring the sensation of heat that lingered even when she went into the dressing room. When she turned to close the door, Felix was still standing there, watching her. She glared at him, and he dropped his head, cupping the cigarette in his hand and lighting it.

She sat on a chair in front of the mirror and gazed blankly into the glass. Felix may not have shown any interest while Sylvie had been dancing, but it appeared that

Monsieur Julien was not the only man in the room who has been affected by her performance. She bit her fingernail and replayed the events of the afternoon.

The pianist was dangerous. The music he had played, the way he had asked if she was a spy; Felix had been playing with her, trying to intimidate her. Or perhaps he was flirting, albeit badly. She didn't like the way her body had decided it appreciated his interest in spite of her best intentions.

She was relieved that despite Céline telling her everyone ate together, Felix did not appear at the dinner table in the room above the club, only appearing again at half past eight and settling himself straight at his piano.

Sylvie had realised at a young age that she had a weakness for dark-haired men, but for more reasons than she could list, she was determined to steer clear of this one.

Chapter Eight

SOE Basic Training, Scottish Highlands

1943

'How would you defend yourself from attack?'
'Shoot the attacker?'

The voice from the back of the gymnasium made everyone laugh, though Sylvie noticed there was a nervous edge to the sound.

Captain Walters, who was leading the day's lessons, grinned amiably.

'In certain situations, and always remember, fire two bullets. The Double Tap as we call it. but guns are useful only in the circumstance where there would be no cover story needed. If you are assaulted walking through the streets before curfew, you can't pull out a pistol and see off your assailant – you would not be carrying a weapon in ordinary life.'

Captain Walters thrust his hands behind his back, linking his fingers and stuck his chest out. Broad and tall, he looked to Sylvie as if his mere presence would see off any attackers.

'Today, we will begin our training in close combat. This is designed to aid you when you have lost your weapon or in situations where weapons are inadvisable. Have you all read the syllabus?'

The recruits nodded and looked about them at the fellow students who would soon become their opponents. Sylvie had memorised the list of sessions until they were seared on her brain.

Body blows with various parts of the anatomy.

How to release oneself from a restraining hold.

Crowd fighting.

Knife fighting.

Disarming an opponent.

Killing an opponent.

The pile of straw-filled dummies did not give much cause for reassurance; the day would be long and hard and most probably involve pain.

'The men among you will no doubt be familiar with the Queensberry Rules. You can forget them now. They have no place in *war*.'

His voice rose, barking out the final word.

'Ladies, you will be taught – and expected to carry out – exactly the same techniques as the men. No soft treatment. No special considerations.'

A couple of the men began to look uncertain. Sylvie wondered if it had occurred to them that the women who sat alongside them at the dining tables and in lectures would be joining them in the gymnasium and they would have to train together.

For the whole morning, they practised blocking blows and grappling with each other until they were starting to become proficient. When they resumed after lunch, they were allocated new partners.

'You won't always be fortunate enough to find yourself up against someone of the same build,' Captain Walters explained.

'Hold on, do you expect me to attack a woman?' asked the heavily built blond man standing beside Sylvie. He looked down at her with uncertainty written all over his face.

'I expect you to attack each other,' Captain Walters replied. 'Gentlemen, unfortunately you will have to overcome your qualms about striking a member of the fair sex. Ladies, you will have to learn how to escape from a man using force.'

'I think most of us have done that once or twice already,' interjected a statuesque woman from the back to general laughter. Sylvie joined in. Fortunately, she'd never been in the position of having to fight off a man; she'd made some inadvisable choices with regards to boyfriends, but the only injuries had been to her heart or ego.

'Strength isn't everything,' Captain Walters reminded them. 'Surprise can buy you an advantage. Now we will teach you how to maximise that.'

He clapped his hands sharply and the room stood to attention.

'Same drill as this morning. Take turns and begin.'

Nantes, France

1944

The first night was a success. Sylvie danced for two of the numbers with the promise that the following evening she could join the girls for more when she had learned the routines. When she was not dancing, she served drinks at tables, a smile fixed on her face as she dodged roving hands and tried to listen out for snippets of conversation that might be useful. By the end of the evening, she was ready to drop, having been on her feet for most of the day. As she walked away from the club, she stifled a yawn. She was starting to see why Céline spent most of the morning in bed.

'Wait a second, mademoiselle.'

Sylvie hesitated. The voice had spoken in a confidential manner and sounded familiar. She turned slowly round, adjusting the bag tucked under her arm as she did so. The man who had called her name was silhouetted against the dim streetlight. He wore a familiar hat with the brim pulled down over his face, but there was enough light among the shadows for Sylvie to recognise him.

'Felix?'

The pianist took a step closer. His long Mackintosh coat was undone, and he put his hands into the pockets of his trousers. There was a slight swagger in his walk. Perhaps he hoped he resembled an American film star. Sylvie had seen him watching her as she danced with more open interest than when he had accompanied her audition. She disliked acknowledging that she was aware of the audience members during a performance so had tried not to make eye contact with him, but she had a vivid picture of the intense watchful gaze from his violet-blue eyes.

'What do you want to talk to me about?' she asked.

'I wanted to congratulate you on your performance,' he said. 'I didn't get a chance earlier.'

He had found her interesting, she suspected; a new dancer might be a possible conquest, and now he was deciding to make his move. She took another step and let her eyes slide surreptitiously from side to side. The street wasn't completely empty, but they were isolated enough that if the pianist decided not to take no for an answer, she might be in a sticky situation. He took another step closer. Voices from further down the street were coming a little closer. The sound of singing with a slight slur suggested patrons of other bars were making their way home.

'You had a strange way of showing it earlier in the day, accusing me of spying, and making innuendo.'

He frowned, but Sylvie couldn't tell whether that was because of her reference to innuendo or spying. Her nerves jangled. What if *he* was a spy? A member of the Abwehr or, worse, the Gestapo. A man of his age who was by all appearances perfectly healthy should be fighting for his country. There must be some reason he was not.

'I should go,' Sylvie said. 'It's almost curfew and I need to get home.'

She continued walking, which brought her alongside the entrance to another alley. Felix sauntered alongside her as if he had no cares in the world. She felt his eyes on her and kept hers firmly on the darkened pavement.

'Have you settled into your accommodation?' Felix asked. 'Do you have far to go?'

'I'm not going to tell you that.'

Sylvie felt a little of the tension in her shoulders melting away. She was more certain now that this was a clumsy attempt at seduction. Perhaps Felix didn't often need to waste his time with conversation. He was good-looking and had a debonair air about him. Sylvie had already felt the tug of his charm. She didn't doubt other women – women who weren't as determined as she was to avoid letting any man break down her walls – would gladly slip into his arms and bed.

'My room is very pleasant, thank you.' She tucked her coat a little tighter around herself and left her arms folded across her chest. 'Although I am far from ready for visitors, before you ask.'

Felix gave a deep chuckle. He had an appealing laugh and the sound made Sylvie want to smile in response; it went well with his well-shaped mouth. Annoyed that she had even noticed that detail, she shifted the weight of her bag under her arm to make the opening more accessible and began to rummage inside. If the pianist had any bold ideas, then the heavy brass rings that she could slip onto her hand would soon change his mind. In other circumstances it would have amused her to think she might conceivably take him by surprise and do him serious injury, but now she was tired and wanted to get to bed.

'Nicely evaded, mademoiselle,' Felix said. 'Don't worry, I'm going home myself now. I wasn't presuming to invite myself up for an apéritif.'

Sylvie narrowed her eyes. 'Surely an apéritif is what you have at the start of the evening. This one is almost over.'

He laughed again and leaned against the wall with his hands in his trouser pockets, pushing his unbuttoned overcoat back. 'I know that. In my view, it doesn't matter how late the evening starts if it shows promise.'

'Well, this one doesn't,' Sylvie said firmly as she began to walk away. 'I'm tired. I don't have time for fooling about.'

'Neither do I,' Felix said, following her. 'I merely thought I would introduce myself properly and see how you are finding Nantes. Have you seen the Loire by moonlight, for example?'

The hairs on the back of Sylvie's neck stood on end. Her footstep faltered and she slowed as a band of iron around her chest seemed to cut off her breath. That was the start of the code phrase that would allow her to confirm the identity of her contact. She had memorised the reply she had to give and what the counter reply to that should be. She let go of the knuckleduster and closed her bag.

She knew Marcel was English, well-built and with blond hair. Hair colour could be changed, but Felix was too lean.

Moreover, unless he was the best actor in France, the dark-haired man who was standing before her with such an infuriating expression on his face was definitely French.

It could just be a coincidence that he had asked that question. Or worse, it was a trap. Marcel hadn't appeared, and Sylvie still had no explanation why. If Felix knew the code, then he either knew Marcel or where he might be. The question was whether he was an ally or the man responsible for the agent's disappearance.

There was the sound of a door creaking open and then voices in German wishing someone good night. A female voice answered and then the door slammed. On their way to Céline's apartment the night before, the singer had pointed out the discreetly painted black door with a bouquet of dried roses hanging in the window three doors down from the club. She had explained it was a brothel for the sole use of the German officers.

'Singing for them is not so bad considering what we could be doing,' she had remarked. Sylvie had agreed, imagining the lives of the unfortunate women forced into prostitution for the occupying forces. She had heard rumours. Been warned.

Footsteps were heading their way.

The pianist growled and stepped smoothly round in front of Sylvie. 'I don't have time to fool around either, mademoiselle. Tell me: have you seen the Loire by moonlight?'

It was unmistakable now. He had used the same question twice. Whether or not it was a trap, Sylvie had little choice but to respond or run, with all the complications that would entail. She had waited two days without contact. This was not the way she was supposed to meet Marcel, but perhaps it was the only way her contact could safely get in touch.

'I couldn't see it clearly because of the fog,' she answered in a low voice, giving the phrase she had memorised.

'What is going on there?' came a voice speaking in French but heavily accented with German.

'You should be careful you don't fall in,' the pianist answered. The counter response.

'Who is that?' the German shouted. 'Stay where you are!'

Sylvie looked at the pianist in panic. It was too appalling to think that she would be discovered at the same moment she had finally made contact.

She tensed, expecting him to seize her by the wrist and hand her over. She braced herself to run. Felix's lips were set in a firm line, and his stance had become alert.

'Friend not foe,' he muttered as he tucked Sylvie's arm under his. He moved swiftly, pulling her down the alley into the darkness. Sylvie gasped in surprise, followed by a yelp as she skidded on something she had to hope was mud. Felix pulled her upright, lifting her easily with his hands beneath her armpit, and backed her against the wall.

'Forgive me for what I am about to do, mademoiselle,' he whispered.

He pushed his body up against Sylvie's, one hand at her waist and the other over her breasts. His fingers fumbled with the buttons on her blouse and deftly slipped beneath the silk. She gasped in shock as his fingers brushed against the mound of her breast and something scratched the delicate skin.

Felix removed his hands. He put them either side of Sylvie's head, holding her firmly, and kissed her. She didn't have time to protest as his lips frantically moved against hers. The scent of vanilla and lavender from his cologne mingled with the taste of tobacco. Rich and seductive.

The burst of pleasure that shot through her as their tongues tangled was jarringly good, but she was damned if she was going to kiss him back. She squeezed her hands between their bodies and dug her nails into his shirt front. As Felix pulled away from Sylvie, she bunched her fist and delivered a punch to his jaw. His head jerked, then he straightened back up. Their eyes met and she just had time to see the anger boiling in his before a burst of light blinded her and made her screw her eyes tight shut.

'What is going on down here? There are ten minutes until curfew.'

They both looked, blinking, to the end of the alley where a figure stood in silhouette holding a torch raised to shoulder height.

'We are just having a bit of fun,' Felix said. 'No harm in it.'

He rubbed his palm across his jaw and glared at Sylvie.

'Is he telling the truth, *fräulein*?' The German marched into the alleyway. 'I take a dim view of rape.'

Sylvie shook her head. She slipped out from between Felix and the wall. 'It was not my idea of fun but I don't need help.'

'I wasn't going to rape her,' Felix exclaimed. 'We're just making friends. We work together.'

'You are both from the club.' The German flashed his torch across both their faces. 'I saw you playing tonight. And you danced. Is he telling the truth or should I arrest him?'

'No!' Sylvie exclaimed. This was a dreadful tangle. An enemy officer was threatening to arrest her contact. The pianist had not endeared himself to her, but she knew which side she was on. 'I mean, don't arrest him. He misunderstood what I said and thought I agreed to something I didn't.'

'Then either he should pay more attention or you should make yourself clearer,' the German said. 'You! Get home,' he barked at Felix.

Felix slid his eyes towards Sylvie and raised his brows. She gave the smallest nod she could. He adjusted his hat and nodded his head stiffly to the officer, then walked away. He paused at the end of the alley to look back one final time before disappearing. Sylvie looked properly at the German officer.

'I recognise you. You were at the club tonight. On the table at the back.'

'That's right.' He nodded seriously.

He was a blushing young man who had sat in the corner of his group looking as if he would have preferred to be anywhere else while his companions applauded and drank. He'd been one of the party who she had encountered in the street on the first night she had arrived.

'You didn't enjoy yourself?'

The officer looked down at his hands. 'I enjoyed the music. Some of it is very new to me.'

'But not the dancing?' Sylvie asked.

He looked at her with his head on one side. 'Oh no, *fräulein*. The dancers were very good too. Very pretty.'

There was an earnest air about him that Sylvie found oddly endearing. But he was a German, so what was she doing practically flirting with him? True, she had agreed to use any opportunity to find out secrets, but this young man hardly seemed the best use of her time.

'Where do you live, *fräulein*? Do you need someone to take you home?'

'No.' The last thing Sylvie needed was to call attention to herself or give a member of the German army knowledge of where she lived. 'That is, no, thank you. It is very close and I am fine.' To emphasise her words, she straightened her hat and coat. She sighed. 'The only damage is to my stockings. One of them has a run in it.'

The German's eyes dropped to her legs. He was young. A year or two older than Sylvie at most.

'I'll be fine, but thank you.'

She walked past him, holding her breath until she reached the street. A shadowy figure in the recess of the brothel doorway caught her attention as she stepped out. She craned her head and the shadow receded deeper into the doorway. Despite being told to leave, Felix had lingered to see if she was safe. She nodded and he slipped away silently. Impulsively, Sylvie looked back at her unlikely German knight in armour. He was adjusting the torch and pistol at his belt and looked at her with narrowed eyes.

'Perhaps I will see you at the club another night.'

'Perhaps,' he said. 'Go safely now. Good night, *fräulein*.'

Sylvie walked to the end of the road in what she hoped was a casual manner. She pulled her coat around herself and tightened the belt, although the night was warm. When she had crossed the street and rounded another corner, she began to stride out, determined to lose the German if he happened to be following her.

Chapter Nine

Sylvie entered her lodgings quietly and closed the door with barely a click. From Madame Giraud's room came the sound of a gramophone playing a creaky old waltz. She walked up the stairs on tiptoes. Even though her landlady was half-deaf, Sylvie didn't want to risk being noticed and invited in for a chat and reminisce.

Once in her room, Sylvie hung her coat on the back of the door, kicked off her shoes and sat at the table. Only then, when she was as sure as reasonably possible that no one might be watching her, did she reach inside her brassiere and pull out the piece of paper Felix had pushed there when his hand had fumbled against her breast. For a moment she simply held it, reliving the sensation of his fingers brushing against her flesh. She curled her lip and shuddered. He might be an ally, but she had no regrets for punching him hard.

The paper was folded twice and was torn from a piece of sheet music. Sylvie opened it with growing anticipation.

There were very few words on the paper, but it felt like the most significant message she had ever received.

The name of a café and a time, and finally one word.

Marcel.

Felix was not Marcel. He couldn't possibly be, but in Marcel's absence he might be the only link she had. Sylvie memorised the name and time of the meeting before carefully rolling the paper into a cylinder lengthways. Her room contained a small gas ring with a single burner. She lit the gas, held the cylinder over the flame and watched the paper burn to ash. There was a knock at the door.

'Sylvie, are you there? Can I talk to you, please? Let me in.'

Céline's voice. She sounded as if she was holding back tears.

'One moment,' Sylvie called.

She looked at the small pile of ash in her hand. She had intended to tip the small pile out of the windows so no one would be any the wiser, but couldn't do that with Céline waiting. Sylvie tipped the ash into a small pan, added water and some of the coffee grounds from her tin. It was really too late to be drinking coffee, but until there was absolutely no trace of the message she would not be at ease. In any case, after the excitement of the night, she would not sleep easily. She left the pot to boil on the ring and opened the door.

Céline stood there in her lace and satin nightgown with a slightly more sensible dressing gown over the top.

'Where have you been? I've been listening out for you. I thought you left about the same time I did.'

Céline sounded almost accusatory as she stared at Sylvie with a plaintive look in her eyes. A flicker of irritation raced through Sylvie as she felt like a fourteen-year-old girl under her stepmother's gaze. She had every right to be wherever she wanted to be and was about to answer to that effect when she caught herself. It wasn't Céline's fault.

'I was fixing my shoe. The buckle came loose. Then I started walking in the wrong direction and didn't even notice until I'd gone almost a mile. It took me ages to find my way home.' Catching herself babbling, she paused. *Never over explain*, she reminded herself, *it smacks of having something to hide.* She smiled at Céline. 'I'm making coffee. Would you like a cup while you tell me what's wrong?'

Céline nodded and sniffled again. She sidled in, shoulders drooping and a handful of handkerchiefs clutched to her face.

'I fought with Alphonse again. He told me I should have worn my red hat like he wanted me to. I told him I wanted to wear my blue one, but he said it makes me look old.'

Sylvie listened absent-mindedly, nodding and making sympathetic noises as she poured the coffee. How silly to have quarrelled over a hat and got into such a state. She had no idea who Alphonse was, but he was right; blue really didn't suit Céline.

The two women sat at the small table and sipped the sludgy brew. Céline continued to talk, sharing more of her romantic troubles than Sylvie could ever hope to remember. She didn't appear to notice anything untoward in what she was drinking. If anything, the burnt ash added a depth of flavour that had been missing in the weak chicory-adulterated coffee Sylvie had been used to. It reminded her a little of the first taste of real coffee she had ever tried sitting on her mother's lap as a child aged eight in the evening sunlight. She had felt so grown-up.

Instantly, she was transported back across years to a café in a square of a village she had long forgotten the name of. That had been a good day. They had sung songs and Mother had danced in the arms of the man from the theatre who dressed as a woman when he performed slightly racy songs. She smiled to herself, lost in the memories, until Céline tugged at her sleeve.

'What do you think I should do?'

Sylvie blinked. 'Wear the hat you want to wear and tell Alphonse to jump in the Loire,' she said. 'That's what I would do if a man told me what to wear.'

Celine laughed and sniffed again. 'You're so daring. I bet you tell men all the time to do exactly what you say, and if they don't you up and leave. The way you faced off against Felix earlier was wonderful. I wish I was as confident as you.'

Sylvie smiled, remembering the impact of her palm against the pianist's cheek, and gathered the cups. She left them on the table by the coffee can and ushered Céline out.

'I learned the hard way that men aren't worth the tears they make a woman shed. Go to bed, Céline. I'll see you tomorrow.'

She ushered the singer out and went to bed herself, but as she had anticipated, she couldn't sleep. Her first night as a performer had been a success, and she had finally made contact with someone who could lead her to Marcel. What a pity he seemed so objectionable. Now her real job was about to begin.

The café was one of those indistinct little establishments that littered every French city. Tables for two or four spilled out onto the wide pavement with more inside, while a row of six chairs were set at the bar to the rear. Sylvie had dressed for the rendezvous in her red coat and teal blue hat. Perhaps the conversation with Céline had prompted the choice of outfit because unlike Céline's pale blonde colouring, Sylvie knew the colour set off her chestnut hair. Halfway to the café, it struck her she had dressed to impress the man she was meeting, but there was no time to go back and change.

The pianist had taken a table right at the back of the café by the door into the kitchen. As Sylvie entered, he rose from his seat and came to greet her. He rested his hands on her shoulders and leaned forward to kiss her on both cheeks as if they were old friends. Sylvie caught his eye as he moved from one cheek to the other and glared. He removed his hands and pulled her chair out for her to sit down.

Sylvie had worried she would be conspicuous, but if anything she was underdressed. Each table appeared to be occupied by a more flamboyantly dressed woman accompanied by an older man in a suit. There were no German uniforms to be seen. As new dresses were hard to come by, the women of France had decreed that hats would be as vibrant as possible. With the number of feathers and flowers on display, it was like walking into an aviary or tropical garden. There would be a lot of pet parakeets missing their tails! The clientele did not look to be suffering under the occupation.

'What sort of place is this?' Sylvie asked as she sat and drew her chair to the table.

The pianist gave her a long stare. 'The sort of place an ambitious woman might come to try to meet a patron or a new *friend*.'

'You mean prostitutes,' Sylvie said. She glanced around again. If these women were whores, then they were not like the sad scraps who Sylvie had seen hanging around street corners.

'I'm sure they would not term themselves that,' Felix replied, wrinkling his brow in disapproval. 'These aren't the sort of women who will give you a quick once over in an alley behind the Hôtel de Ville. They have greater ambition than that. More class.'

'So why did you suggest meeting me here?' Sylvie asked.

'Because it is somewhere two people of the opposite sex may converse without causing comment.'

'Why not talk to me at Mirabelle though?' Sylvie asked.

Felix raised his hand and motioned to Sylvie to stop talking, then began waving his fingers lazily about in the air until a waiter appeared.

'Coffee or something stronger?' he asked Sylvie.

Sylvie smiled politely. 'Whatever you choose.'

He ordered coffee and two glasses of pastis. Spirits? At half past ten on a Saturday morning? Sylvie inwardly rolled her eyes. This was obviously a rite of passage or test of some sort. She waited until the waiter had gone, then folded her arms on the table, leaned forward and fixed the pianist with a firm stare.

'Why didn't you talk to me at the club rather than insisting I come all the way across the city?'

He narrowed his eyes and copied her movements so they were face to face across the table. His eyes remained fixed on hers, and, once again, she felt the stirring of attraction beneath the confrontation.

'Why didn't you give me the response straightaway?' he asked. 'That could have solved a lot of problems. You put us both in danger last night.'

'I didn't know if it was a trap,' Sylvie answered after a moment. 'You don't match the description of the man who is supposed to contact me. Are you Marcel or merely a messenger sent by him? Is your name Felix or is that a codename?'

'I'm not Marcel,' the pianist admitted. 'Felix is my real name. I don't have an alias.'

Sylvie narrowed her eyes. Was this a trap? She took a slow breath to calm the rising flicker of anxiety. She resisted the urge to look around at the other patrons, knowing that would cause suspicion in itself, conscious that just because there were no German uniforms did not necessarily mean there were no Germans. Anyone in plain clothes would be infinitely more dangerous.

'What is your connection to Marcel?'

Felix leaned forward. 'Marcel and I know each other well. We have worked together on numerous occasions.

He has provided useful aid and equipment to people I know.'

'You're in the Resistance?' Sylvie asked in an undertone.

He sat back, folding his arms across his chest. Equipment would mean weapons, explosives, ammunition. She couldn't imagine the man before her risking his life.

'Where is Marcel?' Sylvie asked.

A look of worry crossed Felix's face. 'I don't know. I saw him five nights ago. He mentioned a new woman was coming and to look out for you. He told me what the exchange to verify you was and that you would be working at Mirabelle. I have not seen him since.'

His eyes narrowed. They were very blue, Sylvie noticed, and in contrast with his dark hair. He was a good-looking man. Something that no doubt he knew himself. He leaned forward and stared at her.

'Why did you wait so long before asking me?' she asked. 'Marcel was supposed to meet me three nights ago.'

'Much better for you to cool your heels for a day or two than immediately be arrested as a spy, don't you agree? I wasn't sure you were the person I needed. Marcel vanished, then you arrived and made rather a flamboyant entrance at Mirabelle in the company of a party of Germans after all. You match the description Marcel gave me, but you might be a German spy trying to infiltrate the Resistance.'

Felix drummed his fingers on the edge of the table. Sylvie bit her lip. She had been so concerned as to whether she could trust Felix that she hadn't really considered that it went both ways.

'I am who I say I am, though, of course, a spy would say that as well.'

His lips twitched into a smile. 'Mademoiselle, tell me, are you French or English?'

'I'm French,' she said, then amended. 'But I've travelled here from England.'

He sat back, seemingly satisfied.

She sat back and sighed, closing her eyes briefly. Astonishingly, she felt tears beginning to gather behind her closed lids and an ache spreading up the back of her neck. 'I cannot prove it, and I have no way of contacting home. I'm stranded here.'

When she opened her eyes, she found Felix staring intently at her with what she suspected passed for a sympathetic look.

'Don't despair, Mademoiselle Duchene, you are the only dancer who has started recently, so I took the chance that the agent had to be you and that you are what you say you are.'

She let out a low sigh of relief. 'What I am unsure about is why you introduced yourself in such a farcical manner. You could have spoken to me like a normal person rather than stalking me through the streets.'

His expression darkened. Obviously, he did not like being accused of foolishness. 'I wanted to see how you would react. You must understand, mademoiselle, that England sends us agents and we have no option but to trust that you are on our side and capable of doing what is required. Seeing how agents react to unexpected circumstances gives me an indication of their mettle. I cannot afford to risk that by putting my trust in unsuitable people when I am fighting for my country.'

He sounded so arrogant. At his suggestion that she might be inadequate, Sylvie bristled.

'France is my country too,' she snapped, 'and you do not get to judge if I am worthy enough to fight for her.'

'You really are French?' She felt his eyes roving up and down her face and nodded.

He rested his elbows on the table, linking his hands with his first fingers extending towards Sylvie. The waiter arrived with black coffee in two small cups. He placed down two shot glasses and poured pastis into them before leaving.

'Which first,' Felix asked, 'coffee or a toast?'

Sylvie sat back and folded her arms. 'Why do you assume I want to toast with you?' she asked.

Felix looked surprised. 'We are allies and colleagues. Why would you not?'

He reached for the nearest glass of pastis. Sylvie pointedly picked up her coffee and sipped it. It was hot and wet, but that was about all that could be said in its favour. She longed for the days when cream, or even milk, had been readily available. 'We are allies, that is true, but that doesn't mean I have to like you. I am choosy about the men I drink with.'

'And why do I not measure up to your standards?' Felix asked.

'Groping me hardly recommends you to me.'

'That was not part of my plan,' he admitted. 'If you had given the response when I asked, we would never have drawn attention to ourselves. You will discover when you have been at this game a little longer that plans sometimes have to change with a moment's notice.'

He raised one brow and gave her a sardonic look. Sylvie leaned forwards again and placed her hands on the table close to his. To anyone in the café, it would hopefully look as if they were about to hold hands.

'How do you test the mettle of a man?' Sylvie asked.

'Sometimes I accuse them of spilling my drink,' Felix said. 'I see how they handle themselves in a potential fight. Sometimes I challenge them over the supposed flirtation with a lover.'

'I'm disappointed,' Sylvie said, pouting. 'I was hoping to discover you slip your notes somewhere equally personal about their bodies?'

Felix raised his brow and then burst out laughing. His eyes gleamed. 'Very good, mademoiselle. You can count that as a win. A point to you. Fortunately, it has not been necessary for me to get within fondling distance of any of Marcel's male agents.'

'It will not be necessary for you to get that close to me again,' Sylvie warned. 'Save your toast for another time. You treat this as a game, but I am not interested in games. I am here to do what needs to be done, and nothing more. Tell me what I need to know and let me be gone.'

She drained her coffee cup in one, bravado and annoyance overtaking caution, and leaving her with a burnt tongue. She held in the grimace of pain, determined not to reveal any emotion to the cocky bastard sitting opposite her. Felix stared at her and pressed his lips, then he grinned.

'You're right,' he said. 'It isn't a game, but sometimes we have to lie to ourselves to make the truth bearable. I will drink to you, Mademoiselle Duchene, even if you will not join me.'

He raised his glass to her and drained it.

'I will ask around and find out what I can. I might be able to reach another of Marcel's contacts who can verify you are who you say you are. If I do, then I will pass word to you at the club tonight or tomorrow.'

'Thank you,' Sylvie said.

'If you don't want that, I'll drink it,' he said, gesturing to the shot glass. 'I don't want it to go to waste.'

'Feel free.' Sylvie shrugged.

She stood and gathered her bag and gloves. Felix rose and lean forward to kiss her cheeks in the traditional manner of parting. As he kissed her second cheek, he leaned a moment longer than necessary and whispered in her ear.

'You acquitted yourself excellently last night, in case you are interested. You throw a good punch. My jaw hasn't ached like that for a long time.'

She pulled away. He sounded amused, and when she looked into his eyes, they were dancing. Her lips turned traitor and curved into a smile. She forced it away.

'I'd be happy to repeat the experience any time you would like.'

Felix grinned, and for a moment Sylvie found herself liking him. She walked out into the sunshine and away from the café. The meeting had gone better than she had expected. A mild flirtation and the crossing of linguistic swords with Felix was merely a thin scraping of icing on top of a very small cake. Felix might be a little full of his own importance, but she believed he was genuinely an ally, and she felt more optimistic than she had at any time since arriving in Nantes.

Now she had only one other task to occupy her: successfully infiltrate the dance troupe.

Chapter Ten

Poitiers

1928

'Pass me my hairbrush, *chérie*.'

Angelique waved her hand in the direction of the dressing table. Sylvie rummaged among the cigarette boxes, vials of perfume and open pots of face paint and took the brush to her mother.

'Can I brush it, please, *Maman*?' she begged.

'Not tonight, *chérie*. I'm running too far behind time, and the curtain will rise soon. In the morning, I promise. And tomorrow night.'

Angelique popped a kiss on Sylvie's forehead and patted her daughter's cheek.

'You can do my hair too, *ma poupette*,' called Soraya, one of the other dancers, kindly, taking Angelique's brush and running it through her sleek bob. 'We all appreciate your help.'

Sylvie bit her lip. She wasn't a doll, though the twelve-strong troupe that Angelique danced in treated her as one. She was their mascot or pet. To have so many grown women paying her attention was nice, but she wasn't one of them. Yet.

She settled on the stool beside Angelique and fingered a strand of the long fringe that fell from the thigh-length skirt of Angelique's costume. She watched in admiration as Angelique separated her black tresses into plump rolls and secured them in place with feathered combs, longing for the day when she could pin and wrap her own hair in the same manner. She would be ten soon – that must nearly be old enough.

She sighed. One day, the feathers and spangles would be hers. The powders and lipsticks and heels. It was what she wanted most of all. *Les Filles Luciole*: The Firefly Girls, named for the final number of the show where they wore leotards with radium-paint covered beads that glowed under the lights as they danced. It was the most magical thing in the world.

She trailed her fingers over the tassels on the short cloak that hung around the back of Angelique's chair and pictured of the day she could join them.

'How is your dancing, *chou-fleur*?' A voice called from the other end of the dressing room. Rosetta was one of Sylvie's particular favourites, a beautiful woman with the glossiest, tightest curls of black hair Sylvie had ever seen. Sylvie would never even dare attempt to fix

Rosetta's hair which required a hot comb to straighten it.

Sylvie stood once more and began to dance one of the routines with high kicks and tapping heels. She received a loud round of applause and began to dance the Charleston.

'Keep rehearsing, *poupette* and you'll be joining us soon. I'll teach you the Black Bottom tomorrow night,' Rosetta promised.

There was a knock on the door. Sylvie rushed to answer it. One of the stagehands stood there, almost hidden behind a huge bouquet of roses and carnations.

'A delivery for Mademoiselle Duchene. Flowers!'

Sylvie took the heavy armful and carried the bouquet to her mother. The other women gathered round, cooing and chattering.

'Who are they from this time?'

'Another admirer, you little *nénette*!'

Angelique laughed and read the card. 'Monsieur Clement. I'm dining with him tonight.'

'What about Oncle Henri?' Sylvie asked. 'Won't he mind?'

Angelique shrugged. 'He might, but as we're moving on to another town at the end of the week, I won't have to put up with him sulking.'

Sylvie frowned. 'Won't you miss Oncle Henri?'

Angelique leaned forward and patted Sylvie's cheek. '*Ma petite*, men are nice to have around, but they will leave you. Don't allow yourself to become too attached to one or they will break your heart.'

'What your mother means is use them before they use

you,' commented the woman on the next stool. She twisted her ginger curls and wrinkled her nose until the freckles stood out against her pale skin. 'Isn't that right, Angelique?'

'Completely. And I cannot suffer a man who sulks!'

'Not even if he has the tortured soul of an artist?'

'Perhaps then!'

The women all laughed. Sylvie didn't join in. She had liked Oncle Henri, who brought her candied ginger when he visited Angelique and showed her the watercolour sketches he made of the river. He was not her real uncle, of course. Mother had no brothers or sisters. Before him there had been Oncle Albert, Oncle Vincent, Oncle Martin...

Lots of uncles. Whenever The Firefly Girls came to a new town, it didn't take Angelique long to find a handsome or rich man to take her dancing and dining. It made Angelique happy and meant her eyes didn't contain the sadness that tore Sylvie's heart whenever she saw it.

A bell rang out, calling the women to the stage. There was a sudden flurry of women adding final touches to their makeup or outfits, then they rushed out, leaving Angelique alone with Sylvie.

'Go to sleep, *chérie*,' she said, cocking her head to the small camp bed pushed into the far corner of the dressing room where Sylvie's storybook and cloth rabbit were waiting. Sylvie had spent most nights she could remember falling asleep in different dressing rooms while the troupe performed, then being woken to return to lodgings late at night. She found it harder to fall asleep in silence than to the background murmur of voices and strains of different music.

'I'll wake you when I come back from dinner. I love you.'

'I love you too, *Maman*.' She gazed up at her mother. She couldn't give her a hug without risking damage to the flimsy wisps of chiffon and gauze that made up her costume, so she settled for touching her fingers lightly to Angelique's soft roll of hair. Sylvie's hair was lighter than her mother's, a nice brown, but without the gleam that came with blackness. She must have her father's colouring.

'Did you love my papa?' she asked.

'What a strange question,' Angelique said with a gentle laugh. Her eyes grew misty and the amusement fell from her face. 'Yes. I did. But he couldn't stay with me.'

She dropped a kiss on Sylvie's forehead. She hurried away but turned back at the door.

'Remember, *ma chérie*, keep your heart safe when you're old enough to give it away, but don't be too quick to do so.'

Nantes, France

1944

'Have you seen my stocking? I can't find it anywhere.'

It took Sylvie a moment to realise the dark-haired woman standing in front of her dressed in an open negligee and lingerie was actually talking to Sylvie.

The last time she had been surrounded by members of

her own sex had been when she was training for her role in SOE. Before that it had been at boarding school, but the camaraderie she had expected to find from her experiences of living with The Firefly Girls as a child were nowhere to be seen. She'd been too sophisticated and bohemian. Too French. She had found little in common with the well-read and academic English girls with their sensible plaits and enthusiasm for sport. She kept herself to herself, which resulted in a reputation for being stand-offish.

Now, much to her delight, after a few nights of working at the club, she found herself welcomed into a world of female confidences and gossip. The small dressing room that was shared between the five women was a hive of activity and chaos. It was smoky and loud, littered with the clothes, makeup and jewellery of too many women crammed into a small space in front of two mirrors. Sylvie had sat and watched in awe at first, putting on her powder and cream, slightly nervous of the glamorous women she shared the stage with. It occurred to her that this world would be as hard to infiltrate as the covert society she had been thrown into. If the women of Angelique's troupe could see her now! If only her mother had lived to see her daughter follow in her high-kicking footsteps. Sylvie gazed round the room. All white faces. Where were Rosetta and Soraya, she wondered? Still dancing in France, or had they fled to England where it was still safe to have dark skin?

'Sorry, Emily. I don't think I've seen your stocking,' Sylvie replied, twisting round on the stool to look beneath her.

'Never mind, there it is.' Emily lunged beside Sylvie and

picked up the wisp of nylon from beneath the mirror. How it had got there was anyone's guess. Emily perched on the stool beside Sylvie and began to carefully roll the stocking up her leg.

'How are you enjoying working here?' Emily asked. 'You were in Rouen before, weren't you? Was it a big troupe?'

Sylvie felt a rush of trepidation. This was the first time she had been really asked anything about her past and the first test of whether her cover story would hold. She shook her head. 'Angoulême, most recently. Vannes for a little while before that. I travelled about the north before it became too awkward to move around. I've worked in all size troupes, but this is the smallest.'

Deflect the attention from yourself. Get your questioner talking about themselves.

She remembered the advice from training. 'How long have you been working here?' she asked Emily.

'About half a year,' Emily replied airily. 'But I've known about the club for years. I trained as a ballerina but, of course, the Germans don't like our ballet, so it isn't popular now. This is the next best thing, but it took me a long time to persuade Papa and *Maman* that dancing was not akin to prostitution.'

'My mother was a dancer, so she always understood when I said I wanted to dance too, but my father would have said the same as your parents,' Sylvie said. She faced Emily. 'He would have a fit if he knew what I was doing now.'

'Doesn't he?' Emily asked, leaning forward with wide eyes and obviously hoping for gossip.

Sylvie cursed herself inwardly. One minute of conversation and she was already spilling secrets. Nothing harmful in this one though. 'He died last year. His heart gave out.'

'I'm sorry to hear that. That must have been hard on your mother?' Emily asked. She really was relentless. How fortunate Sylvie had rehearsed her past until she would not make any mistakes.

'She died when I was a child. But before then I travelled with her around the theatres with the troupe she was in. The Firefly Girls. Those were fun days. We almost went to Paris once.'

She smiled at the memory, then applied her lipstick in a perfect pout. In the reflection, she noticed the door open. Felix stuck his head through. Emily squealed his name aloud and covered her breasts with her hands. It caused more of a fuss than if she had quietly wrapped her negligee around her because all the attention in the room turned to her, Felix's included. Feeling ungracious, Sylvie wondered if that had been her intention, but he looked away quickly. He caught Sylvie's gaze in the mirror, and as he did he rolled his eyes. Clearly, he shared Sylvie's thoughts. It felt odd to find herself in this silent agreement, and she shifted uncomfortably. Two days had passed since their meeting in the café, and he had said nothing more to her than civilities as they passed in the corridor or over the evening meal.

'What do you want, Felix?' Céline asked, making her voice low and husky. She sauntered over and placed one hand on her hip and the other on the doorframe, barring his way but ensuring the only woman he was looking at was her. 'I'm out of cigarettes if you've come begging. Or were you just trying to get a look at us in our slips?'

'I have my own cigarettes and I see enough of you all when you are onstage,' Felix said, folding his arms. In the mirror, Sylvie watched Emily readjust her clothing with a covert glare towards the doorway. Interesting. There was a touch of jealousy there. Had the pianist flirted with Emily before moving on to Céline, or had Emily hoped he would make a move and been disappointed? Whatever the reason, she didn't seem to like Céline flirting.

'I came to tell you Monsieur Julien says it's should be busy tonight, so bring your best smiles.'

Felix withdrew his head. Céline shut the door behind him and faced the other women.

'Arrogant *andouille*!' she muttered in an undertone. She brightened and exclaimed out loud. 'Men! I don't know why we bother!'

Sylvie joined in the murmurs of agreement and went back to making up her face. When she had been training for SOE in England, she had worn the barest touch of powder and lipstick; sometimes not even that if the lessons were in combat. Now, applying stage makeup took concentration to produce the desired effect.

'Save us from sullen men,' Adele remarked with a laugh, smoothing rouge over her porcelain cheekbones.

'Unless they have the soul of a poet,' Sylvie added, remembering the old joke from years ago. She wondered where the rest of the Fireflies were and if any of them were still dancing. One of the things that had saddened her most about being whisked away to England had been losing the warmth and care of those women. She'd scoured the papers for any mention of them but had found nothing.

'He's always sullen,' Emily whispered. She seemed to have been speaking more to herself than Sylvie, because as Sylvie turned her head towards her, Emily drew her head down. It suggested the relationship between the two was longer standing than she first thought.

'He does seem moody, when he isn't flirting with customers or Céline,' she remarked to Emily who had sunk onto the stool.

Emily bit her lip. Poor girl, she looked so wistful, as if she was about to cry. Sylvie's heart went out to her, and she wished she could snatch back the reference to Céline. Being in love with someone who was not interested was a horrid feeling.

'This terrible occupation has changed all of us. He's bitter about life,' Emily explained, flicking out her hem expressively. 'He hates the Germans for what they have done and thinks their coming here to drink and dance is an insult. I've told him to keep hope, but he doesn't believe the Allied forces will ever free us. He has no time for the Resistance either. The incident of the Fifty Hostages saw to that.'

'The Fifty Hostages?' Sylvie wrinkled her nose, sensing something she should have known about. She felt a pang of remorse at pushing Emily to talk about Felix when it was clearly a sensitive subject but she couldn't pass up the opportunity to find out as much as she could about the man who so far was her only hope of contact with Marcel's network.

'It happened a few years ago. That's why there is no Resistance to speak of here,' Emily explained. 'When everyone saw what had happened, people gave up. Now most of us try to live day to day and hope for the day it is over, but Felix's memory is long, and he won't forget.'

She wiped her eye and Sylvie looked away discreetly. The girl was far too sweet to be concerned about someone who had barely noticed her. Anyone could see they would be a bad match.

'Let Felix stew in his own *bouillon*,' she said firmly.

Emily gave her a washed-out smile. 'Can I borrow your lipstick, please, Sylvie? Mine has run out, and I don't know when I'll get another.'

Sylvie passed over the tube, pondering Emily's words. She was none the wiser as to what had happened to the hostages to make Felix so surly, but Emily was wrong about there being no Resistance. Unless Felix was lying after all and trying to trap Sylvie. But what would be the point of that? She had said enough to incriminate her if he was a double agent working for the Gestapo. It was more likely Emily didn't know what went on outside the walls of the club. That was how it should be, of course. The more people knew, the greater the risk to everyone fighting for freedom.

Sylvie jabbed her hairpins in determinedly. Sitting and gossiping or dancing was all very well, but she was not doing the job she had come here to do, and until she was, she would never be satisfied.

'Is this seat free?'

Sylvie looked along the row of empty stools. Despite Monsieur Julien's early hopes, it had been a relatively slow night. Felix stood beside her.

'They all are.'

He sat beside her at the bar and ordered a beer and another glass of wine for Sylvie from the bartender, who had been wiping glasses and chatting to Sylvie. When it arrived, Felix cocked his head at Sylvie then winked at the bartender. 'Leave us in peace, Alphonse.'

Alphonse took his cloth and moved to the other end of the bar, grinning. It was obvious he was giving them some privacy for whatever Felix was planning.

'*Santé!*' Felix said, raising his beer. 'Will you drink with me yet or are you still angry because of the other night?'

Sylvie picked up her glass and sipped the wine. 'I'm thirsty.'

She looked at him over the rim. 'Have you got any news for me or is this a social conversation?'

'Can't it be both?' Felix murmured. When Sylvie raised her brows, he put his glass down. 'I have a task for you.'

The hairs on the back of Sylvie's neck stood on end. 'What sort of task?'

'An item has been delivered that I need. You will collect it from an address and return it here to me.'

Sylvie lowered her voice and leaned towards Felix. 'Should we be talking about this here?'

'No one is listening, and anyone watching will assume we are getting to know each other better.'

'Or that you are trying to get to know me better,' Sylvie pointed out. 'I don't think I'm giving them the impression that your company is welcome.'

'If you say so.' Felix looked unimpressed by her goading. The moodiness made a brief reappearance. 'Either way, I wouldn't risk talking unless I thought it was safe. At this point, I think it is.'

Sylvie twisted the stem of her glass and slid her eyes in either direction. They were alone at the long bar. Céline and Adele were chatting to a group of Frenchmen sitting at a table by the door and pointedly ignoring the uniformed Germans beside them. Emily and Estelle had gone backstage as soon as the number had ended. A handful of couples were on the dancefloor, dancing to the slow number that crooned from the gramophone.

'What is it you want me to collect?'

Felix raised his brows. 'There is a saying about curiosity and cats. You don't need to know what it is. All you have to do is collect it.'

'I don't care what is inside,' Sylvie lied. Of course she did; who wouldn't? 'I meant, is it something I would need a shopping basket for, for example, or can I slip it inside my pocket?'

'That's a fair point,' Felix conceded. 'You won't need a shopping basket, unless you want to carry one so you don't stand out. Can you do it tomorrow and bring the package here to me by six?'

'Tell me where I need to go,' Sylvie answered.

Felix told her. 'Can you remember that? Tell me.'

'I go to the bakery two streets back from the Chateau of the Dukes of Brittany. When I am served, I order three brioche and ask if I can order a birthday cake for my aunt, Louise. When I pay I should drop my handbag. A man with wire-rimmed glasses will help me pick everything up, and that is when he will give me the package.'

Felix looked impressed. 'Well remembered. Is there anything else you would like to ask?'

'The chateau is used as the German headquarters, isn't it? Why is the exchange being made so close?'

Felix gave a gentle laugh. 'Mademoiselle Duchene, you cannot expect résistants to move addresses simply for your convenience. The bakery has been there for decades and has been a safe location since the start of the occupation.'

Sylvie gave him a brittle smile. He was so damned condescending at times. 'I'll have it for you by tomorrow night.'

The song on the gramophone was coming to an end. Sylvie picked up her drink and walked to the stage.

'Mademoiselle Duchene?'

She stifled a sigh of annoyance and looked back, rolling her eyes and not bothering to hide her annoyance.

'Yes? Did you forget something?'

Felix tipped his head to one side. 'Only to wish you good luck.'

Sylvie blinked. She hadn't been expecting that.

'Thank you,' she said grudgingly. She held his gaze for a moment and a chill raced up and down her back. She shrugged it off and left.

Chapter Eleven

Rouen

1932

'All of them leave.'

Angelique wobbled her way to the windowsill where she kept a bottle of English gin, one hand on her lower belly. 'Men will use you.'

She uncorked the bottle and lifted it, then seemed to change her mind and put it down. Sylvie laid down her book. She stared out of the window over the rooftops of Rouen to the ugly cathedral that stood forbidding grey against an insipid grey sky. Winter was her least favourite time of year.

She could point out that Angelique had never minded the jewellery or bonbons. Each new city still meant a new lover for Angelique, but Sylvie had long since grown bored with the men who came and went. When she had been younger, she had enjoyed the gifts and excursions that she had been included in, but these had gradually stopped. No man wanted an awkward girl of thirteen watching while he tried to kiss her mother.

She moved the gin bottle out of Angelique's reach. It was only ten in the morning and it was far too early to drink anything besides coffee, but Angelique was not well. She put on a brave face but spent most of the day in their rented room, leaving Sylvie to shop and cook before they both went to the theatre to perform.

'I didn't really love them,' Angelique said. 'I tried to, or pretended to, but I believe your father was the only man I truly loved.'

'Please will you tell me about him,' Sylvie asked. She'd begged so many times over the years and didn't really expect the answer to be any different, but Angelique gave her a watery smile.

'I should, shouldn't I? Because, well...'

Angelique walked back to the bed and lay down. She reached for the smaller bottle that the pharmacist had given her. She was supposed to measure a spoonful, but, recently, Sylvie had seen her drinking straight from the bottle as she did now. She was trying her best to ignore the worm of anxiety that wriggled in her belly.

'Your father is English. He was not married when we met, but he was engaged to a woman in England.'

Sylvie felt the blood drain from her legs, leaving her unable to support herself. She found the stool beside the bed and sat before she fell.

'You knew and you still went to bed with him?' Sylvie wrinkled her nose in disgust. Why should she be surprised? Angelique had been with so many men over the years that Sylvie had lost count.

'It was wartime. People behaved differently. Morals were relaxed. We knew straightaway we were meant to be together. We decided it was better to love for a short time than never. I cared for him very dearly, and he loved me too.'

Sylvie chewed her fingernail. It was hardly a rare story. A man and woman thrown together, resulting in a child.

'Does he know about me?'

'Even I did not know about you when he returned to England.' Angelique reached up and patted Sylvie's knee. 'You are the only thing of value a man has ever given me, *ma chérie*. The thing I treasure above all else, and you're growing up so fast. You're almost a woman.'

Sylvie wriggled awkwardly. She *was* a woman, if the red stain on her underwear was anything to go by. She hadn't bothered Angelique with that information but thanked her lucky stars she was surrounded by a host of other women to help her.

'I'll make you some coffee. Then I'm going for a walk. Alone. I want to think about everything.'

'Make better choices than I have, *ma petite*,' Angelique said. 'Once your heart is broken, it is not easily repaired, and each new break is bigger. If you are going to let a man use you, make sure there is some advantage to you too.'

'I won't let anyone use me,' Sylvie assured her.

She'd been kissed on more than one occasion but hadn't loved any of the men. She had enjoyed the way her body had seemed to ripple with delight, but it hardly seemed enough of a reward to risk heartbreak or ruin. She couldn't imagine a man so wonderful that he could make her change her mind.

Nantes, France

1944

The queue was out of the boulangerie door when Sylvie joined it. When she finally neared the front of the line, she discovered that this was because the shopkeeper insisted on carrying out a lengthy conversation with each customer. If the bakery had been there for decades, the owner seemed equally ancient.

She was about to pass through the door when three German soldiers pushed past Sylvie, walking straight to the counter.

'What do you have today, Frau Vallons?'

The woman who had been about to be served pulled her children to one side, hushing their protests. Everyone else ignored the intrusion, suggesting it was familiar, but Sylvie was outraged. She reined in her temper, not wanting to draw attention to herself, and waited patiently. As the three men left, one of them stopped beside Sylvie.

'*Fräulein* Dancer! What a surprise to see you. Do you live in this area?'

It was the young German who had intervened on the night Felix had accosted her. How could she have been recognised on her first mission!

'I like to walk to keep fit for dancing,' she answered. 'I don't know this part of the city, but I saw the boulangerie and stopped for breakfast.'

She was glad she had dressed in a plain skirt and sensible, flat shoes as they added veritas to her tale. She was conscious of the eyes of everyone in the queue on her.

The officer held his paper bag up. 'It's a good bakery. The cakes remind me of ones my *Oma* used to bake.'

Despite her anxiety, Sylvie smiled. In one sentence, the enemy had become a human being with a grandmother who baked cakes. Fortunately, she was spared from further conversation by the queue shuffling forward. She gave a nervous smile and moved along a little.

'It was nice to speak with you, *fräulein*.'

The German left to catch up with his friends. The man in the queue behind Sylvie coughed and glared at her. Being on speaking terms with a German clearly branded her a collaborator in his eyes. If only he knew the truth.

After that unfortunate start, the rest of the mission went smoothly. Madame Vallons was apologetic; it would not be possible to bake a birthday cake at such short notice. Sylvie's aunt would have to understand. Sylvie knocked her bag off the counter, scattering loose coins, lipstick and handkerchiefs everywhere. She knelt to pick them up. As she reached for the silver compact that had been a gift from

Major Buckmaster, she felt something pushed into her hand. The delivery boy who had been sitting on a wooden stool was a young man with wire-rimmed glasses pushed high on his nose. He seemed very young to be involved in covert activities.

'You forgot this, mademoiselle,' he said.

'How silly of me. Thank you,' Sylvie replied. She pushed the packet down into the bottom of her bag, picked up her paper bag of brioche and left. She crossed the road and walked a short distance before leaning against the wall in relief. She took a bite out of one of the brioche, hoping it would calm the butterflies in her stomach. It was good, and she sighed with approval.

'*Es schmeckt gut?*'

Sylvie almost choked to hear her thoughts echoed aloud. It was the German again.

'Excuse me. I didn't mean to startle you,' he said.

'Are you following me?' A chill raced down Sylvie's spine, perspiration pooling in her armpits and lower back.

'Not at all, *fräulein*,' he said. 'That is, I was watching out for you leaving.'

Sylvie's heart began to thump double-speed. 'Why?'

'Not for any reason other than I wanted to confirm you suffered no further ill on Friday night. I wish you had let me take you home. I mean, escort you home. My French is still not good.'

'I am perfectly well,' Sylvie answered, adding as an afterthought, 'but thank you for your concern.'

His face broke into a smile, and he stood more at ease. He had the ice-blue eyes and blonde hair so prized by the

Führer but he looked roughly Sylvie's age, with an earnest look completely free of guile. The overall effect was of an eager schoolboy. Perhaps he was speaking the truth and he was simply concerned for her.

'There was another reason ... I hoped to see you again,' the German continued. 'I wondered if you might like some company. I am off duty until midday, and I know a little of the city. I, too, enjoy exploring.'

Her instinct was to decline, but if she refused his company, it might raise his suspicion. Felix's package was scarcely bigger than a box of cigarettes, but simply knowing she had it in her bag made Sylvie uneasy. She might be walking into a trap. She tried not to look too obviously at his uniform as she tried to detect his role. A small *MV* pin on his collar meant *Militärverwaltung*. Military administration.

'My name is *Verwaltungs-Sekretar* Baumann.' He watched as her lips tried to form the rank, then grinned. 'Please, call me Dieter.'

She had been right; the lengthy title marked him as a secretary. He did the paperwork in an office rather than any fighting.

'Sylvie Duchene,' she replied. 'I can only spare a short while, but I'd like to walk with you.'

He seemed genuinely pleased and held out an arm for her to take. Sylvie gave a small shake of the head, and he dropped it, seemingly taking no offence. Side by side they strolled through the old streets to the Passage Pommeraye. The covered arcade would once have been full of high-end shops where women browsed for gloves and bonbons. Now the boutiques were neglected and windows were boarded up or empty of glass. They walked back through the Place Royale, stopping by the ornate fountain that had somehow miraculously escaped destruction when the Allies had bombed the city.

Sylvie sighed. 'It looks so sad.'

'When the war is ended, Germany will rebuild,' the German assured her. 'The Führer loves France and her people. The Allied forces will see they cannot prevail.'

His voice was confident. Sylvie winced, unsure that the Allies would ever surrender to Germany. She would not be here unless they were planning to resist and free Europe from Hitler's grasp. She wondered again what she was carrying in her bag and felt a rush of pride at the small, insignificant part she was playing.

The German – Sylvie found it hard to think of his name even in her head – was an interesting guide, displaying his knowledge of the city without boasting, and for a time, Sylvie forgot she was in the company of her enemy. It was only when they emerged in front of the imposing medieval fortress of the Chateau of the Dukes of Brittany that it struck home.

The castle had been built to inspire awe and demonstrate the power of its owners. It still managed to fulfil that admirably, even when the walls and turrets were adorned with the flag of the new occupiers. The drawbridge was guarded and soldiers were stationed along the battlements at regular intervals. Seeing the flag and men sent a shiver of hatred through Sylvie. That sensation was immediately followed by dread that she had been tricked and would soon disappear within those walls, never to be seen again.

'Isn't it magnificent?' the German said. 'I come from a small town in the foothills of mountains, and we have nothing so large or old. Can you imagine the lives that were lived there?'

Sylvie shook her head in wonder. Hundreds of years. It was too long to comprehend. How had the citizens of Nantes felt when other enemies had assailed them? Did they bow down or fight?

The original medieval buildings had been added to later in the castle's history. High, white buildings that looked a couple of centuries old stood inside the outer walls. The German pointed at the large building facing into the courtyard.

'I work in that room.' He indicated a small window on the second floor. Sylvie felt a small flicker of relief in her belly that at least he did not work in the dungeons, which she imagined to be home to the Gestapo.

'What do you do?' Sylvie asked

'I assist with transportation arrangements for men returning home and workers going to Germany. Sometimes I examine the letters that the soldiers send back to their families to make sure that none of them are accidentally giving away information that could be of use to our enemies if they were intercepted. My work is very dull.'

Sylvie's scalp prickled. He might describe it as boring, but it seemed to be precisely the sort of information that SOE might be interested in knowing.

'So you learn their secrets? Who is having a secret

romance and lying to his girl back home about being faithful?'

'Mostly the letters are very mundane. Men ask for news of their families or reassure their mothers they are well. Occasionally, they boast about outsmarting the Resistance or defeating the Allied forces, so I must censor those even though they are made-up. But yes, sometimes I read declarations of love from men I know have lost their wages to the brothels or have a French mistress.' He frowned. 'It isn't principled or kind. They will return to their homes and what will become of the women and their children here in France?'

Sylvie was about to say something scathing, then considered his words. Her mother had been a French mistress to Sylvie's English father. Angelique had always sworn that the love affair between her and Arthur Crichton had been mutual and intensely passionate. Her father had not abandoned Angelique or Sylvie financially, when he could easily have done; he'd sent money, despite having a wife in England to support. She felt a little quiver of shame that she had been so resentful of him. She was aware she'd retreated into her memories and was ignoring the German.

'Who reads your letters?' she asked, giving a little laugh.

'I'm not sure. Not that I have anyone back home to declare my love to.'

He held her gaze for a moment, then his cheeks grew slightly pink in a very endearing manner. A slight shiver passed over Sylvie; just a murmur, but enough to alert her that whatever opinion her mind might have of the German standing in front of her, her body was seeing only a man. A warm breeze caught her cheeks, lifting the hairs at the back of her neck that had strayed from her chignon. She pushed them back into the net, thinking how long it had been since other fingers had stroked her flesh with tenderness and passion.

'The weather has suddenly changed,' the German observed. 'It was cold at night until recently. Nantes is nice in the summer. When the war is won, this will be a pleasant place, I think.'

When the war is won. Of course he did not entertain the thought of defeat. How pleasant it would be for anyone French was entirely a different matter, however idealistic he sounded. Sylvie kept the thought to herself.

'How long have you been here?' she asked.

'I arrived in October 1942,' he said. '*Feldkommandant* Hotz was assassinated the year before that and the new commander requested new staff.'

Assassination? Why didn't she know about this?

'I didn't hear of that.'

The German looked at her and Sylvie wondered if she had blundered. Was it something every man, woman and child in France knew?

'I was living in Tregastel with my *grand-mère* then. It is a small village and she did not approve of newspapers or a radio. We missed a lot of what happened in the early days.'

'It was a dark time,' the German explained. 'I understand his murder was unpopular even among the Nantais. Forty-eight men were executed in retaliation. Communists and socialists; troublemakers. Now things are more settled. There are no uprisings and the streets are safer to walk.'

Sylvie bowed her head. Forty-eight lives for one. A signal to all that the Germans were in control.

'I have to go,' she said. 'I was very tired last night after the performance, so I want to take a nap before this evening.'

'Of course. I should return too.'

The German reached for her hand and kissed it. 'I have enjoyed myself walking with you. Perhaps we might do it again when I am off duty? There is a *botanischer garten* which is becoming beautiful now. You understand me? With many flowers.'

Against all odds, Sylvie had enjoyed the morning. She'd been instructed to find out any useful information, and if she could do that while spending time in the German's company, then that would kill two birds with one stone.

'The *Jardin des Plantes*. I've heard of it. That would be pleasant,' she agreed.

'I will come to Mirabelle again. I enjoyed watching you dance. *Auf wiedersehen.*'

Sylvie walked home feeling the shape of Felix's parcel against her ribs, picturing the look on his face when she presented it to him. No doubt he would be as arrogant as ever. It struck her as odd and slightly traitorous that she felt more in common with the shy German clerk than the résistant.

The sentries at the checkpoint were carrying out spot checks for contraband, but Sylvie's luck was in. She passed her identity papers over, keeping her face carefully neutral.

Nervousness might attract attention, but equally, being overly friendly or eager to help would seem odd. Before the sentry had time to ask to see what she was carrying, an old man wheeling a bicycle slipped and his basket of fruit went everywhere. The sentry rolled his eyes and held out his hand to Sylvie. He thrust her papers back at her impatiently and immediately turned on the old man who was scrabbling about the road for his fruit. The sentry loomed over him, shouting orders to hurry. He aimed a kick at the old man's back.

'Leave him alone'! Sylvie cried. The sentry stopped, more in surprise than any inclination to obey. Not turning her back, Sylvie picked up a couple of apples and handed them back, then righted the bicycle. The old man caught her eye gratefully. She was the only one who had bothered to help him. Everyone else in the line had their heads down, trying to avoid notice. Sylvie hurried on, ignoring the man's thanks. To intervene had been foolish; she could have drawn more attention to herself, and with the package for Felix in the bag, that would have meant ruin for more than herself.

Chapter Twelve

Sylvie returned home and lay on her bed, arms outstretched and feet dangling over the end. Now that she was off her feet, she discovered how tired she was. She had walked a long way when she included the spontaneous trip around the streets with the German. Her blouse clung to her body where she was damp with perspiration, and her hair was coming loose.

The room was too warm and stifling after the fresh air. A beam of sunlight was making its way across the floor through the slanted skylight. She dragged the wooden chair beneath the skylight and tried to open it. The catch was stiff and hadn't been opened for a long time, but it eventually gave under her efforts, sending a fine powder of rust drifting down over Sylvie's hair.

The window opened just enough for Sylvie to peer through when she stood on tiptoes. She took a deep breath and released it with a long sigh of pleasure. The air smelt warm and fresh, far enough above the streets that the fumes had dispersed. Her room was at the back of the building and the window faced away from the city, over a cobbled yard. Although the roof was slanted inside, the pitch outside was much narrower and there was a gutter not too far below the windowsill.

Inspiration struck. She shut the window and fastened the catch. It did not look as if she had tampered with it. The ledge would be an ideal place to secrete things she didn't want anyone to find. A nail and a length of string would mean she could hang things out of the window to rest unseen on the gutter. If she could get a waterproof container, such as the biscuit tin she had delivered for Marianne, anything she put in there would stay dry and hopefully escape discovery.

She replaced the chair, then took out the small package that she had collected from the bakery. She weighed it in her hands. It was lightweight, not much larger than a packet of cigarettes, and wrapped in plain brown paper. Despite what she had told Felix, she was curious to see what she was carrying, though decided it was better not to know.

That evening, Sylvie arrived at the club early. She could have sworn she had heard the strains of Felix's accordion as she had crossed the street, but Felix was not in the club, nor upstairs in the first-floor room where the staff ate. She encountered Monsieur Julien as she went back into the stairwell to go downstairs. He was coming from the floor above, the entire space of which was his private accommodation. She froze, aware how suspicious it looked for her to be sneaking around, but Monsieur Julien seemed as surprised as she was.

'Mademoiselle Duchene, can I help you?'

The sound of a gramophone followed him down the stairs. Sylvie recognised the song as 'Summertime', sung in the rich, languid tones of Billie Holiday. The song was perfect for the warm afternoon, conjuring up both smoky clubs and warm beaches at the same time. Jazz was banned, however, and Monsieur Julien was right to be wary. A word in the wrong ear could see him fined, or worse.

'I was hoping to speak with Felix. I have a song to suggest to him.' She raised her eyes upwards. 'I wish I could suggest that song – it's beautiful.'

Monsieur Julien relaxed.

'He's in the attic.'

Monsieur Julien pointed to the staircase he'd just come down, very much like the one that led to Sylvie's room at Madame Giraud's, then went downstairs. She hadn't realised the building continued further upwards than Monsieur Julien's apartment.

Monsieur Julien had not asked questions, though her excuse had been flimsy. He knew she was connected to SOE. Did he also know Felix's role or play a bigger part than she assumed? It was tricky knowing who could be trusted.

The stairs led to an open attic space. A skylight in the roof, similar to the one in Sylvie's room back at Madame Giraud's, allowed her to see it was cluttered with boxes, crates, piles of curtains and a clothes rail with old dance costumes. The gowns were beautiful; a collection of taffeta and feathers, silks and sequins. Sylvie forgot her errand and spent a few minutes raking through them. It was a crime that they were hidden up here, going to waste. She made a mental note to ask Monsieur Julien if she could use them. Reluctantly, she turned her attention to her true purpose and looked for Felix.

Half the attic – the space that would be over the family room two floors below – had been partitioned off with a door set into it. The door was ajar, so Sylvie picked her way past the detritus and knocked.

Felix's voice rang out. Wary and sharp. 'Who is there?'

'Mademoiselle Duchene. Sylvie.'

There was silence.

'I can go,' she said.

'No. Come in.'

Sylvie had expected another room full of litter from the club, but she walked into a bedroom apartment. Felix was lying on the bed underneath a small window set into the end wall. He lay propped on a pile of pillows and his accordion was at his side. A small table stood beside the bed with a jug of water and an open bottle of red wine on top. She had clearly caught him at a moment of leisure. His feet were bare, and this caught Sylvie's attention more than anything else.

He was dressed in casual trousers with the braces down and the legs rolled up to the knee. The top two buttons of his shirt were undone and the sleeves were also rolled up. His legs and arms had a downy sprinkling of light-brown hair except for a puckered, circular scar on the flesh of his right calf. He oozed sex appeal, and it didn't take much imagination to imagine him in the bed rather than on top. He made no move to get up off the bed. It was a double, which somehow didn't surprise her.

'Is this where you live?' she asked.

He narrowed his eyes.

'It is as good as anywhere. The rent is cheap, it's quiet, and I don't have far to go home at the end of the night. Do you have something to say about it?'

'The night you attacked me in the alley, you said you were going home. If you live here, that was a lie.'

Felix swung his legs over the side of the bed.

'First, I didn't attack you – I was the one who ended up with a bruised jaw, if you recall. Second, I *was* going home – which I did after I left you – I just didn't tell you where that was.' Felix gave her a wolfish smile, though his eyes remained hard. 'Did you think this is just where I bring my women to make love to them?'

Her belly gave a little somersault. She stared around the room.

'Make yourself at home,' Felix said sarcastically, following her gaze.

It was clearly meant to deter her from being nosy, but she took it as an invitation and, ignoring his scowls, she continued to look around. It was her first insight into his life. The bed had rumpled sheets but with a homemade blue-and-red-patchwork counterpane folded neatly at the end. Against the far wall, beneath the sloping roof, were two chairs and a table that held a paperback book, a pack of cards and a second, unopened bottle of wine. Black socks and a white vest hung over a clothes horse to dry. The wooden floorboards in the centre of the room had been covered with a frayed, but obviously good-quality, oriental rug. The walls were decorated with French and American film posters. *La Regle Du Jour* and *Guele D'Amour* hung alongside *Gone with the Wind* and *King Kong*. It was more homely than Sylvie's room, and unquestionably the room of a man. She pointed at *The 39 Steps* and smiled at him.

'That's one of my favourites.'

'Spies and romance. A good choice,' Felix replied. 'Have you seen everything you want? When do I get to see your bedroom in return?' His eyebrow rose and he gave her another of the smiles he obviously thought made him irresistible.

'You don't,' Sylvie said. 'I have not really made it my home yet. I haven't had the chance.'

She needed to remedy that. Some flowers in a vase, a picture to liven the walls. Anything that would impress her personality on the room. Permanence. Something she'd never really had wherever she lived.

Felix nodded. 'You should. Any visitors would expect it to look more than temporary. And I don't mean any men you invite back.'

His voice carried an edge of warning. Unwelcome visitors, he meant. The Gestapo or the almost as hated French *milice*, who worked alongside the Germans to foil the Resistance. She was doubly glad she had already found a hiding place out of the window.

'I live in an attic room too, so I'd have warning, I hope, before anyone climbed the stairs. I've taken how to keep things safe into consideration, but you're right, I haven't made it a home. Talking of which…'

She brought the package out of her bag and held it towards him. He took it from her and weighed it in his hands.

'Well done. Any trouble?'

'None at all.' He didn't need to know about her morning walk in the German's company. She wanted to keep that secret to herself.

'What happens to the package now?' Sylvie asked. She was desperate to find any more people who might be able to help her. With Felix as her only point of contact, the world felt too precarious.

'Now this happens,' he replied. He put it on the table and opened it painstakingly slowly. Sylvie drew closer and peered over his shoulder. Inside the brown paper was a cigarette carton. Felix glanced round, and upon seeing that Sylvie was looking over his shoulder, he smiled.

'I can tell you're desperate to know what is inside. That could get you killed, you realise. You're a courier, so all you need to do is pass the messages and take the items. If you can convincingly deny you know what you carry, you will be safer.'

'Do you think that excuse would save me if I was caught?' she asked drily.

Felix was silent for a moment, then shook his head brusquely. 'No. The crucial thing is, would it save other people?'

'When we were being trained, they taught us to try to

hold out against questioning.' She bit her lip and took a deep breath. Questioning. Torture.

She shuddered, remembering how long she had endured the simulated interrogation back in England, and closed her eyes. The ordeal had lasted a morning at most, and no lasting harm had been done. Would she be strong enough to bear true pain? When she opened her eyes, Felix was watching her closely, his brow wrinkled with concern. It was odd to see that the man who was either surly or seductive had access to other emotions, especially such sympathetic ones.

'You do a brave thing by coming here, Mademoiselle Duchene,' he said.

'Are you laughing at me?' she asked.

'No. I mean it.' He stepped a little closer to her and reached for her hand. Sylvie's pulse sped as she allowed him to take it.

'You come to my country to fight beside us when you could stay in England and wage your war from overseas. It takes courage to give up your old life and begin anew like you have.'

'France is my country too,' Sylvie murmured. Her voice sounded distant and dreamlike in her ears, drowned out by the pulsating rhythm that had sprung to life. 'Or it was once, long ago, when I was younger. This is not the first time I have given up an old life. When my *maman* died, I said goodbye, I thought forever. Now I am not sure where I belong.'

'How many lives have you lived?' Felix asked in a low voice. 'Where would you like to belong?'

His fingers moved in a circle in her palm; a gentle pressure that, nevertheless, sent a tremor along her arm, where it amplified and spread inside her ribcage, halting the breath in her lungs. Was he going to kiss her? The pull towards him was undeniable and from the way his eyes widened, she sensed he was equally attracted to her as she was to him. She was conscious of tilting her head, waiting for his lips to find hers. She ached to be kissed. By Felix.

By anyone.

Felix put a hand to her cheek and gently pulled her towards him while the other slipped around her waist. She inhaled deeply and the scent of his cologne caught her attention. That wonderfully rich vanilla and lavender woodiness that was so intriguing. A memory stirred. The last time she had smelt it had been when he had kissed her in the alleyway on the night he had first made contact. The recollection of that unasked-for kiss and the fumbling at her blouse quenched the burgeoning desire.

She slipped from his gentle hold and stepped back out of temptation's way. Not that she was tempted any longer. He was a man who thought nothing of teasing and flirting and using kisses to achieve what he wanted. How stupid she would be to succumb to that temptation!

Felix wrinkled his brow, looking confused at her sudden coldness.

'Not a good idea,' Sylvie said.

'You have had a change of heart?'

'A change of head,' she corrected him. She tapped her temple with a fingertip. 'I don't think it would be wise to kiss you.'

'Why not? Are you afraid you might not want to stop?'

Oh yes, she was, very much so. The thought of them touching each other any more intimately made her hot.

'I don't have time to think about romance,' she said.

Felix raised an eyebrow. 'Who mentioned romance? I just want to take you to bed.'

Sylvie gaped at him. Such bluntness was unnerving. And a little exciting. It made a change to have a man openly admit that was what he wanted rather than try to win her round with charm until she fell for it. It was too tempting.

'I'll leave you alone to open your package,' she said, raising her chin and giving him a cold stare.

Felix shrugged and straightened his collar. He appeared to take the rejection on the chin. Why wouldn't he, of course, when it was just another kiss to him?

'In this case there is no need to leave me alone. You can see what you carried.' Felix picked up the cigarette box and opened it to reveal cigarettes.

Sylvie furrowed her brow. 'Where is the message? What was I carrying?'

Felix waved his hand in the manner of a stage magician revealing a hidden rabbit.

'This is what you were carrying. My cigarettes.' He put one between his lips and let it dangle while he struck a match and lit it.

Rage boiled inside Sylvie. She had been so nervous carrying the package around all day. She had believed she was doing something worthwhile to help the cause she believed in.

'Is this some kind of joke to you?' she asked incredulously.

Felix took a drag on the cigarette, inhaling through pursed lips and blew out a long stream of smoke. 'It's not a joke at all. I was running short. Getting hold of these on the black market isn't easy.'

'Is that what I am?' Sylvie spat. 'A messenger to get your contraband from the black market? This is not a game to me!'

She gave an exclamation of annoyance and turned on her heel to leave. Felix stepped smoothly round her, blocking the path between her and the door.

'No, it isn't. Nor is it a game for us. It was a test.'

He pinched the end of the cigarette between finger and thumb, then stuck it behind his ear. 'You appeared from nowhere knowing the codes and names of contacts. You entered the club in the company of four Germans. You are a pretty woman who seemed eager to please and anxious to be of use, but that doesn't mean a thing. The Germans use female agents, too, on occasion.'

Sylvie folded her arms and glared at him. He held her gaze levelly.

'So you concocted this charade?'

He nodded. 'I wanted to be sure you were who you said you were before I trusted you to with a real task. The men and women I work with are risking their lives, and I won't jeopardise that. For all I knew, you might have gone straight to the German authorities and that would've been the end of us.'

He gave her a penetrating look. 'I thought at one point

that is exactly what you were doing. I assume you did not tell your German friend this morning what was happening, otherwise we would have been raided by now.'

'How do you know about that?' Sylvie's cheeks grew hot. 'Did you have me followed?'

'Better than that,' Felix admitted. He folded his arms, mirroring Sylvie's stance, and his lip curled into a sneer. 'I followed you myself.'

Sylvie's mouth fell open. She closed it quickly. He couldn't have. She would have noticed, wouldn't she? Stupid, stupid! She should have spotted that she was being tailed. Her cheeks flamed. She took a deep breath, hoping they were not as red as they felt. She couldn't stand the thought of Felix seeing her so discomforted.

'I think I recognised him from the club,' Felix said. 'Am I right?'

Sylvie nodded. 'We met by chance. He was the man who intervened down the alley when you accosted me. He wanted to check I had recovered from that ordeal and asked me to go for a walk.'

'That *ordeal*?' Felix rolled his eyes.

'His words, not mine,' Sylvie spat. 'I'm more than capable of taking care of myself as you saw.'

'I don't doubt it,' Felix said. 'One advantage to using female agents is that the average German cannot contemplate a woman being so daring or unfeminine.'

'What would you have done if I had handed the package over?' Sylvie asked, ignoring the implied insult at her femininity.

Felix stepped back towards the bed and relit his

cigarette, not taking his eyes off Sylvie. 'I would have shot you where you stood.'

She shivered. There was no menace in his voice. No emotion at all. His words were entirely factual. He would have killed her rather than let her betray him, and he would be right to do it. She wondered if she had the iron in her blood to be able to do the same.

'Why did you go with him?' Felix asked.

Sylvie turned to face him. 'Because he invited me. I couldn't think of a good enough reason to refuse. I could hardly tell him I had to hurry back and hand over a mysterious packet, could I?'

Felix looked sceptical. Sylvie's temper flared.

'Did you even stop to think how terrified I must have been carrying what I thought could have been explosives or arms while I wandered round with a German, having to appear normal!'

He dropped his head, and she was glad he could not see the emotion she was sure must be visible on her face. She took a deep breath, clenching and releasing her fists until she felt calm enough to speak without her voice shaking.

'Not so terrified that you couldn't shout in a German's face over some apples.'

'You saw that too?'

He nodded.

Sylvie glared. 'And you didn't think to help the old man when he was kicked?'

'Sometimes you have to ignore the small wrongs to right the bigger ones.'

They were glaring at each other. Felix's eyelid flickered, but Sylvie was the first to look away.

'It's hard to stand by and watch.'

'You'll have to learn to if you want to survive.' Felix took another drag on his cigarette. He smoked it angrily, as if resenting its very existence and trying to suck the very life from it. 'It gets easier.'

'So now do you trust me?' Sylvie said.

'I think so.'

Sylvie shouldered her bag. 'Then I think we are done here. Unless there is any more shopping you wish me to do?'

She meant it to be an insult, but Felix gave a wide grin, the humour appearing from nowhere. 'If you could find me a bottle of good brandy, I wouldn't say no to that.'

'Fetch it yourself.' Sylvie walked to the door.

'Mademoiselle, there is something else.'

She paused in the doorway. Felix sauntered across the room towards her and leaned down confidentially.

'Marcel has returned.'

The hree frustrating days passed before Felix whispered to Sylvie that the rendezvous spot was the *Jardin du Plantes*, coincidentally the same place that the German had mentioned. Sylvie wore her dress of dusky pink rayon with a scooped neckline and small white collar. The repairs beneath the armpits where the fabric had worn thin from use by the previous owner didn't show too much and it almost fitted her perfectly. It went with her gold cross necklace very well. She curled the front of her hair and pinned it beneath the brim of her teal hat, while the back fell in a looser chignon.

Her appearance drew a whistle of appreciation from Felix when they met in front of the Cathédrale de Saint Pierre and Saint Paul. It sounded completely spontaneous and unforced, so she accepted it with a smile and toss of the head. Felix was dressed in a sober brown overcoat and hat that made him look very respectable. She told him so as she took his offered arm, and they set off walking in good humour. Although she would not have chosen to spend her time in Felix's company, Sylvie had to admit they made a handsome couple.

They retraced some of the route Sylvie had taken with the German, but the experience could not have been more different. Where Baumann had seen the prospect of unity, Felix saw only the destruction that had been wrought on the town of his birth. Sylvie's comment on how the fountain statues had escaped melting down resulted in a bitter retort that many had not.

He glared at her. 'You sound like a collaborator. Your German friend looks on the world with the eyes of an idealist, and one who is on the side of the oppressors. Of course he will see what he wants to.'

The muscles in his forearm grew rigid, and Sylvie withdrew her hand. They walked stiffly side by side in silence until they reached the entrance to the garden. Sylvie folded her arms and barred his way.

'What's wrong?' Felix asked.

'Felix, if we're going to appear inconspicuous, we need to be more relaxed. Do you think you can stop grimacing? Otherwise we look like a couple about to divorce.'

He pursed his lips and said nothing, but held out his arm again for Sylvie to scoop hers through. As they approached the open lawn along a sandy path, Sylvie accepted that it had been sensible to wait rather than rush the meeting. Sunday afternoon was a peaceful time. Morning church services had finished and people were able to forget about the privations of war for the time between lunch and evening Mass. There were plenty of families and groups enjoying the sunshine as they strolled around the shrub-lined paths of the ornate botanical gardens. Ageing men played boules, and elderly women sat on benches in the sunshine.

Life seemed normal, if one was able to ignore the swastika flags on poles where the Tricolore had once fluttered and the soldiers standing at checkpoints. Uniformed Germans of both sexes walked around the gardens, mingling with the French. They were always there: a presence in the corner of the eye and back of the mind.

Now that they were arm in arm again, Sylvie and Felix did not stand out in the slightest. It took all Sylvie's resolve not to stare around too openly as she and Felix wandered through the gardens, wondering which of the men she passed was her contact. A slight pressure of Felix's elbow nudging her ribs indicated they must be within sight.

'Why, Monsieur Pauly! I have not seen you for weeks!'

Felix gave a cry of delight as he hailed a tall, bespectacled man who had been sitting on a bench in the shade with an easel and palette of paints. Monsieur Pauly stood and the two men embraced, rapidly kissing each cheek.

'Felix Lambert, what a pleasant surprise. Please, will you introduce your friend,' Monsieur Pauly asked. He was in his mid-thirties, tall and broad with short, sandy-blonde hair. He fitted the description of Sylvie's contact.

Felix obeyed with a charming smile. 'This is Sylvie Duchene. She dances at Mirabelle. Marcel is a painter.'

Marcel gestured to the half-completed watercolour on his easel. He'd been preparing to paint the rose garden and ornamental pond. The pencil sketch was well proportioned and Sylvie wondered if he had done it himself. He was currently dressed in slightly shabby, wide-legged trousers and a beret that fitted with the persona of an artist, but Sylvie could imagine him playing rugby at one of the public schools where so many of the officers seemed to have come from.

'A struggling artist in my free time. I make my living painting doors and windows.' He lowered his voice. 'Your field name, if you please, mademoiselle.'

'Sylvie Duchene.' She took his outstretched hand and added in a whisper. 'Field name Monique.'

'Marcel Pauly. Field name Hubert,' he replied. 'Shall we all walk together? The camellias are still in flower.'

It was a good choice of destination because the winter-flowering plants were a less popular destination than the rose garden or the neat paths edged with blossoming shrubs. They were alone there, and if anyone had been hiding within earshot, they would have been spotted immediately amid the thinning foliage.

'I'm so sorry I was not here to meet you on arrival,' Marcel said in English. 'Circumstances interceded.'

She had expected the cut-glass tones of the upper classes, so was surprised to hear the broad Yorkshire accent that came out of his mouth. He reminded her of her father, who had sounded similar, and she felt a sudden stab of longing for the clifftop house on the Esplanade in Scarborough. At some point, she would like to ask where Marcel was from, though doubted he would tell her. Marcel Pauly was not his real name and like her, if interrogated, he would stick to his cover story for as long as it was humanly possible, withstanding whatever methods were used to prise the truth from him.

'Don't worry,' she replied, also in English. 'It's all worked out thanks to Felix here.'

She wondered if Felix, walking on her other side, could understand what they were saying. He had clearly recognised his name and looked round suspiciously. Marcel repeated what Sylvie had said in flawless French.

'I understand your words,' Felix said in halting English. 'It made me surprised to hear them because she has not thanked me for my help. I don't know if I have been very helpful after all.'

Sylvie felt a little guilty. It was true; she had not thanked him for going to the effort of finding Marcel for her. The trouble was she found him so irritating a lot of the time, with his silly flirting and the exploit of the cigarettes.

'You have been very helpful,' she admitted. 'Please allow me to buy you a drink when Mirabelle is open.'

'You will drink with me?' Felix grinned, switching back to French.

'Just one,' Sylvie cautioned. She wagged a finger at him. The sunshine was making her playful. 'And no more foolish errands.'

Their eyes met and she saw humour dancing in Felix's. The atmosphere seemed to grow friendlier and the future seemed brighter.

'Errands?' Marcel asked. 'Sylvie, what has Felix had you doing?'

'He sent me on a test run to see if I could hold my nerve.'

'Which she carried out boldly,' Felix added. 'She has a cool head.'

'He wanted to be sure I am who I say I am,' Sylvie explained. 'With you vanished and me appearing suddenly, he was suspicious and cautious.'

'It rather exposed a weakness in our methods of contacting new agents,' Marcel said. 'Felix, I'm glad you intervened. Is this a sign you might be persuaded to take a more active role in operations again?'

'Perhaps.'

Felix stuck his hands in his pockets and walked over to one of the planted borders; it was clear to see that Marcel had touched on a nerve. Marcel shook his head subtly and drew Sylvie away, leaving Felix to stare at the flowers.

'There is accommodation, but, of course, you did not have the address. It will still be available if you want it. Have you been staying at the club?'

It had never occurred to Sylvie to consider staying at the club. There might be space. Monsieur Julien lived there, and, of course, Felix had his room in the attic. No. Sharing a house with Felix might lead to things she was doing her best not to imagine.

'No, I found a room with one of the other girls. I've paid for a month so I'll stay there as I am settled.'

'As you wish,' Marcel said. 'You'll receive pay for your accommodation. I'll arrange things with my woman so she can let the room go.'

Felix wandered back over to join them. His face was

carefully neutral, as if he was taking great pains to make it so.

'Where have you been?' he asked Marcel. 'Can you tell us?'

Marcel lit a cigarette and took a few short puffs. 'I'd taken a shipment of arms up the river towards the coast near St Nazaire. I planned to meet with some men from the Resistance from up that way to pass them on. We were ambushed.'

He glared at the cigarette in his hand and bunched it into his fist.

'Somebody knew we were coming. Tipped off the SS. Fortunately, the circuit had good lookouts who got to us in time and as far as I know no one was captured. We had two tonnes of plastic explosives, fuses and detonators.' Felix drew closer as Marcel continued. 'As soon as we heard the first gun fire, my contact and I had to abandon them. I pray everybody else made it out alive. Three good men died though. One you knew, Felix: Marc with the moustache.'

Felix swore under his breath; a single expletive that exploded out of him violently. Marcel broke off and stared intently at the sprawling camellia plants with their fading blooms. Sylvie glanced at Felix. His face was white with anger. Their eyes met, and she was startled to see that his were slightly moist.

'Was he a friend?'

He gave a violent shake of the head. 'Our paths crossed once or twice, but we shared the same purpose and every man lost is one to mourn.'

Sylvie remembered Emily's comment that he had always

been angry and sullen. Each death of a man he knew must be a splinter in his heart. Feeling the anger and grief welling inside her at the fate of strangers, she understood how easily it would be to become bitter towards the world. No wonder Felix could think only of destruction as they had walked to the gardens. It was too long since she had been in Brittany, but if she was faced with such sights… If the clifftop house in England fell to the enemy…

Impulsively, she stepped closer to Felix and reached a hand to his arm, wanting to offer solace and perhaps to draw comfort herself. He tensed and his eyes grew wide. She'd overstepped the mark. Before she could draw back, Felix covered her hand with his and gave a gentle squeeze. His palm was warm over the back of her hand. She was acutely conscious of the way his fingertips brushed against the side of her wrist, leaving a tingling sensation on her bare skin that gave her chills. His eyes flickered to hers, dark lashes ringing the azure depths. There was no anger and no scorn in them; none of the habitual flirtation, only acknowledgement of their shared despair and sadness.

'What happened after the ambush?' he asked Marcel.

Marcel walked to the end of the pathway. Sylvie and Felix fell in behind him, walking arm in arm. Feeling the weight of Felix's arm linked through hers was more reassuring than she expected it to be.

Marcel looked both ways, then sat on a low wall. 'I spent two days hiding under debris in a bombed-out barn, waiting for the heat to die down before it was safe to leave. I had to abandon my bloody – pardon me, Sylvie – my blasted bicycle and get back here most of the way on foot.'

The picture Marcel was painting of night-time ambushes and gunfights was alarming. Carrying packages through the streets of Nantes was risky but was nothing in comparison. Sylvie hugged herself surreptitiously and felt the solidity of Felix leaning gently against her. She looked up and his mouth quirked to one side in a wry smile that said more than if he had spoken aloud.

'Where are the explosives?' she asked. 'Did they fall into enemy hands or will they need retrieving?'

'They're safely collected by now, I hope. I haven't heard from anyone. The cell will have gone to ground for now. I went straight to see my wireless operator when I came back to Nantes so he could check in with London and tell them what happened. I'm waiting to hear if there is any news from HQ when his next scheduled messages arrive. That should be tomorrow afternoon.'

Marcel tilted his hat back. 'Sylvie, as soon as I have something for you to do, I'll send word. The message will come from Tante Louise or Oncle Hubert.'

'Thank you. I want to be of use as soon as possible. I don't feel I have done anything worthwhile yet.'

'You're dancing at the club, aren't you?' Marcel said. 'Did our mutual acquaintance back home mention that there might be opportunities to gather intelligence from the patrons in ways that are not open to male agents?'

He looked at her meaningfully.

'They did. I'm happy to do that.'

'She's already started from what I have seen,' Felix said. When Sylvie shot him a confused look, he folded his arms, a sardonic look on his face. 'The officer from the bakery?'

Sylvie flushed. 'A German named Baumann. He came to my assistance on the way home one night,' she explained to Marcel, who had watched the exchange with a frown of confusion. She saw with satisfaction that the reference to assistance had struck home with Felix, who glowered.

'I didn't expect to see him again, but we met by accident. He works in the chateau in an administrative role overseeing transportation. I don't have to see him again if it won't fit with your plans for me. I probably won't anyway.'

There was no point in mentioning Baumann had promised he would return to the club.

'Now, I really must be going,' Marcel said.

Sylvie took his outstretched hand and shook it once again. 'When the wireless operator sends a message through with his next skeds, please can he explain what happened to me and why I didn't make contact before?'

'Of course. If I had been in contact with Felix before I sent my report and had heard you were here, I would have done it then. No doubt there will be people back home anxious to hear that you made it here in one piece.'

Sylvie made a noncommittal sound of agreement. Every agent wrote a series of letters before being sent on their missions, kept safe at SOE headquarters, to be posted to family regularly so questions weren't asked about their absence. Sylvie had dutifully written to her stepmother in Scarborough, but the only tie to Maud had been Arthur. Now he was dead, the two women had little in common. Dennis would be highly unlikely to care. At least Uncle Max would be pleased to hear she was safe.

She thought back to the conversation she had had with

the German. He had said there was no sweetheart for him to write home to. Perhaps that had been what had drawn them to each other; an inkling of the loneliness and affection each was lacking.

Marcel strolled off in the direction of his easel while Felix and Sylvie walked the opposite way, taking the winding path up around the back of the camellia garden towards the glasshouse. A pair of blonde women wearing sober grey skirt suits walked past arm in arm. They openly stared at Felix. Sylvie tossed her hair back and looped her arm through his possessively. Felix tipped his hat at the women and gave them a charming smile. They hurried on, whispering to each other.

'I'm glad to see you French women still outshine these dowdy German *frauen*,' Felix said loudly. 'They scurry around like little mice in those dull grey clothes.'

Sylvie smiled and checked her hair was still in place. She resolved to search the attic costumes for some spare feathers for her hat. Defiance through clothing was a subtle form of rebellion, but one she enjoyed.

'Do you have anyone special waiting back in England?' Felix asked. When she tilted her head up, she saw he was looking down at her intently.

The fact that the answer was so depressing meant her initial response was to tell him in no uncertain terms that it was none of his business who or what she had left behind, but she was actually feeling kindly towards him. He'd been perceptive enough to notice that she had avoided answering Marcel in any great detail. They'd both taken moments to offer support to the other in the course of the afternoon, and he didn't look as if he was trying his seduction routine. His question had sounded casual, and perhaps he was just making conversation.

'Don't you know we're not supposed to share any details like that?' She tilted her head so her hat brim hid her face.

'It would hardly break your cover,' Felix said. 'Do you have a lover waiting at home?'

'No, I don't,' Sylvie admitted, head still down. 'No one is waiting for me.'

'Not at all? I would have thought a pretty girl like you would have a sweetheart or two and a trail of broken hearts left behind you.'

He sounded surprised. That stung. Her love affair with Dennis had ended badly, and the only broken heart in Sylvie's past was her own. She whipped her head up to look at Felix. His eyes were bright and it seemed the habitual seducer she recognised was back.

'Of course you would expect that,' Sylvie said scathingly. 'I imagine a man who spends his time trying to sweet talk every woman he meets would be incapable of believing a woman wouldn't have one or two followers hanging on.'

She was feeling irritable again. She'd actually been enjoying his company, so why did he have to ruin it with meddling talk of sweethearts and trying to poke into her business? She stalked ahead to the busier part of the garden. It didn't help to see couples strolling arm in arm. Felix caught up with her and took hold of her elbow.

'I didn't say followers. I asked if there was anybody special.'

She shook him off irritably. 'You know the difference? I'm surprised. It hardly seems to bother you who you spend your time with. Any of the women in the club will do, from what I've seen.'

She frowned, hearing her own vitriol. Why should she care what Felix did with his time or how many women he flirted with as long as he didn't try including her in that number?

Felix frowned too. 'At least I have some standards. Perhaps you prefer to spend your time consorting with Germans like your friend from the bakery. *Collaboration horizontale* is a popular pastime, I believe.'

'Standards! You couldn't even resist trying to charm those mice back there.' Sylvie clenched her fist at her side. 'The walk I took with Herr Baumann was as blameless as you and I walking together now. Less blameless, in fact, because he has never tried to kiss me or shove his hand down my blouse!'

'So far...' Felix retorted. 'Though I'm sure it won't be long before he does if you're intending to carry on *cultivating* him as Marcel suggested.'

His voice dripped with distaste.

Sylvie rounded on him furiously. 'If I am instructed to do so ... than I will. But believe me, I will take as little pleasure in it as I did when you kissed me.'

She walked off, determined to ignore him if he called after her or followed.

He did neither and that increased her tetchiness. Thank goodness Mirabelle didn't open on a Monday, so she would have a couple of days to calm down. His questions had stung, but that was not his fault. He couldn't have known how deeply the remarks about people waiting at home would cut her to the core. As she made her way back home, she realised this war-torn, occupied town and the friendly people in Mirabelle held more attraction for her than England ever had.

Chapter Fourteen

Boulogne, France

1933

'We'll be in Paris this time next week, *chérie.*'

Angelique lay back on the pillow and smiled.

'Yes, *Maman*, we will.'

Sylvie was glad Angelique's eyes were closed so she did not see the tears in Sylvie's. She stared pleadingly at the white-clad nuns, with their unsettling combination of severe habits and kindly faces. The sister in charge of the ward made the sign of the cross over her breast.

Too soon.

Too quick since Angelique had first complained of the pain in her abdomen six months previously that medicine could not cut through. Then a hard lump began to swell in her once flat belly, and the doctor said there was nothing to be done. Now all that mattered was to keep Angelique comfortable and free of pain for as long as possible.

'Paris will be beautiful,' Sylvie said. 'We'll join the troupe soon. Rosetta wrote to me that she wants to copy Josephine Baker's number from *Zouzou*. She wants me to help teach it to the rest of the girls. You can learn it too.'

'You know I can't, *chérie*.' Angelique's eyelids flickered open. She reached for Sylvie's hand. 'You should create your own dances. You have talent. I would like to have seen them. I wanted to see you grow up and become a better dancer than I ever was.'

Sylvie bit her lip. Angelique was reconciled to her death more than Sylvie. Fourteen was no age to become an orphan.

'When I'm gone—' Angelique murmured.

Sylvie started. It was as if her mother had read her thoughts. 'That won't be for years, *Maman*. But don't worry, Rosetta and the girls will look after me. They won't let any harm come to me.'

Angelique smiled fondly at her daughter. 'I've written to your father. He is coming for you.'

'I don't want him here!' Sylvie exclaimed. 'He's nothing to me. I don't want to see him.'

'I do.' Angelique fumbled for Sylvie's hand. 'I would like to see him one last time. He wired me to tell me he is coming as quickly as he is able.'

Sylvie sat back down. All around, the nuns ministered to other patients with the efficiency they had shown ever since Angelique has been admitted to the hospital. It seemed impossible that everyone else's lives were continuing as normal when Sylvie's whole world had been ripped out from beneath her.

'I'm sure he will come soon,' Sylvie said. 'Go to sleep now. I promise I will wake you as soon as he arrives.'

'You're a good girl. I'm so proud of you. I wish your father could have known you better, but you will have all the time you need now.'

Sylvie laid her head on the bed, her cheek touching Angelique's hand. When she next awoke, it was daytime, and a soberly dressed man stood at the end of the bed.

'You must be Sylvia.'

'Sylvie. Not Sylvia,' she corrected.

'I'm Arthur Crichton. I'm your father,' he said in halting French.

He didn't have to explain who he was. Parts of Sylvie's life that had, up until then, made no sense suddenly became clear. Her tip-tilted nose was his. The lips were the same. The gingery brown hair that peeked beneath the rim of his hat had mixed with Angelique's dark locks to create Sylvie's chestnut that glinted with hints of tawny in summer. He was definitely her father.

Sylvie stared at him, silent. He was a stranger. He was a man with a wife who had abandoned a pregnant woman to fend for herself. Who had not ever seen his child. How worthless. No wonder Angelique had never had a high opinion of men.

'I'm sorry I have not met you before,' Crichton said, 'but all that will change now. We'll have lots of time to get to know each other.'

'How?' Sylvie's voice was hollow.

'Because I'm going to take you home.'

'To Brittany?'

Crichton smiled. 'To England. You're coming back home with me as soon as your affairs here are completed. You're coming to live with me now.'

'But I can't go to England!' Sylvie protested. 'I'm about to become a front-row dancer. The troupe is waiting for me. We're going to Paris.'

Crichton looked apprehensive. 'Your mother took you with her because she had no choice, but I did not expect her to let you join the troupe. That is not suitable for a child of your age. But now I am here, you don't need to do that any more. You can get an education.'

'I have an education,' Sylvie said. Her eyes filled with tears. Hot and angry. She wiped them furiously on the back of her sleeve, not wanting him to think she was weak. 'I can read and write and I am quicker with money than *Maman* is.'

She looked at the figure of Angelique, still and small beneath the smooth sheet, and now the tears began to fall freely. This man who had fathered her then run away thought he had a claim on her. Rage and sorrow gave her the strength to speak to Crichton in a way she would never usually dare address an adult.

'I don't want to go with you. I don't know you. How dare you come here now and tell me you are taking me away!' She turned back to face him and raised her voice, not caring that she was causing the nuns to stop and stare at her. 'You come here to see my mother, but you have never been here for her.'

Crichton's expression hardened. He walked around the bed and gripped Sylvie by the shoulders, turning her round to face him. Sylvie let out a gasp of pain and shock at being handled in such a way, and he released her instantly.

'I'm sorry.' He took off his hat and rubbed his fingers across his temple. His hair was thinning on the top, and there were lines that furrowed his forehead. Sylvie guessed he was older than Angelique by at least ten years. Her mother had always liked older men, and Arthur Crichton would have been handsome fifteen years ago.

'This was not how I planned to meet you. This is not the place. Come with me and we can talk. I won't keep you from your mother for long. Please.'

It was the *please* that did it. Sylvie kissed Angelique's forehead. The skin was so cold now. Barely a person any more.

'We'll be back soon, *Maman*,' she promised.

When she moved away, Crichton made a move towards the bed. He caught Sylvie's eye and hesitated, raising an eyebrow, asking her permission. It was a small gesture, but she appreciated it, and a little of her resentment towards him scraped away.

'Yes, you may,' she said.

Angelique lifted a hand and Crichton clutched it tightly, bringing it to his lips. His body convulsed. He bent over the dying woman and spoke to Angelique in English. Sylvie didn't understand a word of it, but his tone was gentle, and Angelique murmured something back in the same language.

Sylvie realised she would have to learn English and, as

that thought struck her, a sense of defeat began to creep up on her. If she was thinking that, she was already starting to accept she would have to go with him.

Obediently, she followed him out of the hospital to a nearby café, which was considerably more expensive than the ones Angelique usually took her to. Angelique had always allowed Sylvie to order coffee but when she asked Crichton, he ignored the request and ordered Sylvie cake and hot chocolate.

She ate politely, though her stomach felt too knotted for the food to be able to fit inside her. The chocolate was thickened with cornflour and tasted rich and sweet. Comforting.

'That was not how I wanted our first meeting to be,' Crichton said again. 'I was going to tell you about myself, but I think that is the wrong way around. What would you like to ask me?'

Sylvie gave him a hard stare over the rim of her cup. He looked tired and his overcoat was crumpled. If he had come from England to Boulogne, he must have taken an early crossing. Where on earth did one start asking the questions that tumbled around in her head?

'Do you still have a wife?'

'Yes. She's called Maud.'

'Does she know about me?'

Crichton took a sip of his café noir before answering. 'Yes, she does. She has for a few years. I had to explain why I was sending money abroad.'

'You sent money? To my mother?'

'Of course. I may have been absent, but I wanted to support you.'

Sylvie sipped the chocolate thoughtfully. She had never realised that. Crichton took another sip of coffee. He was looking a little more alert now the caffeine was having an effect and his French was becoming more fluent the longer he spoke.

'Maud and I have no children of our own. Maud wasn't – we weren't – ever able to. She'll welcome you into our home. We live in Yorkshire, by the sea. You'll have your own room. We have dogs and horses. We have a tennis court too. I can teach you to play.'

A home. Sylvie's skin prickled. She had spent her life moving from place to place, boarding house to hotel. Never a home. It was a strange idea to be permanent. This felt like something in a moving picture where the poor heroine was whisked off to fortune and happiness. She had become little orphan Annie, to be adopted by a millionaire. But there was an arrogance in Arthur Crichton's assumption that she would be happy to give up her entire life to fall in with his plans.

'But The Firefly Girls. I belong with them,' she explained. 'I love dancing. I want to dance and create dances.'

Crichton laughed, shaking his head indulgently.

'Travelling from place to place? Living from a suitcase? Associating with acrobats and musicians, female impersonators and suchlike. No. You are fourteen but look like you could be eighteen from the way you dress and do your hair.'

Sylvie reached a hand up to the sleek waves. Even though she had slept at Angelique's side, they were still set. 'Mother did them for me. She always liked us to look the same.'

Crichton smiled kindly. 'You look so very alike. The way you move and your voice. It was quite a shock to see you. But it is time to become yourself, Sylvia. You could be so much more than a dancer in a touring sideshow. I'm offering you a home and a future. A chance to become a proper English young lady. Children should not be doing the jobs of adults.'

His voice had become commanding. He'd been a soldier, and whatever he did now, he had the air of being used to being obeyed.

'Angelique wants you to come to me. That's why she contacted me.'

Sylvie nodded reluctantly.

Angelique had loved Arthur Crichton and probably still did. No man she had been with had ever measured up in her estimation or heart to him. For her mother's sake, she could try for a year or two. No one said she would have to stay forever.

'We should go back to the hospital,' she said. 'I want to stay with *Maman* until she is gone. After the funeral,' she said in a dull voice, 'I'll come with you.'

***

Nantes, France

1944

'Monique? Monique? Where are you?'

Sylvie and Céline paused to look at the teenage girl holding a leash with a broken collar on the end. She was standing beside the drinking fountain in the small square around the corner from their apartment, peering around.

'I'm looking for Monique,' she said to the two women, turning desperate eyes on them. 'Can you help me?'

Céline shrugged and switched her bag of groceries from one arm to the other. 'Sorry, I haven't seen a dog.'

Sylvie hesitated. The name might be a coincidence, but it was an odd choice for an animal. Also, the girl hadn't specifically said Monique was a dog; it was just a conclusion one might jump to.

'Does anyone know you are out looking?' Sylvie asked.

'Tante Louise sent me,' the girl said.

The hairs on Sylvie's neck prickled. Too coincidental for two names.

'I don't mind helping you search. I have a little time free,' she said. 'Céline, be a friend and take my bag too. Leave it outside my room, and I'll take it in as soon as I'm back.'

Céline raised her perfectly shaped eyebrows in surprise. 'I thought we were going to fix your hat before we go to work. You won't have time.'

It was only one o'clock. There would be plenty of time to

search for a dog and fix a hat before they needed to leave for the club. Céline didn't want to spend her time looking for a dog, which suited Sylvie fine.

'I feel sorry for her. It won't take long,' Sylvie said. 'I had a dog once, and I would have cried for weeks if Pepe had run away.'

She hoped the story would not motivate Céline to help. She quickly passed over her basket before the singer could change her mind. 'Don't eat the whole pastry before I get back,' she said, referring to the precious slice of glazed cherry tart they had managed to buy by pooling their money and foregoing eggs.

Céline carried on towards the apartment, shaking her head as Sylvie's foolishness. As soon as she disappeared inside, Sylvie turned to the girl.

'Let's go back down the hill to see if Monique is there.'

She led the way and sat on a wall beside a small empty café. The girl was skinny and flat-chested with her hair in two plaits. She wore a summer dress with a patched skirt that had been lengthened with fabric of a different colour. She looked about thirteen but with rationing meaning so many people were underfed, she could have been anything up to sixteen. Sylvie would later discover that she was almost eighteen, but at the time she appeared too young to possibly be involved in Marcel's undercover world. Then again, the delivery boy at the bakery had been young too.

'I think you might have something to tell me. Am I right?' she asked hesitantly. 'Is Monique a dog or a person?'

The girl smiled and rolled up the dog leash. She tucked it under her arm.

'I have a message for Monique. Your Tante Louise would like you to visit her at her house on Rue La Cholière. Do you remember which number she lives at?'

'I don't know,' Sylvie admitted.

'Number twenty-three,' the girl said. '*Maman* asks, can you visit before tomorrow noon?'

Sylvie had no idea who the girl's mother was, or whether the message was even from her mother.

'Of course. Tell your mother I will. Thank you.'

The girl skipped off without a backward glance.

Sylvie was elated as she climbed the stairs to her room back at the house. At last, a real job for her to do. She gathered her hat and the slice of tart and knocked on Céline's door.

'We found the dog,' she announced. 'A silly little ball of fluff. It was cowering in a doorway.'

Fortunately, Céline seemed less interested in the dog than the tart and the hat. No further mention was made as they gossiped and stitched feathers onto their straw hats and ate slivers of cherry tarte.

Sylvie avoided Felix at the 'family dinner' that evening. Two days had passed since their argument, but she still felt a lingering annoyance at him for his suggestions that she would willingly go to bed with Baumann. He seemed happy to ignore her too, even though they sat beside each other at the large, round table over dinner. He spent his time flirting with Céline so overtly that Emily, sitting on

Sylvie's other side, became so sullen she barely said a word.

Poor Emily! Her love was not only unrequited, but went completely unnoticed. She must not realise how obvious her emotions were, but she had an expressive face that couldn't mask anything. If her dark blue eyes had been pistols, Céline and Felix would both have been lying dead. Sylvie felt quite sorry for her, remembering how she had writhed in frustration as she had spent nights waiting for Dennis to ask her to marry him. Of course he never had.

Sylvie ground the end of her baguette into the napkin, then wished she hadn't because crumbs went everywhere, wasting some of the precious bread.

'Some men are so fragile that they can't survive unless a woman is paying them attention,' she whispered to Emily as she scooped up the breadcrumbs and tipped them into her bowl of potage. 'You're better off with no man than one like that in your life because as soon as they become accustomed to your adoration, they start looking for it elsewhere.'

Felix raised his head sharply.

'You are talking from experience?' he asked. 'Or is that a general statement of damnation on all men?'

Sylvie gripped her water glass too tightly. He'd been listening even though he had appeared rapt in what Céline had said, and she hadn't realised. She was nowhere near as observant as she needed to be, and now he'd pounced on her slip. With his question about whether she had anyone special, she had let him see far too much of her.

'You can decide for yourself whether my judgement on your sex is unfair,' she muttered.

There was an uncomfortable silence. Emily toyed with her napkin, Monsieur Julien and Alphonse stopped talking. Even Adele and Estelle, who sat together whispering, looked up.

'Sylvie helped find a dog today,' Céline said brightly. 'Tell everyone what happened, Sylvie.'

Casting her friend a grateful look, Sylvie recounted the tale, elaborating on the description of the fictitious bichon frise.

'She had ever such an amusing name, didn't she? Madeleine. No, Mariette.' Céline frowned. 'Monique! That was it. A dog with a human name.'

Sylvie felt Felix's eyes on her. He was the only other person in the room to guess the significance of the name, and she trusted he wasn't so stupid as to comment on it.

'Some people are strange, I suppose,' she said lightly. 'Anyway, the girl found her dog and went home. Can you pass me the wine please, Estelle? We don't have long before we have to go change for tonight.'

Estelle passed the wine and conversation resumed, but Sylvie could feel Felix glancing in her direction through the rest of the meal. When it was over, he stood behind her and helped pull her chair out.

'Is there anything I should know or that you need help with?' he murmured in her ear.

'If you haven't been contacted, then assume not,' Sylvie whispered. She gathered the soup bowls and piled them up. 'I'm not incapable, and I don't need your help.'

He looked affronted. 'I didn't say you were.'

'No, you didn't. That was rude of me,' Sylvie said.

'I accept your apology,' he said smoothly, inclining his head towards her.

'I didn't give you one,' she said.

He put his lips close to her ear to whisper his answer. 'Nevertheless, I accept it.'

He took the bowls from her. His fingers brushed over hers. He'd done it deliberately, she was convinced of it, and it was even more annoying that even though she was irritated by him, his touch still made her quiver. He gave her an exaggerated smile.

'You'd better go get dressed. There will be an audience ready to charm.'

'And you should do the same,' Sylvie replied. She returned his smile with one she hoped was equally charming. 'There might be some mice for you to catch.'

He laughed out loud, dipped his head and sauntered off into the kitchen with the bowls. Sylvie turned to go and saw that both Céline and Emily were waiting in the doorway. They might not have heard the details of the exchange, but they had clearly seen the way Sylvie and Felix had been whispering and would doubtless have drawn their own conclusions about what had been going on. And from their faces, neither of them was very happy about it.

Chapter Fifteen

Scarborough, England

1933

If Sylvie had been asked to describe the exact opposite of Angelique, Maud Crichton would have been the result. She was short with intelligent, grey eyes behind wire-rimmed glasses, ruddy cheeks and curly red hair that was tamed into submission by numerous pins. She wore plain, mannish-looking clothes and told Sylvie that she spoke plain sense.

'I read classics at Oxford University,' she told Sylvie in flawless French. 'I firmly believe all women are capable of being educated to the highest level.'

Maud was certainly intelligent. Even without Arthur's admission of the truth, she was more than capable of doing the arithmetic required to place the Sylvie's conception after her own engagement. That she was never unkind to Sylvie was something the girl appreciated from the start.

'We'll start on English lessons tomorrow morning, Sylvia. French will be permitted for an hour each morning and evening, but at mealtimes and all other times, you must speak in English, otherwise you will never learn to communicate.'

Sylvie toyed with her spoon, pushing the heavy sponge pudding around the dish. It was delicious and unlike anything she had eaten before, but her appetite had gone completely, and she couldn't force more than a few mouthfuls down.

It became a world of *Don't, Mustn't* and *Can't*.

Don't wear your hair like that, it's far too adult for someone your age and makes you look fast.

You mustn't sing those songs; I know what the words mean, even if the other guests don't.

And worst of all, *No, we can't go back to France. I am too busy with my charitable causes and your father has his business to attend to.*

Arthur's business was something to do with accounting. He had left the army after the Great War and returned to the profession he had been doing beforehand. The photographs of him in his smart uniform stood alongside his wedding-day photograph, Arthur dressed in a sober suit while a serious-eyed Maud stood beside him wearing high-collared lace and a veil.

Sylvie could not imagine the Arthur in those photographs attracting the high-spirited and glamorous Angelique, however, one of the acts of kindness that Arthur did the grieving girl in her first months in England was to produce a small crumpled photograph and discreetly give it to Sylvie. Maud was out visiting the Young Mothers' Welfare group she had established for the poor women of Scarborough, and Arthur appeared at Sylvie's side when she was struggling over her English lessons.

'I want you to have this, Sylvia,' he said, speaking in French even though it was not the allocated hour. 'Keep it safe and please don't tell Maud of its existence. You'll see why.'

Sylvie took it from his outstretched hand, face down. Arthur looked hesitant.

'Maud is doing a good thing bringing you into our house. She is showing you a great kindness, and I would not see her hurt for the world.'

Sylvie nodded. Despite the rules and strictness, Maud did have a good and generous heart, and Sylvie did not wish to cause her any grief. She took the photograph to her room before looking at it. It was of a younger Arthur, wearing pyjamas and lying in a hospital bed, with one leg raised in some sort of sling contraption. Beside him stood a pretty girl dressed in a stiffly starched nurses' apron and cap. They were holding hands and gazing at each other with such expressions of love that Sylvie could practically feel the heat in the air between them.

The girl wore no makeup and the dark waves of her hair were concealed completely, so it took Sylvie a moment to realise she was looking at her mother. She clutched the photograph to her, and tears fell freely. She dabbed them away with a tissue. Crying openly was something else

Maud disapproved of, saying a woman could be as emotionally strong as a man and that this sign of emotion was one of the things holding the women of the world back. Nevertheless, Sylvie cried, letting her grief well up and spill over. When her body finally ceased mourning and it felt she had no more liquid in her to expel, she looked at the photograph carefully once more.

This Angelique was only three or four years older than Sylvie was now. Her face was young and pretty, but her eyes showed a seriousness and determination that was alien to Sylvie. The carefree, lively and flirtatious woman whom Sylvie had always known had somehow managed to rein in her impulsiveness well enough that she could become the serious creature caring for injured men in a battlefield hospital.

She put the photograph safely with the only other one she had of Angelique – a publicity shot for *Les Filles Luciole* of her mother onstage, dressed in a flowing gown with a train of feathers, showing most of her shapely legs. The two images could not have been more different, and seeing them side by side gave Sylvie unexpected hope. If Angelique could emerge from the plain cocoon of starched aprons and caps to become the brilliant butterfly Sylvie had known all her life, then she too could burst free from the restrictive English life at some point and return to the one she had known and loved.

When Maud and Arthur decided that Sylvie had learned enough English to be able to attend school, they sat side by side and explained the plan to her over Sunday lunch.

'By boarding you will learn how English girls behave,

Sylvia. You will pick up the language much more easily and make friends of your own age. It is better than living with only Maud and I for company,' her father explained.

'The Mount is an excellent school, Sylvia, and York is a fascinating city. I attended it myself, and from there I secured a place at university,' added her stepmother.

Sylvie accepted the decision eagerly. 'It will be almost like being back with the women in The Firefly Girls,' she explained.

'Not quite like that, I hope,' Arthur said.

'But they provide for extracurricular classes. You could have ballet lessons as you like to dance,' Maud added kindly.

Sylvie dressed in her own stiff uniform of pinafore, blazer and straw hat to travel to York. She had packed the two photographs into her suitcase to take with her.

She didn't dislike the school, but after assuming the glut of female company would be reminiscent of The Firefly Girls, she discovered she was mistaken. Her tales of life in the theatres and clubs, and the varied people she had known, were met with raised eyebrows and scandalised giggles from her classmates and stern rebukes from the staff. The two precious photographs lay concealed in the frame behind one of Sylvie, Arthur and Maud underneath the whalebones at Whitby. Sylvie couldn't see them, but it was enough to know they were there.

Her father and stepmother had insisted on calling her *Sylvia*, as if this somehow changed who she was. She would answer to it, but in her heart she remained Sylvie. This was her cocoon and one day she too would burst free from it as Angelique had done.

Nantes, France

1944

To make matters more awkward for Sylvie, Baumann arrived at the club at the beginning of the evening. As soon as the door was unlocked, he walked through in the company of a group of other young men in uniform and sat at the table closest to the stage. He was right within Sylvie's eyeline from the stage as the girls began their first dance. Three bars in, he managed to catch her eye and gave her an awkward grin. His shyness was quite endearing. She flashed him a brilliant smile back, which caused his friends to guffaw and dig him in the ribs. Unfortunately, Felix caught it and he gave her such a withering look of contempt that she lost count of the beats and almost missed a spin.

With both men there, she did not feel happy, especially because Felix knew about Baumann and that Marcel had been ambivalent about her encouraging him. It meant that when the first set was over and the German called her over to his table, she was conscious of Felix's eyes on her as she adjusted the strap of her dress and took a seat. She remained conscious of him moving among the tables, working his charm on various female patrons even as she was introduced to Baumann's friends. Valter, Nikki and Valter Hoch (which was not his surname but apparently meant 'tall', to distinguish him from his shorter friend, Baumann explained). Valter and Nikki were both *Unteroffiziers*, which would make them corporals, and Tall Valter was an *Unterwachtmeister* the equivalent to a sergeant.

'You danced well,' Baumann said.

'Thank you, Herr Baumann. I'm learning the routines now,' Sylvie replied. In truth, they weren't hard to learn. She spent a lot of her free time choreographing more complex and interesting ones that she hoped to suggest as possibilities.

'Please, call me *Dieter*,' Baumann said. 'Let me pour you some champagne,' he said as Alphonse the waiter brought over a bottle and five wide-rimmed coupes.

Sylvie raised her eyebrows. Mirabelle did not sell the highest quality, but even the smallest and cheapest bottle would have cost more than she could afford.

'It is my birthday,' Baumann explained, seeing her surprise. 'It is an extravagance, but one my friends are happy to pay for.'

'In that case I accept, and happy birthday, *Dieter*,' Sylvie said, emphasising his name.

Dieter filled a coupe and passed it to her. He and his friends raised theirs and drank. Sylvie took a sip and sighed appreciatively as the cold, tangy fizz filled her nose and slipped down her throat. She'd had champagne before, on her twenty-first birthday, and it was every bit as delicious as she remembered.

'Lovely. Thank you.'

Nikki said something in rapid German, his face a wide grin. Sylvie couldn't understand all of it, but caught the word *kosten* and *vögeln*.

Cost and *fuck*.

There was an embarrassed silence. The two Valters looked intently at their drinks. Baumann went red. The meaning was clear. Nikki looked around, hands up and a bemused look on his face. Sylvie put the champagne coupe down and pushed her chair back. Dieter shook his head apologetically, but before he could speak, Felix appeared at the table. He put one hand on the back of Nikki's chair and leaned forward ever so slightly. He spoke quietly, in fluent German. He smiled all the time, but his eyes were hard. Nikki made a move to stand up, but Dieter put a hand out and stopped him. Felix gestured to Monsieur Julien, who was watching from the bar, and Nikki settled down.

'Glück an deinem geburtstag,' Felix said to Dieter.

He walked away. As soon as he had disappeared behind the curtains, Nikki drained his glass, slammed it down and stood.

'There are better women elsewhere,' he sneered and stormed out.

Adele and Céline appeared at the table and laughingly pulled the two Valters onto the dancefloor, leaving Sylvie and Dieter alone.

'What did Felix say?' Sylvie asked.

'Did you understand what Nikki said?' His cheeks were brick red.

'Some of the words.'

'The piano player told Nikki that he had got the wrong idea about this club, and the women who work here. He said also that even though we are occupying your country, we should not assume we get to have your women.'

Sylvie drew a shaky breath. What was Felix thinking of speaking to an officer in such a way?

'I don't want there to be trouble,' she said.

'There won't be, at least not for your piano player. Tall Valter is Nikki's superior officer and will speak to him tomorrow. He doesn't have sisters like Valter and I have, and sometimes he forgets how to respect women.'

Sylvie looked towards the dancefloor where Tall Valter was dancing with Céline, towering over her. His hands were roving across her back and his face wore a look of surprised delight. The dancefloor was filling up with couples.

'I would like it very much if you would dance with me,' Dieter said.

Sylvie needed to change into her dress for the second half of the evening, but he had been abandoned by his friends on his birthday.

'How old are you today?' she asked.

'Seven and twenty.'

He looked younger. Sylvie was struck again by the innocence that seemed to radiate from him.

'I'd like to dance too,' she said.

She let him take her by the hand and lead the way to the dancefloor. Dieter put one hand on her waist and took hold of her hand and they began to dance the Java. After his shy manner and awkwardness around her, Sylvia had unfairly assumed he would be poor at dancing, but surprisingly he had good rhythm, and she found herself enjoying dancing with him. Céline caught her eye and gave her a wink as they passed, spinning in the arms of their partners. For a few minutes, she allowed herself to get lost in the music and the beat, unconcerned by the fact that by spending time in his company, she was running the risk of her true identity being discovered.

The only thing that threatened to spoil the atmosphere was when she caught sight of Felix as he came back from behind the curtain and took his place at the piano. He shuffled his music and appeared to be absorbed in it, but Sylvie caught him looking towards the dancefloor with a frown on his face. *Let him watch*, she thought, twirling in Dieter's arms with a laugh. She was doing nothing wrong.

When the song came to an end, Céline patted Tall Valter on the arm and made her way to the stage with a backward glance over her shoulder at him. She raised her eyebrows at Felix and tossed her head disdainfully. Sylvie winced. Most likely Felix's ire had been directed at that couple, not at her and Dieter.

'One more dance?' Dieter asked hopefully.

Céline began to sing in her sultry tones.

'*J'attendrai*'.

A slow and dreamy number.

'One dance. Then I have to go get changed into my next costume.'

Sylvie rested her arm on top of Dieter's and took his hand. To dance as they had been would not fit the rhythm or the mood. This needed something more intimate; a slow foxtrot. He put his other hand around her waist, drawing her a little closer as he led her around the floor, weaving among the couples who remained.

Sylvie stared at Dieter as they danced. His hair was blonde, almost white, but it was his eyelashes that fascinated her. They were the same colour as his hair, and against his tanned complexion and icy-blue eyes they almost disappeared.

Ice-blue eyes. Such a clichéd way of describing them, as if he was a character in a cheap paperback thriller, but it was all Sylvie could think of. She kept looking back into them as they danced. It surprised her at how much she was drawn to him. Dieter was perfection personified. Handsome and tall. The sort of man the Führer would have admired.

Sylvie turned cold. Exactly the sort of man who had conquered France. Even as beguiling as she found him, she must not allow herself to forget that. As soon as the last notes of the song ended, she unwound herself and stepped back.

'Thank you. Now I really must go and get changed.'

'I must not let you be late.'

'Are you going to stay and watch for the rest of the night?'

'Of course,' Dieter said. 'I am off duty tomorrow afternoon. Would you please join me for another walk and for some lunch? I have not yet been to the botanic garden and I would like to. I know a good restaurant that opens its doors at midday.'

Sylvie hesitated. She had no idea what missions Marcel would give her when she met him the following day and could end up with plans that she could not cancel in favour of lunch. Dieter took her hesitation as reluctance.

'Or another day,' he said. He looked crestfallen. 'Unless you do not wish to.'

She couldn't think of a reason not to that wouldn't seem unfriendly. What harm could it do? If she was given an unavoidable task, or Marcel decided the engagement was a bad idea, she could send a message and plead illness.

'I do wish to but I have to go shopping tomorrow morning and it can take such a long time to queue in every shop.'

He waved his hands as if dismissing her worries. 'Then I could request a table for one o'clock.'

'Tomorrow will be perfect. Thank you, I would like that,' Sylvie replied. 'Shall I meet you here or outside the chateau?'

'The chateau?' Dieter frowned and glanced towards the two Valters. Nikki slipped in through the door and joined them. He adjusted his trousers and leered as he spoke to the other men. Had he been to the brothel down the street? Sylvie's stomach heaved as she imagined the poor woman forced to suffer Nikki using her to satisfy himself. The only consolation was that, given how long he had been gone, it must have been over for her quickly. Nikki flashed Sylvie and Dieter a look of hostility.

'I think the restaurant will be better,' Dieter said. 'Do you know the Theatre Graslin? It is a short walk to the restaurant from there. Come straight to the restaurant, La Cigale, and I will be waiting for you.'

'Then until tomorrow,' Sylvie said.

Dieter kissed her hand. 'Until tomorrow.'

She hurried backstage to change. She had her first chance to do something really useful rather than traipsing about on Felix's damned errands, and she had gained a lunch engagement with a handsome young man in the bargain. It had been such a long time since anyone had tried to court her; despite knowing she was only doing it for information, she had to admit she was a little excited at the prospect.

Chapter Sixteen

Leeds, England

1942

'Y ou're the new girl, aren't you?'

The young man with whom Sylvie had almost collided as she left the filing room was dressed in a smart three-piece suit. Sylvie recognised him as Mr Radcliffe, the most junior of the partners in the solicitor's Key, Fry, Fforde & Radcliffe. She had briefly encountered Mr Fforde when he had popped in to her interview with Mr Fry, and she had been offered a post in the probate department, which Mr Fry led. Mr Radcliffe took charge of conveyancing.

'I started last month, sir,' Sylvie replied. 'Miss Crichton. Sylvia.'

She'd lived with that name long enough to get used to it,

but it still rankled. Her school certificates were in that name, as was her bachelor's degree from the University of Leeds.

'Call me *Mr Radcliffe*,' he said, bestowing a gracious smile on her. '*Sir* sounds awfully formal. I might like to end up in the House of Lords one day, but not quite yet.'

He had an easy manner about him and Sylvie found it easy to provide the laugh which he was obviously waiting for. She adjusted the bundle of files in her arms, being careful not to disorder them. Mrs Kent, her supervisor, had a sharp tongue, and on Sylvie's first day, she had impressed on Sylvie her expectations of punctuality, personal neatness and professional rigour. A pile of files that was not neatly lined up so all the edges were in perfect unison would receive a sharp reminder about standards.

'You're in Old Kent Road's department, aren't you?' Mr Radcliffe said. 'I can always tell from the way her girls hold their folders. I'm surprised she doesn't pass offenders over to Fforde in the criminal department for prosecution.'

Sylvie frowned. She was fairly certain that the partners shouldn't be sharing nicknames with the clerks like that. It was impertinent to Mrs Kent, who had been with the firm since Mr Fforde joined in 1926 and was in her late fifties. She deserved more respect from her employer, especially as he was ten or more years her junior.

'Oh, don't pull that disapproving face and make me feel like a naughty schoolboy,' Mr Radcliffe said. 'Everyone loves Miss K, and she knows we couldn't do without her. She knows I'm teasing when I call her that. Good to see some sense of loyalty though. I bet you were head girl at your school, weren't you?'

'Far from it,' Sylvie retorted. 'I spent half my first year repeating my prep because my handwriting was so bad and the next half being told to stop dreaming and start marking the ball in hockey!'

It was Mr Radcliffe's turn to laugh. 'You look so prim and proper too!'

Sylvie wriggled inwardly. Of course she looked prim, she'd chosen her work wardrobe to give that effect entirely. Gone was the Sylvie who had dreamed of chiffon and feathers, replaced by tweed skirts and crisp cotton blouses.

'I should take Mrs Kent the files,' she said.

'Of course.' Mr Radcliffe nodded and she passed around him. The corridor was narrow and she couldn't help but brush up against his sleeve. She supposed he could have backed up against the wall, but he didn't. She smiled up at him shyly before walking away. As she reached the door to the office where she worked, he called after her.

'Oh, Miss Crichton?'

She looked back. 'Yes, Mr Radcliffe?'

'I thought I'd take my sandwiches to sit and look at the river this lunchtime. If Old Kent Road lets you out, would you care to join me? I can answer any of the questions about the firm that you might want answering.'

Sylvie felt a blush starting to creep around her neck. If she understood correctly, he was asking her out. She looked at him standing there, waiting for an answer. He was unremarkable to look at, but his eyes crinkled attractively and he had a charming smile. He was a good ten years older than she was, but as her mother had told her, the age

didn't matter if there was a feeling, and there definitely was a feeling stirring inside her.

'I think I'd like that,' she answered.

'Good. Tell Mrs Kent I'm plundering her department and that you'll be an hour.' He walked off along the corridor, hands in his pockets and whistling.

Sylvie watched him turn the corner. She wasn't sure what plundering involved, but she was looking forward to finding out. Mrs Kent received the message with an expression of displeasure and Sylvie almost decided against meeting Mr Radcliffe, but there was enough of Angelique left in her to give her the courage to ignore the disapproval and the inevitable gossip that would follow.

Sandwiches in the park soon evolved into lunch in a corner café. Then into lunch in a nicer establishment, more suited to where a junior solicitor might take a woman he was trying to impress. *Mr Radcliffe* became *Dennis* and tentatively kissed Sylvie as he walked her back to the office. Lunches turned into dinners, and dinners to dances at the 101 Club. The Blitz, that awful campaign of bombing, had seemingly ended and spirits were high.

On their fifth dinner date, Dennis admitted he was married but unhappily and was estranged from his wife. While he lived in the flat in Leeds, his Catholic wife had returned to her parents in High Wycombe. In the argument that followed, Sylvie almost broke off the affair, but Dennis begged her to meet him for dinner once more so he could explain.

'Our marriage was a mistake, Sylvia darling,' he swore, reaching for her hand across the table. 'We were too young.

Edna won't divorce me because of her faith, but we live separate lives. As soon as I'm able, I shall begin the proceedings myself and then I'll be free to marry. I want to be with you, Sylvia.'

Sylvie was in love. Completely, deliriously and wonderfully in love for the first time. The young men she had dallied with at university meant nothing. The stagehands and musicians in France were a distant memory. The expression of remorse on Dennis's face swayed her. The eyes that threatened to brim with tears before he blinked them away sealed the deal.

'I want to be with you too,' she said.

As Sylvie danced in Dennis's arms at the 101 Club while the band played swing, he pulled her close and murmured against her neck.

'Why don't you come home with me tonight?'

'You keep asking me and I keep saying no,' she murmured. 'What makes you think I'll change my mind tonight?'

'Because now you know the truth and you forgave me.' He drew her closer so she could rest her head against his shoulder. 'We can't have a wedding yet, but we can make that vow to each other privately.'

He swung her round, and she did a graceful twirl followed by a slide. Dennis caught up with her and nuzzled her from behind. He manoeuvred her round so they were both facing the band and the row of girls dancing on the stage.

'You dance so well. You could easily be a professional. You've got the sort of body that's made for moving.'

Sylvie looked longingly at the dancing girls.

'I could have been, in another life,' she said, raising her voice over the music.

Dennis laughed and whisked her into another smooth slide across the dancefloor. Over his shoulder, Sylvie kept her eyes on the women in their silk and sparkles. What wouldn't she give to be up there with them?

What would she give? Would she exchange her good job and a comfortable room at the boarding house that Maud's friend ran to be back onstage? She shouldn't want to, but the music caught her and moved her, lifting her like a wave.

She wanted that exhilaration to continue, needed something to make her feel that elation. When the band finished their final number and Dennis had collected her coat, she slipped her arms around his neck and kissed him slowly.

'I'll come home with you tonight,' she said.

His face lit up, and he drew her into a deeper, longer kiss, enfolding her inside his Mackintosh. Sylvie was shivering with excitement by the time they reached Dennis's flat in a smart mews building that had escaped the bombing, though the houses at the end of the road had not been so lucky.

She didn't have time to investigate the flat as he led her by the hand straight through into a bedroom. He didn't even bother to turn on the light and they undressed each other in darkness, feverishly kissing all the while. Dennis pulled her down onto the bed and straddled her.

'I don't know if you know what to expect,' he

murmured, as he twined his fingers in the strap of her brassiere and began to ease it down over her shoulder.

Sylvie had never told him she wasn't a virgin, but then she had never told him that she was either. He just assumed it. She considered correcting him but, well, some men preferred to think that they were a woman's first, and it did not really matter to her. She'd lost her virginity to an arts undergraduate called Oliver on the night war was declared. She had no idea what had happened to Oliver since, and he didn't really matter.

She put her arms around Dennis, drawing him down closer to whisper in his ear.

'I'm sure you'll teach me everything I need to learn.'

Afterwards they lay in the dark, warm beneath the blankets. Sylvie felt she fitted into the crook of his arm as if she had been made for it.

'Conveyancing is so damned dull,' Dennis said. 'No one wants to buy a house when they're worried the Luftwaffe might flatten it at any moment. I might go seek my fortune in one of the government departments rather than hang around Leeds forever. You could come with me and we can set up together.'

It would be good to do something more productive for the war effort. Of course, life had to go on, but when Sylvie saw the women in WREN or WAAF uniforms heading to their shifts, she did feel that she could be doing more. Moving to London would provide better opportunities.

Then Sylvie remembered the countless men her mother had loved and lived with, and though it was tempting, that would be the end of promises of marriage. She wasn't that

naïve. Besides, her father and Maud would never permit her to do something so scandalous; she had tried too hard to become the respectable English lady they wanted her to be.

'We could do that...' Sylvie said. She leaned over him and planted a kiss on his lips, then smiled in the darkness. '...when you're free to marry. The second Mrs Dennis Radcliffe might move to London with you, but Sylvia Crichton is staying right here.'

Nantes, France

1944

Sylvie began to change, slipping out of the sequin-covered short green skirt and cropped top. The first costume she had worn was playful, but the second set of dances called for a slinkier gown of black silk and lace with a red silk scarf. It reminded her of the clothes The Firefly Girls had worn as the Twenties changed into the Thirties, although hers was shorter and more revealing with thin straps edged with rows of beads.

She reached her hands around the back, struggling slightly to do up the top button that was in the middle of her shoulder blades. The door opened, allowing a brief burst of laughter and music to blast through, then closed behind her.

'Can you do this for me, please? I can never reach the top button.'

She glanced into the mirror, but instead of one of the girls, Felix stood there.

'Can't you knock? I could have been naked,' she exclaimed. He averted his eyes – a touch belatedly, in Sylvie's opinion. 'I'm not, so you don't have to look at the floor. What do you want? Shouldn't you be onstage with Céline?'

'I can take a minute.' He leaned against the wall beside the door. 'After seeing the way you were dancing, I assume your honour is intact and your composure is fine, but I came to ask how you were after being insulted. Here let me do that for you,' he said, noticing she had started to struggle with her buttons again.

'There is no need,' Sylvie said. 'I don't need your help.'

'Always take help if it is offered freely,' Felix said.

'Is that what you were doing when you intervened?' Sylvie asked. The latent anxiety that had been hovering in her breast ever since Felix had confronted Nikki flared again. 'That was so stupid! Didn't you think what could have happened if you spoke like that to a German officer?'

Felix's eyes flashed. 'I did think,' he said. 'My initial instinct was to punch him and throw him out of the club.'

'He would have had you arrested,' Sylvie exclaimed in horror. 'You might have been executed!' She had visions of Felix being manhandled out in handcuffs, dragged into the depths of the chateau, never to be seen again.

'That's why I didn't do it, but I wasn't about to stand by and listen to that sort of talk,' Felix said. He glared at the

room in general. 'Did you understand what the Unteroffizier said about you?'

'Some of it,' Sylvie admitted. 'An insult like that was hardly enough to risk getting yourself imprisoned or executed for, especially when you disapprove of what I've been asked to do and most likely agree with his estimation of me.'

'I don't agree with him!'

'Well, that comes as a surprise to me!' Sylvie muttered.

Felix stuffed his hands in his pockets and stared intently at the floor.

'How come you speak such good German?' Sylvie asked.

'I made the effort to learn. It comes in useful. When you are clinging beneath a railway carriage, trying to lay explosives without being seen, it is important to understand what the men searching for you are saying.'

'You need to take more care,' Sylvie said. Her blood chilled at the thought of what Felix described. She could imagine him in the darkness, teeth gritted and brow furrowed in determination.

'I'm used to danger,' Felix replied. 'I've lost friends and allies, and I know what might happen if I am caught. Some things are worth taking risks for.'

'I don't consider rudeness to a woman one of them,' Sylvie said.

He raised his head, chin jutting forward and a determined look in his eye. 'It is a matter of principle.'

'You sound like a knight talking of chivalry. I would not have taken you for a romantic.' Sylvie gave a gentle laugh.

But actually, having someone leap to her defence had felt unexpectedly good.

Felix sneered. 'Those men who occupy the chateau now understand nothing of chivalry. The dukes of days long ago would not have tolerated them.'

Sylvie folded her arms, staring at him gravely. 'I can live with an insult to my honour, such as it is, but I couldn't live with knowing you had died as a result.'

Felix drew closer to her, moving slowly and carefully as if he expected her to run from him like a cat startled by a dog. 'You would care if I was shot?'

There was more to that question than he was asking aloud. Sylvie took her time before answering. The fear that had shot through her when Felix had confronted Nikki had been surprisingly intense and urgent. She met him halfway across the room.

'I would care if anyone dies as a result of something I had done,' she answered, raising her head to look into his eyes. 'You need to be alive to continue your fight. That's the most important thing to both of us, don't forget. What happened to minding your own business and ignoring small wrongs like you told me?'

Felix didn't meet her eye.

'I can gather my own apples,' Sylvie said gently.

'You're right.' There was a catch in his voice. 'Let me do your button up. You need to be onstage soon – your audience will be waiting. After all, you need to continue with your mission to charm our German patrons, don't you?'

Sylvie turned around to face the mirror. Felix stepped

behind her and looped the button through the hole. His fingers were cool against Sylvie's skin, and she gave a little shiver. Felix leaned closer to her, staring over her shoulder into the mirror to look at them both. He'd finished fastening the dress but didn't take his hand away. His touch was electric; a surge strong enough to power lights. The delicate skin over Sylvie's spine began to flare with heat. She met the eyes of his reflection. Raw desire burned in them.

'I suppose you're more used to undoing dresses than fastening them,' she remarked.

His eyes flickered. 'I think you have a lower opinion of me than I deserve, but I can do that too if you would like when tonight is finished.'

His hand began to drift from the buttons up the curve of Sylvie's bare spine to the nape of her neck. She didn't stop him. When had she last felt an attraction this powerful towards any man? Not since the early days of her affair with Dennis. Why the hell shouldn't she allow herself to give into it a little?

Because she'd had enough of charming, easy-talking men.

'I've told you, I'm not going to do that.' She turned around to face him, realising how unconvincing her voice was. 'Thank you for your help earlier, even though it was not asked for.'

He accepted the thanks with a nod. 'We started off on the wrong foot, didn't we?'

'We started off on the right foot, then it went wrong when you accosted me and kissed me,' she reminded him. 'That was unnecessarily dramatic.'

'I know, but the opportunity presented itself, and I'd wanted to do it since I first saw you walk through the door.'

Sylvie blinked in surprise. 'Really?'

'Oh yes, but I could hardly just say, *"excuse me, Mademoiselle, may I kiss you?"* could I?'

His voice was as rich as velvet. He stared into her eyes with a gaze that was steady and unblinking. A hard ball of desire was tightening in Sylvie's stomach, overcoming her determination not to fall for another sweet-talker.

'You might not have been punched if you had,' she murmured.

Maybe his talk of chivalry had appealed to the romantic in her because she put her hands on his shoulders, drawing him a little closer, and stood on her tiptoes. She kissed the corner of his mouth, nothing more than a moth's-wing touch. A trace of stubble scratched her lips, rough and enticing. His hands tightened around her body and he pulled her to him, mouth searching for hers.

The door handle rattled. Instantly, they jumped apart. When then the door opened and Emily came in, they were standing a little apart, Sylvie fiddling with the combs in the back of her hair and Felix standing with his arms crossed, leaning against the mirror and looking bored. Emily's brows knotted as she looked from Sylvie to Felix. She couldn't possibly suspect anything, but Sylvie felt as if everything they had briefly done was being replayed on the wall like a cinema reel.

'Why are you backstage? Everyone is waiting,' Emily said to Felix. 'You need to come now. So do you, Sylvie.'

'Thank you, little one,' Felix said, patting her cheek as he ambled past her. Emily narrowed her eyes angrily.

Sylvie followed the pair of them out, not wanting to catch Emily's hard stare. It was difficult enough seeing Emily's sadness as she watched Céline and Felix together, and Sylvie didn't want to be responsible for the poor girl knowing he preferred yet another dancer instead of her. Assuming, of course, that was why Emily was watching them. It seemed unlikely she was an informant for the *milice*, but Sylvie had to remind herself that spies were everywhere and she could put her trust in no one.

Chapter Seventeen

It took Sylvie over an hour to walk to Rue La Cholière. She'd have to see about getting a bicycle if she was going to be travelling around the city. Number 23 was a narrow house that reminded Sylvie of places Angelique had rented when she had been short of money. Outside was a two-wheeled cart laden with pots of paint and a tub of brushes and a sign proclaiming the owner to be *M. Pauly, Paintre*. The door was opened by an old woman dressed in an outfit that would have been fashionable thirty years before.

'I'm here to visit Tante Louise,' Sylvie said.

The woman gave a wide smile devoid of teeth and ushered Sylvie up to a top-floor room before disappearing. Inside, Marcel was playing cards with another woman. He was dressed in paint-spattered overalls and a shirt with the sleeves rolled up. The woman had blonde hair streaked with grey and was probably in her early forties. She reminded Sylvie of the girl who had passed the message on.

They shared the same light-brown eyes and mild expression.

'Thank you for joining me,' Marcel said. 'You had no trouble finding the house?'

'None. I was careful to check I was not being followed. I doubled back once or twice and visited the small church at the bottom of the hill, then went the other way out of the churchyard.'

'It's wise to assume you're being followed. We have a number of safe houses, but this one is by far the best. Madame Barbe – Louise – and her daughter Claire are resourceful and loyal.'

'Do you mean the girl with the dog leash?' Sylvie asked. 'She was very clever to find me as she did rather than coming into the shop.'

Madame Barbe looked pleased. There was a knock at the door. Marcel reached beneath his chair and drew a pistol beneath the table. Sylvie tensed. Her hand went to the necklace and the hidden L-pill.

'Come in,' Louise called cautiously. The old woman appeared, carrying a tray with thin slices of cake and glasses of clear, brown liquid. Louise took it and ushered the old woman out with profusive thanks and assurances that they did not need anything else.

'My mother-in-law,' she explained in a voice that was little more than a whisper. 'She has lived with us since my husband died in the first weeks of the war. I'll go sit with *Belle-mère*,' Louise said, smiling at Marcel. The look that passed between them was the purest form of love Sylvie had ever seen. A lump formed in her throat. No one had ever looked at her in that way. Once Louise had left the room, Sylvie caught his eye and he shrugged. His eyes were sad.

'It can't last, I know,' he murmured in English.

He didn't elaborate and Sylvie didn't ask. There could be any number of reasons why he believed a relationship with Madame Barbe was doomed. It was unfair to leap to the conclusion that he had a wife and half a dozen children back in England, and even if that was true, it was not her place to judge. He had sounded genuinely sad, but she couldn't help thinking how easy it was for men to find women who would ask no questions. She wondered how often the Englishman found the excuse to visit the safe house, and if Louise suspected he was an English agent not simply a French résistant.

'Is there any chance I can get a bicycle somehow?' Sylvie asked to clear the awkwardness.

'I'll see what we can do. Now, to why we're here,' Marcel said. 'Britain informs us that a number of airmen have been shot down and Nantes is on the route being used for the time being to get them to safety. Our intention is to steal food stamps to give to them when they pass through.'

'Won't that leave families short?' Sylvie asked.

Marcel took off his spectacles and cleaned them on his shirt front. 'That can't be helped, I'm afraid. We need the stamps and there is no other way of obtaining them.'

The long queues for stamps snaked around the town hall where French workers counted out and handed over stamps to the recipients under German supervision. Even if one of the workers was so inclined, there would be no opportunity for her to hand over more than was allocated.

'We have a contact in the town hall who has told us everything we need to know about where the tickets are kept and how to gain entry. The Resistance will be carrying out a raid on Thursday night and simultaneously creating a diversion. Felix is the best marksman we have and will be covering the town hall from an advantageous building,' Marcel explained.

There was no reason why Felix shouldn't be good with a rifle, but it wasn't something Sylvie associated with the musician. Imagining him as a sniper took some doing.

'What do I have to do?' Sylvie asked, eying the pistol that Marcel had placed on the table after the old woman had left. It felt like years since she had handled a gun, but in reality, it had only been weeks since the lessons in marksmanship. Marcel saw her looking and slipped the gun out of sight. She wasn't sure whether to be relieved or disappointed that she wouldn't get to put her training to use in the field.

'I will be waiting with others to receive the tokens when they have been obtained. We'll split them and send them out to different locations around the city, along with decoy packages. You will need to be waiting outside your apartment at five in the morning to accept one of the genuine packages. Do you have somewhere safe to keep it hidden for a few days?'

'Yes, I found somewhere that I don't think—'

Marcel cut her off with a wave of the hand. 'Don't tell me. The less I know, the better. I trust you to take care of them. In a week or so, I will pay a visit to Mirabelle to give you further instructions,' Marcel said. 'It looks to me as if the paintwork needs touching up on the front windows and I'm cheap, so I'll have an excuse to be there.'

'I can't argue with you about the paint,' Sylvie said. 'Does Monsieur Julien know who you are?'

'He knows I am with the Resistance, but not that I am English. He never takes part in activities. Mirabelle has been a safe house on occasion and he lets us plant agents there. His brother is deeper into the organisation.'

'The butcher?' Sylvie asked.

Marcel smiled. 'That would be quite an apt alias for Tomas. He's had a reputation as a bottle-drunk fighter for years.'

The church bell pealed twelve.

'I need to go,' Marcel said. 'I have a job for you now. Deliver this pile of magazines to the bookshop on Allée du Port Maillard and tell Monsieur Tombée, the owner, that Louise enjoyed them. Be careful not to change the order they are piled in. There is nothing concealed within the pages and no marks anywhere, but the order of the publications is the code itself.'

'That's very clever,' Sylvie said. She picked up the piles and slipped them carefully into her bag, making sure not to accidentally rearrange them. 'There is one more thing I should run past you. I have been invited to lunch this afternoon by the German I met – I mentioned him to you the other day.' Her cheeks flushed a little. 'I hope you don't disapprove of me meeting him.'

Marcel looked thoughtful. 'You said he works in the Department of Transportation?'

'That's right. He might not be a ranking officer himself, but he has friends who are officers in the *Heer*. An Unterwachtmeister and two Unteroffiziers. They might talk to him about their work.'

She said it more in hope than anything else. Marcel might think Dieter too poor a source and order her to focus her attention on attracting one of the others instead. She would have to grit her teeth to pretend to find Nikki appealing.

Marcel drummed his fingers on the table top. 'London have asked us to try to discover the capacity for the submarine base at St Nazaire. We have put the word out to men in that area, but if he has any information on that, we'd use it. Otherwise, it is always useful to know the ins and outs of the rail network: when and where shipments are planned for. Continue cultivating him until there is a better target. I doubt it will cause problems for you working at Mirabelle to have an admirer. Yes, you can make your lunch date.'

'Thank you. If I find out anything useful, I will let you know.'

He walked her to the door and grinned. 'You should take advantage and make sure you eat well at your suitor's expense. The German forces have commandeered almost all of France's food for themselves. It's your duty to claim some back for the French.'

Rue Allée du Port Maillard was close enough to the chateau that Sylvie had time to take the books on the way to meeting Dieter. A plump man with white, curly hair looked up from the volume he was reading and gave her an enquiring look over the top of a pair of small, wire-framed glasses.

'Monsieur Tombée?'

'Yes?'

Sylvie handed over the magazines. 'These are for you. Tante Louise enjoyed them.'

The bookseller thumbed through the titles with an air of deep concentration, then looked up and beamed at Sylvie.

'Thank you, mademoiselle. All is in order.'

Sylvie left the shop. She had no idea what message she had relayed and didn't want to know. Presumably it had been good news, given the man's smile. She glanced at her watch and walked faster. She would be on time if she hurried and hoped Marcel would make good on his promise to find her a bicycle.

—————

There was a checkpoint at the square in front of the theatre. Sylvie waited in line to hand her papers over, the curdling feeling in her stomach growing stronger with each step she took towards the front of the queue. The checkpoint was not too busy. Good for ensuring she would be on time, not so good for slipping through without being questioned or having her bag searched. When the queues were greater, the sentries in charge of examining papers did not pay as much attention.

'What is your purpose here today, *fräulein*?'

The sentry turned Sylvie's identity paper over, examining it closely. She took a breath. There was always the worry simmering just beneath the surface that the forged papers would be spotted.

'I am going to La Cigale. I am meeting a friend for lunch.'

'Who is this friend?'

Sylvie gave Dieter's name and rank, glad she has practised the tongue twisting syllables of the German title. The sentry looked her up and down and wrinkled his nose disdainfully. He handed Sylvie's paper back.

'Proceed.'

Sylvie stepped through the checkpoint.

'Whore!'

Sylvie stiffened and turned around.

The culprit was the middle-aged woman who had been in the line behind Sylvie. She had muttered the word loud enough for Sylvie, the guards and the other people queueing to hear. The woman sneered, sniffed and spat on the ground. A couple of bystanders murmured in support. Sylvie walked away, head down and cheeks burning with shame.

She arrived at the restaurant with time to stop around the corner and reapply her lipstick and smooth her hair. Her hand shook as she fumbled in her bag. She was apprehensive anyway, but the confrontation had shaken her more than she would have expected.

She might be making a terrible mistake. A chance meeting and walk was one matter, but this was a *date*, to use the American term. In the eyes of the French it put her firmly into the despised category of a collaborator, and she felt like one. Women who consorted with the enemy were the lowest of the low. In eyes of the woman in the queue, Sylvie thoroughly deserved the insult. Sylvie didn't blame her for the contempt, but she wished there was a way of explaining that she had a purpose to fulfil. She pulled herself up straight. She had a job to do, and she doubled her resolve to find some useful information from Dieter.

Chapter Eighteen

La Cigale had the look of somewhere that had once been elite, with elaborate Art Nouveau styling inside and out. An immaculately dressed waiter showed Sylvie to a table for two against a mirrored wall where Dieter was waiting. When he saw Sylvie, his eyes lit up.

'You look very beautiful.'

'I would have worn something nicer if I had realised how fancy the restaurant would be,' Sylvie said, gesturing down at her dusky pink dress.

She was out of place. Most tables were occupied by at least one man in Nazi uniform with a female companion. The women were dressed in understated outfits and subtle accessories that, nevertheless, screamed of money. It reminded Sylvie of the café where she had first met with Felix, and his cutting comments about women seeking patrons. Of the other female diners, how many of them were paying for their lunch with sex?

Dotted among the *Heer* and *Kriegsmarine* uniforms were

the grey of the *Schutzstaffel* with their lightning bolt double-S insignia: a chilling presence that was almost enough to put Sylvie off lunch. Her neck went clammy. She had walked into the lion's den, and if her identity was ever going to be discovered, it would be here.

Dieter must have seen her unease because he leaned forward and whispered confidentially, 'I also find it unnerving to see them.'

Sylvie's eyes widened. He was admitting something that no loyal party member should voice.

'They remind me of the keenest boys when I joined the *Hitlerjugend*. I am ashamed to say I was a sorry member because I preferred reading to pursuing outdoor sports. My father was the mayor, so I was given an easier time. My brother is a gunner in the *Luftwaffe*. I wanted to be a librarian. I am afraid I was always a disappointment to him.'

Though Dieter was criticising himself for lacking the drive he should have possessed, the fact he mentioned it at all gave her something to ponder.

'My father expected better of me too,' she confided. 'There was too much of my mother in me for his liking.'

Dieter ordered for them both. The portions were generous, though the food was unfamiliar. A piece of braised pork covered in a creamy sauce arrived, accompanied by thick white noodles and greens of some sort. The morning's events had dulled Sylvie's appetite, but mindful of Marcel's earlier comments, she ate with simulated enthusiasm. The dish tasted bland, but presumably this was something favoured by the homesick

Germans; being able to taste cream made up for any lack in flavour.

'Is this what you eat in Germany?' she asked.

'Food from the mountains. The *Spätzle* here are almost as good as my Oma's cook used to make.'

For a moment, Dieter's eyes misted over as he reminisced about home. Alongside his admission that the SS presence unnerved him, she was struck by an insight: he did not really want to be here. There had been rumours of Germans being persuaded to switch allegiance and work as agents for British Intelligence. Sylvie might have found someone who could be turned. She noted it away carefully in the back of her mind to mention to Marcel later.

'My *grand-mère* did not want me to travel away from her village because of what I might encounter. She wanted me to marry and settle, but I loved dancing too much. Now I wonder if I should have stayed in Brittany.'

She forced herself to picture a kindly old woman with a black dress and the traditional Breton lace *coiffe bigoudène* balanced on her head. There had been no loving *grand-mère*, of course – Angelique's mother had disowned her as soon as her pregnancy began to show – but lies were more convincing when the teller believed them. The woman she pictured was the one who had admitted her into Madame Barbe's house.

'I do miss Brittany sometimes. I miss oysters and *coquilles St Jacques*, and big pots of mussels with wine and onion,' she said wistfully.

Dieter pulled a face. 'I've never eaten mussels. They

look...' he looked around, waving his hands expressively, searching for a word to describe them. '*Schleimig.*'

'Slimy. Yes, but fresh and salty.' Sylvie sat back in her chair, memories crashing over her. 'By the sea they are best of all. One summer my mother's dance troupe was in Saint Nazaire. Her lover taught me to pluck mussels using the shell of another.'

She hadn't picked a memory from England. No food or place from her life in Britain appealed to her sense of longing for the past. France was everything. But now she was on the subject of the coast, it was a natural way to introduce the subject that Marcel wanted to find out about.

'Saint Nazaire was not my favourite place to visit. The estuary was very flat and the tides were too strong to swim in. Now I hear there is nothing left of the town, and the whole coast is now made of concrete. Is it true?'

Dieter hesitated before answering, and Sylvie wondered if she had been too blatantly curious, but then he shrugged, and she relaxed.

'The U-boat pens are there. They are made from concrete, it is true. The British destroyed the dry dock, but they couldn't destroy the pens because the design is too strong.' Dieter looked grave. 'I haven't been there, but I imagine you would not recognise it. Of course it has changed, but this is a change for the better. France will play an important role in the new Reich. Times are hard at the moment, but when the war is over, France will be prosperous.'

Sylvie looked around the restaurant. It was easy to say that with a full plate.

'I've seen it happen before,' Dieter said earnestly. 'After the Great War. Saarland, my home, was held by the French. It was fifteen years before we were returned to our true motherland.'

He seemed to grow taller in his seat, standing to attention in an unseen parade ground.

'And it is better now than before?' Sylvie asked.

'Nowhere is as good as it should be. Most of our men have gone to fight. The work has to be done by the French labour force, and they are lazy and unwilling.'

Dieter looked at her, his pale blue eyes full of a fire that lent them a ferocity and passion they didn't usually possess.

'My mother told me about the Great War and how the French controlled the mines. Troops came from everywhere to patrol the streets. Britain, Italy, Sweden... I grew up seeing the uniforms everywhere of men who were not of my country. Our homeland was not ours.'

Like the French children growing up now with German uniforms on the streets causing them terror, Sylvie thought. She was mystified by how he could not see that the childhood he described was what the homeland he loved was inflicting on the rest of Europe.

'I was born not long after the end of the war,' Sylvie said. 'My mother was happy it was over and the death had stopped. She could stop nursing and return to dancing. She would be sad to know we are at war again.'

The atmosphere changed, growing tense.

'What about your father?' Dieter asked.

Sylvie looked him in the eye. Even without the

complication of Arthur Crichton's nationality, that was not a matter she wanted to share.

'I think she was happy he was over and done with too. As I said, I was not the daughter he would have hoped for, and she was definitely not the wife!'

Dieter held her gaze for a moment, then broke into a fit of laughter. Sylvie joined in with giggles that came naturally in response to the infectious sound of his laugh.

'What is so funny?'

'You Frenchwomen are outrageous,' Dieter explained. 'The girls I grew up with would never say such a thing. All my sister wants is to be a *hausfrau* and raise children. It was the same with the girls in my village.'

'Is that what German men want from their women?' Sylvie asked.

Dieter began to play with his napkin. 'I don't know. Maybe not all German men.'

The expression in his eyes was one she had seen on the face of other men. It made his meaning clear whether or not he realised it. He wanted Sylvie. And against all odds, she found she did not mind.

She did not hesitate when Dieter offered her a dessert and had to stop herself moaning with genuine appreciation when a delicate slice of cake was placed before her, consisting of six layers of sponge held together with chocolate cream.

Chocolate!

Sylvie licked her lips. 'This is heaven.'

Dieter smiled over the top of his less appealing looking dumpling with custard that was apparently called something like a *Germknödel*. She was glad she had chosen the chocolate cake, but was almost regretting her gluttony by the time two small cups of coffee arrived. Three courses felt like a banquet after the slender rations she had been used to for so long, and her stomach was beginning to ache.

'This is proper coffee too.' She sighed with pleasure after a sip of the bitter, black liquid.

'Of course,' Dieter said with a smile. 'La Cigale is a good restaurant, and they serve the best food. The food in my *Soldatenheim* is very pleasant but dull.'

Sylvie felt a flicker of irritation. The boarding houses for soldiers had once been hotels or pensions for more welcome visitors. Even though the *Wehrmacht* had commandeered the majority of the food supplies, it was their French hosts who were expected to foot the bill for the occupying forces. All at once her enjoyment diminished, replaced by an overwhelming sense of guilt. She'd eaten half a week's rations in one meal. The cost must be immense.

'How can you afford to eat here?' she asked. 'I'm sorry, that is rude. I just didn't imagine a secretary would be very well paid.'

To her surprise, Dieter blushed a little. 'My family is wealthy. I have money of my own. I don't have many things to spend it on, but good food is one of my pleasures.'

He signalled the waiter and paid the bill.

They walked to the botanical garden. Instinctively, Sylvie avoided the camellia paths and they settled on an iron bench in front of the glasshouse. Unlike the Sunday when she had visited before, there were few people strolling through the gardens.

'I thought there would be a greater army presence in Nantes,' she remarked. 'I am surprised that there are not more patrols marching night and day through the streets.'

'If you were to go further along the coast, there are more garrisons,' Dieter said. 'Paris is very busy, of course.'

Sylvie looked at the sky. 'I've never been to Paris. I was going to once. I nearly did, but...'

She wrinkled her nose, feeling the prickle that meant tears were not far away. Too many painful associations. The loss of her mother and an entire change of life. Of who she had been.

'Before my mother died. But then she died and I never went.'

'I am sorry to hear that,' Dieter said. '*Jeder einmal in Paris*. That's the promise they have made. I will go one day. Perhaps you will too.'

She smiled at his kindness.

'Perhaps.'

He licked his lips nervously, then swiftly leaned towards Sylvie and kissed her cheek, his lips landing like a butterfly alongside hers. Caught off-guard, she stiffened. Dieter pulled away, his expression one of mortification. His face began to glow scarlet down to the roots of his white-blonde hair.

'I'm sorry, *Fräulein* Duchene,' he said. 'I don't know what came over me. I should not have done that. I must go. Goodbye.'

He stood and walked off, head down and hands bunched at his side. Sylvie watched him go. Thoughtfully, she raised her fingers and touched the spot that Dieter had kissed. There was something sweet and innocent about him. He had lacked any of the idea of slowly building up to a kiss – she suspected he was probably a virgin. For a fleeting moment, she had caught a glimpse of the boy he had been before war had transformed him into the enemy, and she was intrigued.

A rich boy. A mayor's son who showed slight glimpses that he had reservations about some of his country's actions before the propaganda took over again. A reader who became a secretary with a desk job rather than go into battle.

She wondered if he would have liked the woman she had been in peacetime. She'd worn so many faces living in France, then England, and now back in France that she was not sure now who that woman had actually been.

Chapter Nineteen

Ensuring Céline did not discover Sylvie's night-time exploits on the night of the planned raid was a problem that occupied Sylvie right up until the very morning of the event. Even though she was not expected to be directly involved with the break-in of the town hall, she woke having slept badly, feeling nauseous with anticipation, like she had been drugged.

As she was stirring hot water into a tisane of chamomile flowers, a solution came to her. As well as the cyanide pill, agents were given barbiturates and amphetamines to either keep them awake or help them sleep. Sylvie hadn't used any, but one of the pills would ensure Céline slept soundly.

She crushed one to a fine powder and wrapped it in a twist of paper, ignoring her conscience telling her it was wrong to do what she planned; there were more important matters at stake. If anything, she was doing Céline a favour, because if she did happen to wake and discover what Sylvie was doing, she would need to be silenced.

The weather grew hot and stormy through the course of the day. By late evening, the sky was black with thunder clouds that burst in torrents of rain that battered the roofs and pavements, bouncing back up to soak everything. There could not have been a more perfect night for a raid if God himself had arranged it. No one would be outside if they could help it. The soldiers on patrol would huddle in their greatcoats, wishing they were indoors and hopefully paying less attention to shadows.

Céline and Sylvie sheltered in the doorway as Mirabelle closed, hoping the rain would ease, but it showed no sign of it. Sylvie saw Felix slip out through the side door, dressed in a dark coat and beret. The crates and piles of rubbish had been moved, suggesting the door was deliberately kept blocked unless needed. He looked towards the front of the alley, and their eyes met. One eye flickered in what might have been a wink before he slunk away down the alley, collar up and beret pulled down low to ward off the rain. Sylvie's blood chilled to think that whatever risk she was running, his was so much greater.

'Let's run for it,' she shouted to Céline over the noise of the rain. They held their umbrellas low and did their best to dodge the puddles and streams that ran down the old streets, but they were both cold and shivering by the time they reached home. The circumstances could not be more perfect.

'Come in for a drink,' Sylvie suggested as they stood in the hallway, shaking water off their umbrellas and coats. 'I want to ask you about some ideas I have for a new dance. I've saved a little wine.'

Céline readily agreed. Sylvie described the dances The Firefly Girls had performed while she warmed cheap red wine on her gas ring. Whenever Céline could, she turned the conversation to what she might be able to sing while the girls were dancing, and after being interrupted one too many times Sylvie lost her qualms about drugging her friend. She gave the wine a stir.

'Oh dear, this smells very sour. I'll add some chamomile and honey. I miss nice wine. It was so lovely to drink champagne the other night.' she added wistfully.

'What happened to not accepting drinks from the enemy?' Céline asked.

Sylvie examined her fingernails. Céline could never be allowed to suspect her real motive for accepting Dieter's hospitality. 'I don't know. It's wrong, but he's clearly going to keep coming to the club and he seems quite nice. He was very angry at the way his friend spoke to me. I had such a lovely lunch too. There was proper chocolate cake! I wish I could have saved some for later.'

'I miss chocolates.' Céline sighed. 'When the war is over, I'm going to eat until I burst.'

'Do you think it will ever be over?' Sylvie asked. 'That the Allies will win, and we'll be free of Hitler?'

'Or the Nazis will and we'll have their sort of peace. If they do, perhaps they'd ease the regulations and we'll have more freedom.'

'I'm not sure that counts as free,' Sylvie said. 'Standing in line to have our papers pored over as if we're doing something wrong just by walking down the street.' She hid her surprise. Céline was talking as if she was happy to accept that outcome. Didn't she see the boarded-up shops and houses belonging to families who had just disappeared? Or what happened to those who stepped out of line?

'They won't need as many checkpoints or curfews if they don't think we're going to fight back. I know it's awful now, but this can't last forever, can it?' Céline asked. 'I don't want them to win, but nothing seems to be changing.'

Sylvie stretched out her legs. 'Did you ever consider joining the Resistance?'

'Hiding in fields and laying bombs? Not for me.' Céline examined her nails. Unlike Sylvie's, they were perfectly shaped and polished. 'For girls like us, the best we can do is find a man who can give us a good time. That's why you'll do well to keep Herr Baumann onside.'

She gave a mischievous smile and toyed with one of her blonde curls. 'Perhaps you could see if one of his friends might like to come out with me. We could all go together and eat as much chocolate cake as they'd be willing to buy.'

'Perhaps.' Sylvie poured the hot wine into cups with her back to Céline. She stirred in a smear of honey and crumbled a few chamomile flowers on the top. Surreptitiously, she added the white powder to Céline's cup and gave it another stir before turning around and passing it to her.

'Which one of Herr Baumann's friends would you like him to ask?' She hoped Céline had better taste than to suggest Nicki.

'Oh, I don't mind.' Céline gave a coquettish shrug, then

wrinkled her nose. 'The tall one, I think. He was a good dancer.'

'Then I'll do my best.' Sylvie curled her knees up and raised her cup. '*Santé*!'

They clinked cups together and drank.

'Oh dear, I don't think that has worked very well,' Céline exclaimed with a cough.

'Maybe not,' Sylvie agreed, wrinkling her nose. 'It needs a lot more honey. Still, it's a shame to let it go to waste.'

She took another tentative sip. Céline did likewise. The honey should have left no taste of the sleeping powder, and hopefully it was just the bad combination of chamomile and red wine that Céline meant; the strong flavours guaranteed that any trace of the sleeping powder should be masked. But Sylvie wasn't sure if a sip or two would be enough; she needed to keep Céline drinking.

'Won't Felix mind if you go out with Valter?' she asked.

Céline took a bigger sip. 'Felix? He doesn't get to say who I go dancing with.'

'So you are not serious about him? I thought you were together when I first came to the club.'

'That's crazy talk.' Céline gave a genuine laugh. 'I'm not serious about any man. Felix is only one of many, and I like him the least – he's too serious. Do you like him?'

Sylvie's heart lurched. She buried her nose in the cup. 'He's nice to look at but rude.'

Céline yawned. Sylvie noticed her posture was beginning to loosen and she was slumping into the chair. Sylvie gave a huge yawn herself. It was important Céline did not suspect why she was suddenly becoming tired, or that she was alone. It was maddening that they had only just begun to discuss Felix but now she had to bring the conversation to an end before Céline collapsed in the armchair for the night.

'I feel so tired. I should go to bed now,' Sylvie said. 'I think the chamomile is making me sleepy. You can take yours with you and give me the cup back tomorrow.'

'No need,' Céline said. She drained the rest of the wine and stood, wobbling slightly. 'Oh dear, I feel tired too. Is this what running in the rain does to us?'

The two girls clutched each other and giggled. Even without drugs in the wine, Sylvie's nerves were so stretched that she was more lightheaded than she would be on such a small cup of wine. Céline dropped her head onto Sylvie's shoulder and gazed up with heavy-lidded eyes.

'Do you know Adele and Estelle are lovers? They think no one knows, but I saw them kissing once.' She brushed her lips over Sylvie's cheek. 'Do you think kissing a woman is different to kissing a man?'

Sylvie leaned back. This was definitely something she did not need to deal with now.

'I don't think I care to find out, thank you, Céline.'

Céline giggled and allowed Sylvie to escort her onto the landing. She patted Sylvie's arm and leaned in.

'You should go to bed with Felix. He's a good lover. Very…' She raised her hands, holding them some distance apart, and giggled. Her voice was beginning to slur more obviously. 'I think your German would be too scared to touch you with the lights on. I don't think you've ever been made love to well.'

'Yes I have,' Sylvie said, a little shocked at the intimacy of Céline's announcement. 'I just don't like to talk about it. Why do you think that?'

'I've seen the way you dance. You want to be expressive, but you hold back.'

Sylvie manoeuvred Céline onto her bed, said goodnight, and went back to her own room. She sat on her bed hugging her knees, listening to the rain hammering down. Out in the darkness, windows were being broken and locks were being forced. Men were risking their lives. Felix would be waiting with rifle at the ready.

Sylvie lay back, picturing the intensity of his gaze when he was deep in thought that always made her heart stir. Had she ever truly lost herself in passion? Dennis had always turned the light off before undressing, and even in daytime, he had drawn the curtains when they made love so they were in semi-darkness. It had been exciting at first, but as it went on, there had been an air of caution to it.

She wished she had never brought Felix's name into the conversation because Céline had effectively given her blessing; the balance between restraint and temptation was tipping firmly one way.

The alarm clock vibrated, waking Sylvie with a jolt. In the silence, it sounded desperately loud. She reached her hand under the pillow to where it was hidden and muffled it. She had never believed she would be able to sleep with the anticipation and nerves, but by two in the morning, she had felt her eyelids drooping and had decided to close her eyes for a moment. How fortunate that she had put the clock beneath her pillow because she had slipped into a heavy sleep, no doubt helped by the wine.

She was dressed, so it took seconds to slip on a dark sweater and her slippers. She tiptoed downstairs, remembering to avoid the middle of each step, which had a tendency to creak. The sleeping powder should keep Céline knocked out until morning and Madame Giraud was practically deaf, but it was still unnerving to be sneaking around. She reached the front door without awakening anybody at four minutes past five.

She sat on the doorstep and shivered in the grey light of the morning. The rain had eased to a fine mist. It was colder than she had expected given how hot the previous day had been, and she wished she had brought a blanket to wrap herself in.

Presently a figure slunk into view, dressed in dark trousers and a sweater. He had a beret pulled down forward over his face. She thought at first it was Felix, and her heart skipped a beat.

'Duchene?'

'Yes.'

The stranger tossed her a rolled-up newspaper tied with string, then hurried off. Sylvie crept back to her room, not at ease until she had closed her door behind her. She stuffed the roll into the biscuit tin and put that in a string bag, then hid it outside the window. Satisfied with her work, she felt the weight of tension drop from her shoulders. It was twenty-two minutes past five. She put on her pyjamas, went back to bed and slept more peacefully than she had for many nights.

A knocking woke her from a dream. She had been in England, waltzing with Dennis until he had told her he needed to go and play the piano in London to earn food tokens. The fug of sleep cleared and she remembered where she was. Céline was at the door, looking grumpy. She pushed her hair back from her cheeks and winced.

'You too, Sylvie? My head feels awful. It's almost eleven and I only woke up about ten minutes ago! What did we drink last night?'

Sylvie wanted to laugh with relief. It seemed Céline didn't suspect there was any reason out of the ordinary why she had slept so well. She ran her fingers through her own hair, which still had a couple of grips in the roll at the front, and leaned against the door.

'I don't know how I could have slept this long. My head feels awful too. I don't ever want to smell chamomile again!' She opened the door wider. 'Let's have some coffee. Even chicory will taste better than that horrible cocktail we drank last night!'

Chapter Twenty

Marcel's trailer, laden with tins, was parked outside Mirabelle when Sylvie arrived. The windowsills were now smooth and glossy black. Monsieur Julien had brought a stool outside and was smoking a hand-rolled cigarette as he watched the painter at work. Beside him was propped a bicycle with a wire basket on the front that looked so old it could have found a home among the exhibits in the British Museum.

'My friend here has persuaded me to employ him.' Monsieur Julien puffed at his cigarette. 'He says it is for the greater good of our cause. I say it costs me money, but there we go.'

He flicked his cigarette end into the gutter and went inside. Sylvie took his place on the stool.

'I've brought you a gift,' Marcel said, indicating the bicycle. He leaned down beside Sylvie to load more paint onto his brush. 'Is the delivery safe?'

'Perfectly. No one will find it unless they search my room inside and out.'

Marcel grunted and started to paint over the wooden boards covering the glass.

'Maybe I'll do a mural here. Dancing girls like our faded beauty on the sign. Tomorrow afternoon, take it to Tomas Julien's shop. He'll be expecting you.'

His switch of subject confused Sylvie momentarily. She pictured arriving at the butcher's shop with the sign from the club. Marcel grinned when she explained.

'It takes a while to get used to subterfuge and keeping so many thoughts in your head. When this is all over and we're back home, we must meet and you can tell me how you got into this business.'

Back home. There was a thing. Her room and the club felt more like home after a few short weeks than Arthur and Maud's house ever had. She wasn't sure if she wanted to go back. Even with the threat of exposure and capture hanging over her head, she was more alive than she had been for years.

'You mentioned at Madame Barbe's house that Monsieur Julien lets you place agents in his club. Is there another agent I don't know about? Felix hasn't told me anything.'

She hoped the slight heat that washed over her at Felix's name didn't manifest into a blush on her cheeks.

'Felix wouldn't. His loyalty is absolute.' Marcel said. 'Though in this case, he did not know of her identity. My woman was the dancer you replaced.'

Sylvie blinked. 'Marie-Elaine? She fell pregnant, I believe.'

Marcel frowned and continued to paint the window, not looking at Sylvie. 'She didn't fall pregnant – that was just the excuse she gave so her leaving Mirabelle would not be questioned. She had become a little careless and attracted the attention of the *milice*. She was taken for questioning and brazened it out, but it shook her nerves too much. I thought it wise to withdraw her before she was arrested and revealed who she really was. I arranged a route for her as far as Lyon – the network there would have helped her reach Switzerland and from there to England.'

'Would have?'

Marcel laid down his paintbrush and shook his head.

'She never arrived in Lyon. I hope one day I will hear from her, but…'

Sylvie grew cold thinking about it. Marie-Elaine would have known and accepted the risks when she joined SOE, as Sylvie had, but it meant the authorities were aware that the Resistance were working in Nantes.

'You didn't think to tell me this?'

Marcel shrugged.

'It happens. Perhaps I should have warned you. Would it have changed anything you have done?'

Sylvie bit her lip. Confidences over wine with Céline. Emily's probing questions. It was always possible one of the staff might have informed the *milice*. She might have been more wary if she had thought officials had already been interested in the club.

'Does Felix know who Marie-Elaine really was?' she asked.

'No. I only took him into my confidence that you would

231

be arriving because I had to leave Nantes. As far as anyone at Mirabelle knows, Marie-Elaine left in disgrace when she discovered her pregnancy and went back to her village. If there is anyone who knows differently, they are keeping it close to their chest.'

Sylvie thought back to the first day she had danced and the conversation that had taken place around the table with the other women.

'The other girls think Monsieur Julien is the father of Marie-Elaine's baby,' she told Marcel. 'It doesn't seem fair on him.'

'He knows, and he finds it highly amusing,' Marcel said. He leaned in close. 'In these dark times, it is good for a man like Antoine to be connected intimately with any woman, if you understand what I mean. It alleviates suspicion of a different kind.'

A man like Antoine. It took Sylvie a moment to understand his meaning.

'He's a homosexual?'

'Here and now is not a time to be indiscreet,' Marcel said darkly.

'I'm not shocked. Or disapproving,' Sylvie added. 'I knew other men of that inclination when I toured with my mother in the cabarets and theatres.'

Marcel cocked his head at the painted sign with the dancing woman on it. 'You might like to ask Antoine how he came to own so many elaborate costumes.'

'He was Mirabelle?'

Marcel's mouth twitched. 'I have never asked why he

chose that name but I believe mirabelles are small, sweet plums that one can fit in the mouth whole.'

'That's so rude!' Sylvie laughed in delight. 'Antoine was a female impersonator! I really would not have guessed. Well, I should be going in. It is my turn to cook the family dinner.'

She went up to the kitchen and began to assemble what she could of a cassoulet, slicing the sausages thinly so that everyone would be sure to get a few pieces and stirring them in the pot with chicken bones and haricot beans that had been soaking overnight. By the time the meal was ready, the rest of the staff had appeared and the apartment was filled with bustle. Monsieur Julien joined Sylvie in the kitchen, adding dried herbs to the pot. Sylvie proposed her new dance routine ideas, which he received enthusiastically.

'Perhaps we could alter some of the costumes upstairs,' she suggested. 'Your costumes, I mean.'

'Our friend Marcel has a loose tongue,' he sighed. 'Yes, I suppose I have no use for them any longer. Those days are gone and even if they return, my figure is not what it was. Take them with my blessing, my child.'

He picked up the wine and carried it out with a slightly theatrical flourish. Sylvie followed with the iron pot and placed it down on the table. As they ate, she glanced around her. Adele and Estelle, side by side as always, two blonde heads bowed in conversation and what Sylvie now knew was more than friendship. Monsieur Julien with his inclinations kept secret. Céline flirting with Alphonse in her customary carefree manner. Felix, for once, sitting beside

Emily. She was fretting over a vibrant coloured bruise that he sported on the side of his face in quite an intrusive manner, but he seemed to be accepting her fussing with good humour and more tolerance than he usually did.

And there sat Sylvie among them, laughing at the jokes and joining in the songs, demonstrating new dance steps to the beat of forks on cups, all the time with her real identity hidden. And it was so easily hidden now. Cool, cautious Sylvia Crichton, buried deep beneath the Sylvie she felt she could always have been. Might have been if she had not been taken from France to England.

These people had become her family. She was accepted as one of them. She wondered what other secrets were being kept and what the future might hold for them, whichever side of the conflict triumphed. And what would become of Sylvie herself? She had twice given everything up and started a new life, and this one would be hardest to give up of all.

They finished eating, and Felix and Monsieur Julien began to clear everything away. Sylvie pulled her silver compact out of her bag and checked her hair.

'Oh,' Emily said, wandering over. 'Did you find that in the bibelot box?'

'It was a present from my godfather. Which box would it be in?'

'In the cupboard beneath the stairs. Monsieur Julien puts everything customers lose in there in case they come back. Hair slides, handkerchiefs, that sort of thing. If enough time passes without anyone claiming them, he lets us have them. I saw the compact three or four weeks ago and meant to take it because it was so pretty, but when I looked it had gone.'

'It definitely wasn't this one.' Sylvie briefly showed it to Emily, then closed the lid and slid the compact into her bag. Emily's gaze followed it.

'One of the others must have taken it,' Emily said with a disappointed glance at Sylvie's compact. 'Or the owner must have come back.'

Sylvie went down to the dressing room thoughtfully. She could only think of one person who might have a compact like that. The missing SOE agent, Marie-Elaine. She hoped Marie-Elaine had taken it before she fled and that before too long she would appear safely in Lyon.

Sylvie delivered the package containing the food tokens to Tomas Julien's butcher shop as the shop was closing for the afternoon. She was greeted at the door by a large young man who was in the process of sluicing out the shop floor with a pail of water and a mop. He wore an expression that suggested the task needed a lot of concentration.

'The butcher is my father,' the man said slowly, in response to Sylvie's query about the whereabouts of the butcher. His voice was ponderous and it seemed to take him a long time to consider what the correct reply was. 'I will go now and bring my father to you. Don't touch my mop. It is mine.'

Sylvie promised not to, and the son lumbered off inside. Tomas duly arrived and Sylvie handed over the parcel. He was very like his brother, Antoine, though built on a larger frame with less elegance of movement.

'I'll see these get to where they need to be,' he said. He gave Sylvie a parcel in exchange, wrapped in brown paper and string.

'Three trotters and a rabbit. Don't ask where they came from but give them to Antoine with my compliments and tell Marcel yes to tomorrow night.'

Sylvie gingerly placed the parcel in the basket of her bicycle. She had intended to spend the afternoon in bed trying to catch up on sleep, but the day was uncomfortably hot, with no clouds to give respite from the baking sun. She didn't relish the thought of the meat warming on her table at home. The trotters could sit in a pan of cold water in the kitchen at the club until the following day before needing to be dealt with.

When she arrived at the club, Marcel was outside again. He had made good on his promise of painting a dancer on the blacked-out window. Felix was leaning against the bollard at the end of the alley, chatting and observing the progress.

'Here's the muse herself,' Marcel said as Sylvie leaned her bicycle against the drainpipe.

She stood back and examined Marcel's handiwork, struck by how good an artist he was. The woman on the window did look a little like her, though more curvaceous and with a sultry expression and pout that promised all sorts of delights were on offer. She seemed to be finding it hard to keep the strap of her dress up too as it had slipped over one shoulder, so the black, slinky dress was held up by the jutting of her breast alone.

'Very flattering!' she remarked drily.

'You missed her glare,' Felix said, laughing. He left his position by the wall and came to stand at her side. 'This Sylvie looks as if she actually likes people rather than pretends to. She's smiling.' He put his hand on his heart and gave her a look of mock distress. 'She never does that to me.'

Sylvie couldn't help grinning. Playfully, she put her hands on Felix's shoulders, noticing how his body tensed at her touch. He was wearing the cologne Sylvie liked.

'Don't tell me to smile. Give me a reason to do it,' she said in a breathy, seductive voice, catching another hint of the cologne. As his eyes widened, she dropped her hands and stepped back.

'I have a bag of pigs' trotters from Tomas that really needs to be dealt with. There is a message too, Marcel. He says yes to tomorrow night.'

'Good. I think I'll watch the show tomorrow. Felix tells me you are rather good.'

She left them to continue their conversation and went up to the kitchen. The club was deserted and silent aside from faint strains of forbidden jazz floating down the stairwell from Monsieur Julien's apartment.

She left the rabbit wrapped up for someone else to deal with, the sight of the dull, black eyes making her feel melancholy, and put the trotters in the largest pan with cold water and salt. She looked forward to the prospect of a pork terrine in a day or two. As she finished, Felix appeared at the door to the kitchen.

'Do you want something?' she asked.

He stood, arms folded in the doorway. 'Marcel asks that you stay behind after the show tomorrow night when Tomas is here. He wants to know how your lunch with your target went.'

He gave her a penetrating look that suggested Marcel wasn't the only one keen to hear the details. Sylvie wished she had briefed Marcel the previous day when Felix would not be around to hear her report.

'All right. Tell him I will.'

She took the cast-iron pan by both handles, bracing her back to support the weight. She should have put it by the window before filling it with water because it was far too heavy now.

'Let me do that,' Felix said, coming fully into the room. He reached around her and put a hand on one handle, covering Sylvie's. She felt a tremor of longing and slipped her fingers from beneath his. She could feel warmth rising from his body, acutely aware of how close he was standing.

'I can't lift it with you standing there,' he murmured.

True. If he reached for the second handle, he would be trapping her between the pot and his body. Her heart hammered; the sudden increase in rhythm making her lightheaded. It was constantly unnerving that his mere presence close to her had such an unsettling effect on her. Reluctantly she stepped aside, her waist brushing against his forearm.

'That's better,' Felix said. 'Where do you want this?'

'By the window, please,' she said. 'The breeze will hopefully keep it cool. It's very hot in here.'

Felix lifted the pot, arms tensing and muscles thickening and straining beneath the cloth of his shirt sleeves. They'd feel like warm iron to touch. Sylvie tried to ignore the flicker of excitement that ignited in her belly at the thought. As he walked across the kitchen she stared at his back. Slender and straight, tapering slightly at his waist. She blew upwards to try unsticking the hairs that had stuck to her forehead and fanned herself with her hand. Felix looked round at the sound, forehead wrinkled in puzzlement.

'The heat,' Sylvie explained.

He grinned and crossed back to where she stood. He brushed the hair back from his face, then reached out and straightened a tendril that still clung to Sylvie's cheek.

'You do look quite overheated. It will be cooler upstairs. When the skylights are open, there is a fine breeze. Would you like to join me for a glass of wine?'

Her heart hammered. 'In your room?'

He gave a slight nod.

'Just for wine?' she asked, narrowing her eyes. If he answered something different, she might go anyway.

He looked deep into her eyes, radiating sincerity. 'Just for wine.'

'Then yes, I'll come.'

'Good. I'll go tell Marcel you will join us tomorrow. When you've finished what you are doing here, come find me upstairs.'

Once he had gone, Sylvie scrubbed the countertop then rinsed her hands. She smoothed her hair back, securing a stray pin. Footsteps on the stairs told her Felix was heading upstairs. She rummaged in her bag for the silver compact. England and SOE training felt a very long time ago. She put a little powder on her nose and considered adding a touch of lipstick, but decided against it. After all, she was only going to share a drink with a colleague. Nothing more than that.

Chapter Twenty-One

While Sylvie had been occupied in the kitchen, Felix had pushed his table into the middle of the bedroom so they could sit at it and catch the breeze. He was right; the room was cooler than the rest of the club as the open skylights allowed a breeze to circulate.

'Tell me about your lunch with the German,' he suggested. 'Was it as useful as you hoped?'

'Why do you want to know?'

He gave an offhand shrug. 'Consider it a trial run for when you tell Marcel. There will be other men there who will want to know too and won't want to waste their nights on talk of the menu.'

While he found glasses and a half-bottle of white wine, Sylvie described in great detail the food they had eaten and told him of Dieter's family background. If he was going to be silly, she would respond likewise.

'Is that all you managed to accomplish with your afternoon?' Felix said sarcastically, leaning over her to put the glasses in the middle of the table. She could tell his patience was beginning to wear thin.

His arm brushed hers and the rising tide of excitement ebbed and flowed again. He filled the glasses and took the chair beside her, stretching his legs beneath the table. They brushed against Sylvie's, and once again she felt a frisson of excitement and a quiver, this time leading upwards, the vigorous throb between her legs taking her by surprise.

'I also learned the submarine pens at Saint Nazaire are more heavily guarded than we thought,' she said. '*Verwaltungs-Sekretar* Baumann believes they are so well built from concrete that they are indestructible.'

'Well done. I don't think we would ever have learned that the military sites would be more heavily guarded than a town without you to beguile the enemy.'

He'd been good humoured, even flirtatious, outside and in the kitchen. Now his irritation took her aback.

'It was more useful than spending it lying in bed with a bottle and an accordion,' Sylvie retorted. They glared at each other.

'He won't spill secrets just like that,' Sylvie said. 'Not during a walk in the gardens.'

'You took him to the gardens?'

Felix clinked his glass down roughly, knocking it against Sylvie's. They both reached out at the same time to prevent it falling, and their fingers clashed. Sparks of electricity shot up Sylvie's arm as if she'd stuck her fingers into a socket. Felix moved his fingers lower to grip around the stem. Sylvie wondered if he had felt the same rush of excitement at contact that she had. She withdrew her hand thoughtfully and put it in her lap, rubbing her thumb over the forefinger.

'Yes, he wanted to visit them.' She snatched up her glass of wine and took a long drink, emptying it. 'Is there a reason I shouldn't have taken him? Are they particularly sensitive to operations?'

'No reason that would affect the course of the war.'

The atmosphere was intimate. The street outside was quiet and despite the breeze, the room was warm. She wanted to undo the top button on her blouse and let the breeze cool her neck, but that would send a signal she was not yet certain she wanted to broadcast. They made eye contact, and Felix quickly turned his face to the window. He gave a soft laugh and looked back at her.

'Another glass of wine?'

'If you can manage to be civil and not grill me over my afternoon with *Verwaltungs-Sekretar* Baumann, I will.'

'If you don't describe your lunch with Baumann any more, I might manage it,' he replied.

Sylvie refrained from pointing out he had asked her to. 'That bothered you?'

'Yes.'

Sylvie held her glass out to him. 'Why? Because you disapprove of those methods of getting information?'

'Because I dislike thinking of him with you.'

The frankness of his answer was unnerving. And attractive.

'Why did you become involved in the raid for food stamps?' she asked. 'I thought Marcel said you didn't do that sort of thing.'

His jaw tightened. Shoulders set.

'It's none of my business. You don't have to tell me,' she said.

He took another drink and leaned back in his chair, staring at nothing. When he finally spoke, his voice was low and he still didn't meet her eye.

'I used to take part but haven't for a long time. When the occupation first happened, I was filled with fire. Then I become despairing and angry. I was content to carry messages, but I refused to become involved.'

'Emily once told me that you were always sullen. You seem a little less so now.'

Felix made a sound in his throat that was somewhere between irritation and amusement. 'Emily told you that? Do you discuss my character often? Am I the talk of the dressing room?'

Sylvie flushed, remembering some of the intimate details Céline had shared. Her eyes slid to his lap, and she forced them back to his face, appalled at herself.

'Not all the time. Did you really tell Marcel I'm a good dancer?' Sylvie asked, seizing on something to change the subject.

Felix shrugged and looked a little embarrassed. 'It's true. You are good. You should be leading the troupe, not Estelle. You've also changed since you have arrived, you know. You've become different somehow. I've seen it.'

Sylvie banged her glass down in alarm.

'Oh, no! Don't worry.' Felix captured her hand and held it, running his thumb over the palm in smooth circles. Her heart thumped, breath coming faster at his touch. 'I don't mean that your secret is obvious to anyone, but something has become free inside you. I've noticed in the way you move. In the way you dance.'

He dropped her hand and walked to the furthest wall to stand below the skylight in the breeze. He leaned against the wall and folded his arms, giving her an appraising look.

'From the first time I saw you dance, I knew that you had the capacity to be seductive and sensual, but it was hidden. Now you hide it less well.'

His lips curved into a smile. Seductive and sensual. Did he realise how well that description applied to him now? Sylvie looked into his eyes. They filled her vision, deep, questioning, and promising. She licked her lips and swallowed nervously.

'If you could have seen me a year or two, even six months ago, you would not recognise the prim and proper English woman. I had become the girl my father wanted me to be. When I came to France, I remembered who I had once been and who I wanted to be again.'

'Would that Sylvie have punched me?' he asked, grinning.

'She might have,' Sylvie replied. She stood and walked towards him, aware that by making that move she was sending a clear signal. 'If you pushed her against a wall and kissed her without permission.'

'And what would the Sylvie now do if I asked permission?'

Sylvie smiled. She tilted her head back a little. 'If you asked?' She smiled. 'Are you asking?'

He stepped towards her. 'Yes, I am.'

'Then yes,' she replied. 'You may.'

Felix put his forefinger beneath her chin and tilted her head back. He didn't push her against the wall, but very slowly he leaned forward and pressed his mouth against hers. His lips were gentle. Hesitant. Exploratory. Nothing like the frantic aggression with which he had pushed himself against her in the alleyway. This time she gave no resistance but welcomed his touch.

Their bodies brushed as he moved closer to slip his arm around her back, finally lighting the fires that had been building within her. Delicious friction sent pulses of pleasure through her limbs, sensations that she had become a stranger to. Each small contact was enough to send a thrill stamping throughout Sylvie's body, radiating from whichever place they touched but always, without fail, culminating with a pulsating sensation between her thighs. She sighed, lifting her hands and burying her fingers in his hair, cleaving to him as their mouths danced a slow tango.

All too soon, Felix pulled away. After teasing and tempting for weeks, was that all he was going to give her? She wanted more, but maybe it was up to her to take it. She pushed closer to him, letting their bodies brush fully against each other and wrapping her arms around his neck. She felt the hardness in his groin jutting against her hip bone. Knowing he was hard for her excited her more than she expected. It made her breathless. The longing for someone to touch her, the pent-up lust that she had not really been aware she was housing begged to be allowed to the surface. Felix grunted. He removed her hands from around his neck and held them to her side.

'What's wrong?'

'You're dangerous for me, Sylvie. I don't want to stop at kissing you, and if I take you to bed, I won't want to let you go,' he murmured. 'I shouldn't have even done that.'

'But you wanted to. So did I.' The sudden refusal left her desperate for more. She twisted her wrists, still held loosely within his hands, and ran her fingernails along the underside of his forearms.

'We don't have to go to bed together. We can stop at any point.'

He tightened his grip and brought her hands up between them both, holding her eye sternly.

'I think it will be harder to stop than you realise. Go downstairs, Sylvie. Talk to Antoine or practise your dances for tomorrow night. If you stay here, we'll do something we regret.'

To come so close and now to be thwarted was unbearable. The libido that had been so long dormant has awakened and was more than she could bear. She put her hand on his chest, feeling the muscles tense.

'Why would we regret it?'

'I said no.' He took her hand from his arm and held it against her waist. 'It isn't that I don't want to – believe me, I want you more than any woman I've kissed for quite a long time.'

'What then?' She folded her arms across her chest, staring him down. 'You teased me and flirted until I wanted it too. Now you back away because you're scared of what might happen?'

'Yes, I'm scared,' he admitted. His eyes burned into her. 'Aren't you?'

She shook her head, mystified. He put his hand in the small of her back and guided her to the door, shutting it firmly behind her. She didn't go downstairs immediately, but sat and stared at the rows of abandoned costumes from Monsieur Julien's former life. What did Felix have to be scared of?

She was not expecting him to marry her; assuming she survived detection, she'd be going back to England at some point in the future anyway. Another throb in her belly made her reel. Not desire this time, but sadness at the idea of giving up everything here.

She heard his door open and looked round, guiltily.

'You're still here?'

His voice was tense.

'I was looking at these,' she said, gesturing to the costumes. 'I wasn't waiting to tempt you again.'

She stormed downstairs, not looking back. It wasn't that she particularly cared about Felix, she told herself, but the assurances felt hollow. Their kiss had been so good, and she had felt closer to him than ever before.

It was closeness she craved, she told herself, and she had been stupid to even let her guard down that much. Now all she was left with was a feeling of her own stupidity and a well of frustration that somehow she needed to get rid of and no way of doing it.

Maybe that was something to be scared of after all.

That evening she avoided his eye. It was difficult because he seemed determined to do his best to catch hers. Monsieur Julien had agreed to her new ideas for numbers, which seemed to be well received by the crowd. She had devised a solo Monsieur Julien had allowed her to include towards the start of the second set that required a theatrical beginning, including a duet with Felix; he on piano, her dancing in response to the rhythm of his melody. It reminded her of the first day she had danced and the way she had tried to prove that she was capable of passion.

Knowing that they wanted each other added an extra spice to the dance. Once, Sylvie would have drawn her instincts inwards and controlled herself, but now she gave her desire free rein, pouring her longing into the movements. Felix never took his eyes from her, his hands finding the keys from memory. And from the applause, it appeared the audience were equally swept away. Afterwards, Sylvie accepted the generous congratulations of the other dancers.

Mirabelle closed an hour earlier on Wednesday nights as the number of patrons midweek was too low to justify staying open longer. The dancers changed and left. Marcel had been sitting at a table towards the back and now came forward. Almost as soon as the door had closed, there was a knock and Tomas Julien entered, accompanied by another man with deep auburn hair and a bushy moustache who he introduced as Bernard.

There were six of them altogether. They sat in the back room in Monsieur Julien's office on bar stools and chairs brought in to fill the room. They huddled together by the light of a small table lamp. Monsieur Julien closed the door and took a seat. Marcel stood at the head of the table.

'Gentlemen ... and lady, let's get started. First, I would like to hear from Sylvie about what she has discovered. She had been spending time with a German officer in the hope of finding something out.'

She repeated her account, leaving out the details of the walk in the garden and the lunch that she had told Felix in order to plague him.

Marcel looked unimpressed. 'Is that all you found out? Perhaps you should pick a higher-ranking target or work a little harder to get him to spill more secrets.'

'Perhaps Sylvie is not as good a seductress as she believes,' Felix said. The comment was directed to Marcel, but his eyes met hers.

'I wasn't trying to be a seductress,' she said tightly, with an eye roll added to show her disdain.

'It is demeaning for a Frenchwoman to be lowering herself to this,' Tomas said. 'I have names for women who behave in such a way.'

'So do I,' Felix said sharply. 'I call them brave patriots. She isn't doing it for her own pleasure.'

Sylvie shot him a look of surprise. She wondered if he had forgotten that he had made the same accusations when they had walked in the gardens. Felix frowned, which emphasised the bruise on his face.

'What did you do to your face?' Bernard asked.

'I've been meaning to ask too,' Marcel said. 'It was not in your report to me.'

'Perhaps Felix has been trying to seduce a German *frau* and wasn't as good as he thought he was,' Sylvie scoffed.

Felix put his fingers to the bruise. 'I had to leave my lookout point in a hurry and was not looking where I was running. I collided with a couple of drunks in the dark. One took exception and threw a punch.'

'Did you return it?' Tomas asked.

Felix folded his arms defensively as if he was unhappy with the affair. 'I had a revolver in my coat pocket and a balaclava up my sleeve, and I was leaving the area where a raid had taken place. I wasn't going to do anything that invited attention. It was easier and quicker to let them have their fun.'

'So you let yourself be beaten!' Sylvie leaned towards him, looking him up and down. His white shirt was open at the neck and she could see a few dark hairs scattering his upper chest. 'Are you hurt anywhere else?'

'Would you like to look and find out?' Felix said, leaning over the table towards her. He gave her a wink. 'I can show you later.'

'Enough,' Monsieur Julien said wearily. 'Listening to you two, I feel like I'm in the rehearsal for a third-rate romance play.'

They both sat back, though the tingle that raced up and down Sylvie's spine took longer to subside than she liked. She forced herself to concentrate. This was a job. Flirting with Felix was all too tempting, but she was determined to be professional.

Chapter Twenty-Two

Marcel tapped his fingers on the table. 'Sylvie, I question whether it is worth you pursuing Baumann as a target. Can you see any other benefit?'

She leaned back against the wall and stared into space, reliving the afternoon. Dieter might not be the most useful target, but he didn't feel threatening. He hadn't tried to get her into bed, which Uncle Max had warned her might happen.

'He's strange. The way he talked – I don't think he entirely believes that what Hitler is doing is right. He is a civil servant, not a soldier. It could be something we can use. A double agent who has access to letters sent back to Germany and works in transportation would be very useful.'

Marcel steepled his fingers.

'You're in a better position than anyone else to work him, but if you're going to waste your efforts for no gain, then I'll have to ask London for advice on a better use of your time. You have a week and no more.'

'I'll do my best, though he hasn't visited the club since the day we had lunch. I may have blown it.'

The men looked at her with interest, clearly wanting elaboration.

'He kissed me, and when I didn't kiss him back he left.'

'Why didn't you kiss him back?' Marcel asked. 'That seems like a wasted opportunity to get closer.'

'He took me by surprise,' Sylvie said.

Felix flashed her a look. 'You didn't punch him?'

'You mean did I assault a member of the Nazi Party in public? No, for some reason I decided against that,' Sylvie retorted.

Felix grinned. He was maddeningly attractive. Maybe it was the summer heat or the wine taking charge, because she tilted her head on one side and gazed through lowered lashes.

'Also I know him a little. I'd be less likely to punch someone who isn't a complete stranger.'

He said nothing, but raised his glass to his lips and stared at her over the rim as he drank.

'Let's move on to more important matters,' Tomas growled. 'I don't want to spend all night watching them circling round like a pair of dogs on heat.'

Sylvie flushed, and Felix began examining his thumb. Tomas was right; they should not be flirting when they should be thinking of more serious things. Monsieur Julien raised his hands and shrugged as if to say, 'He's right'.

'First, there will be increased drops of arms. Something is in the pipeline, according to England. Something big.'

'What?' Sylvie leaned forward, excitement coursing through her.

'I'm not privy to that,' Marcel said, 'But we need to be ready to mount an assault if and when we are given the word. Whatever happens won't start here, but it might reach us. Sylvie, you'll be responsible for making deliveries across the city a few at a time. Taking weapons and explosives.'

She nodded. By now she felt confident enough to walk past checkpoints, knowing her identification papers would pass. It seemed years since she had shaken with trepidation at carrying Felix's stupid cigarettes.

'Now, onto the second matter.' Marcel took out a rolled document and unfurled it on the desk. The paper showed the plan of a set of buildings. 'The raid to obtain food tokens was a complete success. England have suggested – as we are such a well-coordinated unit – we carry out an act of sabotage on a factory on the outskirts of town on the other side of the river.'

'Owned by a French company,' Tomas said, frowning.

'The factory owner is known to have been sympathetic to collaboration in the early days of occupation and gave his factory over without too much hesitation. I don't think anyone should feel guilty,' Bernard said. 'Others on the inside are more loyal to France and have provided us with details we need.'

He walked around the room to stand over the map. He

was a large man and had to ease his way past the table. He began to make soft marks in pencil at various points.

'Three of our men will enter here during the day and leave with the workers. They go in with bags and come out with bags, but throughout the day they change the explosives and fuses for rags and tools. Our second team go during the cover of night before curfew. They will be responsible for detonating the charges.'

He paused while everyone absorbed his words.

'Sylvie, this is where you come in,' Marcel said. 'A woman waiting at the factory gates for her sweetheart to meet her for an illicit liaison won't attract attention. You will keep a lookout for the night patrols, and signal when they pass, and it is safe for the team to leave the factory.'

Bernard spoke again. 'Felix, as you have embraced a more active role, you will—'

Before he could tell Felix what his role would be, there was a rapid knocking on the front door. Sylvie froze. Marcel held his hand aloft.

The knocking came again.

'Sylvie? *Fräulein* Duchene, are you there?'

Sylvie drew in a sharp breath. Dieter.

'Who is calling you?' Tomas asked.

'It's the one she spoke of who keeps sniffing around her,' Felix said.

Tomas drew out a revolver. 'I'll get rid of him.'

'What are you doing?' Sylvie exclaimed. 'You can't shoot him! And what if he isn't alone?'

'You should never have used the club.' Tomas glared at Marcel. Bernard rolled the schematic up and began to glance around for a place to hide it. Pointless. If the club was being raided, there would not be a drawer left unopened or a box missed.

'There is no need to kill him,' Sylvie said. 'I'll go out and see what he wants. 'The rest of you go out the door into the alleyway while I distract him.'

'The door is blocked from the outside,' Monsieur Julien said. 'We only move the rubbish in advance if we know it will be used. Can you climb out of the window in the dressing room?'

Felix raised an eyebrow and glanced at Bernard. Despite the severity of the situation, Sylvie wanted to giggle. There was no way the man could fit through the tiny window.

Dieter's voice came once more.

'Give me five minutes with him,' Sylvie begged. 'I'll make him go.'

Marcel nodded curtly and gestured towards the door. Sylvie straightened her hair and walked back out to the curtain that separated the backstage area from the rest of the club. She called in a bright voice, 'Who is it?'

'It is Dieter,' he replied. 'I saw a light on.'

Sylvie looked at the bar. A single lamp had been missed and was suffusing the room with a pearlescent light. On shaking legs, Sylvie made her way to the front of the club. She closed her eyes and took a deep breath, trying to hold down the feeling of nausea. It had been their foolishness that has caused this. She stopped and put her hand to her throat, fingering the reassuring coldness of the cross and the pill encased within. She heard a foot step behind her and glanced over her shoulder. Felix stood in the shadows.

'What are you doing?' Sylvie whispered.

'Protecting you,' he hissed back. He moved slightly and Sylvie caught the glimpse of metal in his hand. 'I'm not going to let him take you.'

Sylvie gave him a quick smile. Knowing he was there meant more than she could express in words. She walked stealthily to the front door and slowly turned the key.

Dieter was waiting. He peered over her shoulder suspiciously. 'What is happening in here? It's after curfew.'

'What are you doing here?' Sylvie asked, ignoring his question and greeting him with a smile. 'I haven't seen you for a few days. I was worried I had upset you somehow.'

He looked a little less stern. 'I arrived after closing time. I hoped to see you tonight, but I missed you when the other women left,' he said. 'I waited at the *Strassenkreuzung* at the bottom of the hill to see if you would walk past, but when you didn't, I walked up and I saw the light was still on.'

'Oh.' Sylvie forced another smile. 'I was talking to Monsieur Julien about a new routine for the show.'

Dieter didn't smile. 'You're keeping something from me. I can feel it.' His voice held an edge of steel that Sylvie hadn't heard before. It chilled her. 'For what reason do you not let me come in?'

Sylvie tightened her hold on the doorframe. If she let him in, she would be signing his death warrant or theirs. He would never be able to leave alive once he saw the gathering of men. He was the enemy. He had been kind, but that was because he found her attractive. She'd been foolish to even consider that he might have sympathies towards the French, or that he would not hesitate to have her arrested if there was a need. Frantically, she thought of any excuse, and inspiration came to her from the most unlikely place. The picture on the wall that Marcel had painted. Something illegal that one might want to hide, but which would only result in a fine.

'We are listening to jazz. It's been banned. Please don't reveal our secret.'

She spoke clearly enough for the men listening in the back to hear her words. She moved aside to reveal Felix, who stood glowering in the corner. He'd had the sense to conceal his pistol.

'Jazz?' Dieter narrowed his eyes. 'The music?'

'Nantes is the French home of jazz,' Felix said. 'After the Great War ended, Theatre Graslin was host to the first jazz concert, played by American soldiers.' He gave a tight smile. 'An entirely black regiment.'

Dieter pulled a disapproving face. Sylvie thought briefly of Rosetta, whose father had brought his family back to France after the Great War had ended so he could continue playing the saxophone, saying it was a country where men of his race could be free. Could Rosetta's father have been one of the men Felix referred to? Again she wished she knew what had happened to Rosetta when war had been declared.

Dieter peered past Sylvie into the centre of the room. 'Where is your music? I see no sign of it here.'

He was alert. Tense. This was a side to him that Sylvie had not seen before; however friendly he was and whatever the attraction between them, he was a German and would not hesitate to have them all arrested.

She'd done precisely what she had assured Uncle Max wouldn't happen and allowed his friendliness to blind her to that. Dieter drew his pistol from its holster. Perspiration pooled at the base of Sylvie's back. He looked from her to Felix and back again.

'Is it just the two of you?'

Now Sylvie detected a return of the Dieter she knew, because there was a hint of humanity and jealousy in his voice. It would have been simpler to have told him that she and Felix were having a private liaison.

'Not just us. Monsieur Julien and a few of his friends.'

'We are in the back room,' Felix said. 'We wouldn't be so stupid as to play it here where it could be heard from the street.'

Sylvie tensed, hoping that Dieter would believe Felix.

'I want to see,' Dieter commanded.

'Come this way,' Felix said. He cocked his head at Dieter, who gestured towards Sylvie with his gun. Nervously she passed him and slipped through the curtain, not knowing what to expect. She followed Felix into Monsieur Julien's office, where she was relieved to discover that he had obviously heard the exchange and had managed to produce half a dozen records. They were scattered on the table where the map of the factory had previously been and covered over with ledgers, as if he was in the process of hiding them. Bernard's hair had apparently been a toupee, because now he was completely bald and had found a pair of crooked wire-rimmed spectacles, which were now balanced on the end of his nose. As disguises went, it was unlikely to fool anyone but was, nevertheless, a salutary effort. Tomas and Marcel were nowhere to be seen.

'I'm afraid our secret is out,' Felix said. 'This officer knows about our music.'

Monsieur Julien gave up his half-hearted attempt at concealing the records underneath and drew one out with a guilty expression on his face.

'Are you going to report us?' Sylvie asked. She gave Dieter a look of appeal. 'I know we are breaking the law, but please, it is only music. We are doing no harm to anyone.'

Dieter stood rigidly in the doorway. 'Banned music. Negro and gypsy music. Degenerates.'

Sylvie kept her face neutral, hiding her distaste as faces of more friends from her childhood in the theatres floated across her memory. In her peripheral vision, she saw Felix shift his stance, like a guard dog preparing to pounce. His pistol was nowhere in sight, but Dieter still held his close to his body at waist height. If Felix decided to jump Dieter, he would be shot before he reached him.

'I am a musician,' Felix said. 'Petty matters of race are beneath me.'

Sylvie blinked and Dieter looked taken aback. 'I could have you arrested for those words.' He gestured his pistol towards the records. 'Play one.'

Monsieur Julien narrowed his eyes. 'Is this a trap?'

There was a spark of interest in Dieter's eye, and Sylvie suspected he was genuinely interested in listening to the music.

'Go on,' she urged. She reached for the top record. 'This one.'

Felix stepped forward and took the record out of her hand. His fingers closed over hers, a small, reassuring pressure.

'It is my choice today, in case you have forgotten,' he said. 'Please come through to the club, *Verwaltungs-Sekretär* Baumann, and I'll put it on the gramophone there. The quality is better, and for the first time a man hears Al Bowlly, it must be the best conditions.'

Felix led the way, Dieter following close behind.

Tomas appeared from the dressing room and seized Sylvie's arm. 'What? Now we are running a covert jazz club for Germans?' he hissed.

'Better than digging a grave to hide his body,' Marcel muttered, appearing from behind him.

'I don't like it,' Tomas said.

'None of us like it,' Sylvie answered, shaking free. 'But it is better than being arrested.'

From the front of the club came the opening bars of 'The Very Thought of You', a slow, romantic number.

'I have to go or he'll get suspicious,' she said.

She pushed through the curtains, humming the song. It was a good choice. Nothing too harsh or fast. Felix knew his music.

She caught Felix's eye and nodded discreetly. He jerked a finger at Monsieur Julien, who slipped behind the bar and produced a bottle of wine and glasses. As the song played, he passed them around. Dieter took his with a curt nod, his eyes fixed on the gramophone.

Never had the response to a performance been so eagerly anticipated. Sylvie held her breath, sensing she was not the only one. When the record ended, all eyes were on the German. If he sensed, his life was in danger, he made no show of it. He nodded slowly.

'*Sehr gut*. Another one.'

The release of tension was almost tangible. Monsieur Julien changed the record. Sylvie didn't recognise the song or singer, but it was faster with horns and drums. Dieter's brow creased a little. He was less keen on this, clearly.

'Let me show you how to dance,' she said, taking his glass from him and not giving him time to object. She put one of his hands on her waist and took the other, then began to move, showing him simple steps that fitted with the rhythm. She hoped fervently he could not feel the pounding of her heart in her chest. He was a quick learner and she felt the instant he relaxed and began to enjoy himself. From the corner of her eye, she saw Monsieur Julien and Bernard begin to dance too; less intimately but still as a couple might. She laughed.

'I have the most handsome partner,' she said, moving closer to him and gazing up into his eyes.

When the song finished, Sylvie clapped until everyone joined in, Dieter included. Felix quickly put on another record, and the dancing began again. It was the strangest half-hour Sylvie could remember in a long while. Sylvie danced with each man in turn while the others watched and applauded. Dieter appeared to have embraced the music wholeheartedly, though how much of that had to do with the liberal pouring of wine was anyone's guess.

'I see why this music is banned,' he said after a second dance with Sylvie. 'It is stirring. Too disorderly.'

'Talking of disorderly, my wife will be waiting. Goodnight everyone,' Bernard said. He pulled his collar up and left, signalling the night was over.

'*Fräulein* Sylvie, may I walk you home? I would like to speak to you on the matter I came here for,' Dieter said. He put his cap back on and adjusted the belt of his coat.

She could hardly object but Monsieur Julien came to her rescue.

'Sylvie, you told me you would debone the pigs' trotters and press them before morning and you still haven't done that. You can't leave yet.'

Sylvie flashed Dieter a look of apology. 'Can I see you tomorrow? I am free all afternoon. We could walk in the park again.'

'Tomorrow is not good for me. The day after, that will be good,' Dieter said. 'Twelve fifteen at the gardens.'

He took hold of her hand and she expected him to kiss it, but he merely shook it, then stood to attention and nodded at the men.

'Tonight has been … instructive.'

He left, closing the door quietly behind him.

Chapter Twenty-Three

No one moved for what must have been five minutes, then Marcel and Tomas emerged from behind the curtain.

'Well done, everyone,' Marcel said. 'Sylvie, that was quick thinking. So that's Baumann? I see what you mean about the potential to turn him. He has a curiosity for our so-called decadent, degenerate lifestyle. You got us out of an immediate scrape, and hopefully we did enough to allay his suspicion. Keep working on him.'

'She may have thought quickly but knowing that dog is prowling around because of her means Mirabelle is no longer safe. We can't use it again,' Tomas said. He jabbed a finger at Sylvie. 'And we don't need this woman.'

Sylvie felt condemnation oozing from him.

'Sylvie is an important part of our network,' Marcel said. 'All our female résistants play an equally vital part. I say if we need Sylvie, then she comes.'

Sylvie shook her head. 'It doesn't matter. The cause is

more important than whether I am here for the meetings. I'll do what I need to do, and there is no need for me to be present.'

She felt a hand slip into hers, uncurling the fist she had unconsciously bunched.

Felix.

'Sylvie deserves her place at this table,' he said. 'She is risking everything, as we are.'

'And who are you to say that?' Tomas growled. 'A man who has shied away from doing anything for the cause for so long.'

'I'm here now, and that's what matters,' Felix snapped.

'My friends, stop this,' Monsieur Julien said. He reached for Sylvie's other hand, and she gave it, slightly surprised. Then he took hold of his brother's hand. Tomas gave it a little more reluctantly. Monsieur Julien looked from face to face. 'We work together and we fight together. Mirabelle is at your disposal. Use it as you wish, but nobody who fights for France is unwelcome.'

He waited a beat before adding, 'And none of your other meeting places are so free with their wine.'

It raised a laugh and the tension was broken. Sylvie yawned. The unexpected appearance of Dieter had meant the night ended much later than she had expected. Tomas and Marcel left, nodding silently to Sylvie and the two men. Then it was Sylvie's turn.

'Good night, my dear,' Monsieur Julien said. Unexpectedly, he leaned forward and kissed Sylvie on both cheeks. 'You did very well tonight. I bless the day you came to work for me. When all this is over and France is finally free, I would welcome you back with open arms. And please call me Antoine.'

He disappeared behind the curtains with a backwards wave of his fingers, and Sylvie briefly imagined him leaving the stage, dressed in the furs and silks he had abandoned.

Now she was left alone with Felix at her side.

'I should go,' she said, swinging her hands back and forth.

'Yes. You should.'

They stared at each other in silence. Neither of them moved. Then Felix leaned forward and kissed her on the cheek. 'Be careful out there, *chérie*.'

His lips left a burning sensation. He drew back, as if surprised at himself. Sylvie drew the collar of her coat a little closer, turned the door handle and stepped outside. The street was silent and empty, but her nerves jangled and her hand shook as she turned to pull the door shut. She closed the door carefully, keeping eye contact with Felix through the gap until the door was fully closed.

Her legs felt like rubber as she pulled her hat down and walked to the bottom of the road. Her heels sounded like gunfire in the night, and she stopped abruptly after a few steps.

'Pull yourself together,' she muttered angrily to herself.

She surveyed the street. Every doorway looked menacing tonight. She couldn't be sure Dieter had gone. She couldn't be sure other eyes weren't watching her. She had to relax and behave normally, not slink along looking suspicious. She moved closer to the wall, stepping carefully from each shadow to each sliver of light.

A hand fell on her shoulder and she gave a small cry that sounded monstrously loud. Someone made shushing noises, and she clamped her hand over her mouth.

'Sylvie, it's me.'

Felix, of course. She wanted to sag against him, but he pulled her against the wall into the shadow of a doorway.

'What's wrong? Is someone there?' His eyes were sharp, peering past her into the darkness. 'You were moving so slowly.'

'Nothing's wrong, apart from you scaring me to death just now. Why are you following me?'

He ran his hand through his hair.

'You don't seem yourself. You're on edge. I watched you walking and you looked scared of your own shadow.'

'Why were you watching me?' His must have been the eyes she had felt.

'You looked like you were about to pass out when you left. I regretted letting you leave.'

'I'm fine,' she lied. 'After tonight, I was just imagining figures behind every lamppost. I'm just being silly.'

'I'm not sure I believe you.'

'It's your fault for telling me to be careful!' she snapped. 'If you hadn't done that…'

'My fault?' His brows shot high.

'Yes!' She folded her arms defensively. 'If you hadn't kissed my cheek and called me *chérie* as if there was a reason to be concerned, I would have walked home without a care.'

'If that's the case, remind me not to kiss you again,' he growled. 'I'll just wave you off into the night.'

'Why not? That's what you usually do,' she retorted.

She wasn't being fair. Both of them were still tense after what had happened. It wasn't like him to show such concern over her well-being, and it wasn't like her to care how he behaved.

Far in the distance, somewhere towards the edge of town, a door slammed. A female voice cried out and was cut off abruptly. Felix pulled her to his chest, his frame as tense as she felt. Their eyes met and Sylvie recognised the same questions in Felix's. A raid, or just a domestic argument? He eased his grip a little but didn't let her go.

'Felix, give me your gun,' Sylvie whispered.

'What?' His hand flew to his waist. 'No!'

'I don't have one. I'd feel happier walking home if I knew I could defend myself.'

'No!' His brows came together. 'I'm not giving you a weapon.'

'I know how to use one,' she hissed. 'Don't turn into Tomas and assume I don't know what I'm doing.'

He glared.

'Don't insult me by comparing me to that *balourd*. I'm sure you know how to use one, but if you were found with a weapon, that would be the end of you for certain. You'd be better taking your chances unarmed.'

Sylvie brushed the hair from her brow, hating the way her hand trembled. She'd crawled on her hands and knees through darkened woods but never lost her nerve like this before. 'You're right. Tonight just shook my nerve. I'll be fine going home.'

She turned away, but Felix caught her by the hand. 'There's another option... You could stay at Mirabelle...'

His thumb pressed into the base of her wrist, over her hammering pulse.

'...With me.'

His eyes were bright. Sylvie felt a tingle run through her. The sort of ecstasy she hadn't experienced for so long. Every limb, every nerve screamed to accept.

'When we kissed before, you told me to stop,' she pointed out. 'Why have you changed your mind?'

'We risk our lives daily. None of us know how long we may live and life is too short to waste. When the German appeared tonight, I thought we were going to die, and I wished more than anything else I had kissed you properly. I regretted letting you go the second you walked out the door, and I've spent every moment since wishing I had done differently. I'm not going to let you go tonight.'

'I shouldn't.' She didn't move.

'What's stopping you?' Felix asked.

'I don't know.'

He stepped closer to her.

'This is wartime. We might die tomorrow.'

'We might have died tonight,' Sylvie said, shivering a little.

Felix's lips quirked into a crooked smile. 'The *petite mort* is all, I hope.'

He took her hand and began to walk back to Mirabelle. She didn't make any effort to object. He closed the door behind them and drew the bolt across, shutting out the world.

'Watching you dancing with Baumann was a death in itself,' he murmured, bringing his forehead down to touch Sylvie's. He slipped one arm about her waist and began to move as if he could still hear the music that Sylvie had danced to before. 'It took all my strength not to wrench him from you.'

She laced her fingers through his and slipped her other hand to his lower back. He was an excellent partner, steering her confidently around the dancefloor, taking charge. Would he be the same in bed? Anticipation rippled through her.

'I danced with you too,' she reminded him.

'You did, and it was magical. Do you realise that's the first time we've danced together?'

'No it isn't.' She rested her head against his chest as she had done when they danced. He started to move the palm of his hand in a slow figure of eight over her back; from shoulder blade to shoulder blade, down her spine and round above her buttocks and then back up. It felt delicious.

'You've never danced *with* me,' he said. 'You danced *to* me when you performed that first afternoon, and even *at* me, as if you wanted to spite me, but tonight was the first time we danced together. And now I've danced with you, I don't want to ever stop.'

'Nor do I,' Sylvie said.

They moved slowly, bodies pressed close, listening to the memory of music inside them and around them. When Felix sought her lips with his, Sylvie moaned with longing and kissed him eagerly. The last vestiges of resistance burned away. She could be dead by the weekend. Arrested.

Imprisoned. Interrogated. If Dieter had any suspicion they were lying, or even if he mentioned what he had done, everything could be lost. Or she could be sent back to England at any moment if SOE found a better use for her.

If she made love with Felix, there would be no repercussions. Almost none.

'I can't have a baby,' she cautioned him. 'I don't want one.'

He gave a soft laugh against the top of her head. 'What sort of Frenchman would I be if I was not prepared for that precaution. Don't worry, Sylvie, *chérie*, the only things I intend to give you tonight are fond memories.'

He kissed her again, and she wrapped her arms around his neck, burying herself in his warmth. He pulled her towards him, holding her tightly against his body. She felt again the hardness of his erection and tilted her hips towards it. He growled, put both arms round her waist and lifted her off her feet.

'Come with me now or we will end up making love here on the stage and Antoine would take exception to that.'

Sylvie laughed, lightheaded with exhilaration at the prospect of what was about to happen. Still kissing each other, they stumbled through the curtains and upstairs to Felix's room, smothering giggles as they went past the door of Antoine's apartment.

Felix backed her into his room and they tumbled onto the bed, limbs tangling and bodies crushing. He began to unbutton the front of Sylvie's dress while she pulled his shirt from his waistband and unbuttoned the flies. They continued kissing and undressing each other, moving in and out of the shadows and moonlight until they were both clad only in their underwear. She ran her hands from his chest down to his belly, feeling the sharp quickening of his breath as her fingers played at the waistband on his briefs.

'*Mon Dieu*, you're beautiful,' Felix breathed. He put his hand on the flat of her belly, fingers spread teasingly wide. 'Tell me how you want me to touch you?'

'Tell you?' Sylvie opened her eyes. Felix was looking at her with a furrowed brow.

'Don't you know? Please don't tell me you're a virgin.'

'I'm not,' Sylvie said. She pushed herself up onto her elbows. 'It was just a bit of a surprise – no one has ever asked me that before.'

The idea of speaking out loud and telling him where to touch her felt, not exactly shameful, but peculiar to her.

'Then your lovers have all been selfish pigs or very bad,' he said decisively.

'That's not fair. I've had some very good lovers,' she retorted.

Dennis has never asked her to do such a thing – she could not imagine him telling her to be so free – but he had made her happy in bed.

'Do you remember Antoine saying that you were not performing from your heart? I think the same is true when you are in bed. I have seen what's inside you coming to the surface, only to be snatched back under control at the last moment.'

'Why does that take speaking?' She asked. She trailed her hand down the length of Felix's stomach until she reached the bulge between his legs, then squeezed gently. He growled and she smiled in triumph.

'See, you didn't need to say anything at all.'

'Because I want to hear the words from your lips.' He breathed heavily. 'I have spent enough nights lying here imagining you were with me. Now you are, I'm not going to let it be anything other than unforgettable.'

He knelt with his legs either side of Sylvie, gazing down at her. He hooked his thumbs under the elastic of her brassiere straps and stroked the sides of her breasts with his fingertips. 'Lighter or firmer?'

Sylvie pushed herself further forward, arching her back so that her whole breast was in the palm of his hand. 'Firmer,' she whispered.

Felix's eyes gleamed. He eased the fabric down until Sylvie's breasts were bare and stroked her nipples. The sensation was electrifying.

'Lighter!'

'Good. Now I'm going to kiss you again. Then I'll show you how I like to be touched. We'll take it from there, and you're going to show me with your body exactly what you want and exactly what you want me to do.'

'I can do that,' Sylvie said, pulling him down towards her. 'With complete pleasure.'

Chapter Twenty-Four

The sky was turning mauve when they finally both conceded that they had exhausted each other and needed to rest. Felix lay on his back and pulled Sylvie into the crook of his arms. She let her limbs flop and grow heavy against him. He had been an energetic and creative lover, and the night breeze across her sweat-slicked skin made her shiver. He tucked the blanket over her shoulders snugly and dropped a slow kiss onto her lips.

'You are a wonder, Sylvie. I know this can never be anything more than an affair, but while you are here, if you want me, as long as you want me, I am yours.'

Her heart ached. Her entire body ached with longing. Could she stay forever? It was impossible, surely? She has false papers and at any time could be discovered. But still the prospect of staying was enticing, like a length of wool dangled before a kitten.

'What about all the other women?' she asked. 'What about Céline?'

'What about her? She's a flirtation and nothing more. It looks good for the club and gets the patrons in the mood if there are couples looking like they adore each other.'

She snuggled her head next to Felix's neck and kissed his shoulder blade.

'Well, she told me you were a good lover and she was right.'

'She did?' Felix rolled over and looked at Sylvie in horror. 'You women share secrets men never would! When did she tell you that?'

Sylvie recounted the conversation where Céline had asked her to find a friend of Dieter's to go to dinner with.

'I wanted to make sure you would not be upset if she went for dinner with someone else.'

'How considerate you are,' Felix said. He put his hands behind his head and looked over at her with a wry smile.

'You cared enough about my feelings to hesitate before finding her a date, yet you thought nothing of how going out with Baumann yourself might make me feel, and I cared much more about that than anything Céline might do.'

'You know anything I might get up to with Dieter is purely for any information I might get out of him,' Sylvie protested. She got out of bed, dragging the top sheet with her like a toga, and poured herself a glass of water. She didn't want to be thinking about Dieter. Until she had spoken to him and reassured herself he had believed the story of the illicit jazz club, she would not rest easy. There was also the matter of what he had wanted to speak to her about.

'I wish you didn't get up to anything with him,' Felix muttered. 'You haven't done this, have you?'

'No, and I wouldn't. Flirting is one thing, but making love to him is another.'

'Are we making love?'

'I don't know.'

The interview with Max and Miss Atkins played inside her head like a film reel. How blasé she had been about seducing men in the cause of the war. How cold Sylvia Crichton must have been.

'Have you ever made love? With someone you loved?' Felix asked. He climbed out of bed, strolling across the room as if his nakedness was nothing.

'I thought so, but I think in the end I was making love to him while he wasn't making love to me. The man I was with before I came here...'

She felt a lump of fury in her throat at the memory of the last, unpleasant exchange with Dennis. It took her by surprise. She barely thought of him any more, and certainly not with regret. If things hadn't ended, would she have returned to France? She wouldn't have met Felix, that was certain.

Felix put his finger to her lips and pouted. 'I'm not sure I'm ready to hear about your other lovers, *chérie*.'

She bit the tip of his finger lightly, and he made the same breathy, growling noise in the back of his throat that he had let slip in a moment she had been caressing him particularly intimately.

'Not even to know whether you're better or worse?'

'Oh, I know that,' he said, grinning and stroking the finger down her neck.

'I think it is better not to name things and just enjoy them,' she said.

'I can agree to that.' Felix drew her close, wrapping his arms and legs around her, bare flesh against bare flesh.

'You have quite an effect on me, Sylvie.'

She looked down between them, then up again and batted her eyelashes coquettishly.

'So I see.'

Felix grinned wickedly. 'I thought we agreed we were too tired for any more of … whatever we're doing.'

'We did, but you seem to be awake again, and we can change our minds.'

He laughed and swept her into his arms, crossing the room to the bed in two great strides and tumbling down on top of the sheets.

'It's lucky for us the club doesn't open until this evening,' he said as he wriggled himself into the cocoon of sheets Sylvie was wrapped in. 'We can stay awake or sleep as long as we like now.'

For today at least, Sylvie thought. She had promised to meet Dieter tomorrow, although now was definitely not the time to mention that to Felix. The future didn't matter. The past and Dennis didn't matter. She kissed Felix, losing herself in the pleasure of his lips and pushing thoughts of everything and everyone else from her mind.

Leeds, England

1943

Sylvie visited Dennis the day after her father's funeral in Scarborough. She travelled back to Leeds in the mourning clothes she had borrowed from one of the typists at Key, Fry, Fforde & Radcliffe on the fateful day when the telegram arrived informing her of Arthur Crichton's death from a heart attack.

Dennis's idea of being sympathetic to Sylvie's loss was by not immediately taking her to bed, but making her a soda and Tanqueray first, which they drank sitting side by side on his sofa. Sylvie secretly longed for a cup of tea or, even better, real coffee. She knew Dennis had a tin hidden away, acquired illicitly through the black market.

Once they had finished the gin, Dennis led her to the bedroom. Even though it had only been a week since Sylvie had left for Scarborough and the funeral, Dennis's lovemaking was frenzied. He nuzzled against her neck, sucking at her earlobe as he thrust until he was spent. Afterwards, they lay in bed, the late-August sunshine banished by the heavy blackout curtains he had drawn as soon as they entered the bedroom.

'Was it dreadful, Sylvia darling?' he asked.

'Funerals are always dreadful.'

'Did you cry?' He fondled her breast, slightly inappropriately considering the subject.

'You know I don't do that. It was less awful than Mama's funeral.'

She rolled over and leaned on her elbows, tracing a fingertip over Dennis's bare chest. She'd been visiting the flat more and more, staying for a week at a time on occasion, but had refused Dennis's pleas, suggestions and occasional demands that she lived with him as man and wife. The flat was his, not a joint home. She was tired of borrowing drawer space and not owning more than could fit into a single room in someone else's house.

'Maud has got three refugees and is enjoying having young children around. She hinted a number of times she'd like me to take the rest of my things. I think we might do more to help the war effort than we are doing.'

'I don't see myself piloting a Spitfire! Are you planning to drive a tank?'

Sylvie swatted him playfully on the arm. 'Of course not, but we could both look for work in London like you said before. There must be work in offices or suchlike.'

Dennis put his hands behind his head and gave her a strange look.

'Sylvie, where is this leading?'

He should be pleased, not silent and growing tense. Drawing a deep breath, Sylvie carried on. Maybe she wasn't being clear enough.

'I know I have been dillydallying about moving in with you but I think now might be the time. I don't inherit much, I'm afraid – almost everything goes to Maud – but I'll receive two hundred pounds now and a small yearly allowance. It would be a good start for married life, and, of course, when Maud dies…'

Dennis sat up, glaring. 'Damn it, Sylvia, we can't get married!'

He never raised his voice and the vehemence was shocking. Her stomach felt acidic.

Couldn't? Or wouldn't?

'You're never going to leave Edna, are you?' she said. 'She won't divorce you and you don't have the guts to make the first move.'

'The thing is, Sylvia, wartime makes you realise what's important.' Dennis hung his head. 'Edna and I owe it to one another to give it another go.'

The full meaning of his words took a minute to sink in. Sylvie sat up too, hugging the counterpane around her knees. She'd made the decision to stay with Dennis when she knew he was married. She had imagined he would string her along with promises of marriage and had become resigned to it. Why should he force the divorce when Sylvia was content to let him eat her cake while he had his own elsewhere?

But she had never expected this.

'You're going to reconcile with Edna?'

He looked at her sorrowfully. 'I have to. You only get one shot at life, and I couldn't bear to think I had wasted mine.'

'I'm a waste?' Sylvie exclaimed. She pulled up the strap of her slip and began to climb out of bed. Dennis grabbed her hand and pulled her back towards him. He held her close, pressing against her as if he was about to start making love to her. He buried his head against her hair so she had to strain to hear his muffled words.

'No, Sylvia, you've not been a waste. I've adored every moment we spent together, but I have responsibilities. There's Edna, of course, but there is also Maximus.'

'Who is Maximus?' Sylvie asked, wriggling out of his suffocating embrace. 'A pet dog?'

Dennis managed to look both reproachful and shamefaced at the same time. 'Maximus is our son.'

'You have a child!' Sylvie dragged herself free and climbed out of bed, fumbling for her clothes that lay scattered on the floor.

Dennis sat on the edge of the bed, elbows resting on his knees.

'I didn't know Edna was pregnant when we parted. She didn't tell me about Maximus until he was a year old. I've never even met him.'

'Why didn't you tell me as soon as you found out?' Sylvie asked.

'Because I love you. I hoped there was a way around it, but there isn't.'

Sylvie sank down onto the end of the bed. This was her life story in a twisted form. A man who did not know he had fathered a child, and a woman who he should never have been with. The difference was that, in this case, Edna had a legitimate claim on Dennis that Angelique hadn't on Arthur. Sylvie had no claim at all.

Her eyes blurred with tears. Ordinarily, she forced herself to keep them in, to be unemotional and controlled, but now she let them fall.

'Oh heavens, Sylvia. You never cry. Don't be sad.'

She heard Dennis moving across the bed towards her and held up her hand to ward him off.

'I'm not sad, I'm furious. You let me go to bed with you when you were planning to leave me! How could you?'

'I wanted to make love to you one last time.' He was practically whining. Pleading. She felt nothing but scorn for him, and it helped her stem the tears. She dragged her hand across her face, no doubt smearing powder and mascara with the tears she cleared. She folded her arms and stared Dennis down.

'What an absolute fool I am. You wanted to make love to me again? Did you stop to consider whether I would want that?'

'I'm sorry. But Sylvia, dearest, I love you.'

She looked at him. His face was a picture of anxiety. The mouth that she had always described as sensitive was trembling weakly. She couldn't even bring herself to despise him. It didn't seem possible to fall out of love instantaneously, but now she had. He looked pitiful. He *was* pitiful: a sad little man who made excuses and lied.

Later, the heartache would happen, but for now she was able to be as cold and unemotional as she always was. Thank you, Arthur and Maud, for that discipline!

'You have to do the right thing by Edna and Maximus,' she said coldly. 'I wouldn't dream of stopping you going back to your wife, and certainly not where there is a child involved. If you wouldn't mind, I would like you to leave the flat for a little while. An hour should be long enough for me to gather everything and be gone before you come back.'

His eyes grew dull with defeat. 'I'll go into the offices. I took the day off but there is plenty to do.'

He began to dress. Sylvie left him to it and went into the living room. It was a Thursday. Thanks to Mrs Kent's kindness on hearing of the funeral, she wasn't due back at Key, Fry, Fforde & Radcliffe until Monday. Now she discovered she couldn't bear to go back at all. Everybody would know about the end of the affair, and she would not be able to face the looks of judgement or sympathy. She felt nauseous at the thought. There was a stack of notepaper on the bureau in the corner. She poured a gin and tossed it down her throat, then wrote a few lines. When she heard Dennis leave the bedroom, she went into the hallway and held out the note.

'Mr Radcliffe, please accept my resignation. I shall send a formal letter to Mr Key by the end of the week.'

'Sylvia, there's no need to do that.'

'There's every need.' In a flash of defiance she added, 'And my name is not Sylvia.'

He took the letter as if he were in a dream. 'What will you do for money? You can't intend to live on what you get from Maud?'

'I don't know, but I'll find something. Maybe I shall join the WRENs or WAAF. I should have been doing my part for the war effort instead of typing up letters about house sales! Even Maud has taken in her refugees, and I've wasted my time with you!'

She turned her back on him and stared at the wall until

she heard the front door pull shut. In actual fact, it took less than an hour to get her belongings together. Paperback books, clothes, makeup; everything that didn't fit into her overnight case went into the rather fine suitcase that she tugged out from underneath Dennis's bed. She'd send it back to him at some point when she had no further use for it.

With the remaining time, she dug out Dennis's precious supply of proper coffee and brewed a pot. She drank it all and left the dirty cup in the middle of the kitchen table. Fortified by the first decent cup of coffee she could remember in years, she redid her makeup and regarded herself in the bathroom mirror.

Eyes bereft of emotion but no longer red from crying stared back at her. She could do without Dennis. Without any man. She locked the front door behind her, posted her key back through the letterbox and walked out of Dennis's life forever.

At the end of the road, she stopped and sat on a bench. The adrenaline that had flooded her thanks to fury and shock was beginning to wear off, and now she was feeling wobbly. In the space of an hour she had lost her lover and resigned her job. The annuity from Arthur would not be enough to get by on and pay her rent in the boarding house.

She needed to do something worthwhile to help with the war effort. How did one go about that? She could go back to Maud in Scarborough and offer to help with the refugee children, but she baulked at that idea. Thinking how she would have felt if Dennis had presented her with

Maximus to raise, she was acutely conscious of how much her presence must have been torture to poor Maud.

The name sparked a memory. Major Max Swift – Uncle Max – had come up from London to attend Arthur's funeral.

'You look and sound English through and through now, my dear. Your father would be so proud of what you've become,' he had told her over the cold collation at the wake.

She had smiled, knowing he meant to compliment her, and they had parted on good terms but not before Uncle Max added, 'If you ever decide to help the war effort a little more directly, I work for a department that will always have work for a bright young woman with excellent French.'

She had no idea what work Uncle Max might have for her, but anything was better than being unemployed, and if she could use her French, then that would be even better. Uncle Max had given her a card with his number, so she went to the telephone box at the end of the road. While she waited for the operator to make the connection, she felt excitement bubbling inside her.

Arthur, Maud and Dennis had all wanted her to be Sylvia. They had all tried to mould her into the woman they thought she should be, but now there was no one with a claim on her. There was a hairline crack in her cocoon. She was ready for a challenge. She was ready to become Sylvie again.

Chapter Twenty-Five

Nantes, France

1944

When Sylvie returned home in the middle of the morning, Marcel was leaning against the wall opposite the *épicerie* with a cigarette in his mouth. He had a sketchbook in his hand and had begun a pencil drawing of the shopfront.

'You must have gone out early. I've been waiting here since the *épicerie* opened to speak to you.'

The back of Sylvie's neck grew warm. She'd never been one of those girls who spent the night with men to then blithely return home the following morning still wearing an evening dress, but here she was. She swore she could detect a faint trace of Felix's cologne beneath the violet water she had dabbed behind her ears.

'It was so late, I stayed in the club,' she said, hoping that would be sufficient detail. Marcel narrowed his eyes, and she got the impression he suspected something, but he made no comment.

'I hope you're fit enough for another late night,' he said. 'We've had a communication from England. There's going to be a drop by air tonight. As soon as Mirabelle closes, cycle to the village of Sautron and wait by the cross at the edge of the forest. You'll be met there. Take what you are given and leave as quickly as you can. You won't have a weapon, so if there is trouble, try to evade it.'

What would she do? Hide under a pile of wood? Climb a tree? It made her shiver to think of what she might have to do. She'd better wear something warm.

'What will I be collecting?' she asked, eying the basket on her bicycle. She estimated it was large enough to fit a small suitcase. Unlike Felix, who had been scathing about her wanting to know, Marcel answered.

'Radio equipment including new crystals, rolls of film and a consignment of bullets.'

'Quite a shopping list!'

'Indeed. The package with the bullets will be the heaviest. Drop that in the empty milk churn outside the dairy on the road back from Sautron. Bring everything else back here. Tomorrow morning, take the package containing the film to the bookshop where you took the magazines and give it to the owner. Someone will collect the radio equipment from your room over the next day or two. Probably a young man with red hair. Good luck, Sylvie.'

He packed away his sketchbook and grinned.

'And maybe spend some of this afternoon in bed ... getting some sleep.'

With a growing sense of nervous excitement, Sylvie followed the directions to the village after that evening's performance. Two men were waiting for her just beyond the crossroads. One older and one roughly her own age, both dressed in dark clothing.

'Turn your backs a moment, please,' she instructed them.

They grumbled but obeyed as she changed in the bushes from the dress she had worn to leave Mirabelle into trousers and a dark-blue sweater and scraped her hair underneath a flat cap. She stowed her clothes and bicycle under a crop of bracken and followed the men into the woods. As they followed a narrow pathway deeper into the forest, it occurred to Sylvie that in any other circumstances, putting herself into such a position with strangers was incredibly risky. Well-brought-up young women did not go into dark places with men they didn't know. If her stepmother could see her now, she would have a fit. The danger would not come from these companions, however, but from German patrols if they had got wind of the drop. So many links in the chain and only one had to be loose for disaster to strike.

They moved silently. There was no point in making conversation. They were there for one purpose only. After around a mile, the path split. They took the right fork, pushing through the undergrowth. Finally, the trees thinned. The older man raised a hand.

'We wait here.'

They crouched down and he handed Sylvie a canvas satchel. They waited long enough that Sylvie lost track of time. She stifled a yawn. Normally, by now she would be in bed, falling asleep after the long evening of performing. Two late nights in a row was not good for her. The moon was a thick waxing crescent and threw enough light on the sky that when a silhouette passed overhead, it caught Sylvie's attention. She tensed and shifted position so that as four crates dropped from the sky on the silently billowing of silk parachutes, she was ready to run forward to retrieve them.

She was surprised to discover the three of them had not been waiting alone. As she and her companions raced forward, three other groups appeared. One of them was a woman. She and Sylvie exchanged a nod and smile. She could be SOE or French; Sylvie would never find out, and it didn't matter. The résistants converged on the crates. One man produced a crowbar and wrenched them open. The contents were swiftly divided up. One crate contained rifles. Another was full of tins the size of house bricks. Sylvie was handed a surprisingly heavy package for the size. The bullets. She slung it in the canvas satchel and stowed two other brown-paper-wrapped packages with them.

'Gather the silk,' instructed one man. Sylvie and a man from a different cell began to roll it tightly. It would be buried in the woods away from the clearing.

Everything seemed to be going according to plan until a

rapid burst of gunfire cut through the trees. Everyone froze, mid-activity. It had come from the opposite direction to where Sylvie had come from. There were distant shouts in German, then French.

'Everyone, leave now!'

Sylvie wasn't sure who had given the order, but the résistants scattered. A couple of them drew pistols, heading towards the trouble. The younger of Sylvie's companions grabbed her by the elbow as they all ran back into the woods, crashing through the bushes to escape. There was no point looking back to check if they were being followed. They'd discover that soon enough if flashlights blinded them. She only realised as they lay face down in the bushes that she was still holding the bundled parachute in her arms.

'Drop it,' the older man muttered. 'There's no time to bury it.'

'If I leave it, they'll know which direction we went,' Sylvie answered in a whisper. He gave a curt nod. She bundled it and stuffed it inside her jumper.

The gunfire had resumed, and it seemed from the shouts that the bursts were being answered by French fire. Sylvie bit the inside of her lip until she tasted iron. To Sylvie's immense relief, the fight didn't seem to be coming closer. The younger man cocked a thumb, and painstakingly the trio crawled through the woods on their hands and knees, only moving into a low crouch as they reached the fork in the path.

Keep moving. Keep moving. One more minute. One more minute. For France. For England. Keep moving. Keep moving.

One more minute. One more minute. For France. For England.

The repetition had helped Sylvie during training when her endurance had been pushed to the limit in training exercises, crawling through fields during the freezing-cold Scottish winter. Now, she muttered it under her breath over and over, thanking Sergeant Walters for putting them through their paces.

The journey back to Sautron took them twice as long as their trek to the drop site, and when at last they came to the road, Sylvie wasn't the only one who gasped with relief. The three of them clasped hands and the youngest produced a hip flask. They passed it round, taking turns to toast the others. The flask contained a strong liquor of some sort, probably homemade, and was the most welcome thing Sylvie had drunk in weeks.

'When is your child due?' he asked, pointing at her stomach.

Sylvie looked down. The silk parachute had bunched under her jumper and did indeed look like a pregnant belly. She began to laugh and found that once she had started, she could not stop. The shock of the night's events was catching up with her. She clasped her hands over her mouth and tears rolled down her cheeks.

'Go home and go to bed, mademoiselle,' the older man told her kindly.

Sylvie unearthed her bicycle. She rearranged the silk into a more becoming bump and stowed the packages in the basket. She dropped the bullets at the dairy as instructed and cycled home on deserted dark roads. Fortunately, the house was silent as she crept upstairs and she had no awkward encounters.

The time was just past three in the morning, according to her alarm clock. Definitely time for bed, though she felt too alert. Tomorrow, she had to meet Dieter. The fact that she had not been arrested since his visit to the club must be a good sign, but it was one more thing to think about.

She stored the packages in her hiding place outside the window and changed into her pyjamas. She spread the silk on her bed on top of the sheet and lay on it before pulling her sheet over her. The silk felt cool and soft against her skin. She imagined what it would be like to lie on it with Felix, their bodies sliding over the cloth. With him in her mind, she was not even aware when fantasy became dream, and she fell asleep.

She overslept. Hardly surprising after such a late night, but it set her off on the wrong foot. The silk parachute was twisted around her legs, and she had to untangle it. It had seemed a good idea the night before to turn it into something, but now it was just one more thing she would have to hide. When she had time, she would cut it into smaller sections and smuggle it into the club. She could hide the pieces on the clothes hanger inside one of Monsieur Julien's costumes until she had time to deal with them. With luck, anyone who saw it would assume it to be the lining of the costume.

The scent of the forest clung to her. As she rubbed the

hard soap over her skin to try to get a lather, she couldn't stop thinking about the men in the forest who had run towards the sound of gunfire not away from it. Her instructions from Marcel had been very clear not to get involved in any fighting, and she had followed them to the letter. Even so, she felt a deep stab of guilt as she wondered what had become of the men.

This was both the tragedy and the genius of the Resistance. Members only knew the names of a handful of other people in the organisation. Even at the highest level of command, each cell leader knew only those in his immediate band. Sylvie had not even learned the names of the two men she had worked with and shared a drink with; they would not be able to identify her beyond a vague description, and in turn she would be unable to do the same to them. The men and woman she had barely glimpsed in the forest were safe from her, and she was safe from them.

It meant she would never discover the fate of those who went to fight and most likely gave their lives in the forest. She hoped fervently that most of them had escaped, or if they had not, that their deaths were instant and painless.

She had intended to wash her hair but had run out of time and settled for dabbing eau de cologne along the roots and running her brush through the strands to freshen it. She rolled her hair into a victory roll on the top and pinned the back neatly. She decided not to cycle partly because she could wear a nicer dress, and partly because she had discovered that the muscles used for pedalling were entirely different to those used to dance. The prospect of climbing back into the saddle made her wince.

She retrieved the package of film, which was small enough to slip into her bag. The bookshop was in a small street at the rear of the chateau, about a fifteen-minute walk from the *Jardin du Plantes*. She should have enough time to deliver the film to the bookshop and then walk across town to meet Dieter. Céline was chatting to Madame Giraud when Sylvie went downstairs; Sylvie called good morning and hurried on, humming to herself.

The first indication that something was wrong was when she reached the end of Allée du Port Maillard. A large group of people were milling around the end of the road. Sylvie edged closer and worked her way through the crowd. Whatever was happening, she didn't have time to waste before going to meet Dieter. A roadblock had been set up and two privates in uniform stood to attention, rifles poised and ready.

A black van was parked in front of the bookshop and two men dressed in the blue uniform of the *milice* stood by the open rear doors. A fist gripped Sylvie's hand as she stepped closer, pulling her back. She went cold, thinking she had been discovered but an old man standing at her side had been the culprit. He raised a finger and wagged it at her, shaking his head silently.

She stepped back into the huddled group with her mind whirring. She had to let Marcel know, but she had no idea whether it would be safe to visit him. Worse than that, she was carrying a package of film and was about to go meet Dieter. It was highly unlikely he would search her bag, but there could be absolutely nothing to cause him suspicion.

While she was vacillating, a door slammed open. Sylvie

tensed, expecting to see Monsieur Tombée marched out, but instead two *miliciens* emerged from the dress shop next door, dragging a middle-aged woman between them. She was handcuffed but kicking and struggling to escape. Two more officers followed, half carrying an even older woman with wispy grey hair. Both prisoners had a defiant look in their eyes and were fighting their captors. A murmur of anger and despair surged through the crowd. Clearly these women were well known in the area.

'What's happening?' Sylvie whispered to the man standing next to her. He shrugged.

'They are mother and daughter. They own the clothes shop. I don't know what their crime is said to be.'

Said to be. A chilling phrase. They could be guilty or innocent, or the charge might have been completely fabricated. However true or not, the reason for their arrest was announced by a *milicien* wearing the double yellow stripe of a company commander. He faced the women and spoke in a loud voice so the crowd could hear.

'Therese and Anne-Therese Brodeur, you are under arrest for publishing and distributing seditious materials with the intention of inciting civil disobedience.'

The elderly woman spat on the ground at his feet. Sylvie wanted to cheer her bravery but kept silent. To show any support would be tantamount to suicide. Instead, she stood with the rest of the crowd, watching silently. How much courage would it take to raise a voice in solidarity? How many voices would be needed to inspire the crowd to act?

Something was coming, Marcel had said. Whatever it

was, it would most likely not come soon enough to save these two women.

Another man exited the building, his arms full of rolls of poster-sized paper and small blocks of wood that looked like printing blocks. Sylvie's heart sank. In this case, it seemed the charges were true. He dropped the equipment onto the floor and produced a box of matches. The two women watched as their apparatus was set alight before they were manhandled to the waiting van. As the daughter's head was bent to push her in, she twisted to look back at the crowd.

'*Vive la France! Vive la Resistance!*'

The soldier raised his hand and delivered a blow to her the back of her head, and she slumped down. She was lifted and thrown inside, the door was closed and the two women were driven away. The *miliciens* who had not gone in the van joined the two German privates that had been standing guard at the roadblock.

'Get back to your homes – there's nothing to see here!' one shouted. The crowd began to disperse. Reluctantly, Sylvie backed off too, casting a final look back at the pathetic bonfire. The bookshop would have to wait. It would be the height of stupidity to attempt to do the drop at the moment. She would have to return once she had spoken to Dieter and hope to see the bookseller. For now, it seemed the bookseller was safe, but the probable fate of those brave women haunted her as she walked across town.

Chapter Twenty-Six

As Sylvie arrived, she could see Dieter pacing back and forth in front of the gates to the *Jardin du Plantes*. He was looking nervous, and when she walked towards him, he twisted his hands together before kissing her on the cheeks in the French fashion. He was wearing cologne. Either he had never worn it before or Sylvie hadn't noticed.

'Dieter! I'm so sorry I am late.'

'You look tired,' Dieter said, peering at her. 'I hope you have not been working too hard.'

She couldn't tell him the real reason she was exhausted, and the arrests were raw in her mind.

'I saw something horrible on the way here. It upset me more than I thought.'

She told Dieter about the arrest of the two women. She watched his expression carefully, hoping to see the smallest indication of sympathy in his reaction, but he looked unmoved. He raised his jaw and gave her a severe look.

'If they committed crimes, they must be punished. They

would have known the consequences before they started their treasonable endeavour.'

'All they did was make posters. That's hardly assassinating the *Feldkommandant*!'

'What if their posters caused someone to try? Peace depends on people obeying the laws.'

Something in Dieter had snapped to attention. He stared forward, eyes fixed on a distant point, shining with belief. When he became that man, he could have been on a poster himself, extolling Hitler's vision of the perfect *Herrenvolk*. Every time she wondered if there might be enough in him to bring around, the kernel of indoctrination burst forth.

Sylvie stepped back, shaking her head sadly.

'One of the women was so old,' she murmured. Madame Brodeur's sentence would probably be execution in any case, but her treatment beforehand might finish her off before the firing squad could do their job.

'Sylvie, don't let what you witnessed this morning upset you.' Dieter flashed her a look of concern, and the zeal in his eyes vanished. The party spokesman had vanished, and the man was back again. 'If you do nothing wrong, you have nothing to worry about.'

Sylvie wasn't sure if he genuinely believed that innocence was a shield against arrest, or if it was simply a line he repeated as any upstanding citizen should.

His brow creased. 'Sylvie, what you were doing the other night was very risky of you and stupid. If it had not been me who had seen the light beneath the door, you would have been taken for questioning without a doubt.

You could have been in the situation of those … *unfortunate* women you saw this morning.'

He sounded genuinely upset, but Sylvie noted the adjective. There was a little sympathy for the women beneath the cold exterior after all.

She put her hand on his arm. 'Dieter, I need to thank you for what you did the other night. You could have reported us. I owe you a debt of gratitude.'

'You were very fortunate I was the one! A group of French men and a woman meeting in secret! Do you know what it could look like?'

Sylvie's skin grew clammy. She tried to calm her breath before speaking so her voice didn't betray her.

'What?'

He avoided her eyes, looking beyond her ear. His neck was growing red. 'That you were working as a … a prostitute.'

Sylvie's muscles sagged with relief. She felt the need to laugh bubbling up inside her, relief spilling out. Never before would she have imagined being described as a whore was the lesser of two evils.

'You thought Monsieur Julien might be running a secret brothel?' Her voice was shaking. She hoped he would think she was offended rather than relieved.

'It is fortunate – I know you would not do such things,' he said, smiling in a way that caused ripples of shame to wash over her. 'Shall we walk?'

He held out an arm for her to take and she slipped her hand through.

'Did you find the music enjoyable?' she asked.

There was a long silence before he answered. He shouldn't have enjoyed it, but he obviously had. The laughter in his eyes as they had danced and the way he had naturally found the rhythm had been proof of that. But to admit appreciating music that was scorned as degenerate? Played by people of inferior races who could not be allowed to affect the purity of his country? How terrible it must be to feel such a conflict between the truth he felt and the 'correct' answer.

'The music was strange,' he said finally. 'I think it would take me a long time to understand it, but yes, I had an enjoyable evening. I very much enjoyed dancing with you.'

He stopped abruptly. 'I came to the club the other night because there was something I wanted to say. I have wanted to for a while now. *Fräulein* Duchene, I love you.'

Sylvie blinked and took a step back and saw the briefest flash of hurt in his eyes. He clearly expected a different response.

'You love me? I don't understand… We only met each other recently. We've only been out together once. Twice, if you count when we met by accident.'

His face was serious. 'I've spoken to you at Mirabelle. We've danced together. It sounds stupid, but that is all it took. I knew as soon as we first walked together through the streets that you were the only woman I ever want to be with.'

He took both of Sylvie's hands, holding them tightly, and for one awful moment she thought he might drop to one knee and propose marriage.

'Say that you feel something for me too.'

He stood before her in the uniform of the enemy. The oppressor. She should feel no qualms about disappointing him, but Sylvie had never seen anyone looking less oppressive. He looked eager and boyish. Endearing. She did like him at times, but that was as far as her feelings went.

'What you're feeling isn't love,' she said as kindly as possible. 'It is infatuation or the excitement of first love. I've felt it before and it fades.'

'But perhaps not always,' Dieter said.

That was true, at least. What he did not know – what he could never know – was that she had only spent time with him at all to try to make him spill secrets so she could use them against him. She'd grown fond of him, but at Mirabelle the other night she'd seen the side to him that was her enemy. The friendly dog had bared his teeth.

'It is too soon,' she said. 'And you are German and I am French.'

'Our countries may be enemies, but you cannot help who you fall in love with,' he said. 'It is not uncommon. There would be no trouble.'

His naivety was both endearing and frustrating. For a German man, perhaps not. For a French woman, almost certainly.

'How long would you need to fall in love with me?' he asked. It was pitiful to see him standing with hope and despair mingling in his eyes. 'A month? A year? Am I pressing you too quickly? We should take more time to get to know each other better.'

He walked over to the lake and stared into the water. He beckoned her over.

'I would like to propose something to you. I have a friend who arranges the leave rotas. His family own a farm. If I promise to have workers sent to help on their land, he will grant me a favour and move me to the head of the list.'

The workers he talked about were French, taken and forced to work in Germany under the *Service du Travail Obligatoire* ruling. Dieter was offering to arrange a quick holiday by sending slave labour to his friend and saw nothing wrong with that. He didn't notice Sylvie's lack of enthusiasm, because he continued. 'I could be in Paris in two weeks and you could come with me.'

Despite her revulsion, the moment he said the word Sylvie's imagination started to spiral.

Paris.

The city that had been snatched from her was now being dangled enticingly again. The idea was so seductive she almost agreed, but this would not be the Paris she had dreamed of since childhood. This would be the Paris where jackbooted Nazis goose-stepped past the Arc de Triomphe and Hitler posed proudly for photographs before the Eiffel Tower. She didn't want to see it like that.

'They call Paris the city of love, don't they? There is a guide to the best hotels to stay at. We could visit all the sights. I could take you to see everywhere you wanted to see.'

'I can't just stop working,' she said. She started walking again, and Dieter fell in beside her.

'Of course you can. I can arrange matters so that Herr Julien sees the advantage of letting you come with me.' Dieter reached for her hands again and his lips curved into a smile that was not completely pleasant. 'After welcoming me to your jazz music night, I am sure he would not deny me the chance to take you with me. He is my friend now, after all, and I'm sure he would wish to remain so.'

His voice had hardened. Sylvie wondered if he even knew it had changed, but arranging matters now had a sinister sound to it. Was it a threat? At his touch, ripples of disgust raced over her skin where they hadn't before, like cobweb-winged moths.

'Please don't push me for an answer now,' she pleaded. 'You have given me so much to think of.'

'If you wish. But please let me know your answer soon. I shall need to speak to my friend and arrange matters.'

'I must go,' Sylvie said. 'I need to get ready for tonight. I have another new dance and I want to rehearse it with the other girls.'

'Of course,' Dieter said, all genuine smiles now. 'I can't come to watch you, but I will be thinking of you.'

He turned to go, then paused and looked round, the boyish charm back again. 'When we danced to the jazz music, I felt something I had never felt before. I hope one day you will feel it too.'

She had felt something when she was dancing to the jazz, but not in Dieter's arms. Did that mean she loved Felix? She was uncertain, but if Felix had invited her to Paris, she would not have hesitated for a moment. She couldn't tell Dieter that.

She gave him a gentle smile. 'Who can say?'

He muttered something under his breath and rocked on his feet as if uncertain whether to move. He strode back to

Sylvie, took her head in his hands and kissed her. It was not a good kiss. Even if she had been prepared and willing, he was clumsy, his lips bruising and tongue too eager. She let him do it, too shocked to object. He pulled back and smiled at her, pleased with himself and blithely unaware of Sylvie's discomfort.

'I should have kissed you like that before instead of being timid.'

He moved in again, this time cupping the back of her head with one hand and fumbling into the rolls of hair at the side. He leaned her backward, so she had to cling onto him in order to keep her balance, as if he was a hero in a film, while his tongue explored her mouth. Finally, he released her and stroked a hand down her cheek.

'Don't tell me you feel nothing now.'

She couldn't speak to answer him. That was the worst part. He looked pleased, as if he believed her muteness was because she was overwhelmed by pleasure. She was beginning to get a headache, the pressure building at the back of her neck.

'I'll be waiting for your answer. My *Soldatenheim* is on Avenue Saint-Luce. When you wish to contact me come there and ask for me.'

He strode off with a spring in his step. Sylvie watched him go and sank onto the grass by the lake. She wanted to be sick from revulsion. And fear. There had been a definite threat in his words. Unspoken and perhaps unintentional, but there, nevertheless. She needed to inform Antoine and Marcel as quickly as she could. Tomas had been correct: the club was not a safe place to be, for her or perhaps for anyone.

Before she could warn Marcel, she had to make her delivery of film to the bookshop. She made her way back to Allée du Port Maillard. By now, as she had hoped, the street was almost deserted. A couple of planks had been nailed over the doorway of the dress shop. A scrawny tortoiseshell cat sat outside, miaowing plaintively to be let in. Sylvie gave it a scratch behind the ear, and it twined round her legs. For one moment, she considered taking it home, but Madame Giraud would draw the line at a cat roaming about the house.

The handwritten sign on the door informed customers that the bookshop was closed, but through the window Sylvie could see Monsieur Tombée was sitting at his lectern reading. She tapped gently on the glass, and he beckoned her in.

'Mademoiselle? May I help you?'

They had met only days before, but he gave no indication that he recognised Sylvie. Nor would he until she gave the password.

'Do you have any books for young children?'

Monsieur Tombée peered at her over his glasses. 'What should they be about?'

'Something with angels in it,' Sylvie replied.

He smiled and slipped off his stool, brushing down his waistcoat and trousers.

'I might have something in the back room. Please come and see.'

Sylvie followed him through into a small room that was piled high with books from floor to ceiling. She dug the package of film out and handed it to him. He ran his fingers along a shelf, pulled a volume down and opened it. The book was false with a compartment inside. Once the film was safely inside, he put the book back.

'Are you all right, my dear? You look pale,' he asked.

Sylvie touched her cheek. The memory of Dieter's hands forcing her head back made her shudder. Her headache was getting worse, spiteful fingers burrowing into her brain.

'It has been a trying day. I came here earlier and I witnessed what happened to your neighbours. It seemed safer to wait until now. Has there been any news of them?'

Monsieur Tombée shook his head. 'I have known Madame and Mademoiselle Brodeur for years, and to think I was completely unaware of what they were doing. If I had known, I could have helped them. So many people are keeping secrets from our enemy that the result is our friends can't tell us when they need aid.'

He removed his glasses and wiped them on a pristine white handkerchief. 'I think this had better be my last collection for a while. I wouldn't want everyone's brave work put at risk if the *milice* come sniffing around again.'

'I'll pass that on to Marcel,' Sylvie promised. He was right; as soon as a location was possibly compromised, it was not safe to keep using it.

As she opened the door, the cat dashed between her legs

and leapt onto the lectern. Monsieur Tombée rubbed it on the head.

'I'll feed this boy until they return. It's the least I can do.'

'Do you think they will be back?' Sylvie asked.

He gave Sylvie a sad smile. 'Not really. They were very courageous women, mademoiselle, but I think their journey has come to an end.'

He walked to Sylvie and took her by the hand.

'I sense that you are courageous too, and I wish you better luck than they had.'

'And you, monsieur,' she whispered. 'May we both be the fortunate ones.'

Chapter Twenty-Seven

By the time Sylvie arrived at Mirabelle. her headache was so bad she felt as if she was going into shock. Her head was being squeezed in a vice, and the world seemed too bright. She managed to hold herself together long enough to sneak into the changing room, then sank onto a stool before bursting into tears.

'Sylvie!'

She had thought the room was empty, but Emily was in the comfy armchair tucked away in the corner, reading a book. She gave a cry of astonishment, closed her book with a snap and threw her arms round Sylvie.

'What's wrong? Have you been hurt? Threatened? Assaulted? Was it a man?'

'No. Yes. I don't know. I'm sorry, I'm not making any sense.' Sylvie sobbed, unable to work out which of Emily's jumble of questions she was answering. Emily's embrace was comforting, but there were other arms she craved. More urgently, she needed to share what had happened to her.

'I need to speak to Antoine. Will you fetch him for me, please?' She couldn't ask for Felix too.

If Emily was surprised at the use of Monsieur Julien's first name, she didn't show it. She left and returned with the club owner shortly afterwards. He took one look at Sylvie and fear flashed across his face. He spoke without looking back.

'Emily, my sweet, please go get Sylvie a brandy. She's had a shock.'

As soon as Emily left, he dragged a stool to Sylvie's side and whispered urgently.

'You were meeting Baumann, weren't you? What happened? Are we in danger?'

'I don't know.' Her voice cracked. 'Possibly we are. There have been developments. I need to tell Marcel as well. He was like a stranger. It was horrible.'

Antoine squeezed her knee reassuringly. 'I know where Marcel lives. I'll go myself as soon as Emily brings you a drink. I will not be more than ten minutes.'

Emily returned carrying a glass of brandy, closely followed by Felix. His eyes met Sylvie's, and he froze.

'I got Felix too,' Emily said. 'When Sylvie implied that there was a man involved, I remembered the German you had trouble with before.'

Felix squeezed Emily's shoulder and she tailed off. Sylvie dropped her head. She had not thought their involvement so obvious that Emily would automatically summon Felix to deal with her distress. Again, she felt Emily's scrutiny. The girl was far too concerned with what Felix did.

'Thank you, Emily,' Antoine said. 'Sylvie, I think you need some more air. The window in this room is too small. Come with me upstairs, and we'll leave Emily to her book. Felix, will you carry the brandy for Sylvie, please?'

He took Sylvie by the arm and wheeled her to the door before she could protest.

'Take her up to your room. Don't leave her,' he instructed Felix.

'As if I would!' Felix squeezed her hand tightly to the point of discomfort.

'I'll go get Marcel. Is it safe for him to come here?'

'Yes, for now,' Sylvie answered. 'But please go quickly.'

Felix peered anxiously at her. 'Sylvie, can you walk? Do you need me to carry you? For God's sake, tell me if you are injured. Do you need to lie down?'

She wiggled her hand loose a little and gave him a smile she hoped was confident.

'Yes, I can walk. No, I'm not hurt. I have a headache. I don't need to lie down.'

Emily had come out of the dressing room. Her eyes were large and anxious.

'Felix, what's happening? Are you in danger?'

Felix turned back to her and, to Sylvie's surprise, he took her face and kissed her on the top of the head. 'Nothing for you to worry about. Or mention to anyone. Go on now.'

Emily went back into the dressing toom and Sylvie followed Felix upstairs. Had it only been yesterday morning she had left there after making love with him? She sat at Felix's table, and he pushed the brandy into her hand. He knelt at her side and took hold of her other hand, more gently this time.

'Did you come here from your meeting with Baumann? Did he not believe our story?'

Sylvie sipped the brandy before answering. It warmed as it went down, reviving her spirits a little.

'He believes it. That's not the problem. He told me he loves me and wanted to know if I feel the same.'

'Do you?'

The interruption was curt. Urgent. Felix began to pace round the room.

'Of course I don't. I told him so as kindly as I could. Then he said he wants me to go to Paris with him to see if I can start to love him there. When I refused, he started threatening me. Threatening Antoine. At least I think it was a threat. Then he kissed me, but not like before. Roughly.'

There was a loud thump. Sylvie jerked her head up. Felix had banged his fist against the wall. His face was thunderous.

'You should have let me kill him when I had the chance.' He came back to Sylvie's side and wrapped his arms around her. He held her to his chest, and she could feel the thump of his heart through his shirt.

She felt Felix's arms a cage around her. No, not a cage, because that suggested she would want to break free. A refuge. She was content to be held for as long as he would hold her.

'I felt a little better now. The brandy is working. I feel silly for making such a fuss. Fancy crying!'

'There is no shame in crying,' Felix said. 'The shock can do that.'

There was a cautious knock on the door, then Antoine and Marcel entered. Again, Sylvie tolerated their concerned questions.

'Did he hurt you?' Marcel asked. 'Tell me everything that happened.'

'When I arrived at the bookshop, there was an arrest.' She repeated her story from start to finish. 'Do you know the women?'

'Nothing to do with any cell I know of,' Marcel said. 'It's a damned bad coincidence they happened to be next door to Monsieur Tombée's place. He's been useful. Tell me about the encounter with Dieter.'

Marcel and Antoine exchanged worried looks as she mentioned Dieter's reference to the jazz night and Antoine accommodating his wishes.

'It won't be safe to use the club from now on,' Marcel said.

'I'm sorry. I was stupid to invite him in,' Sylvie said.

Antoine shook his head. 'The damage was done the moment he discovered we were here at all. That cursed light gave us away. I am to blame for that.'

Felix crossed his arms. He had left Sylvie's side as soon as the other men arrived and had taken position by the door. 'Let us agree it was an unfortunate series of events and no one is to blame. The question is, how does Sylvie deal with his proposal without endangering herself?'

'I don't think I am in danger,' she said thoughtfully. Now she was safe in the company of friends, she was able to look at it with clarity. 'I offended him and hurt his pride. He was clumsy. I don't think he meant to hurt me, and I'm not sure his threats are real.'

She ran her hands through her hair, remembering the way Dieter's fingers had gripped into it.

'How could he tell me he loves me?' she exclaimed. 'We barely know each other. I think that's what upset him most, when I told him it wasn't possible to love somebody after a few weeks.'

'Isn't it?' Felix asked in a voice that was low and husky. His arms tightened across his body, the muscles in his forearms visibly tensing. 'Don't you think that's possible?'

Sylvie looked into his eyes. Hadn't she felt what Dieter had described when she danced with Felix? Didn't she long to be with him now? She'd even considered giving up everything in England to stay near him.

'I don't know,' she said slowly. 'Perhaps it is. But not with him.'

She became aware of a gentle pressure on her arm and looked round to find Antoine smiling at her knowingly. 'So we conclude Sylvie does not love this German – which I am sure we are all relieved to discover – but what now?' he said.

Marcel sucked his teeth. 'You mentioned he wants to take you to Paris. Let me contact England and see what they say. There could be an advantage to you going.'

'You can't mean for her to go with him?' Felix exclaimed.

Marcel held up his hand. 'I'm not sure. It might be the best thing to do. There are cells in Paris, so it might be an opportunity for Sylvie to gather information. If Baumann is growing suspicious or decides to be vindictive, then clearing him out of the way for a holiday would be better for all of us.'

'Not for Sylvie. I can't imagine he's thinking of separate rooms.' Felix turned his eyes on her. 'I'm right, aren't I?'

She said nothing. Her stomach had contracted painfully when Marcel had spoken, but what he said made sense. She was here to do a job. She'd said to Max and Vera she was prepared to give everything to the job.

'You don't want to go, do you?' Felix said, his voice filled with disbelief.

'No, of course I don't, but when I took this role, the people who recruited me warned me I might have to do things I'd find unpalatable. I told him I would do what is necessary. If that means I have to take Dieter out of the way to keep everyone else safe, I will.'

Felix shook his head violently, then paced around the room. 'This is what comes of being soft-hearted. I said you should have let me kill him the other night.'

'And if you had done that, where would we would all be now, tell me?' Sylvie snapped.

'Have courage,' Marcel said. 'Remember I said we've had notice to expect more airdrops? A strike of some sort is being planned. Perhaps there will be no need for you to do anything after all.'

'Perhaps,' Sylvie said. 'I hope so.'

Marcel shook her hand.

'I need to go. I'll be in touch as soon as I have work for

you. I'm glad you seem more yourself again. You gave me quite a scare when Antoine appeared at the door.'

Marcel and Antoine left. Sylvie went to follow him, but Felix caught her by the hand and held her back. She turned and found herself swung straight into his arms.

'You came here crying,' he growled. 'That is what his kiss did to you, and now you suggest that you would be prepared to make love to him?'

'I never said *that*. There is a difference between going to bed with someone and making love, isn't there?'

'Yes there is. I know you'll do what you have to, I just want you to be safe. I … care for you, Sylvie.'

'I know. I care for you too.' She touched his cheek, and he closed his eyes. His face creased into softness; both unbearable and exhilarating to see. She felt tears rising again. The hopelessness of her predicament was bearing down again. 'I don't want to go to bed with Dieter. I don't want to do anything with him.'

Felix kissed her on the corner of her mouth. 'Do you want to stay for the night after the show has finished?'

'I want nothing more, but I don't think I should,' she said. 'Céline already wondered where I had been the other night, and last night I didn't get in until far too late. I don't want anyone else getting suspicious.'

She rubbed her eyes. She needed a decent night's sleep. No wonder her head was throbbing.

'Perhaps I do need to lie down for a little while.'

'One minute.'

Felix shook the bedclothes and smoothed them down, then to Sylvie's astonishment he scooped her in his arms and carried her to the bed. He laid her down on top of the sheets, then climbed in beside her and lay back, hooking his hands behind his head. Sylvie rested her head into the triangle of space created by his arm and body.

'Who is getting suspicious?' he asked.

'I feel like everyone is watching me. Emily just found me crying and looks at me strangely whenever I talk to you. I don't know whether it is because she suspects what I'm doing and plans to inform the *milice* or whether she has feelings for you.'

To her surprise, Felix laughed.

'I can tell you now Emily would never inform the *milice* of anything. If she is watching you, it is because she is my sister and thinks I need protecting from fearsome women.'

'Your sister?' Sylvie sat up and stared at him.

Felix laughed again.

'My half-sister, I should say. We share our mother. My father died in the first year of the Great War, when I was five, and my mother remarried a year after it ended. So yes, Emily cares for me, but not in the way you are thinking of.'

A dead father and a remarriage. It definitely explained Emily's interest in Felix's dealings with women, and, perhaps, some of Felix's surliness.

'My mother died when I was fourteen. My father was already married, so it is not quite the same, but it hurt me. Was that what made you so angry, having your father replaced?' Sylvie asked.

'Not in itself. My stepfather is very wealthy – he owns factories along the river. Of course, now they have been requisitioned by the Germans, but before the war they produced canned fish. He wanted me to work my way up to become a partner in the canning business. I could not think of a worse life than sitting in an office dealing with orders and supplies. We clashed as I grew up. On politics, religion. On everything.'

He looked at her out of the corner of his eye. She gave him a slight smile, silently urging him on.

'When I was thirteen, I had a bad bout of influenza and spent months convalescing, unable to leave my room. It gave me the time to practise music. As soon as I was old enough, I left home and decided to use my music to earn my living. I joined the *zazou* movement – listening to swing and jazz in underground clubs, learning to play, making connections. Choosing to live in attics and garrets with Jewish and black musicians and other "morally questionable types" that society deplored.'

His voice became mocking, and Sylvie wondered which of his parents had called them that.

'Your stepfather disapproved?'

'And my mother. She could not understand it. I was a rich man's son now, with the prospect of a secure job, so why I would ever want to be otherwise? But I never forgot how we had lived before, in a modest set of rooms among working people. The sort of people who work on the production line for her husband, earning a fraction of his profits. Sometimes I wonder if my principles were created entirely to oppose my stepfather's. How much do we choose our paths to spite our parents?'

Sylvie chewed her fingernail thoughtfully. She'd embraced the chance to return to France, not to spite Arthur and Maud, but in spite of them. Felix rolled onto his stomach, propping himself up on his elbows. Sylvie did the same and they lay side by side, the lengths of their body touching. Felix dropped his head so that his hair flopped over his face, concealing it.

'As Bernard said, when Germany invaded France, my stepfather favoured appeasement and I did not.'

Something slotted into place like a piece of a jigsaw Sylvie hadn't known was missing.

'Does the factory we are intending to blow up belong to your stepfather?'

He smiled grimly. 'I'm the one who put Bernard in touch with the contacts he needed. Not such a good stepson, but hopefully a better patriot.'

'Emily told me you don't believe in what the Resistance do.'

'That's what I've told her. I don't want her thinking I'm involved and letting something slip to my mother. It would break her heart to think I was putting myself in danger. Emily's too. Even though she's younger, she likes to cosset me. I think she tries to make sure I don't fall prey to a scarlet woman who will break my heart. I hope she doesn't work out the truth that I've become even more active than I was before.'

'Why have you become more active again?' Sylvie asked.

'It feels right. Seeing how bravely you go about your work made me reconsider.' He gave a half-laugh and looked at her side on. 'I don't know what you did before you came to France, but you left the life you had and the people you loved and threw yourself into the unknown. When I sent you to fetch my cigarettes and you accused me of playing games, it struck me harder than I expected. I think it is called a conscience.'

'Oh!' Sylvie smoothed her hair down, feeling flustered at his words. 'I didn't intend for that to happen. There wasn't much to give up. It was a bit of a rash decision if I'm completely honest. My lover ended our relationship and it meant I had to leave my job. I didn't really have many other options.'

It sounded pathetic. She should have rushed to defend France as soon as war was declared. Even what little she had done in England had been sorely lacking in patriotism. She had made up for it since, she hoped.

She took Felix's hand, and he linked his fingers through hers. Long and shapely. They couldn't belong to anyone other than a musician. A warm rush coursed through her as she remembered him touching her so intimately.

'I, too, had lost my way and needed reminding that France needed me. I suppose I could say that it was a man who set me on the path towards SOE.'

'Then I should thank him for putting you on the path towards me, *chérie*,' Felix said. He put a finger under her chin and tilted her head up, looking deeply into her eyes. 'Even if he was clearly not an expert at pleasing you.'

'I never said he wasn't.'

'I deduced it myself.'

Felix took hold of her leg and unbuckled her shoe, tossing it onto the floor. He kept hold of her foot and ran his thumbnail along the underside. Sylvie squeaked in surprise. It tickled, but delightfully so.

'What are you doing?'

'You have such elegant feet.'

He began to massage it, and Sylvie moaned with pleasure. 'That feels so good. I've walked far too much and dancing every night is not good for them. Don't stop.'

She lay back and closed her eyes.

'No one has ever done this before,' she purred.

'I told you your lovers were incompetent,' Felix replied. 'Open your eyes, *chérie*. I want to see you watching me.'

She obeyed, feeling his fingers working in firm circles on her instep and stroking her ankles, taking each toe in turn. His touch was so intimate and methodical, she was surprised to feel herself becoming aroused. His smile widened, and she realised he was aware of the effect he was having. He knelt at the bottom of the bed and began to move his hands further up her legs. He kneaded and stroked, fingers moving further and further up, all the time fixing her with his gaze.

His hands disappeared beneath her skirt to the top of her stockings, further up to her knickers. He wriggled his thumb beneath the silk and ran it over the crease of her thigh before moving it to the soft mound of hair. He eased her legs further apart and smiled, wolfish and devilishly attractive, and knelt between her knees. He ran his tongue slowly over his lips suggestively.

'Did your lover do *this*?' he asked.

Sylvie shivered with lust. Surely he didn't mean to put his tongue where his fingers were currently exploring? She shook her head. If she tried to speak, she was sure all that would emerge was a stream of nonsense.

'In that case, let me introduce you to the perfect way to take your mind off your troubles...'

Felix was right.

What he did to her – what they did together – rid Sylvie of all capability of coherent thought. Afterwards, she lay spread-eagled, limbs growing heavy and peace settling over her. Felix lay at her side, arm drooped casually over her waist.

'As much as I would love to stay here and make love to you, it's my turn to cook tonight so I should make myself presentable. If you want to stay here and rest for a little while, you are most welcome.'

'Thank you.'

'My room is yours whenever you need it. So am I,' Felix said and kissed her lightly on the temple.

She felt his weight lift off the bed and heard him moving around the room, humming a sad melancholy tune as he brushed his teeth and changed into a fresh shirt.

Her eyes began to droop shut, and when she woke she was alone with Felix's bedspread tucked over her. It was a small but kind gesture. She buried her face in it, inhaling the scent of his cologne, then climbed out of bed and adjusted her clothes.

Another room with a temporary promise. It seemed that was all life intended to offer her, but she didn't mind. While Felix was happy to have her, she was happy to be with him.

Chapter Twenty-Eight

As Marcel had warned, there were increased airdrops from the RAF. Again, Sylvie found herself cycling at top speed to a location out of the city once Mirabelle had closed. Then there was the race to retrieve and divide the contents before their presence was detected, working almost silently in the company of others, united by their common aim. She didn't recognise any of the faces, and the pang of sadness at not knowing who had lived or died on the previous drop caught her unawares.

The men and women shook hands, nodding to each other in respect at a task well done before vanishing into the darkness back to wherever they had come from. Whatever was being planned had to succeed.

Sylvie delivered her parcels to Tomas at first light. He would send them out as smaller deliveries wrapped in butcher's paper and hidden among shopping. Some, Sylvie would deliver in person. By now, she was confident enough to walk past the patrols of Germans and even smile at them, while in her bag, beneath the makeup and shopping, was enough plastic explosive to blow them all to pieces. Tomas had apparently decided Sylvie was trustworthy and forgiven her for allowing Dieter into the club because when she handed over the parcel, he patted her on the hand, asked her to give his regards to Antoine and sent her away with a Toulouse sausage that he took no payment for.

She took it to the club and shared it with Felix, frying it over a gas ring and eating it in his bed. As the morning sun passed overhead, she caught up on missed sleep while he read or hummed compositions. They spent the afternoon lazily making love, talking and dancing to the strains of the records that crept through the floorboards from Antoine's rooms beneath. In years to come, Sylvie would remember it as a day of perfect peace. There was nowhere else to be and nothing urgent to do.

As night fell, they lay together and stared at the moon rising through the sky light. It had been a perfect day, and now it promised to be a perfect night. A comfortable bed, the warm arms of a lover and the sweet smells of warm summer air. In less than a fortnight it would be June. Lying in Felix's arms, she could almost believe there was no war being waged. No occupation. No Germans walking the streets. No Dieter waiting for an answer.

'Tomorrow night is the attack on the factory,' Felix reminded her. 'Are you prepared?'

'I don't have much to do. Only stand around outside looking as if I'm waiting for someone. Maybe I will ask Antoine if I can borrow one of his wigs. I think I'd like to be a blonde while I wait for my illicit lover.'

'Your illicit lover! How shocking,' Felix said. 'Do you have many?'

'I have one other,' Sylvie laughed. She slipped her arms about his waist from behind and nibbled his ear. 'Watch out for him, he can be very moody but he plays the most wonderful music.'

'He sounds best avoided.' He twisted around. 'Are you fond of him?'

'Yes I am,' Sylvie answered.

He rolled over, pinning Sylvie down with the weight of his body.

'Good. Because he is very fond of you.'

How much of her sudden antipathy towards Dieter was due to the harsher side of him she had seen, and how much was due to her burgeoning relationship with Felix? She caught herself midway through the thought and brought herself up sharply. It wasn't a relationship. They'd been to bed together a handful of times.

He'd said he was there for her for as long as she wanted him, but he'd made it clear he knew she would be leaving eventually. This was wartime, and nothing was certain.

She would be an idiot to expect anything more.

A note arrived at Sylvie's apartment midway through Monday afternoon. Madame Giraud brought it up, muttering darkly about being a messenger at her age. A scribbled line from Tante Louise asked Sylvie to call as a matter of urgency. She left at a run and caught up with

Claire Barbe three streets away. They walked on opposite pavements, not acknowledging each other. As they neared the house, Claire sped up. Marcel's trailer and bicycle were waiting outside in the road, and Claire had left the door ajar. Sylvie made her way upstairs as she had before.

Marcel was sitting alone and rose to greet her.

'There has been a change of plan for you, Sylvie.'

'For tonight?' She settled into the second dining chair. 'I'm ready to go to the factory as instructed. Where do I go instead?'

Marcel sipped his tisane.

'You aren't going to be involved at all.'

'Why? If it is because of my behaviour the other day, you don't have to worry.' Her face grew hot. 'I haven't lost my nerve, Marcel,' she protested.

'I know you haven't. Don't worry, that isn't why I'm moving you from that mission. Something more urgent has arisen that I can only entrust to someone who knows everything about what we do. We received a sked early this morning informing us that a wireless operator from *Seamstress*, the cell near Arcachon has had his cover blown. Fortunately, he was alert enough to realise and the rest of the network has gone to ground. The man's alias is Henri Chevalier, field name Edouard. He evaded capture and has made a run for it. He's working his way up the country and will be in Nantes tomorrow.'

He waited while Sylvie digested the news. This was what every agent feared: exposure and capture. That was why agents took steps to make sure as few people as possible knew their real identities.

'What do you need me to do?'

'Meet him off the train at seven twenty-five and take him to the safe house on Rue de Venus. For one night, he will stay there. I'm afraid it will be a long journey across the city, but it is the safest location I can think of at short notice. It couldn't have come at a worse time, coinciding with tonight's plans.'

He fished into the bag at his feet and produced a small silk handkerchief with a printed map; easy to hide and easy to burn. 'Give him this map and send him on his way to the Couronne bar in Angers. I've kept a few of the food stamps from the raid, so you can give him them too.'

'I understand.'

She put the map and food stamps in the hidden pocket of her bag while Marcel told her the series of phrases that would confirm Henri's identity, and she memorised them. She had to admit she was relieved at the change of plan. She'd had enough of late nights but escorting an agent across the city wouldn't be easy.

The train was delayed by almost half an hour, and by the time it disgorged its passengers, Sylvie was growing more and more vexed. She waited at the end of the platform behind the ticket barrier with a small bunch of flowers, anxiously looking around. Felix would be preparing to go wait at the factory, not knowing Sylvie was no longer taking part in the mission. He'd be watching for her from his post and not know why she wasn't there.

Her irritation soon became concern. No one matching the description she had been given appeared in the first rush of travellers eager to return home. The second wave of older or slower passengers made their way through the gates and still no one appeared. As Sylvie began to worry she had arrived for the wrong train, she saw a man hobbling down the platform. He had one arm over the shoulder of another passenger and was dragging his right foot, which looked to be twisted at an angle.

He was holding a small, black suitcase and was dressed in a smart, well-fitting suit. He had a neat moustache and beneath his hat she could see fair hair. This must be the man she needed to meet.

'Edouard, what have you done?' Sylvie exclaimed, stepping from underneath the light.

The man's brow furrowed. Perhaps he was not the right man after all. She waved her flowers around, drawing his eyes to them. She could almost see the thoughts working behind his sharp grey eyes. She began the first part of the exchange.

'Don't tell me you forgot the flowers for *Maman's* birthday?'

Comprehension dawned in his eyes. He slapped his forehead in exasperation.

'I must have left them at the market stall!'

The counter phrase.

'It's just as well I bought some,' Sylvie replied. The final part of the exchange. He looked relieved.

'Hello, Monique,' he said. 'Your hair is not blonde any more, so I almost didn't recognise you!'

He gestured towards her, speaking to his aide. 'My sister is here, monsieur!'

His French was good, but to Sylvie, knowing his true nationality, it sounded like something learned rather than natural.

'Edouard, what did you do to your leg? Were you drinking again?' She folded her arms, crushing the flowers.

'Your brother injured himself when he arrived to catch the train,' the other passenger said. 'He almost threw himself into the carriage.'

Henry limped over to the ticket office and leaned against the windowsill.

'Thank you for helping him,' she said to the passenger. 'I'll look after him now. Come on, Edouard, mother will be wondering why we are late.'

They waited until the helpful passenger had gone through the barrier, then Sylvie hooked his arm around her shoulder and helped him to walk. He swallowed, wincing as he tested the weight.

They made it around the corner to where Sylvie had left her bicycle before she noticed the perspiration pooling on his forehead.

'Are you in a lot of pain? You can speak in English if you do it quietly.'

'I fell running to catch the train and did my ankle in. I've hurt my knee too. I didn't think I would make it to the station.'

'Why were you running?' Sylvie asked in English.

'I'd been making my way from the safe house and got the feeling I was being tracked. I took a few detours to throw them off, then got lost. I made the train by the skin of my teeth and fell on the platform.'

He exhaled and rolled his eyes, as if he was describing a minor inconvenience, and gave a smile. Sylvie repressed her urge to shout at him, but he must have sensed her mood because his smile dropped.

'I made a hash of it, didn't I? Then made a spectacle of myself getting onto the train! People will remember.'

'Let's hope you lost them, otherwise the authorities will be looking in every town the train stopped at.'

Sylvie put the suitcase in the bicycle basket. It stuck out awkwardly in a manner she knew would draw attention to it.

'You can sit on the saddle and push with your good leg,' she suggested. 'I'll walk beside you. We'll move quicker that way.'

He climbed on and pushed with his good foot and freewheeled down the road for a few yards. Moving at that pace, they would be lucky to cross the city before curfew.

'There's a checkpoint at the end of the next street as we are nearing the Nazi headquarters. Do you have your papers to hand?'

'Yes. I'm now Christophe Bartine, a seller of cosmetics from Bordeaux. I think I'm too old to be your brother if anyone asks.'

It was true. He was nearer to forty than thirty.

'You're my second cousin in that case.'

The checkpoint was busy, with a long line of people who had come from the station and were returning home. Sylvie and Henri joined the line, adopting the same neutral expressions as everyone else. It was strange how easily oppression had become a minor, daily inconvenience rather than something to dread. As they grew nearer to the front, someone spoke loudly behind Sylvie.

'The dancer who is definitely not a prostitute!'

It was Nikki.

Sylvie's heart sank. He was the last person she would have liked to encounter. He was not part of the checkpoint staff but was standing at the opposite side of the road in a doorway, watching the line of people have their identity cards checked and bags searched.

'Hello, Nikki,' she said, giving him a weak smile.

'*Unteroffizier* Sattler, not Nikki!' he snapped.

He marched across to Sylvie. With each step he took, she felt a jolt of anxiety.

'My friend *Verwaltungs-Sekretar* Baumann is very upset. He told me that he believes you no longer wish to see him.'

Sylvie sagged in relief. His attention was personal, not official.

'I didn't say that,' she protested. 'I just said I could not go to Paris with him. It was too soon. And I'm not that kind of girl. I'm sorry he's unhappy.'

Nikki sniffed, disbelievingly. His lip curled into a sneer.

'Not that kind of girl? After he kissed you the way I told him to, I wonder if you are any kind of woman at all!'

He stepped closer to Sylvie, looking over her so she had to look up into his face.

'Why are you here instead of at home? Who is this with you? A lover? Is this the reason you are rejecting *Verwaltungs-Sekretar* Baumann?'

'I'm not rejecting Dieter,' Sylvie protested. The lie made her flinch inside. Marcel had still not told her what London had said, but she would have to tell Dieter something soon.

'This is my cousin. I met him from the train. He's staying the night here before carrying on.'

Nikki held his hand out. 'Your papers, *fräulein*.'

Sylvie passed over her many-times folded identification paper. She had no worries they would be spotted as false, but even so her hand shook a little. Nikki held it up, turned it over, peered at the photograph.

'You do not take care of this as you should. Look how the edges are ragged! Perhaps I should fine you for your lack of care.'

A spark of contempt flickered inside Sylvie. This was bullying. He was trying to intimidate her. Nikki passed them back over, and she put them away. He turned to Henri, who had stood silently throughout the exchange, showing no interest and holding the bicycle handle.

'Now, your papers.'

Henri drew them from his inner jacket pocket and handed them over. Unlike Sylvie's it was folded only once and was clean. It looked too fresh. Sylvie braced herself. Discovery was surely moments away.

'A cosmetics salesman?'

'Yes. I have the finest quality products. Things any woman would be pleased to receive as a gift. Would you care to see some samples?' Henri patted the suitcase and smiled eagerly at Nikki.

'Another time.' Nikki held the paper out in front of Sylvie. 'You should learn from your cousin, *fräulein*. This is how you should take care of your identity card. He has more pride in his belongings than you do.'

He passed it back over to Henri and gave Sylvie another cold stare.

'My friend has been waiting for your answer for far too long. I suggest you give it to him soon. You may proceed.'

Sylvie and Henri rejoined the line for the checkpoint. Neither spoke until they were through and safely on the other side. At the corner, Sylvie looked back, glancing over her shoulder, then immediately chastised herself. Never look as if you are worried about anything. Don't give people a reason to suspect you. However, she was relieved that Nikki was no longer looking in their direction but still watching the line of people.

Henri grimaced. 'There is a story there, I feel. Is this bad?'

Sylvie bit her thumbnail. 'I hope it isn't bad. I think he was just being vindictive towards me. I've been working on a man in the administration system, but he started to get a little too fond of me and wants me to take a trip to Paris. I've been delaying answering, but I can't put it off for much longer.'

'Let's get moving. I'm as much of a danger to you as you are to me, and it's a long way to the safe house.'

She set off, Henri freewheeling at her side. They had not gone more than a couple of streets before Henri called her to stop a moment. His complexion was sallow and he was starting to sweat. He climbed off the bicycle and limped to a wall and sat down. He rolled up his trouser leg and swore. Sylvie peered over and did the same. His ankle was

332

swollen, but that was nothing compared to his kneecap, which was bulging sideways through his skin at an angle it was never meant to take. Sylvie felt vomit rise in the back of her throat, and she clasped her hand across her mouth urgently. A wound gushing blood would have been better than this.

'I think it is dislocated,' he groaned. 'How far is it to the safe house?'

His voice was taut. He must be in considerable pain.

'A little over two miles, and the final part of it uphill. You can't freewheel that,' Sylvie said. 'You'll never make it there on that leg.'

She sat on the wall beside him, running the options through her mind. Her own apartment was almost as far in the opposite direction. Tomas's shop was closer, but he would be out on the factory attack and explaining to his son would be too complicated. There were not many places in the centre of Nantes where she could hide him.

A detachment of soldiers marched past, boots drumming in unison, and Sylvie winced. The encounter with Nikki had shaken her, and she felt hunted. There was one obvious place, but she was reluctant to take him there after she had already brought too much attention to it. However, this would only be for one night.

'I work at a club a short walk from here. I'll have to take you there.'

It took almost half an hour to reach Mirabelle, and, fortunately, the street was almost empty. The door to the club was locked, but the window on the second floor was wide open. Sylvie instructed Henri to wait in the alley while she threw a handful of gravel overarm and called Antoine's name. His head appeared.

'I left my purse here,' she called. 'Can you come down and let me in? I won't take long.'

He disappeared, and shortly afterwards, she heard the bolts scraping back. She whistled beneath her breath to Henri and he lurched around the corner and through the door. He slumped forwards to his knees, gave a cry of agony and slumped face down. Sylvie rolled him over. He had fainted. While they waited for him to recover, she explained the situation to Antoine.

'I didn't know where else to bring him. I'm so sorry.'

'Never be sorry for doing the right thing, child.'

Henri began to stir. Antoine brought him a glass of water mixed with brandy. 'I should start billing you for this brandy,' he said with a smile to Sylvie as she held the glass to Henri's lips.

'My case,' Henri murmured. 'It can't be left outside.'

Sylvie fetched it and when she returned, Henri was leaning up against a table, holding the glass. She was relieved to see he had more colour in his cheeks. With Henri going up backward, seated on his bottom, Sylvie and Antoine managed to get him up to Antoine's apartment and onto a sofa where they removed his shoes, socks and trousers. All three of them regarded the swollen ankle and knee. The leg was a mess of swellings and the beginnings of bruising. Antoine wrapped Henri's knee and ankle in wet towels and raised the leg on a stool.

'It is testament to your courage that you endured walking this far,' he said, shaking Henri's hand.

'Without Sylvie and her bicycle, I wouldn't have. Which reminds me, please give me my case.'

Sylvie handed it over. Henri opened the case and produced a smaller case of lipsticks and powder compacts, a jar of cold cream and other assorted cosmetics.

'When I started to suspect I was being watched, I began to get a few things together. I've got a few important pieces in here I wouldn't like to fall into the wrong hands. Disguised to look completely innocent, of course.'

He unscrewed the lid of the cold cream and offered it to Sylvie. She dipped a finger in and discovered that while the cream was real, the jar did not go deeper than her fingertip. It had a fake bottom. Henri laughed at her astonishment and prised the inner jar free to reveal green putty. The scent of almonds filled the air. The cavity was filled with plastic explosive.

'This might be useful to someone. I had to abandon my wireless set, but I have the crystals safely concealed. I've got some damned good painkillers in here somewhere as well. I'm going to take a handful, and then I want you two to have a bash at putting my knee back in shape. I know you'll have done some medical training down in Kent, Sylvie.'

'I've never had to try on a real person,' Sylvie said doubtfully. 'I'd rather leave it until tomorrow and ask Marcel for advice or you could end up crippled for life.'

'Good thinking, girl,' Henri said. 'In that case, I'll trouble you for another brandy and try to get some rest.'

'Leave him with me,' Antoine said. 'Go home and go to bed, child. Tomorrow, get word to Marcel about what has happened, and we will put the matter into his hands. There is nothing more you can do tonight.'

He was right that she could do nothing to help Henri. She rode home, keeping to the back streets with her mind full of worries. Henri had been ready to leave when the time came. Thanks to careful planning, he had managed to evade arrest. Perhaps it was time for Sylvie to make plans herself.

As soon as she arrived home, she pulled open the window and dragged her tin from its hiding place. She had enough money saved to buy food and accommodation for two or three days, as well as the rest of the sleeping pills she had dosed Céline with, alongside the amphetamines. She unpicked the seam at the base of her handbag and put the money and pills inside the lining.

As she sewed the seams back together, there was an abrupt rumble in the distance, like a roll of thunder. Shortly afterwards came the wail of sirens screaming across the city. She ran to the bathroom and leant out of the window, craning her head to look out over the city. She laughed with delight. The sky beyond the river glowed with fire. The men had done their task and the factory had been blown up.

Chapter Twenty-Nine

Sylvie visited the Barbe residence shortly after eight the following morning. She suspected that even if Marcel did not spend his nights there, Louise would know how to locate him. As it happened, he emerged from a bedroom looking a little guilty at being found out. Sylvie wondered whether admitting to sleeping with Felix would ease his conscience at all. He had dark bags beneath his eyes and looked exhausted. He plodded around the kitchen brewing ersatz coffee in a pot.

'I've only been in bed for a couple of hours. I waited at a rendezvous point by the bakery, hoping to see that everyone was accounted for. I had to leave at five when the workers arrived or I'd still be there now,' he explained.

He hadn't said *safe,* and the fact he had left unwillingly was sinister.

'Did everything go according to plan? I saw the fire from the explosion lighting the sky.'

'The attack itself was a success. I have no complaints

there. A lot of machinery will be out of use indefinitely.' He dropped into the armchair and his expression changed from satisfaction to despair.

'Two of the men who detonated the explosives were shot as they left the factory grounds. They ran almost straight into a patrol. Felix took out the gunman before he could shoot the third, and another three of the soldiers for good measure, but the alert was raised.'

He broke off. A hand gripped Sylvie's heart, squeezing it until she felt it had stopped beating and would never start again.

'Is Felix...' Sylvie sank onto the empty chair, hardly able to ask. 'Did he escape?'

Marcel looked grave.

'By the time the remaining soldiers had worked out where he was based, he had fled the scene. There was no trace of him when Tomas went to look hours later.'

All sound and colour leached out from the world. 'And since then?'

'No word yet, but don't give up hope.'

She nodded. She'd keep clinging on to the belief that he was safe until there was proof that he wasn't.

'You didn't come here just to ask about last night, did you?' Marcel asked.

Sylvie rubbed her eyes. She'd almost forgotten her purpose. More bad news to impart. Marcel filled two coffee cups and gave her one. She sipped it automatically, for once not minding the weak, bitter taste of chicory.

'Last night did not go according to plan for me either, I'm afraid.'

Marcel greeted the news of Henri's injuries and failure to reach the safe house with predictable frustration.

'I'm not angry at you,' he reassured her. 'You did your best, Sylvie, and on balance you made the right decision to take him to Mirabelle rather than trying to get to the safe house. The couple who own it are older and wouldn't be able to cope with having an invalid on their hands.'

He sipped his cup of coffee, staring into the cup as if it held the answer. 'I shall have to arrange for messages to be passed along the networks who will be waiting for him that there has been a delay. It makes things so much more complicated, especially after last night's mixed success.'

Sylvie nodded, but her heart was leaden. The partial destruction of a factory hardly seemed to balance the death of two men and Felix's disappearance.

'There seemed to be more soldiers on the streets when I cycled over.' A direct result of the bombing or her imagination? The authorities would be looking for the culprits. Any movements would be difficult.

'Henri won't be able to ride a bicycle until his knee heals,' she pointed out, trying to find the best of the matter. 'He'll have to stay put for a while, which will give things time to settle down. Do you know a doctor who we can trust to treat his leg?'

'Yes, I think I know a man who can be trusted to keep his silence, as long as Henri can convincingly play a Frenchman while he is being treated. Go home for now, Sylvie. I'll send word if we need you.'

'Shouldn't I go to Mirabelle?' she asked.

Marcel gave her a penetrating look. 'What would you do there?'

'I don't know. See how Henry is? See if Felix has returned home?'

'No, I think I'd rather you went home for the morning,' Marcel said. 'I have nothing for you to do right now, and the fewer people on the street the better.'

Sitting in her bedroom and waiting for news would be unbearable.

She gripped her coffee cup. 'There's something else you need to know. Henri and I had an encounter with one of Baumann's friends at the checkpoint. He told me Baumann is waiting for my answer. Have you received any word from England concerning my situation with Baumann?'

Marcel pursed his lips. 'Major Swift thinks you should end it. You should definitely not agree to visit Paris with him. The Gestapo are much more adept at identifying fake papers than a spiteful jobsworth like Baumann's friend, and there is nothing to be gained from you putting yourself closer to them. We have enough agents in the capital already risking exposure.'

A weight lifted from Sylvie's shoulders. She had not realised how much she had been dreading the opposite verdict.

'Thank you.'

'London suggests if Baumann continues to place us under threat, we remove you from the situation.'

A pit opened in Sylvie's stomach. 'Remove me? I don't want to go anywhere.'

Marcel frowned. 'I know there are compelling reasons for you to stay, but that is irrelevant.'

'What compelling reasons do you mean?' Sylvie asked. She already knew the answer.

'You know what I mean. Or rather, who.'

She couldn't admit it, but her face must have been enough because Marcel sighed.

'I've known Felix Lambert for over two years, and in the past month or two, he has become a changed man. What I've seen recently is enough to tell me you've become close.'

He walked to the window and looked out. Sylvie leaned on the windowsill beside him. Louise Barbe and Claire were standing in the street chatting with a neighbour. He turned back to Sylvie and gave her a sad smile.

'I'm sorry, Sylvie, but we can't always have what we want.'

If Felix was even still alive...

She pushed the thought deep inside her. 'I'm useful here. I'll deal with Baumann in a way that won't endanger anyone. I don't want to go.'

He gave her a stern look. 'You are here to do a job. For your own safety and that of the network and our friends in the Resistance, if you need to be moved, I will move you. Do your best to smooth things with the German, but remember, you're English and whether it happens sooner or later, one day you'll be leaving Nantes.'

Sylvie sighed. 'I'll go to the *Soldatenheim* this evening before I go to the club and speak to Baumann.'

'Good. We don't want Baumann coming for another

impromptu visit, especially as Henri will be at Mirabelle for the time being. Do what you need to do. But be cautious.'

She gathered her belongings. Marcel walked her to the door and took her hand.

'I'm sure Felix will be safe. He's quick-witted and brave. He'll do everything he can to remain alive.'

She nodded, throat too full of grief to dare speak. She'd found happiness with Felix, but all too briefly.

By the time she reached home, she felt too weary even to cycle. As she neared the square at the bottom of the road, she heard her name in a low, urgent hiss. It had come from down an alley. Felix stood in the shadows.

She out a sob, let the bicycle fall and ran to where he stood, seizing him in her arms.

'Where have you been? I thought you must be dead!'

Felix wrapped his arms around her and held her tight, kissing her face and hair, squeezing her breath from her body.

'I've been hiding since last night. I didn't dare go home in case somehow I was being followed or Mirabelle was being watched.'

'Why did you come here?' Sylvie asked.

'I had to see you,' Felix said.

Sylvie's heart soared. He had come straight to her. But his next words brought her down to earth.

'I need you to provide me with an alibi. You must say I spent the night here. Do you mind?'

Sylvie forced her face into a smile that felt unnatural. 'I don't mind at all.'

'Thank you,' Felix said. 'What's wrong?'

'When you said you had to see me, I thought you meant...' Sylvie tailed off, feeling silly.

'I did.' He laced his fingers into hers. 'I do. There's no one but you I wanted to see. No one else I even considered.' He peered behind her into the street. 'I don't want to talk here. Is it safe to come into your room?'

'Madame Giraud will be working in the *épicerie*. I don't know where Céline will be, but we can be quiet.'

She led the way, and he followed her up to the front of the building, walking silently on the other side of the road. Sylvie didn't dare look round in case it attracted attention to him. She left the door open, and he followed her up into her room. They saw no one and as soon as the door was closed she sagged onto the chair, her reserves of resilience giving out.

'I'm so relieved you are safe.'

She began to sob. Felix put his arm around her. They held each other silently, their bodies cleaving together with urgency spoke for them. Something had changed in the moment Felix had appeared in the street. They belonged together and nothing, not even Marcel, could change that.

Eventually, Felix shifted, tucking her into the crook of his arm. He smelt like a man who had spent the night sleeping in a field, but even so there was still the musky warmth and hint of his cologne. His hair and face were filthy with mud, and he looked even more exhausted than Marcel had done. He eased out of his jacket and shirt and dropped them to the floor. Sylvie fetched a bowl of water and he washed off most of the mud from his face and hair then scrubbed his shirt until it looked more presentable. He hung the shirt over the back of a chair to dry.

'Tell me what happened,' she prompted.

Felix leaned back and looked at the ceiling. 'I saw the patrol arriving, but I had no way of warning the men leaving the factory. They ran straight into them. Where were you?'

'Marcel needed me for something else,' Sylvie explained. 'If I had been there, they would be alive now.'

'It wouldn't have made a difference. I don't think the Germans realised they were saboteurs, but they opened fire anyway when they saw them running. If you had been there, you would have been caught up in it. You might have been killed too.'

He made a noise in his throat, leaned over abruptly and drew her close, gripping tightly. He was silent for a while, then loosened his grip.

'I shot two or three, which gave our third man time to run. Then the explosives went off. While the patrol was preoccupied with the explosion, I ran. I know it was the correct thing to do, but part of me wanted to stay and fight to the death. So many men have died, and I've been powerless to stop it.'

The crack in his voice tore into Sylvie. Such bitterness and recrimination.

'It wasn't your fault.' She laid her hand on his arm, and he looked at her bleakly. She thought back to something Emily had said.

'Felix, who were the Fifty Hostages?'

His face crumpled. 'Where did you hear about them?'

'Emily mentioned them.' Dieter had too, but Sylvie didn't want to speak his name to Felix. 'She said that is why you were bitter.'

'When *Feldkommandant* Hotz was assassinated, I had been part of the faction that had argued against it. The plan seemed reckless, and the consequences were uncertain. Unfortunately, our arguments were proven right. As a result of the assassination, forty-eight men were rounded up by the German authorities and executed in retaliation. Eighteen of the men were from Nantes.'

He broke off and made a sound in his throat that sounded like a sob. Abruptly, he climbed off the bed and stood underneath the skylight. He put his hands against the wall and pressed his forehead between them, overcome by his memories.

'Did you know the men involved?' Sylvie asked quietly.

His eyes grew bright. 'Some of them were men I had drunk with and argued with. My brothers in the struggle to free our country. The youngest was seventeen. Only a boy. They went to their deaths, and I walked away free and blameless. I should have been among them.'

He passed a hand over his face, then looked at her bleakly. 'My stepfather, naturally, did not know I had ever been involved. To his knowledge I was an upstanding citizen. If it had just been his opinion at stake, I might have continued meeting with the remaining men, but my mother had already lost my father. I could not bear to see her distressed any further by losing a son, so I walked away from the groups I had been involved in. I should have been stronger and kept fighting.'

His raw honesty tore at her. She couldn't remember a time when Dennis would have spoken so freely or with such self-condemnation. There had always been a reason to blame someone else. Always an excuse. Beneath the sullen exterior and the flirtatious club pianist, Felix was a hundred times more worthy.

'It wasn't cowardly to walk away when you did not believe in their cause,' she murmured. 'Why die for something you did not believe in?'

She tiptoed over and put a hand on his shoulder. Felix looked round. His eyes were hollow with grief. Sylvie put her head against his back and her arms round his waist.

'You were not to blame then, or for what happened last night. Or you might have been caught. Then I would have known you were dead, not believed missing.'

'How *did* you know I was missing?' he asked. He turned around and put his arms around Sylvie, holding gently.

'I had to go see Marcel this morning, and he told me. I don't ever want to feel like that again.'

'Like what?' Felix asked.

'Like I had lost you.'

'You haven't lost me. I'm here.' He kissed her tenderly, then pulled away and looked into her eyes. 'I'm not going anywhere. Now, tell me about last night. What did Marcel ask you to do? Why did you have to see him this morning?'

Once again she told the story of Henri's misfortune, this time leaving out all mention of Nikki.

'A setback, that's all,' Felix said. 'There will be other ways of getting him to safety. Marcel did the right thing sending you home. There is nothing you can do now. Nothing there, at least.'

He smiled meaningfully. And then they were kissing. A slow, deep, burning kiss that contained more than any words could. They slipped onto the bed, clinging together. This was more than a craving for his body and for pleasure. She needed the whole of him.

Felix drew away first. He rolled onto his side and leaned up on his elbow to look down at her.

'Sylvie, I would love to make love to you, and it pains me deeply to admit this, but I am exhausted. I was in hiding for half the night. I hid on the riverbank beyond the city and then crossed back when I reached countryside. I feel like I ran halfway to Calais!'

Sylvie grinned. 'I don't mind. Your pride will recover and then you can prove to me how great a lover you are.'

'What time is it?'

Sylvie looked at her watch. 'Not even noon.'

Felix smiled, then yawned. 'Do you mind if I rest here?'

'I don't mind at all. I'll be here when you wake up.'

He kicked off his shoes and stretched out on the bed, rolling onto his side. It was only made for one person and a small person at that. Felix filled it, but there was space for Sylvie to lie if she rolled in close behind him. She watched as his muscles relaxed and his body became loose and heavy. Watching him sleep made her feel tired herself. She kicked her own shoes off and slipped her hand over his waist, finding his hand and lacing her fingers through his. Felix gave a gentle snore and Sylvie smiled.

It struck her that this was the first time she had ever had

a man in her own bed. She had so often spent nights with Dennis in his flat, but he had never visited the room Sylvie rented in the boarding house. Sharing her space was a novelty. She wasn't sure how she'd explain it to Céline or Madame Giraud if they were discovered, but she decided she'd think about that later. She snuggled close into Felix's back and then she, too, slept.

Sometime in the afternoon, Sylvie was awakened by an urgent tapping on the door. Felix was still fast asleep, so she slipped out of bed, slightly muddle-headed, and opened it.

Céline stood there. She took in Sylvie's slightly dishevelled appearance, with her blouse crumpled and untucked from her skirt and her hair coming down from its curls. She looked concerned.

'Have you been in bed? My lord, that's not like you. Are you ill?'

Sylvie smiled and tucked a hairpin back in. 'I was having a nap. What do you want?'

Céline tried to look past her. 'Can I come in? I've got a rip in my new stockings and I need to borrow a needle and thread.'

'Wait there, I'll get it for you,' Sylvie replied.

She tried to close the door but was prevented by Céline taking hold of it. Her brow creased, and she leaned forward to whisper.

'Is something wrong?'

Her concern was touching but inconvenient. 'No, but

my room is a mess. I'll get you the needle and thread. Wait there.'

She may have got away with it if, at that point, Felix hadn't rolled onto his back and given a loud snore. Sylvie looked at Céline guiltily and saw amusement on her friend's face.

'A man?' she mouthed. She giggled and put her hand over Sylvie's. 'You don't have to hide it from me if you have got someone in there. I won't tell Madame Giraud. It isn't that German from Mirabelle, is it?'

'No!' Inspiration struck Sylvie. She leaned forward conspiratorially.

'It's Felix.'

Céline's mouth fell open. 'Sylvie! I never thought you would take my suggestion seriously. How long has he been here?'

'Since last night,' Sylvie said. 'You mustn't tell anybody. I've been trying to keep it secret.'

'You mean this isn't the first time?' Céline asked sharply.

'The first time I brought him here, but not the first time I've been to bed with him.'

Céline patted her hand with an excited smile. 'I promise. Your secret is safe with me.'

Sylvie gave her the needle and thread and shut the door. She sat beside Felix and blew gently on his face until his eyes fluttered open. He gazed blearily at her, then gathered her into his arms.

She told him about the visitor. 'Céline will be incapable of keeping it secret. By the time we arrive at Mirabelle, everyone will know we've been hidden away here, misbehaving ourselves since last night. You'll have an alibi without me even needing to provide it.'

'Perfect. And she doesn't suspect I haven't been here all that time?'

'I don't think so.'

'In that case, the only thing left to do is ensure that she is telling the truth in part.'

Felix tugged Sylvie down towards him.

'I think it's time we made love, my darling, don't you?'

It was early evening before they left Sylvie's bed and Felix went home to Mirabelle with a kiss.

'I will see you very soon, my darling. Let's hope Céline is as loose-tongued as we hope and we are the subject of scandal.'

Sylvie kissed him back, feeling slightly guilty because she was not intending to go straight to the club. She had something else to do first.

She waited until Felix had gone, then made her way to see Dieter.

Chapter Thirty

Dieter's lodgings had once been the Hôtel Villeneuve Sud. Now the sign above the arched doorway had been replaced with the word *Soldatenheim* in large black letters, announcing that it was now in possession of the army.

From inside, Sylvie could hear loud music and German voices raised in conversation. She rang the bell and asked for Dieter. He appeared at the door shortly afterwards, and he broke into a smile when he saw Sylvie.

'Sylvie! What a surprise. Would you like to come in?'

She raised her eyes to his and was saddened to see the happiness in them. His smile was so warm that for a moment she forgot the revulsion that his kiss had caused her to feel.

'Can we walk together?' she said. 'It sounds very busy in there.'

'Yes, we are relaxing. Today has been very busy. Did you hear about last night?'

'Last night? No, I have been in bed all day unwell.'

Dieter waved a hand dismissively. 'It doesn't matter. A minor inconvenience to us. A walk would be pleasant.'

They walked along a wide boulevard lined with trees, past a couple of cafés bustling with life as chairs and tables filled with uniformed Germans spilled out across the wide pavements. At the end of the street was a small square, with grass and rose bushes in the centre to form a small public garden. Sweet fragrance filled the air and the temperature was cool thanks to the shade that had been provided by the trees throughout the day. The neighbourhood was old and elegant, built for the wealthy citizens of Nantes. No wonder the occupying forces had claimed it for themselves.

Sylvie put her bicycle on the ground and sat beside Dieter on a stone bench. He leaned towards her eagerly. She licked her lips nervously, then began.

'Dieter, you asked me last time we met if I could ever love you.'

His expression became joyous, then his face fell. 'You aren't smiling as you say that.'

Sylvie took his hand. 'I'm sorry. I really do like you. I am fond of you. But I don't love you.'

Dieter grimaced. 'You could try to love me. I told you, Paris could help.'

His eyes looked so despairing that Sylvie's heart broke a little.

'I don't think love is something that can be forced. You either feel it, or you don't.' Her heart swelled. At that moment, she knew with complete certainty she loved Felix. 'I can't go with you. It would be wrong.'

Dieter frowned. 'You talk of force... I could make it difficult for you to refuse me.'

He clenched his fist, and she drew her hand free. His voice had taken on a hard edge. Sylvie was reminded unpleasantly of Nikki. How much of Dieter's malice was due to his friend's influence as opposed to his own nature showing through when he was feeling thwarted?

'Yes, you could,' she agreed. 'You could make my life very unpleasant indeed. But that wouldn't make me love you. And you know that.'

She walked away from him. Her legs trembled, but she tensed her muscles to keep it from showing.

'You could do as you threatened the other day and make me fear for my safety. You could hurt Monsieur Julien or close the club. You could force me to go to bed with you.'

He frowned. 'Do you have another lover?'

She wanted to laugh. German, French or British, men had that sense of egotism in common. He would find it more damaging to his pride to think there was a better man than that she had been leading him a dance in the cause of France.

'It follows that because I don't love you, there must be another man?'

'Nikki told me you were walking out yesterday evening with a man who you said was your cousin. Was that a lie?'

Sylvie's limbs turned to ice at the mention of Henri. She glanced back towards the *Soldatenheim*. Did Nikki live there as well, or had he rushed to visit and share his news with Dieter yesterday? Either way, the result was the same; another person knew of her connection to Henri. When his description was inevitably circulated, Nikki would remember and Dieter would wonder.

'It wasn't a lie. Christophe is my second cousin. He stayed one night, with an aunt on his father's side. I barely know him, let alone love him!'

'Who then? The piano player who flirts his way around the club? Who gropes you in an alley but then defends you against implications of prostitution?' Dieter stood and scuffed at the grass with his boot. 'I've seen him looking at you with the same feelings I have. But then he looks at every woman that way. You'll break your heart if you want him to love you.'

He was clutching at straws, or trying to lash out, feeling wounded, but he couldn't know how deeply his words hurt her while simultaneously causing her heart to skip a beat. He thought he'd seen love on Felix's face. Admitting she loved Felix might be enough of an explanation for why she would not be with Dieter, but she couldn't bring herself to do it. If he turned violent, it might be Felix he took his resentment out on.

'There's no one else.'

Thinking that he might be vindictive was enough to send rage bubbling up inside her. She fixed her eyes on him and folded her arms.

'Last time we met you kissed me to hurt me, or impress me, or something I can't even contemplate, but it was not to show me you love me. You scared me with your talk of revealing secrets and making life difficult for me. I've tried to ignore it because you can be gentle and kind. I tried to convince myself it didn't matter that you are German, but whenever we speak, you say something that reminds me we are on opposite sides of a war and you will always choose your side over me. As I must choose mine over you. I won't be one of those women dripping with furs who parade through Paris on the arm of a man who has killed her countrymen.'

He raised his eyebrows. 'I have killed no one. I work in an office.'

'But what about your actions? The other day, you suggested sending workers to labour in your country so we could go on a holiday! How could I go to Paris with you, knowing what others have been forced to do in order to secure our trip?'

He raised his brows. Clearly that was something that had not occurred to him. She carried on, speaking gently.

'You can't possibly understand what it is like for me. You talk of a great future for the Reich, while I have to stand at checkpoints and let men with guns rifle through my bag.'

'But the future *will* be greater. Peace will come. Order will be restored.' Dieter had the look of a man under a spell. His eyes shone with belief in the new world Hitler was creating.

'Will it be greater for *everyone*?' Sylvie's voice rose. Now she had started, she couldn't stop. The words tumbled out incautiously. She might be signing her death warrant but carried on regardless. It was the only way she could think to end things once and for all in a manner Dieter could never dispute. Part of her was overjoyed to use him as a proxy for all the checkpoints and hunger, the fear and hatred she felt towards the Nazis.

'What about the people you send to labour in the fields in Germany? How will the lives of those men and women be better than before you came? How can anything be better for the men and women who have lost their lives fighting?'

She was breathing hard and realised she had clenched her fists. She watched Dieter's face change from surprise to fury, then incredulity. He swung round towards her, finger pointing at her face like a revolver.

'That sort of talk is subversive. I could have you arrested.'

Sylvie lifted her head. If he thought a threat like that would intimidate her, he was wrong.

'Like the old women I told you about? You could. After all, I'm just as guilty of thinking what they did, even if I haven't made any posters. But if you do, it would confirm why I am right to reject you. Remember what you told me about seeing the enemy soldiers on the streets of Saarland as a child? You are one of those men now!'

He stepped back as if she had struck him, and his eyes creased. Sylvie clenched her fists in frustration. How could he not see the parallels?

'Sylvie, I am not your enemy,' he said, opening his arms. She took a step backward, out of his reach.

'Aren't you? The choice is yours to make. Decide what sort of man you are.'

Now she had vented everything, she felt drained but elated. She picked up her bicycle, positioning it between them in case he decided to assault her with another kiss as he had done in the gardens.

'Please don't visit Mirabelle again. I think it would be bad for either of us.'

'I think you are correct. And I think you had better leave now,' Dieter said coldly. 'You have to get ready to dance after all.'

Sylvie nodded at him. She cycled away, shaking. So much for letting Dieter down gently. She was reasonably certain she had done enough to ensure he would not return to Mirabelle, and she had to hope she had not made an enemy for life.

A few streets across, she got off her bicycle and sat on the edge of a fountain, clutching her stomach. She felt physically sick and was shaking. There was no way on earth she could dance tonight. She went home and climbed into bed. The sheets were still crumpled from making love with Felix earlier and she wrapped herself in them tightly, wishing he was at her side. She had to hope that Dieter would believe her when she said Felix was not involved.

She was awakened by a hammering on the door. It was pitch black outside her skylight, so it must have been quite late. She froze. Possibilities tumbled through her mind. Dieter had discovered where she lived, or she had been connected with one of the attacks. Henri's whereabouts had been discovered. Whatever had happened, there was nothing she could do now to evade the visitors.

The knocking came again, more urgently.

'Sylvie, are you in there?'

She clutched the pillow to her face and laughed with relief. It was Céline, but why was she hammering so loudly?

'Sylvie, let me in if you're there.' A second voice. Felix.

Sylvie remembered she had not gone to the club. They must have wondered where she was and come after Mirabelle had closed. She opened the door, slightly conscious of her mannish blue-and-white-striped pyjamas. For the first time since that fake interrogation back at SOE training, she wished she had something more feminine. Felix and Céline looked relieved.

'Where were you? Antoine was furious when you didn't show up tonight,' Céline exclaimed.

'Then we all got worried,' Felix added.

He stared at Sylvie with an expression of such intensity that she went weak. He must have experienced some of the same terror she had on hearing about his disappearance.

'I was sick. I don't know if I ate something or if I am ill, but I started going to the club but had to stop and vomit at the side of the road.' She put her hands on her stomach, which did indeed still feel fragile. 'It was so embarrassing. I came straight home and went to bed. I'm sorry I didn't let anybody know.'

'There, I knew there would be a simple explanation,' Céline said. 'Felix was convinced some harm had befallen you. I am going to bed, now we know you're safe.'

She looked at Felix and raised an eyebrow. 'I don't want to know whether you are going to let yourself out or stay here. It's none of my business, but be careful Madame Giraud doesn't find you.'

She swayed off down the corridor. Felix came in and closed the door behind him.

'What really happened?'

Of course he had known she was not telling the truth. She slipped her arms around him.

'I went to see Dieter. I've ended things with him completely. Marcel had orders from headquarters for me to do it.'

She felt Felix tense. He drew her to the bed and sat beside her.

'He took it badly? Did he hurt you?'

She shook her head and explained what had passed between them, leaving out Dieter's comment about seeing love in Felix's eyes. Felix looked thunderous. He pushed himself to his feet and stormed around the room.

'To go to him to say such things could have got you arrested! He could have shot you in the street and no one would have done a thing to stop him. Sylvie, how could you be so reckless?'

Such condemnation broke her. 'I was angry. He stood for every Nazi in France, and I hated everything about him. I didn't care that I might hurt or offend him,' she said. She felt tears brimming and wiped them away roughly. 'Yes, I should've been more cautious, but it's too late for that now. I wanted to ensure he would stay away from Mirabelle and the people I care about. Especially now Henri is there.'

'I hope it worked.' He sat back down and took her hand. 'You were right about Céline, by the way. When you did not show up, Adele and Emily came straight to me to ask if I knew where you were. We are the talk of the club. Any

Gestapo or *milice* officer who asks questions will be met by half a dozen people who genuinely believe they saw us leaving together. You are a genius!'

Sylvie leaned her head against him. For the first time since arriving, she felt Felix's body relax into her. 'As for Henri, tomorrow, if you are well enough to come to the club, you will see for yourself that he is safe for the time being.'

He glanced at the door. 'It's late. I should go. Or would you like me to stay?'

'You should know the answer to that,' Sylvie said.

'In that case I will.'

He stripped down to his underpants and vest without any ceremony, switched the light off and clambered into bed beside Sylvie. She rested her head on his chest, and he put his arms around her.

'If anything was going to give away your true identity as an Englishwoman it would be these detestable pyjamas,' he whispered in her ear.

'In that case I should take them off,' Sylvie said. She started to undo the buttons, but Felix moved her hands and took over. She lay back and let him work his way down from top to bottom. She had never felt less English, and now more than ever her adopted country felt alien to her. It was traitorous to want the war to continue, but once it was over, she would have to return, and she feared that when she did, her heart would break forever.

Sylvie discovered what Felix meant when she arrived at Mirabelle the following afternoon and made her apologies to Antoine for her absence.

He patted her hand. 'Don't worry, my child. Things have been rather busy here. I have had a visit from an old acquaintance who is staying with me. Perhaps you would like to meet her?'

Smiling mysteriously, he led Sylvie upstairs to his private apartment. What she saw when she entered left her open-mouthed. A woman in a long silk dress sat by the window. She had an elaborate hairstyle of brown curls piled high and a perfectly made-up face with scarlet lips and soot-black eyes. It was only because Sylvie recognised the eyes that were twinkling at her that she recognised Henri.

'I am pleased to meet you, madame,' she said, trying not to smile.

'I am charmed,' Henri replied, holding out a perfectly manicured hand.

Sylvie took it. 'Hello, Grandmother, what long nails you have!'

Henri gave her a mock severe look. 'Mind your manners, young woman. You should know better than to taunt your elders.'

He seemed in quite good humour considering how he was dressed.

'But this is ridiculous,' Sylvie said.

'It's not ridiculous. It's very clever. I'm not going to ask why your employer has such a ready supply of female wigs and clothing, but the Germans will be searching for a young man with a moustache, not a middle-aged woman. Besides,

I don't intend to go out like this. I can't parade up and down the boulevards with my leg in the state it is in.'

'How is your leg?' Sylvie asked.

Henri winced. 'Painful. You would not have wanted to be here yesterday when the doctor came and reset my kneecap. There was a lot of language that turned the air blue.'

He lifted his skirt and displayed large bandages around both his knee and ankle. A revolver strapped to his thigh added a surreal touch.

'I can hobble with a walking stick, but I am afraid cycling will be beyond me. I had a visit from your network chief, who has promised to get me out as quickly as possible by some other means. Until then, I'm afraid I'll have to hope nobody comes looking here. Perhaps I should do a number on the stage. I believe I can remember some Gilbert and Sullivan from my university days.'

'I'm not sure our clientele is ready for your "Little Buttercup",' Sylvie said with a grin.

Henri barked a laugh.

Sylvie's smile faded. Ever since she had arrived at Mirabelle, she had been excited to perform each night, but tonight she dreaded it, in case Dieter ignored her request and came to the club. She was anxious all through the family meal and barely ate anything, which at least lent credence to the idea she had been struck down with a sickness.

She was fussed around by the other dancers who showed concern over her illness. She was touched. Having people concerned for her was something new, and she liked it. She was amused when Céline took her to one side and whispered in her ear.

'Is your sickness because you are with child? I know a woman who can fix that very easily. You wouldn't even have to tell Felix. It would be awful if you had to leave like Marie-Elaine did.'

Sylvie said nothing. It might be wise to let that rumour start in case she did have to vanish. She ate some bread, musing on what would happen if she did fall pregnant. They hadn't always been as careful as they had the first time. Angelique had been left with a baby after her affair with Arthur, and she didn't want Felix to ever feel bound to her by that obligation. They would have to be more sensible from now on.

To Sylvie's immense relief, Dieter didn't come to watch, but she spotted Nikki and Tall Valter sitting at the table at the front. Valter seem to be enjoying himself and doing his best to catch Céline's eye, but Nikki never took his gaze off Sylvie. He was clearly trying to intimidate her, and unfortunately, it was working.

He was there the following evening as well, sitting in the same seat with a single glass of wine, arms folded as he watched the performances, and it took all Sylvie's strength not to run off the stage. She plucked up the courage to approach him when the dancers took a break and the audience took to the floor, but as soon as he saw her winding her way through the crowd, he left.

'I've blown everything,' she told Marcel when she visited him the morning after the second visit. She dropped her head into her hands. 'I feel like I'm constantly waiting for arrest or a bullet in the back of my head. I don't think it would take much for him to have a reason. I don't know whether Baumann has sent him or if he's come of his own accord.'

Marcel poured her a small glass of pastis. 'I've had word on the Henri situation. We're meeting above Café Napoleon on Rue Versailles at four tomorrow. Henri should be able to walk that far. If he can't, then our plans will have to change again, so it will be a good test. Let me give your predicament some thought and see what I can do to take the heat off you. Bring Felix with you.'

She left feeling a little brighter, but still unsure what could be done.

She discovered the answer the following day. She and Felix strolled to Café Napoleon arm in arm. They slipped through the door behind the bar and upstairs into a shuttered room where Marcel was waiting. Presently Antoine arrived, accompanied by Henri, still dressed as a woman and now sporting a hat with a short veil. He was limping and supported himself with a stick and seemed glad to sit down. Marcel eyed him appraisingly.

'You can manage this far?'

'I can.'

'Good. We're received word from England. The networks have arranged a route. We are getting Henri out tomorrow night, and Sylvie is going with him.'

Chapter Thirty-One

Felix reached for her hand and squeezed it tightly. She couldn't look at him, but from the corner of her eye, she saw he was staring intently at his wine glass.

'I don't want to leave. There is still work for me to do here,' she said.

Marcel smiled. 'I don't mean permanently – though I am not discounting that if it becomes necessary. Henri can walk a short distance as we see, but he can't manage alone. You'll go as far as Angoulême with him. You'll be away for two or three nights, but it means you won't be fretting over what Nikki might do. You agree with me, don't you, Felix?'

Felix gripped Sylvie's hand tighter.

'It doesn't matter what I think. Sylvie can make her own decisions.' He looked at her. 'But Henri needs someone to take him to safety and you're the best person to do it.'

'I don't want Sylvie risking her life for me,' Henri said.

'I risk my life every day,' she pointed out. Her initial dismay had subsided now she realised her absence would be temporary. She leaned across the table, looking Marcel in the eye. 'What is the plan?'

'Tomorrow night, you begin your performance as usual. Henri will be waiting in the apartment upstairs. After your solo dance in the second half, Henri will join you downstairs. Leave by the door from the dressing room to the alley.'

'I'll make sure the rubbish is cleared from the door,' Antoine said.

'Go along to the road behind Mirabelle,' Marcel continued. 'At the crossroads at the top of the hill, there is a row of buildings that was destroyed in the bombing last year. There will be a lorry loaded with building materials waiting to drive you overnight. You'll have to hide among the building materials, so I'm afraid your night won't be very comfortable.'

'Henri, will your leg stand it?' Sylvie asked, thinking of how he had limped into the café.

'I'll crawl on my hands and knees if I have to,' Henri replied.

'Will Henri be dressed like that?' Felix asked.

'I think it best not,' Marcel said, casting an eye over him. 'Your own clothes and the identification papers you were given before. Sylvie, you will need whatever change of clothes you think is appropriate.'

She nodded. Underwear for two days could be rolled small, a sturdy pair of shoes to change into when she came offstage. A sweater for warmth and thick socks for walking.

'Blue pyjamas,' Felix whispered.

She stifled a giggle and glared at him. 'Behave yourself. We're trying to be serious, and everyone is watching.'

She remembered Nikki staring at her at the checkpoint, like a tomcat intent on catching a mouse, and shivered.

'Won't it be suspicious if I don't go back onstage? We have regular patrons who know the dancers always finish the night together.'

'Sylvie makes a good point,' Antoine said. 'Her absence the other evening caused comment. If she is not dancing, people will wonder why.'

'Do you think you could vomit on demand as you leave the stage?' Felix asked, giving her a wicked grin. 'That would convincingly explain your absence.'

She stuck her tongue out at him playfully.

'We need a diversion of some sort,' Marcel mused. Silence descended as they all considered the options. Henri rubbed his fingers across his cheeks, and something in his gesture ignited a memory in Sylvie.

'Your cold cream with the plastic explosive! We can use that.'

'You are not blowing up my club,' Antoine exclaimed.

Sylvie waved a hand. 'We'll only use enough to cause a distraction. I can lay a fuse to the bollard at the near end of the alley. If I light it before I go onstage, I should have time to dance and leave the stage before it goes off.'

'That could work,' Marcel said. 'Antoine, make sure everyone is evacuated into the street at the front. The more chaos, the better, because that way no one will notice who is or isn't there.'

'I'm sure I will manage admirably,' Antoine said.

'Once everyone evacuates, I will slip down the alleyway and trail Sylvie and Henri to the lorry,' Felix suggested. 'I'll keep watch along the road to cover them leaving. If the Germans somehow discover what's happening and give chase…'

He mimed shooting. Sylvie remembered that had been Felix's role in the raid on the town hall and the factory sabotage. She bit her lip.

'If you're caught with a gun, they'll shoot you,' she cautioned.

He shrugged. 'I know the risks just as you do. I can't stand by and watch you risk your life. If it comes to it, I'll turn my gun on myself rather than be taken.'

Sylvie felt for her necklace and rubbed her fingers over the cross. 'I have my means of escape too.'

'You won't need them,' Marcel said. 'Everything will go well. Sylvie will get Henri to safety and come back within a week. Felix, do that. Now, everyone, time to leave.'

Felix was silent as he and Sylvie walked arm in arm. Just before going their separate ways, they kissed and Felix regarded her seriously.

'What if Marcel is right and you should leave?'

'You think I should go back to England?' Her legs drained of blood.

'My head says yes. My heart breaks at the thought. I picture you being captured and interrogated and my heart wants to explode from my body. You'll be safer in England.'

Felix put his hand on her cheek. 'We both know you'll return home sooner or later. Maybe sooner is better before I fall even more in love with you and can't bear to part ever.'

Sylvie couldn't speak. She didn't know what to say. He sounded distraught, as if loving her was the worst thing possible. He shook his head and walked away, waving an arm to ward her off. He loved her! She should be elated, but Felix was right to view it as a tragedy. The longer they spent together, the harder it would be to part.

———

Even though she had carried out numerous after-hours activities, no evening since Sylvie had arrived at Mirabelle had felt so significant as this one. All the preparations were in place. The fuse was laid along the alleyway to the bollard where the plastic explosive was stuck. Her snakeskin bag containing a fresh blouse and pair of knickers was ready under her stool to snatch up when the time came to leave, and she had worn a sensible skirt and flat shoes to the club, which would aid her flight.

She and Felix had avoided speaking alone, a sense of awkwardness between them creating a barrier. She should have told him she loved him back. He must have taken her silence for reluctance. They passed the bread too politely and sat either side of Estelle as they ate so they didn't have to make eye contact. She would have to deal with that when she came back from Angoulême. All she had to do for now was dance as usual.

As the first number of the evening started, Sylvie plastered on a smile and followed Estelle onto the stage. She scanned the audience for familiar faces. Nikki was in the front row as before, and she hid her distaste. With a jolt, she saw Dieter was sitting at a table at the back on his own, making his way through a bottle of wine.

Sylvie faltered, causing Estelle's hand to become tangled in the end of Sylvie's red silk scarf.

'Concentrate,' Estelle hissed, shaking her hand free.

Sylvie murmured an apology and let her eyes glaze so that the audience became a blur. As soon as the dance ended, Dieter left his table and began to make his way forwards. Sylvie met him halfway.

'I need to speak to you,' he slurred.

He was drunk.

'I asked you not to come here,' Sylvie said. 'Does Nikki know you are here?'

'Nikki's here? I didn't know. I must talk to you.'

Sylvie glanced towards Antoine. 'I have to be onstage again soon. Please let me ask permission first. Wait outside.'

By the time she reached Antoine at the bar, Felix was already there.

'Why is Baumann here?'

'I don't know. I'll have to speak to him. I can't risk a scene.' She screwed up the end of her scarf in frustration.

'Be quick,' Felix said. 'I'll go warn Henri that things aren't going according to plan.'

Sylvie turned to go, but he caught her by the wrist. His expression made her insides melt.

'If you need me, call my name.'

Dieter was leaning against the bollard in the alleyway. Sylvie tried not to look at the waxy green substance at the base and the line of fuse trailing away.

'What do you want, Dieter?'

'You came.' He walked unsteadily towards her. She walked up the street, guessing correctly that he would follow.

'I can't stop thinking about everything you accused me of.' He shook his head. 'I believed in it, all of it. I believed in what I was doing.'

'Believed in what?' Sylvie asked.

'In Germany. In the Führer.'

His face creased in horror, as if he was unable to believe the words coming out of his mouth.

'I grew up in a country where my people were shamed and desperate, then *the Führer* came and promised us a new beginning. A greater Germany. My parents' faces wore hope for the first time. My brother was four years older than me. He was the first boy in my town to join the Hitler Youth. He truly believed.'

His eyes shone, but Sylvie was aghast to see a film of tears. 'Why are you telling me this? It won't change my mind.'

'My brother died on the fifteenth of May, shot down near Guernsey. I received a letter from my *mutti* today.' Dieter's face crumpled. 'What better world is there for my brother? His son will grow up fatherless, his wife without a husband to care for her.'

'I'm so sorry.' Sylvie put her hand on his arm.

He looked at her bleakly. 'Sorry for the death of a German? An enemy who has conquered your country?'

'For the loss of your brother,' Sylvie replied. 'For the grief it has brought to you.'

She looked at him; a broken man. How awful it must be

to lose a brother, and how tragic that it took only such a personal pain for him to question the war.

'Why did you come to me?' she asked gently.

'Because my feelings haven't changed. I love you. Perhaps even more now than ever before. You said things to me nobody else has. You were very foolish to speak to me like that, but brave. You are a woman in a thousand, Sylvie.'

'But I'm still not the woman for you.' She removed her hand. 'I must get back. Please go home. Don't drink any more.'

'I think you are right, I should leave now.' He leaned forward and brushed his lips over her cheek. 'Thank you for your kindness, *Fräulein* Duchene.'

He walked away.

Once he was out of sight, Sylvie ran inside. She collided with someone who was leaving. Nikki. He curled a lip then pushed past her. Sylvie ran into the changing room. Someone had left a box of matches on top of her bag. She lit the fuse and lowered it out of the window, watching as the tiny red glow made its way along. She had eight minutes before it reached the bollard. Eight minutes more to dance.

She adjusted her scarf around her neck and made her way through the curtains. A couple of men in the audience whistled and she flashed them smiles without bothering to register their faces. She kept her eyes fixed on Felix as she crossed to the stage. She clicked her fingers and Felix began to play the introductory bars.

Six minutes.

As she had on the very first afternoon, Sylvie danced her way over to the piano, rolling her hips and shimmying.

Felix slowed the tempo a little and stood, leaning over the piano towards her. She slowly slid the scarf from around her neck and held it at arm's length before dropping it on the floor to a barrage of appreciative whistles. She heard them, but she danced as if he was the only man in the room.

Three minutes.

As the music reached a crescendo, Sylvie strutted and swayed back to the centre of the stage for a final kick and flourish ending in a deep bow. She was rewarded with cheers and thunderous applause.

Two minutes.

Her breath froze in her throat. Dieter was back. He stood by the door, his face a picture of misery. She had never meant for him to witness it. There was no way anyone watching could believe that she and Felix had never made love.

She picked up the scarf and ran off the stage and through the curtains. Henri was waiting in the changing rooms. He rose as Sylvie tore off her heeled shoes and threw them in the corner.

'Are you ready?'

She wriggled out of her dress and pulled on a sensible skirt and blouse.

One minute.

'What did you do out there? I've never heard the audience like it,' Henri asked.

'Later,' she answered, tying her shoelaces.

She picked up her bag and jammed a felt hat down over her hair as best she could. The scarf was lying with her discarded dress. The night might be cold. She picked it up and wrapped it around her throat.

'Let's go.'

There was a loud explosion and hell broke loose.

The blast was louder than Sylvie had expected. For a moment she could hear nothing, then a high-pitched ringing began in her ears, which faded into screaming and shouting from outside. She blinked and came to her senses.

'Quickly, this way.'

She threw her bag over her shoulder, grabbed Henri's travelling case in her free hand and pushed open the door into the alley. Antoine had cleared the larger piles of rubbish, but there was new debris underfoot from the blast. Henri followed her out, lurching as he tried to place his walking stick. Every step he took was accompanied by a grunt of discomfort.

They moved in almost total darkness, the tall buildings blocking the moonlight. Surely the alley was not this long in the daytime? From behind them, at the other end of the alley, came voices mingling. Sylvie heard Céline's voice raised in exasperation. Antoine had done a good job of ushering everyone into the street.

Sylvie and Henri emerged into the street behind the club where they could move quicker.

'Not far now,' Sylvie whispered.

'*Fräulein* Duchene!'

Sylvie froze.

Not him. Not now.

She turned around slowly, hoping to brazen it out. 'Dieter, what are you doing here?'

He stood at the end of the alley, partly hidden in shadows.

'I realised I had left my gloves on the table. I came back and saw you dance. I saw *how* you danced. You told me there was no other man, but after I saw you with the pianist, I knew you lied.'

He looked past Sylvie to Henri.

'I looked for you in the street after the explosion. You did not appear, so I went into the changing room and found the open door to the alley. Now I find you leaving with a suitcase. Both of you, move into the light.'

Sylvie shot Henri a despairing look as they obeyed. Dieter raised his brows.

'Who is this?'

'My cousin,' Sylvie said. 'I'm taking him to my aunt's house.'

It sounded feeble as she said it.

'Another cousin? I don't think so, *Fräulein* Duchene.' Dieter drew his revolver. 'A British spy who disappeared was last seen travelling in this direction four days ago. His description matches your "cousin".'

Sylvie and Henri exchanged glances.

'Are you with the Resistance?' Dieter looked stricken. 'How could I have been so stupid! All the time you spent with me was a lie. You were taking what I said back to pass on to the enemy.'

The sense of betrayal in his voice was gut-wrenching.

'There was nothing you told me that I could use against you,' Sylvie said.

'So I was even useless as a target.' Dieter gave a bitter laugh.

Behind him, a figure appeared in the shadows. Felix had followed as promised. She didn't dare look at him, in case she gave his presence away. Didn't dare show relief. His gun was raised, levelled at Dieter's head. Dieter didn't realise he was in danger.

'I should arrest you.'

'Yes, you should.' Sylvie's lips shook. She clamped them shut.

The pistol in Dieter's hand wavered. He raised it a little higher, pointing it at her heart.

'They'll torture you.'

'Yes, they will.' She took a step towards him, wondering if she could get close enough to attempt to disarm him before Felix shot him.

'I order you to stand still!'

Sylvie raised her hands and obeyed. Dieter's eyes were fixed on her, full of anger.

'If I condemned you to that, I could not live with myself.'

'Then let me go.' She edged closer to him, sick to her stomach with terror, and held her hands out imploringly. The pistol remained pointed at her chest.

'If I do that, I am betraying my country.'

'Then shoot me yourself,' Sylvie said. At least that death would be quicker and less painful. 'You'll have killed a member of the Resistance and be a hero like your brother.'

Dieter gave a sob of anguish. That might be the key. She held her hands out to him.

'Tonight, when you talked about your brother, you bared your soul. Don't let there be more deaths in this war. Walk away and forget you saw me.'

His eyes met hers.

'Please.'

'Go,' he whispered.

Sylvie didn't move, not daring to believe she had heard correctly.

'Now!'

He jerked the pistol upwards towards her, and two shots rang out.

Chapter Thirty-Two

Dieter jerked forward and slumped to his knees, the pistol falling beside him.

He had not fired at her.

He fell onto his front.

Crying his name, Sylvie ran to where he lay and dropped to her knees to roll him over. In the moonlight, she could see blood blooming across his chest like roses. He mouthed something she couldn't hear.

'Lie still,' she told him. She put her hand over the wound but the gushing was already becoming weaker. Dieter's mouth went slack and his eyes rolled back. Sylvie sobbed. Felix appeared beside her, lifting her upright, holding her close. She rounded on him, eyes burning, but he shook his head.

'It wasn't me.'

There had been two shots in quick succession. The 'Double Tap' signature of SOE. Marcel stepped out of a doorway, revolver in hand.

'Sylvie, you have to leave. People will have heard the shot.'

'You didn't have to shoot him. He was going to let us leave.'

'He raised his pistol.'

Marcel must have seen Dieter gesturing towards her with the gun as she had backed away. But only Sylvie was able to hear Dieter's words and see his expression.

'He was a dead man the moment he saw you and Henri,' Marcel said.

Sylvie's eyes blurred. 'What will you do? You can't leave him here.'

Marcel regarded the corpse. 'If he disappears, there will be questions.'

Felix ran his hands through his hair. 'Leaving him here will lead to questions too. Whatever we do, his friends will tell the authorities he spent time here.'

He touched Sylvie's arm. 'They'll come for you, Sylvie.'

Sylvie grew cold. The situation was desperate. A dead officer couldn't be left in the street, but people could not just disappear. Not Germans, at any rate. A woman could though. A couple could. She looked at the waiting truck that Henri was hobbling towards. The thought of sharing it with a corpse was stomach churning, but this was no ordinary corpse; this was Dieter.

'We'll take him with us. Somewhere along the way there will be the opportunity to...' To what? Not bury him? Whatever means they found, Dieter would not receive a dignified ceremony.

'When Dieter's absence is noticed, the authorities will

search, but I'll be missing too. People will assume we ran away together.'

Marcel nodded. 'It might work. We'll get in first. I'll tell Antoine to report your disappearance to the *gendarmerie* at first light. He must accuse Baumann of playing a part in your disappearance. Everyone knows you had been in a complicated affair. Enough people saw you together this evening.'

'But it will only work for a day or two. When you come back without him, you'll be arrested,' Felix pointed out.

Sylvie met Marcel's eyes. She had worked out the implications before Felix. She lowered her head. This was the part of the plan that tore her heart to pieces.

'I can't come back. I'll have to return to England with Henri.'

'No!' Felix reeled as if he too had been shot.

Seeing his reaction, Sylvie willed herself not to cry. 'I've been compromised. I bungled everything with Dieter from the start, and this situation is my fault. I let him grow too close. I got too involved.'

'You did what you had to do,' Marcel said.

His absolution didn't make her feel any better.

'If I come back, the Abwehr, or worse, the Gestapo, will come for me. I don't know if I'd be strong enough to withstand questioning. I'd put everyone else in danger. It's the only way, isn't it, Marcel?'

'I think so. I said before it could become too risky and that time has come. I'll have a message sent to England and get in touch with the cell you're heading to next. We'll do what we can to get you new papers for when you meet the next courier.' Marcel paused and glanced at Dieter's body. 'I'll see if the driver has a tarpaulin to wrap him in. Say your goodbyes quickly.'

Marcel picked up Henri's case and began assisting him to walk the rest of the way to the truck.

'It has to be this way,' Sylvie whispered.

Felix gathered her in his arms. 'I know it's the only course of action. It isn't safe for you here any longer. Maybe not for any of us, but for you especially. Living without you will be painful, but knowing you were dead would be beyond endurance.'

Sylvie sobbed. She pressed her cheek against Felix's chest and held him tight. He buried his face in her hair. 'Dieter asked me if there was anyone else. I told him there wasn't. I lied. There is you, Felix. I love you. I don't want to leave you. It's too soon to say goodbye.'

'Any time would be too soon.' He held her tightly, arms encasing her as if he intended never to let her go. 'Sylvie. *Je t'aime.*'

Marcel coughed discreetly behind them. He was back and holding a piece of sacking.

'The best I can do. Let's get him in the truck.'

Together the three of them carried Dieter to the truck and laid him on the sacking. Henri covered him with another piece. There was nothing left to do. Sylvie and Felix faced each other. It was crucial to get away, but she couldn't bear to leave. She couldn't move. Not towards him, not away from him.

'Come with me,' Sylvie said.

'No.' He kissed her forehead. 'I belong here where I can

keep working to free France. The war will end one day, and there will be a reckoning. I intend to play my part in it.'

She pulled him down into a kiss, lips burning against his. Passion and heartbreak and love melding into one head-spinning moment. She pressed herself against him, trying to memorise the feel of his body, the scent of his skin, the taste of his kiss.

Felix released her. Tears glinted in his eyes, turning them into gleaming orbs of blackness. 'If you love me as truly as I love you, then leave now. Live.'

'Live too,' she whispered.

'I'm sorry it ended like this,' Marcel said, as Sylvie climbed inside. 'Safe travels.'

Sylvie's last sight as Marcel closed the doors was of Felix standing in the moonlight, one hand raised in farewell.

Chapter Thirty-Three

Sylvie huddled down in the back of the lorry amid piles of bricks, covered in a tarpaulin and barely able to breathe. She leaned against Henri, and they held hands. She couldn't look at Dieter. They were driven out of the city and were presumably taking farm tracks and small roads from the jolting of the vehicle. At some point, she must have fallen asleep because the next thing she knew was when the back doors were opened and sunlight streamed onto her face. The driver gave her a crooked smile.

'We'll deal with *that* now.' He sneered in Dieter's direction. 'Strip him. There must be nothing on the body to identify it.'

Sylvie reached for Dieter's hand protectively. It was cold and stiff. She climbed out of the truck and looked around. They were in a wooded valley where the river was wide and slow. Sylvie and the driver carried Dieter, now clad in just his underwear, to the water while Henri waited at the truck.

'It will sink deep and the fish will dine well,' the driver said. 'No one will find it.'

'*He*, not *it*,' Sylvie corrected. Her voice cracked and tears filled her eyes. 'He was a person. His name was Dieter, and he had a mother and father who loved him. He liked to dance and eat sweet cakes.'

The driver spat on the ground. 'What is this? A eulogy? Why does he deserve that when so many French men and women lie unmarked?'

Sylvie lifted her eyes to his. 'Because if we can't recognise our enemy as people too, how will we ever stop fighting them?'

The driver looked unimpressed. 'Back in the truck. There's a mill in the village. I'm to leave you there. I'll dispose of the uniform, but I'm keeping *his* boots.'

Sylvie blinked her tears away. She climbed back into the truck, taking one final look at the river. It soothed her slightly to think of Dieter spending eternity in such a beautiful place. The driver was right. How many in this war would be so fortunate as to have their resting place known and remembered?

From the mill, they were taken onwards in the back of a truck loaded with sacks of flour and left at the gates of an imposing chateau. From there, they were driven in the back seat of an immaculately polished Citroën Traction Avant driven through the afternoon by an aristocratic elderly woman with a severe face and a Bible on the passenger seat. Henri was in obvious pain, and Sylvie thanked her foresight for sewing the sleeping tablets into her bag lining. She dug them out and while he lapsed in and out of consciousness, she could grieve in private as towns and villages passed by unnoticed.

Poor tragic Dieter, whose parents would grow old thinking their son had been so stupid to be taken in by a French dancer and abandon everything to run away with her. She couldn't think about Felix or the grief would be too strong to contain quietly.

They spent the night in the village of Carrouges, deep in the forests of Normandy, and the following morning they exchanged their clothes for fresh ones, not that anyone would have seen what they had left Nantes in. Sylvie hesitated over her red silk scarf. She should get rid of it, but it was the only keepsake she had taken from the club. She rolled it small and put it at the bottom of her bag. They were given new papers, and now Sylvie and Henri were Monsieur and Madame Villiers, with a travel permit to visit Sylvie's sister in Falaise who had recently given birth.

'Marcel has done his work well,' Sylvie said. 'They've changed the route because we're nowhere near Angoulême.'

Henri folded his papers, taking care to make them look more dog-eared than the one that had caused notice in Nantes.

'Do you think your plan has worked?'

Sylvie couldn't answer. Even trying to name the people she had left behind brought tears to her eyes.

After a long day of travelling, they were dropped at a church on the outskirts of Bayeux. A woman who introduced herself as Anne led them down into the crypt beneath the church.

'I'm afraid plans have changed. We had hoped to get you across La Manche, but that won't be possible. We've had word from Britain not to try to move you at the moment. You'll be safe here.'

'Do you know why?' Sylvie asked. She recalled the night drops of weapons. There had been rumours of something big, and this might be it.

'I'm afraid I can't tell you anything.'

'I notice she didn't say whether or not she knew what was happening,' Henri commented drily once Anne had left them.

'Whatever it is, I hope it is worth it,' Sylvie muttered. 'I hope everything has been worth it.'

———

For five nights, Sylvie and Henri hid in the crypt, cut off from the world, the darkness eased only by a single torch. The solid walls surrounding them muffled most sound, but on the second day, the silence was broken by a thunderous roar followed by what could only be an explosion. Henri had been dozing; the final painkiller doing its job, but he woke with a start.

'Something is happening. An air raid, I think,' Sylvie whispered.

'Our side or theirs?'

Sylvie could only shrug. She and Henri held hands, their fearful expressions made into masks by the dim shadows, and listened for anything that could give them a clue, but there was nothing. Sylvie took the cross from around her neck and pocketed it. To wear the symbol in this house of God was a blasphemy when she could not even summon the faith to pray that her friends were safe and that the sacred ground she and Henri were on would survive whatever was happening outside.

On the fifth day, the priest came into the crypt and took them both by the hands, his face radiant. 'You may come out now, my children.'

They followed him up the stairs and stepped into a twilight that seemed impossibly harsh. The square outside the church was filled with soldiers, mingling with the townspeople. Children ran around, playing chase. Sylvie was so shocked at the sight that it took her a moment to realise Henri was pulling her sleeve and laughing.

'These are our boys, Sylvie,' he shouted. He turned and kissed her full on the mouth. 'There are the British!'

'Americans, too,' said a man voice from behind them. Sylvie turned to see a young man strolling towards them. He had dark skin and a neatly trimmed black moustache. He was the first black person Sylvie had seen since arriving in France. If ever there was a symbol that something had changed, the handsome sergeant holding out his packet of cigarettes was it.

'So you're English. The padre tells me you've been working undercover.'

'I'm no' English – I'm Scottish and proud of it,' Henri

said, holding a hand out to the sergeant. His accent has changed into something almost impenetrable to Sylvie's ears. The second surprise in as many minutes. 'Angus McLeish, at your service.'

'Sergeant Aaron Evers at yours.'

Sylvie shook Evers's hand.

'Sylvia Crichton.'

Her voice felt tight in her throat. She wasn't ready to be that woman yet. Perhaps she never would be.

'What happened?' she asked Sergeant Evers.

'Operation Overlord is what happened,' he said. 'We invaded by the beaches. Thousands of us. Your boy Winston once said we'd fight them there, and did we ever! Bayeux is the first town to be liberated, but we're here now and we aren't leaving until Hitler is on the run.' He gestured for them to follow, and they fell in beside him. 'I guess you will want to be heading home as soon as you can. Let me take you to some of yours and they can help you out.'

Evers passed them on to a sergeant major who professed incredulity that Sylvie and Henri had been working and living in France undercover for so long. He, in turn, handed them over to a weary-looking doctor in a hospital tent. Henri – or Angus, as Sylvie would have to remind herself to call him – was taken off to have his injured knee treated. He was warned that his injury was not a priority, and as Sylvie stared at the fifty or more beds all occupied with men, she couldn't help but agree that in comparison, he had got off lightly.

'Strap the wee bastard up so I can stand upright on my own and that'll do me for now,' Angus said. He limped off, talking nineteen to the dozen with an orderly, leaving Sylvie alone with the doctor.

'I'm afraid we can't send you back to England now, Miss Crichton. Operation Overlord is just the beginning,' the doctor explained. 'If you've got any experience of nursing, we'll be very glad of your help. More units will be crossing the Channel, but another pair of hands will be welcome.'

'I'm FANY trained,' Sylvie answered. 'I'll do anything I can to help.'

The doctor shook her by the hand. 'Good to hear it. I'll get an orderly to take you to headquarters and see about finding you a uniform.'

For three weeks, Sylvie worked in the field hospital, tending the wounded as Angelique had done when she met Dennis. She spent long days and hard nights with aching feet and a sore back, bandaging, stitching, soothing and watching the men pull through and be moved to recovery wards or slip away. The work was exhausting and often distressing when the screams of men in pain filled the tents, but Sylvie felt as if something had come full circle. Her mother had been a nurse and a dancer, and now Sylvie was fulfilling the same role, though how Angelique had found time for romance was beyond Sylvie's comprehension. So many bodies passed through her care that she didn't have time to learn their names, barely had time to catch a breath, let alone have anything more than the briefest of exchanges. The cots seemed to stretch for miles, with an ever-regenerating stream of patients.

Whenever she was granted ten minutes of peace, she snatched time to visit Angus. His skills as a wireless operator had quickly found him in demand, and he spent his days relaying messages back and forth to England, his leg propped up on a stool.

'Have you heard anything about Nantes?' she asked as they sat together drinking cocoa one evening in a corner of the makeshift mess. The thunderous explosions and screams of battle had ceased for the time being. It was the same question she asked every time they met.

'Nothing, I'm afraid,' he replied. 'The message that you were travelling with me was the last contact anyone had with the cell. I'm sorry, Sylvia. I know you want to hear something from Marcel, but no news is good news, as they say.'

Sylvie didn't answer. Not if the reason there was no news was because anyone who could give news was lying broken and tortured in a Gestapo cell, accused of murdering a German. Of course, Felix could not have left with her, but not knowing his fate, or that of Marcel, Monsieur Julien and the girls at the Mirabelle, would haunt her for the rest of her life. She leaned against Angus, and he put his arm around her.

'Dinna worry, lass. Our lads are moving further across France by the day.'

His words were intended to comfort her, and she tried to let them and not think of the awful rumours of departing

Germans torching houses and hanging civilians as final acts of aggression.

'I hear that, in some places, the German army are fighting back, but in others they've abandoned towns at the first hint of us approaching. The French are taking up arms and fighting back, whether they're in the Resistance or not. I spent so many hours hauling boxes of weapons through the countryside in the dark for Tomas to distribute, I only hope there will be enough.' She sighed. 'I only hope I *did* enough and my time there wasn't wasted.'

So much hoping. But hoping wasn't enough to win a war.

'Nothing you did was wasted effort, lass. There are some brave men and women in that city, ready to take their country back, and it surely won't be long before it's liberated.'

Sylvie kissed Angus's cheek, helped him to his feet and passed him the pair of crutches he used. She had grown quite fond of him in the time they had spent together.

'I'd better go,' she said. 'My unit is heading off with the mobile hospital in the morning. We've done our turn at the back, and now we're heading to the frontline for a stint treating the first casualties. I'm not sure if I'll be back this way for some time.'

She smoothed down her khaki skirt and adjusted her jacket sleeves. Wearing a uniform again felt constricting but had become normal. The time she had worn gauzy dresses with feathers and sequins felt like a dream that she had obstinately clung on to after she had woken. Only the red silk scarf that she kept tucked in her pillow was proof that she had been there at all. Sometimes, she dreamed of trying to race the army down through France to make her way back to Nantes but that would be suicidal. Besides, without knowing what she would find there, it was a futile gesture.

'It's probably too much to hope I'll end up in Nantes at some point.'

Angus smiled. 'You never know, but don't you want to get home to England? As soon as I get the chance, I'm away back to Stirling so see my wife and bairns.'

He kissed her on the cheek again.

'It was good to meet you, Sylvia. Look me up if you ever come up to Scotland.'

Chapter Thirty-Four

I t was late August before Sylvie returned to England on a ship filled with convalescing soldiers. Someone must have passed on the information because she was identified on arrival and told to attend the Baker Street office. Two days later, her FANY uniform neatly laundered and her hair freshly done, Sylvie presented a written report to the secretary, then sat on a chair in the corridor while it was taken and read, drinking a cup of tea. Some things were worth returning to England for.

After a short while, an efficient young man appeared at her side.

'Major Swift will see you now.'

Uncle Max was sitting behind his desk and greeted her with a smile. 'It's good to see you, Sylvia. You may not have heard because you were travelling, but Nantes was liberated yesterday.'

Sylvie filled with elation. Nantes was free. She closed

her eyes and tried to picture the *mairie* devoid of swastikas, the chateau without sentries on the battlements, Mirabelle without a sea of German uniforms in the audience. Had Nikki and the Valters been captured or killed? Was Dieter's death only brought forward by a matter of weeks, or would he have been spared to return home? She could go mad thinking of possibilities.

'What have you heard from Marcel? Has he sent many skeds since I left?'

'That's classified, Sylvia.'

'Please. Things happened on the night I left. I have to find out.'

Max looked hesitant then said, 'After the brief sked telling us you and McLeish were coming home, we heard nothing for weeks. Three weeks ago, communications started again but only a brief reply to a sked to confirm the local résistants would be able to meet an arms drop. With all the excitement over D-Day, the policy became essential communications only, but our troops are still spreading across France. I'm sure Marcel will be complimentary about your performance in the fullness of time.'

It hadn't been praise she was hoping to hear, but whether her friends were safe. *Librarian* was still in operation in some form, which gave her hope. She would have to cling on to that until she heard otherwise. She would have to believe Felix was alive.

Max straightened the papers on his desk. Sylvie's report was topmost. 'Now, you have a week's leave. You can stay in London and we'll put you up in a hotel, or you can return to Scarborough and report back afterwards. We've found you a role here that will use your language skills. You'll be listening to the reports coming in from France and translating them into English. You'll be working across the road from our office here.'

'You can't send me back to France?'

'Your work in France is done,' Max said. 'SOE did what it was set up to do. Operatives who are still there will continue to support the Resistance and military and coordinate sabotage if necessary, but the army and air force will finish the job. Don't worry, my dear. There is still work to be done here and we need you to play your part.'

He stood, signalling the interview was ended. He leaned over the table and shook her hand.

'Welcome home, Sylvia.'

She knew then that she was back in England for good.

London, England

1945

'What time do you call this?' Mrs Underwood's face was stern.

Sylvie's friend Maisie squinted at her watch but gave up trying to read the time and beamed at their landlady. 'Late?' she slurred.

Their landlady folded her arms and glared sourly at the three girls. 'Very late. My rules clearly say the front door is bolted at ten sharp and yet here you are beating it down at half past one in the morning!'

Sylvie adopted an expression of contrition.

'We're very sorry, Mrs Underwood. But today of all days, you must forgive us. It's VE Day. The war is officially over!'

She had started trying to be grave but couldn't stop from smiling as she said the words.

No more war.

'We would have been back earlier, but the centre of London was so crowded. We had to wait ages until we could get seats on a bus,' explained Susan, the third member of the guilty trio.

For a moment, the girls forgot Mrs Underwood's disapproval as shared memories of the celebration filled them with joy. Strangers hugged and passed around bottles of beer. The bus – when it did arrive – had echoed with singing.

The day Britain had been waiting for had arrived. Papers had been signed ordering the cessation of German operations and the war was officially ended, and no one was going to pass up the chance to celebrate, least of all Sylvie and her two coworkers in the Baker Street office.

No one except Mrs Underwood, it seemed.

'I will make an exception today because of the circumstances, however, I will not tolerate drunken behaviour.' She glanced at Susan, noticing how her Elizabeth Arden Victory Red lipstick was smeared across the side of her jaw. 'And I most certainly will not tolerate loose behaviour.'

The three girls did their best to keep straight faces as they were lectured, and Mrs Underwood allowed them to pass inside, before pointedly bolting the door and returning to her bedroom. Sylvie and the other girls collapsed on the comfy chairs in the small parlour that the boarders were permitted to use the evening between six and ten. They kicked off their shoes with sighs of relief. Three of Sylvie's toes were blistered and her big toenail was bruised from being trodden on as she had been hustled to and fro in the great crush of bodies down Pall Mall.

'I told you we should have gone home with those men from South Norwood instead of trying to sneak back in,' Susan said.

'I can't believe Mrs U didn't go and join in the party,' Maisie said. 'I wonder what it would take for her to enjoy herself.'

'I don't know,' Sylvie said. Her eyes drifted to the framed photographs on the mantelpiece. They included one of a slightly younger Mrs Underwood standing beside a man in the uniform of the Home Guard. 'It's a celebration, but some people don't have as much to celebrate as we do.'

She felt her eyes pricking. The night had been the first time since returning from France that she had felt truly free and happy, but now it was tinged with a sense of melancholy. Were people celebrating in Nantes? How many of her friends were alive to join in? What of the nameless men she had nursed as the field hospitals followed the fighting across France? Not knowing played on her mind.

Maisie nodded understandingly. 'My sister's fiancé died at Caen and she was close to becoming an old maid, but in spring she met a nice coalman from Brockley Park, and now she's expecting a baby. If you lost someone you loved, they wouldn't want you to mourn forever, would they?'

'No. I don't think he would,' Sylvie murmured.

'He?' Susan sat forward. 'He who? You never talk much about what you did, Sylvia.'

'Just a man I knew for a while,' Sylvie said. 'While I was working with FANY. You know what it was like. You meet someone, hit it off, then circumstances get in the way and you lose touch.'

The girls nodded sagely. Susan had been a land girl and driven tractors in Kent before coming up to London to resume her career as a teacher. Maisie had worked in Woolworths in Lewisham. Both of them had plenty of stories to tell of the men they had met. Sylvie shared stories about the nursing she'd done with FANY after D-Day and managed to avoid telling anyone what she had done in the months before then.

But that was the past. She'd been back in England for almost a year and still didn't feel settled. It was time to put the past behind her, one way or another.

———

The next morning, during her tea break, Sylvie slipped out of the typing-pool room and across the road to visit Uncle Max.

'Sylvia, my dear, how wonderful to see you,' Max said. 'How is your head? Were you out on the town last night?'

'Wasn't everyone?' Sylvie laughed.

'I'm glad you popped over. I wondered if you had given any thought to what you plan to do next? Your supervisor, Mr Reynolds, thinks you have potential to become a personal secretary in the Civil Service.'

'How exciting.' Sylvie gave a brittle smile. SOE had no purpose now, and there was no telling how long the Baker Street offices would be in operation. She would be out of a job before long. She wasn't worried. She had excellent references. Dennis had written them and his obvious guilt at the way their affair had ended painted Sylvie in a glorious light. But Uncle Max's suggestion didn't fill Sylvie with as much enthusiasm as it did Mr Reynolds.

'I don't know yet. There are a few things I'd like to put to rest. In fact, that's the reason I came to see you. I couldn't stop thinking about what happened after I left.'

Uncle Max gave her a penetrating look. 'I gather from your cell leader's report that there are certain aspects of your time there you neglected to share with us.'

'*Personal* aspects,' Sylvie replied, feeling her cheeks redden.

'Ones that might have had a bearing on your choice of actions,' Uncle Max said. 'Ah well, it's all done with now.'

'Can you put me in touch with Marcel? I would love to see him again,' Sylvie asked. 'I don't know if it is the done thing…'

Uncle Max smiled. 'There's no reason why not. Oddly enough, he's in town at the moment. If you give me your address, I'll pass it on to his hotel. He's only in London for a few days with his wife, but I'm sure he'd love to hear from you.'

'Yes, please!' Sylvie exclaimed. She tried to hide her excitement but failed. Marcel was in London. That was more than she had hoped for. Uncle Max stood, indicating the visit was at an end.

'Take care, my dear. We must lunch together soon. Maud has invited me to Scarborough for a week in July. It would be nice if you could be there as well.'

Sylvie left, having made promises to try to visit that were vague enough that if she broke them, it would not matter. She found it hard to settle back to work, watching the clock on the wall edge slowly towards five, and rushed home. She spent the evening in her room listening out for the telephone in the entrance hall in case Marcel called. The telephone didn't ring, but at half past seven Maise knocked on Sylvie's bedroom door.

'Sylvia, you've got a visitor. A gentleman by the name of Danby.'

Sylvie closed her book and went downstairs to the front parlour. She gave a cry of pleasure. The name had not been familiar, but the man standing by the unlit fire most definitely was.

'Marcel!'

'Actually, it's Walter Danby,' he said. 'It's good to see you again, Sylvie.'

She was so used to being addressed as Sylvia again that the use of her former name took her by surprise. She rushed across the room and hugged him.

'I can't imagine you as a Walter! I'm so pleased you're safe. I tried to find out anything I could about the liberation of Nantes in the newspapers but there was only a line or two.'

She'd scoured every page of every paper, hoping for something to leap out and put her mind at ease.

'The surrender was unconditional. The Germans blew up the bridges before they left, and planted mines, but barely a shot was fired,' Marcel said. 'You'd find the city much as you left it.'

Thinking of Nantes as she left it made Sylvie's throat tighten. She would cry if she didn't control herself.

'What happened about Dieter after I left? I need to know.'

She gestured to the chairs and they sat opposite each other.

'Everything went according to plan. Felix marched down to Baumann's *Soldatenheim* the following morning and demanded to speak to him, accusing him of abducting you. He caused quite a scene in the lobby before he was thrown out. When Baumann's absence was noticed, the Abwehr raided Mirabelle and your apartment looking for you both. They questioned the staff and your landlady, but obviously no one knew anything.' Marcel's face grew grave. 'When you were not to be found anywhere, they arrested Felix on suspicion of murdering you both in a fit of passion. Apparently Baumann had confided in a friend that he viewed Felix as a rival.'

Nikki or one of the Valters, presumably. Sylvie would put her money on Nikki as a way of taking revenge on Felix for embarrassing him in the club when Nikki had insulted Sylvie.

'Is he…?'

She couldn't bring herself to finish the sentence. She could only imagine what being arrested had involved. While she was hiding in the crypt in Normandy Felix had been undergoing torture. She couldn't bear it. Tears brimmed, hot and smarting. Marcel squeezed her hand.

'He's alive. He was imprisoned for a fortnight. He wasn't treated well, but he never broke. There was no evidence to connect him to your disappearance, and they released him. Perhaps to observe him and see if he led them to you. Perhaps because after D-Day, the Germans had more important things to occupy them than look for a missing civil servant and a dancer. Perhaps because Baumann was not important enough to waste resources on. In any case, the truth is still a secret.'

Sylvie wiped her eyes. Felix was alive. The worst she had feared had not come to pass.

'Poor Dieter,' she murmured. 'To be remembered for eloping with a dancer.'

Her heart broke at the thought of his parents who had lost both their sons and the shame that the circumstances of Dieter's disappearance would bring them. It didn't seem fair. 'I wonder if we could ever have turned him if I'd had more time, or given him more attention. There was something there – doubt at what he was seeing or hearing. Towards the end, I think he was growing close to questioning everything.'

'I had to shoot him, you understand,' Marcel said, clearly reading her thoughts.

'I know. We could not have relied on him keeping our secret. Sacrifices must be made, however unpleasant they are. There were too many others at stake. What of Antoine and Mirabelle?'

'Mirabelle survived without too much damage. Antoine was determined to stay open come what may, especially when the city was overrun with GIs. There were accusations of collaboration as he had welcomed German clientele, but he brazened it out and defended the girls. The last thing I heard, he is intending to employ a whole band to accompany Felix.'

'Felix still works there?'

'He returned to Mirabelle once he was released. He still plays there, though he's changed. I don't think I saw him smile after the night you left, even when the city was liberated.'

He picked up his hat and stood. 'I'm afraid I have to go, Sylvie. My wife is waiting at our hotel. You'd remember her – though, of course, you knew her as Madame Barbe.'

'Louise?' Now it was Sylvie's turn to smile.

'I couldn't bear to leave her. I can't stay in France – I have an invalid mother and a family business that needs rescuing. Fortunately, Louise agreed to come to England with me. We're in London briefly before we head north to Darlington.'

Sylvie took his hands. She hadn't noticed the wide gold band when she had come in.

'I'm very pleased for you both. I hope you'll be very happy.'

'I believe we will be, Sylvie. I hope I can say the same for you.'

Sylvie bade Marcel farewell, wishing him and Mrs Danby the best of luck. Mrs Underwood was waiting in the hallway.

'Miss Crichton, you know I disapprove of men on my premises, especially at this time of night. Who was that?'

'Mr Danby was a friend from wartime.' Sylvie smiled sweetly. 'I met him when I was working as a dancer in a nightclub.'

Mrs Underwood sniffed and went back into her own room. Sylvie watched her go with a weary heart. She disapproved of visitors. She disapproved of gentlemen. She seemed to disapprove of Sylvie's very presence in her house, even though Sylvie was paying a considerable part of her wages for the bedroom in the three-storey Victorian villa on Gipsy Hill. It was probably time to look elsewhere for digs.

Maisie stuck her head out of her room as Sylvie went upstairs. 'Tell me about *him*! He's a dream.'

'He's a friend from the war,' Sylvie said. 'Only a friend, mind. I know his wife too.'

Maisie grinned. 'In that case, you can come dancing with me on Saturday night. Robert has a friend he's dying for you to meet.'

'But do I want to meet him?' Sylvie asked.

Dancing appealed. Another in a series of Maisie's boyfriend's friends looking for a night of fun did not. She went into her room and lay on the bed. She looked around the room and was disheartened by what she saw.

Plain, sensible skirts and blouses hung ready for work the next morning. A book on learning shorthand lay open on the dressing table beside the silver compact from Major Buckmaster. The only bright touches in the room were the red silk scarf Sylvie had been wearing the night she had left Nantes, which she had draped over the mirror, and the poster for *Les Filles Luciole* from her childhood, which she had tacked to the chimneybreast. She gazed thoughtfully at the framed photograph of Angelique and Arthur, which stood on the fireplace beside the poster. Angelique had shown her daughter one life. Arthur had given her another. Both parents had combined to make her the woman she was now, but the future was hers to determine. Her parents gazed at each other with no consideration to the world around them beyond one another.

Only one person had ever looked at Sylvie with such an expression. Only one person had told her she mattered to him as much as he did to her. Angelique had spent years pining for the man she had loved but could not have. The man Sylvie wanted was alive, and she knew where he was. She was not going to live the same life as her mother.

The suitcase she had taken from Dennis's flat and reclaimed from storage on her return to England stood in the corner of the room. In the nine months since she had lived here, she hadn't even bothered to tidy it away and had given up any intention of seeking out Dennis to return it. She eyed it contemplatively, and her heart stirred, blood bubbling with anticipation.

She had spent her life moving from place to place and never belonging. From boarding houses in France with The Firefly Girls to boarding school in England. From Madame Giraud's place to Mrs Underwood's house.

She was not afraid of moving on.

The following lunchtime, she visited Thomas Cook's travel agency and made arrangements to travel to Nantes.

Chapter Thirty-Five

Sylvie arrived on the late-afternoon train and walked from the station. She knew the route well, but it was like walking through a new city. There were no checkpoints and the sight of the Tricolore where last there had hung swastikas made Sylvie's heart swell. It had been the same in every town on the long journey down through France. It was a Friday afternoon in August. Men and women sat outside cafés in the squares and on pavements, a colourful array of summer dresses and lightweight shirts around tables that had once been filled with Nazi uniforms. Like shoots breaking through frozen soil after a hard winter, France was coming back to life.

Not all the businesses had reopened though, giving Sylvie pause for reflection. The windows and walls that had once been daubed with yellow stars and graffiti had been scrubbed clean, but the buildings remained closed; a testament to the horrific, inhuman practices of the all too recent past that had come to light since the war had ended.

People numbering tens of thousands, hundreds of thousands, had vanished into the camps, never to be seen again. The final number might be even greater.

Sylvie had heard from Uncle Max that Miss Atkins was trying to discover the whereabouts of some of the SOE agents that were missing, presumed dead, but her task was a daunting one. Marie-Elaine had never been found. Sylvie was acutely aware that she was, as Monsieur Tombée had hoped, one of the fortunate ones.

Would Dieter have known what had been done to the Jews of France and Germany? She told herself he had shown enough humanity and he would have protested, but deep down she doubted it. He, like so many others, would have turned their face and ignored what was happening under their noses. Maybe he had not deserved his eulogy after all, or maybe it was only that little piece of humanity towards the enemy that gave life meaning.

A girl ran past Sylvie, chasing a dog, breaking through her melancholy reverie. Claire Barbe had chosen not to follow her mother and new stepfather to England but to stay with her grandmother. Sylvie had promised Walter and Louise to pay her a visit while in Nantes. She'd do that tomorrow, but today her mind was fixed elsewhere.

She had booked a room in a newly reopened hotel not far from the *Jardin du Plantes*. It struck her as she made her way across the city that she had left lots of her belongings at Madame Giraud's house. They might still be there if they hadn't all been destroyed in the search for her. She wondered if the Gestapo had discovered the tin outside the skylight and hoped not. It would be one small, insignificant victory if they hadn't. She checked into the hotel and freshened up before making her way to Mirabelle, planning to arrive soon after it opened.

The bollard at the end of the alley where Sylvie had laid the explosive charge had been replaced and the damage from the bomb blast had been plastered over. The sign that hung above the doorway to Mirabelle was new, but the painting of the dancer modelled on Sylvie on the blacked-out window looked weather-beaten and a little worse for wear.

A bit like Sylvie herself.

The front door of Mirabelle was propped open. Music filled the air; the familiar piano now accompanied by a trumpet and a soft, rhythmic drum beat.

Jazz.

Sylvie took a deep breath and walked inside.

There had been subtle changes since she had last been there. The small circular tables now had softly flickering candles in the centres, and the chairs were covered with velvet, adding a sumptuous air. A large gilt-edged mirror hung behind the stage, reflecting the dancers' shapely rear view and the audience back to themselves. Where Felix's piano had once stood alone, there were now three musicians. A tall black man playing a trumpet, a very pale-skinned man with a pencil moustache, and the familiar figure of Felix at the piano with his back to the door. Adele and Estelle were performing a dance while Emily flirted with a customer at the bar, drink in hand.

It was early in the evening, but the air was already hazy with smoke. Colognes and perfumes added another layer, and beneath that were the smells of warm bodies and alcohol. The audience was young and seemed to be mainly couples. The atmosphere was intimate and alluring. No one noticed her, so she stood in the doorway and let the familiar scents and sounds wrap around her like a comforting blanket.

After a few moments, Monsieur Julien appeared, dressed in an immaculate white tuxedo jacket. He surveyed the scene as he walked around the tables, chatting to customers, topping up glasses from the bottles. His eyes fell on Sylvie, and he stopped walking, staring at her as if he wasn't sure she was real. She gave him a little wave, slightly hesitant. She had been responsible for bringing trouble to his club, and it suddenly struck her that she might not be welcome. But her fears were unfounded because he walked across the floor with a smile and enveloped her in a hug.

'Hello, monsieur,' Sylvie said when he released her.

'Beautiful Sylvie!' he exclaimed.

He was being generous. Long hours nursing had given her eyes lines and dark circles that never seemed to fade.

'We've missed your dancing. Are you returning to me?' Antoine asked.

'I'm not sure. It depends on a lot of things, but I'd like to. For a little while at least.'

'You can stay for as long as you want, my dear!' he answered, beaming. His voice carried over the low chatter, causing heads to turn. Emily spotted Sylvie first, turning on her bar stool and almost spilling her martini as she shrieked Sylvie's name in excitement. Her high-pitched voice did what Antoine's had failed to do and drew everyone's attention to Sylvie's presence.

Estelle and Adele stopped mid-dance, then jumped off the stage and pushed through the tables to hug and kiss Sylvie. The audience appeared to think this was some sort of floor show and began applauding wildly. Felix stopped playing, leaving the trumpet and drums to continue for a few more bars before uncertainly tailing off. He turned slowly around and their eyes met. He mouthed her name. She nodded, eyes saying more than lips could. Why wasn't he rushing to meet her too?

Doubt began to creep into her heart. Too long had passed since the frantic declaration of love they had exchanged on that terrible night.

But then Felix bent down and picked up a pair of crutches from beside his stool. Slowly, oh so slowly, he made his way towards her, walking with difficulty.

'They broke his leg in two places,' Antoine murmured beside her. 'Crushed his foot.'

Felix stopped in front of Sylvie, leaning on the crutches for support. His left foot was twisted outwards. His hair had grey in among the black at the temples, and there was a furrowed scar on the side of his face between his ear and cheek that looked like a long burn.

Marcel had said Felix was changed but hadn't warned her about this.

'They did this to you?'

She reached out a hand to touch his cheek. He closed his eyes, wincing, and she withdrew her hand hastily.

'This was my fault.' Her voice stuck in her throat.

He drew a breath and looked at her.

'No.'

His eyes were deeply lined at the corners, but the flash of passion in them almost knocked Sylvie off her feet. The audience was growing restless, realising this was not part of the evening's entertainment after all. Emily, Adele and Estelle were still crowding around Sylvie and Felix. She had made a mistake arriving at Mirabelle now. Not by coming at all, but she should have waited until the club was closed and they could talk in privacy. Now was the wrong time.

'I should have waited until tomorrow,' she said. 'We can't talk now.'

'Are you staying long?' he asked.

'I think so. For now, at least. England, it isn't the place for me. There's nowhere else I want to be.'

She felt a moment to a pang of uncertainty. 'Are you staying with Céline again?' Felix asked.

'No. I have a room in a hotel.'

He took her hand, lacing his fingers through hers.

'Or you can stay here with me. For tonight.'

If she had harboured any doubts that coming back was the right thing to do, the moment he touched her hand they vanished.

'I'd like that,' she murmured.

She wrapped her arms around him, holding tight. Tears start to roll uncontrollably down her face.

Felix leaned against her for support as they kissed, lips burning and bruising with his ferocity. Sylvie became dimly aware that Antoine flapping his hands at the dancers, ushering them back to the stage and giving them a small degree of privacy.

'I didn't know if you had made it to England,' Felix said when he drew away. 'When we had no word, I gave up hope of ever hearing from you. I didn't even know your real name.'

'I should have come back sooner,' Sylvie replied.

He kissed her again, this time softly and slowly. She tasted salt. Her tears or his? She wasn't sure, and it didn't matter. They were tears of happiness and sadness, pain and release.

Céline emerged from behind the curtain. She caught sight of Sylvie and tossed her hair back gracefully, then walked across the room arm in arm with the trumpet player. He was still carrying his instrument and looked confused by the uproar.

'Hello, Sylvie,' Céline said, kissing Sylvie on one cheek then the other as if she had been gone less than a day. She pouted in mock severity. 'You and I are going to have a long talk very soon about keeping secrets from friends! For now, let me introduce you to Eugene Wilkins. He was in the US army but not any more. We're getting married next month.'

Sylvie hugged Céline close. In a changed world, Céline's uncomplicated attitude was reassuring. 'Many congratulations to the both of you.'

'Pleased to meet you, ma'am,' Eugene said in a slow, lyrical drawl. 'I don't think I caught your name but I guess everyone here knows you.'

Sylvie smiled up at Felix. Later, she would sit with him

and they would talk and share the stories of what has happened since they had parted. Sob, laugh, and make love.

They would talk of the past, and maybe the future.

Were the few frantic nights they had spent together in a whirl of passion and danger enough to hold them together after the war had ended? She had no idea if what they had endured was enough to build a life together, but she was willing to take the chance and find out.

If not, her suitcase would be waiting and there would be other rooms.

She shook Eugene's hand and there was no hesitation in her voice when she replied.

'My name is Sylvie Duchene, and I am a dancer.'

Author's Note

When I started researching this book I only had a vague sense of the work of SOE – the Special Operations Executive – and a few of the better-known figures such as Noor Inayat Khan, Violette Szabo and Odette Sansom. It has been a pleasure (if such a word can be applied to the circumstances of their frequently bleak lives and deaths in the course of their work) to learn more about the other women (and men), their training and the parts they played in helping to being about an end to the war in Europe. To head into unknown danger under assumed names requires a degree of courage I can't begin to contemplate. I hope readers will judge Sylvie a worthy tribute to their work and memories. Some of the situations Sylvie finds herself in were inspired by real life incidents reported by members of SOE. Any inaccuracies in the described training or work methods are entirely my fault.

I sent Sylvie to carry out her work in Nantes for two reasons. Firstly because there was no SOE cell based there so I could have free reign with creating mine, and secondly because it is one of my favourite cities to visit. I encourage everyone to get there if possible. The locations mentioned such as the Jardin des Plantes, Passage Pommeraye and Chateau des Ducs de Bretagne still exist, along with the more recent addition of a giant, mechanical, rideable elephant at the Machines de L'Ile which now stands on the site of old factories and shipyards.

I'd like to give particular thanks to: Shell Cunliffe from *The Unlaced Historical Romance Group* on Facebook for suggesting *Librarian* as the name of Sylvie's cell.

My editor Charlotte for receiving my drafts with such enthusiasm and being so supportive. My editor Julia at Mills & Boon for introducing me to Charlotte in the first place.

My son, A1, for telling me which type of aeroplane Sylvie might have flown in (and not showing his exasperation too openly when I asked for the fifth time).

YOUR NUMBER ONE STOP

ONE MORE CHAPTER

FOR PAGETURNING BOOKS

One More Chapter is an
award-winning global
division of HarperCollins.

Sign up to our newsletter to get our
latest eBook deals and stay up to date
with our weekly Book Club!
<u>Subscribe here.</u>

Meet the team at
<u>www.onemorechapter.com</u>

Follow us!

 @OneMoreChapter_
@OneMoreChapter
@onemorechapterhc

Do you write unputdownable fiction?
We love to hear from new voices.
Find out how to submit your novel at
<u>www.onemorechapter.com/submissions</u>